THE PRYCE *OF* AMBITION

KARI BOVÉE

VINCI BOOKS

By Kari Bovée

The Pryce of Murder

Vinci Books

vinci-books.com

Published by Vinci Books Ltd in 2025

1

The publisher and the author have made every effort to obtain permissions for any third party material used in this book and to comply with copyright law. Any queries in this respect should be brought to the attention of the publisher and any omissions will be corrected in future editions.

A CIP catalogue record for this book is available from the British Library.

Paperback ISBN: 9781036706449

Chapter One

LA PLATA SPRINGS, COLORADO

Spring, 1886

I stared into the flames of the blazing fire, sipping my Earl Grey, my mood pensive and overcast with a heavy cloud of apprehension. Bijou, my gold and white Havanese dog, lay at my feet—well, actually *on them* rather, keeping them warm. Darkness bathed the parlor room of my three-room suite, except for the glow coming from the fireplace.

It was early spring, but the morning and evening temperatures in La Plata Springs remained frigid, book ending the warmth of mid-morning to mid-afternoon, hinting at more mild weather to come.

The little mining town, nestled in the La Plata Valley of the Colorado Rockies, had been my home for the last eight months. I could scarcely believe how fast the time had flown.

When I first arrived, I resented the year-long stay mandated by my late husband's will. He required that I leave my New York City life to run the hotel for a year to inherit his substantial fortune. Unforeseen expenses extended my stay to a year and five months, as I had to exchange time for funds borrowed against my inheritance, adhering to the will's terms.

My late husband had written in his will that I leave my celebrity, my theater, and my privileged and lavish lifestyle in New York City, and come to this tiny burg in the mountains to run my namesake hotel, which he had bequeathed to me, for a full year in order to gain my full inheritance. A sum which was, in no uncertain terms, immense.

But, for now, I had to work within the confines of a modest stipend. Because of expenses out of my control, I'd had to borrow money from the estate. In order to keep with the terms of the will, I'd had to use more time spent here as collateral, to make up the difference.

Much to my surprise, I had settled into the provincial community quite comfortably. Once my name had been cleared of murder, that is. An act that had necessitated that I become an amateur sleuth of sorts to get to the truth of the matter. I found that I actually had a talent for investigation, and along with my puritan work-ethic and desire to succeed, I had become known for my Sherlockian prowess in solving several crimes. The notoriety fueled my need for a sense of worthiness and gave me the feeling that I belonged.

But today, those feelings of warmth and accomplishment vanished, replaced by a surge of impending dread. My mother, with whom I'd been estranged, gave word she was coming to town.

I took another sip of my tea and heaved a great sigh as I set the cup back down on the saucer. A wave of coolness enveloped me and with my free hand, I pulled my shawl tighter around my shoulders. In seconds, the smell of pipe tobacco filled the air.

"Good morning, Percival," I said. A bitter chill, and the juxtaposing warm, spicy fragrance always accompanied my ghostly friend.

"Hello, my dear. You're up early."

I glanced out the window at the grayness of impending dawn and then returned my gaze to the flames. "I couldn't sleep."

In my periphery, his transparent form settled into the chair next to me. I turned to look at him. As usual, his luminous eyes regarded me with some intensity. He was classically handsome with a head of dark wavy hair and bore the Byronic quality of masculine broodiness that I somehow found attractive.

"Care to share?" He set his pipe between his lips and inhaled, making the bowl of it glow red.

"It's my mother. She sent word she is coming to town, but gave no mention of when. Her inconsiderateness is beyond the pale. It's in poor taste to tell someone you plan to visit—uninvited, no less—but then to not tell them when is just plain rude. I suppose she expects that when she makes her grand entrance, I will drop everything to entertain her."

"Goodness. You really don't want to see her."

I shot him a look. "What do you mean by that?"

With his pipe firmly between his teeth, he held up his hands in surrender. "I haven't any earthly idea. Don't be so defensive, dear. I didn't mean any harm."

I swallowed, embarrassed at my sharpness. "I'm sorry. It's just that—my relationship with my mother is—complicated."

"What's this about Millicent?" Cordelia emerged from her bedroom, which was next to the parlor, in her dressing gown, her hair disheveled from sleep. She stretched and yawned. "Hello, Percival."

I flinched, still not used to the idea that Cordelia now knew my deepest, darkest secret, that I could see and communicate with otherworldly spirits. A capability that she now shared, because of her near-death experience some months ago. In fact, it was Percival who had brought her back from the brink.

I had held this secret close since my childhood, for fear of ending up like two of my relatives with the same capacity, who'd ended up in an asylum, one accused of insanity and the other witchcraft.

Percival nodded a greeting to her. "Arabella is out of sorts."

"If you are talking about Millicent, I don't blame her."

"Is she really that bad?"

Cordelia and I shared a glance.

"Yes," we said in unison.

Percival raised his brows. "My, my. I know you've shared some of your childhood with me, Arabella, and I realize you feel she was a little over ambitious and controlling. But, with your father abandoning the two of you—"

"Don't!" I held a finger up at him. It was true, my father had abandoned us when I was young, but my love and longing for him was still strong, even after all these years. He was the one person whom I felt truly understood me in this world, and loved me completely, flaws and all. I honestly didn't understand how he could leave me, but had put it up to not being able to live with my mother anymore. In my heart and mind, it was her fault that he'd gone. I couldn't abide anyone—especially someone who never knew him—disparage him.

Percival pulled his chin back in surprise at my admonishment. "I—I'm sorry, my dear—I didn't mean to . . . "

I stood up and set my teacup and saucer on the mantle above the fireplace. "I'm going to get dressed. I have a riding lesson with Clayton in an hour. If you'll excuse me."

"Would you like some help?" Cordelia offered.

"No. Enjoy your tea."

I swept past them, leaving an icy chill in my wake, for which I felt terrible but couldn't seem to help. I wanted to be alone for a few moments. The threat of tears pricked at the back of my eyes, stinging my nose, and an ache rose in my throat. I swallowed it down, determined to resume control over my emotions.

I would carry on as normal. It could be days, perhaps weeks, before my mother arrived. And with any luck, she might just change her mind entirely.

I walked to Archer's Livery, at the far edge of town, unsuccessful in putting thoughts of my mother's upcoming visit out of my mind. If I knew when she was to arrive, I might mentally prepare, but this looming uncertainty was like a dark cloud hanging over my head.

I would have to distract myself, and my riding lessons with the handsome sheriff were indeed a welcomed diversion. Many occasions and various circumstances have tested my friendship with Clayton. One of which was our growing attraction to one another that seemed to go absolutely nowhere. It was both frustrating and yet a relief. Knowing that I was not to remain in La Plata Springs for long, it seemed silly, and even unkind, to embark on a relationship I knew would abruptly end. I had not shared with Clayton that I was to leave at the end of my stipulated tenure—for reasons that confused me. Was it because I secretly wanted to stay and pursue the friendship, or was it because I feared that very thing?

Pushing my uncomfortable feelings aside, which was my habit as I had more important things to do, I put it up to the fact that it really was none of the sheriff's business what I intended to do with my life. In the meantime, I would enjoy his company and his instruction in horsemanship.

"Hello, Mrs. Pryce." A voice shook me out of my reverie. It was Mr. Parkhurst, the blacksmith who ran Archer's Livery, and the forge connected with it. It appeared he was fashioning horseshoes ...I had been so lost in my thoughts of my mother and Clayton, I scarcely knew how I got there.

"Mr. Parkhurst. Nice to see you." I dredged up a smile, still preoccupied with my musings.

He returned the greeting with a wide smile, his teeth glowing white against his dark skin, and his coal-black eyes dancing with merriment. He was a strapping man of approaching middle-age, charming and friendly, and I often wondered why he wasn't spoken for.

"You must be here for another riding lesson," he said. "Do you want me to get Monty tacked up for you?"

"No thank you, I think I should do it myself. I enjoy spending a little quiet time with Monty before our ride."

I enjoyed grooming the snowy white gelding, and he seemed to like it, too. I hated to admit it, but I was becoming attached to my equine friend. He was owned by Mr. Archer, but there was no love lost there. Mr. Archer had several horses at his livery, for the purposes of renting them out or selling them. Clayton had kindly entered into a long-term lease of the horse for my lessons.

"All right then, I'll let you get to it." Mr. Parkhurst bowed gallantly.

"Thank you," I said, and walked toward the livery barn.

Once I had Monty groomed to gleaming and dressed in his saddle, rope halter and bridle, I led him out toward the open area near the river where my lessons took place.

It was a deliciously serene spot, set away from the bustling crowd and surrounded by leafing cottonwoods. The sound of the water rushing against scattered boulders in the riverbed, and the heat of the sun melting the chill from the morning air, soothed my senses. I stood facing Monty, running my hand down his face. He uttered a low nicker, returning my affections.

"Either you're early or I'm late."

I turned to see Clayton, perched upon his beloved Queenie, a beautiful chestnut mare. He looked dashing, as always, in his rugged leather coat and Stetson cowboy hat.

"I'm early," I said.

"Good." He swung his right leg over Queenie's rump and hopped down from the saddle. Settling his hands in his pants pockets, he strode up to me, Queenie following behind. His sapphire gaze settled on mine and I quickly glanced away, afraid of getting lost in it.

"You all right?" he asked, his voice low and with an intimacy that both thrilled and terrified me.

"Of course," I said, shaking my head like his concern was preposterous. "I just have a lot to do today, so want to get started as soon as possible."

"Okay, then. Why don't we start with some ground work?" He handed me his rope lariat.

I nodded and unclipped Monty's reins, handing them to

Clayton. I then attached the lariat to Monty's halter, which I had placed on him before I put the bridle on.

I attempted a variety of quick exercises with Monty, as Clayton showed me, to ensure he remained focused on me. Clayton had explained that once I developed a connection with the horse on the ground at each session, our ride would be much more pleasant and productive. So far, he'd been correct. I had always assumed that when riding, the horse did all the work and the rider was merely a passenger. But Clayton taught me it was a dual effort, like a dance, and both partners needed their attention focused on one another and the task at hand. It was far from a passive endeavor.

Soon, it was time for me to climb on board. I led Monty over to a fallen cottonwood, lined him up next to it, placed my foot in the stirrup and gently got on astride, thankful for the new riding skirt I'd had Cynthia Mayes, the dressmaker, fashion for me.

Clayton instructed me through each of the gaits, stops, turns on the forehand, and turns on the haunches. My heart swelled with pride at how well Monty was responding to my cues. After a circle at the canter, I brought him to a halt with my seat and beamed at Clayton.

"That was impressive, Arabella," he said with a slow smile as he approached us. "You are a quick learner."

My cheeks flared with heat at the praise. "Thank you. Monty is a good boy."

"He's only as good as his rider." Clayton sidled up to us, his chest mere centimeters from my thigh. He looked up at me with those dreamy eyes and a devilish grin. "What would you think about jumping that fallen down tree?" He pointed to the tree I'd used to mount. My heart picked up a staccato at the suggestion.

"Jumping? Oh, I-I don't think — "

"You never know when you might need to jump something when riding in these mountains. There can be all kinds of obstacles in the wild. It's a good thing to learn, and I think you are ready. We'll start small, with that tree. If you go for that bend," he pointed to a curve near the top of it. "I reckon it's only about three feet tall. A piece of cake for Monty."

Apprehensive, I bit my lip, hesitating to answer. I was still flying high from my accomplishments in the lesson thus far, but a niggle of anxiety flared at the idea of soaring through the air on a thousand-pound animal. Would I be able to stay on?

"As you approach at the trot, put your weight in the stirrups and tilt forward to get off his back, let him have his head and he'll do the rest. If you keep your heels down, you'll stay put."

It sounded simple enough. A flutter of excitement welled up in my chest. "All right, I'll try it."

"Okay, then," Clayton said with a wide grin. "I want you to take up the trot and make a circle. Once you've got a steady rhythm, turn him face on to the jump. Keep your eyes and energy forward."

"Right," I murmured, envisioning the plan.

I turned Monty away from him, brought him to a trot and headed for the open space in front of the fallen down tree. I made three large circles, just to be sure the horse and I were in perfect sync. Turning him toward the lowest point of the fallen down tree, I kept my focus forward. As we neared it, I took in a deep breath, waiting for the launch, when something in the distance distracted me from my mission. It was a caravan of several brightly decorated carriages, and colorful enclosed wagons.

Before I knew it, Monty and I arrived at the jump, but I had lost my focus. Right as I thought we were about to take flight, Monty set his feet and ground to an abrupt halt, but I kept going, catapulting right over his head.

Time slowed as I flew through the air and then suddenly, with deafening swiftness, the ground rushed up at me, meeting my body with a bone-crushing concussion of hardness, and then everything went blank.

Chapter Two

"Arabella!" A deep, muffled, faraway voice echoed in my ears. A dense heaviness slowly filled my chest, and I couldn't move. The pressure of something warm pressed in on each side of my face.

"Come on, Arabella. Don't do this to me. Wake up." The voice was becoming clearer, and with it a ringing in my ears and deep resonating pain in my upper body. "God, if I've hurt you, I'll never forgive myself. Arabella, please. Come on."

The weight in my chest and the ringing in my ears persisted.

"Don't leave me, I—" the voice said.

My body tensed and I suddenly, desperately, needed air. I sucked in a lungful, electric shock shooting through my chest.

I opened my fluttering eyelids and found Clayton's beautiful face inches from mine, his blue eyes a stormy sea of anguish. His palms cupped the side of my face.

"Oh, thank goodness," he breathed and sent his eyes heavenward.

I pulled in another deep breath, and this time it didn't hurt as much. The pain in my chest was slowly subsiding. His hands gripped my shoulders, and I let out a yelp. My left shoulder screamed with pain.

"That's where you landed. May I continue?"

Biting my lip, I agreed. His hands did their probing, causing a measure of discomfort.

"Doesn't feel broken," he said. He then tenderly, but firmly, ran his hands down my arms. "Does anything here hurt?" I rolled my head back and forth slowly, telling him 'no.' I squinted my eyes against the pain in my shoulder. He then palpated my legs. "What about here?"

"No," I gasped.

"How about your back?"

My breathing was becoming easier, and the heaviness in my chest had subsided, along with the ache.

"It feels okay," I said, my voice almost a whisper.

"Your head?"

"I'm a little cloudy, but there's no pain."

"Do you think you can sit up?"

I nodded.

He gently pulled me to sitting and then settled in next to me, on my right side. He wrapped his arm around my waist to keep me steady. I leaned heavily against his chest, my head clearing.

"You just got the wind knocked out of you, but I'm worried about that shoulder. I'll have to get you to Doc Tate's."

"No," I shook my head. "I'll be fine."

"Sorry, I'm taking you in."

The clattering of wagon wheels caught my attention,

and I looked up to see one of the caravans, painted bright red, approaching us. The horse pulling it was brilliant white, with a gray mane and tail. A red plume of feathers between its ears fluttered with each bob of its head.

"I say." The man driving the carriage, a wiry figure dressed in a dark suit with a waistcoat of the same crimson as the wagon, pulled the horse to a stop. "Everything all right here?" He had an air of sophistication about him. His thick, shoulder-length, heavily pomaded dark hair was parted on the side and shot through with a single streak of gray that looped over his left ear. His face was handsomely chiseled in long lines, and his gray eyes carried a look of intelligence.

"She came off her horse," Clayton said.

"How unfortunate. May I be of assistance?"

The other two caravans pulled up behind the first, followed at a little distance away by three more.

"I need to get her to the doctor in town. I'm just letting her catch her breath." Clayton explained to the man.

"I'm fine," I said flatly, a little irritated that the two were talking about me while I was sitting right there.

"Victor!" a female voice rang out. "Why have we stopped?"

Suddenly, a young woman emerged from the caravan. She wore a simple dress of pink and green pastel. A matching pink ribbon held a cascade of rich chestnut curls off her face. Even from a distance, I could see that she had a classical elegance reminiscent of the heroines found in old paintings.

"Just a moment, Celine." The man climbed down from his perch and the young woman came to stand beside him.

"Is she hurt?" the young woman asked.

"No," I said a bit tersely. Being an accomplished and

celebrated actress, I was used to being the center of attention. In fact, I quite liked it, but when I was on stage giving a performance. Not when I was to be pitied and fussed over. I attempted to get to my feet. Clayton swiftly rose and, taking my right arm, helped me up. He held me steady while I got my bearings. The ache in my left shoulder deepened with the change of position.

"Are you heading into town?" Clayton asked.

"We are indeed," the man said.

"Could I bother you to take her there?"

"Don't be silly," I said, with a weak wave of my hand. "I can walk."

"It would be my pleasure," the gentleman said with a bow. "Victor Langston, at your service."

"No, really," I pleaded.

"Thank you," Clayton said, ignoring me. "I'll follow behind with the horses."

I shot him a look, which he also ignored, as he led me toward the caravan.

"She can ride in back with me," the young woman gave me a captivating smile. "I'm Celine Dubois."

At the mention of her name, I stopped short. Now that she was closer to me, I suddenly recognized the large, expressive mismatched eyes, one hazel, shimmering with specks of green and gold, and the other, deep blue, the pair of them capturing the light in a way that always added an almost mystical quality to her gaze.

Staring at her, I muttered, "I haven't seen you since you were a little girl."

She smiled at me. "Hello, Arabella."

"Victor, what is going on?" Another female voice rang out from behind the caravan.

I turned to see the woman, and the blood froze in my veins.

"Mother?"

Clayton kept one arm securely around my waist and his other hand on my elbow, steadying me. I was thankful for his support, as my knees had suddenly weakened, feeling like treacle.

"Hello, Bella." My mother pulled her shawl up over her shoulders and then primly folded her hands at her waist. I gaped at her like she was some kind of apparition. She was thinner than I remembered, and her once robust energy seemed a little diminished. I knew she'd be coming to La Plata Springs, but not like this . . . traveling in a dusty caravan? She was a woman who loved her creature comforts, who had nearly broken me as a child in order to have them. I had fully expected her to arrive by private railcar.

"What are you—what is—?"

"Ah!" Victor Langston's face lit up, and he clapped his hands together. "So this is your daughter, Millicent? The famous Arabella Pryce! Pleased to make your acquaintance." He gave a theatrical bow once again.

Three more people emerged from the closest caravans. Two men, one younger and the other older, and a woman.

The younger man had a head of tousled blond locks that seemed perpetually kissed by the sun, falling in a carefree manner that suggested a disregard for strict grooming convention. His wide smile created dimples in his well-chiseled features, giving him a roguish air. The other gentleman had gracefully succumbed to the passage of time. His salt-and-pepper hair and impeccable grooming complemented the sharp, intelligent look in his deep-set eyes. The woman, in her late thirties or early forties, exuded seasoned grace mixed with underlying tension. Her raven hair and austere beauty made her compelling, as if she belonged on stage.

I blinked, still utterly confused by the situation, my shock breaking down my barriers of civility. I gave my mother a pointed look. "Why are you with these people, and who are they?"

Her face hardened. "These people," she said, holding her arm out toward the other caravans approaching, are my colleagues. We are a traveling theater troupe. La Plata Springs just happens to be on our route, so I thought it would be nice for us to perform here."

Just happens to be . . . You've really not come to see me, then? I wanted to say the words out loud, but somehow found the restraint not to do so. I had suspected her motives for coming here in the first place, but now seeing her completely out of context with this traveling theater troupe made the hackles on my neck rise.

"I'm sure the townsfolk will love that," Clayton said, his deep voice resonating through his chest and into my body.

My mother fixed her eyes on him, and they melted in a way that made my jaw tight.

"And who are you?" Her voice dripped like honey. Her gaze traveled from him to me, and then back to him again, appraising our semi-embrace. "I never figured you'd go for a cowboy, dear."

I flinched with embarrassment at her forwardness and wanted to sink into the ground.

Feeling my body tense in his grasp, Clayton chuckled in that deep, mischievous way of his. Somehow, he always seemed to know what I was feeling, and it was both comforting and unnerving all at the same time.

"I'm Clayton Marshall. Sheriff of La Plata Springs. I've

been teaching Arabella to ride, and she fell off the horse. I need to get her to the doctor."

"My goodness, I hope it's not serious, dear." My mother's face clouded with concern—mock concern.

"I'm fine," I ground out.

"Well, let's get you to the doctor, then," Victor said.

I looked up at Clayton and pleaded at him with my gaze. "I'd like to walk. I think it would do me good."

His eyes registered understanding, and he gave a shrug of his shoulder. "If you're certain you're up to it?"

"I am." I gave him an assuring smile.

"Never mind," he said to Mr. Langston. "We'll walk."

"Very well," the gentleman said. "Is there a place we could set up camp?"

Clayton looked behind him at the lovely clearing we'd been using for our lesson. "This is a pleasant spot. Close to town with access to the river. The area is open enough for campfires, and it's beautiful."

"Indeed, it is." Mr. Langston nodded. "We'll get started then."

"Take care, Bella," my mother said. "I'll check in with you later to see how you are doing." I gave her a curt nod, annoyed that she had referred to me by the name she, and sometimes William, had called me. It seemed inappropriately intimate, considering we hadn't spoken in years.

"Let's go, Sheriff. Hopefully, the doctor will be quick. I'll need to get back to the hotel as soon as possible."

My gaze shifted to my mother, and we exchanged an icy glance. I bit my lip, a torrent of emotions assaulting me. I only hoped I could endure her visit with a modicum of grace and patience.

Clayton turned to look at the horses behind us. They were standing together, Queenie dozing in the sun, and

Monty standing alert, his eyes fixed on the group of people and caravans. Clayton whistled, getting Queenie's attention. She raised her head and looked over at him. Then, slowly, she began walking toward us. Monty followed behind her.

When they arrived, he gathered up their reins with his free hand, his other still firmly around my waist. The wobbliness of my knees had subsided, and I felt quite capable of walking on my own, but said nothing. In the presence of my mother and these strangers, I wanted to feel the safety and security of someone familiar. I never would have guessed eight months ago that I would consider the rugged, unpolished sheriff a refuge of sorts. He'd immediately created in me a thrilling but uncomfortable sensation, a threat to my carefully guarded heart. But our relationship had changed since that first meeting. I still didn't know what to make of it, but it had lost that initial discomfort.

I flashed back on the moments after my fall. *Don't do this to me. . . Wake up. . . if I've hurt you, I'll never forgive myself . . . Don't leave me . . .*

"Well, that was interesting," Clayton said, breaking my train of thought. His hold around me loosened. He obviously sensed I was feeling stronger. "Your mother. Here. Were you expecting her? You didn't seem very happy to see her."

I pulled my lips between my teeth, considering what to say or not to say.

"It's a long story. And . . . complicated."

"Right." There was an understanding in his voice that gave me some relief. He wouldn't pry, and I was grateful.

"How's the shoulder feeling?" He changed the subject.

I nodded. "Better. Sore, of course. But, as you said, nothing seems to be broken."

"That's good. We still should get you checked out,

though. I'm really sorry that happened. I hope I didn't push too hard."

I smiled up at him. "You didn't. I wanted to take that jump. I just got distracted and then Monty lost focus, too. It just happened."

"Well, I hope it didn't scare you off riding."

I stopped and gazed into his sea-swept eyes, his words reminding me of who I was, what I had accomplished in my life—with and without my mother. How I'd come to this town, a fish out of water, facing impossible odds when I'd first arrived, and somehow had created a life here, even if I planned to leave.

"I don't scare easily, Clayton. And I don't give up, or back down."

He gave me that amiable smile of his. "Yeah, I know. But somehow I don't think you're just talking about riding."

I set my mouth in determination. "I'm not."

Chapter Three

Dr. Tate secured the sling around my neck. A man past his prime, with graying hair and a slight stoop in his posture, he was still very adept at his job, and his no-nonsense approach to medicine gave one comfort that all would be well in his care. He stood at exactly my height of five feet seven inches, and he lowered his chin to peer at me over his wire-rimmed spectacles.

"Wearing the sling will keep the arm stable, thus putting less stress on your shoulder. Try to keep it on as much as possible during the day. I'm giving you some Arnica to apply directly to the skin around the injured area. It will help keep the bruising at bay, and it also helps with inflammation. I'm prescribing Yarrow Root for pain during the day, and some laudanum to help you sleep at night."

"Is that all?" I asked for clarification.

"I'd try to take it easy for the next couple of days. I see no signs of concussion, but since you took a pretty hard fall, don't overtax yourself."

"Thank you, doctor." I smiled at him with gratitude.

We stepped out of his examining room to find Clayton pacing in the waiting area. He stopped when he saw us.

"Well?"

"She's fine," the doctor said. "Nothing broken, but she'll be sore for a couple of days."

Clayton breathed out a sigh of relief. "That's good."

The door to the doctor's office burst open, and a man with a young boy of about seven entered. A gash on the boy's head oozed with blood. The youngster's face was pale, his eyes wide with fear.

"He was climbing a tree and fell," the man said desperately.

"Take him into my examining room. I'll be there in a minute." Dr. Tate pointed to the door and then turned back to us. "Let me know if you require anything else."

We left him to take care of his new patient. As we descended the three steps down onto the street, Clayton took hold of my elbow.

"Are you okay with walking?"

I laughed. "My legs are fine."

"Just checking," he said, with a raise of his hands.

"And if I wasn't? What then? Would you carry me?" I teased.

He gave me a smirk. "If necessary."

It was clear he aimed to walk me back to the hotel. He probably still felt responsible for my fall, but that was silly. All the same, I wouldn't protest.

As we made our way down the street, I noticed a rather large group of people had gathered in front of the hotel, which was odd. A pang of worry stabbed at my chest.

"What's going on there?" I pointed.

"Haven't the slightest," Clayton said.

I picked up my pace, afraid something was terribly

wrong. There had been so many mishaps at the hotel of late, I didn't think I could bear one more. But as we neared, I recognized the problem. In the center of the group stood my mother, holding court with Celine Dubois at her side. She laughed at something someone said, in that way she did when delighted at being the center of attention. My worry quickly turned into annoyance, which then morphed into something else as I saw Constance Chatterley, the town reporter (and chief gossip) who also owned the La Plata Herald, the local newspaper, standing next to them, furiously writing on her notepad.

A woman in the crowd turned to see us walking toward them. "There she is!"

I marched over and the crowd split, parting like the seas for Moses. All eyes were now on me as I approached my mother with a forced smile.

"Mother, what are you doing?"

"Isn't it wonderful, Mrs. Pryce?" The woman said. "Celine Dubois! In our humble little town. And, to think, your very own mother is her manager. This is so exciting!"

Another, older woman stepped toward me. "My dear, what's happened to your arm?" she said, eyeing the sling.

I shook my head. "I had a bit of a tumble from a horse earlier. It's nothing serious, just a sprain."

She seemed satisfied with my answer, and then continued. "Why didn't you let us know that Millicent Jane's theater troupe was coming to La Plata Springs to perform?"

"I, well, um—I haven't had the chance," I said. In actuality, I did not know she was part of such a sideshow. "They arrived unexpectedly early," I finished.

"I saw your mother on the stage years ago," she said. "Oh, my goodness, that seems like a lifetime away. How wonderful that she paved the way for you, my dear—and now for Miss Dubois!"

My gaze swept the group clamoring around my mother. A man and a young woman sidled up beside me.

"I don't believe we've met," the man said. He was tall, thin, with a long, beaklike nose. He had a wonderfully soothing baritone voice.

"I'm Dale Shay." He gestured with a tilt of his head toward the young woman. "And this is Heather Benavides." She was petite, a full two heads shorter than he. She had wide, expressive dark eyes, and jet-black hair—so black it appeared to have been dyed that color. "We are members of the troupe. It's a great pleasure to meet you, Mrs. Pryce. I've been a fan of yours for some time. It's been a delight to follow your career."

"Well, thank you," I said, pleased with the praise. I waved my hand toward Clayton, who was standing on the other side of me. "This is Sheriff Clayton Marshall."

The three exchanged their greetings, and then Miss Benavides turned to me.

"I have yet to see you perform," she said. "But I've heard all about your amazing shows, and your theater in New York. I do hope to see you on the stage one day."

"I hope so too," I said with a smile. "Are you actors?"

"Yes," Mr. Shay said. "We play two small parts each in this production. We're ecstatic that they've cast us. It's an honor to work with your mother—and Victor of course. They are both brilliant."

"They are," Miss Benavides concurred, looking up at her companion. "It's such a great opportunity for us."

"Dear friends," my mother said loudly, pulling my attention away from the two. She put on her most placating voice. "If you will excuse me. It's been so long since I've seen my daughter. I'd like to catch up." She held her hand toward the beveled glass doors of the hotel.

I clenched my teeth, irritated that she had complete and utter control over the situation. As usual.

I nodded to Mr. Shay and Miss Benavides. "It was a pleasure to meet you."

"The pleasure is ours," Mr. Shay said with a slight bow.

My mother, catching my gaze, tilted her head toward the doors of the hotel. I swallowed down my annoyance at her silent command.

The crowd turned their adoring focus to Celine, and a sharp twinge of jealousy seized me. I wasn't sure if it was because she was younger, had grown even more beautiful, and might pose a threat to my newfound place in this town—and perhaps abroad, or if it was because she had replaced me in my mother's ambitions. A notion which was ridiculous. I'd told myself time and time again that I wanted nothing to do with my mother. Why should I care who she mentored or managed?

I turned to Clayton who looked at me with raised brows, obviously sensing my displeasure.

"I'll see you later," I said quietly. "Thank you for walking me back."

He tipped his hat to me and left, probably glad to escape the obvious tension between my mother and me. I only wished I could do the same.

I breezed past the crowd toward the steps leading to the hotel's entrance, feeling the heavy aura of my mother following me.

Once inside, we walked through the lobby and as we approached the reception desk Mr. Pettyjohn regarded me with keen observant eyes behind his round-rimmed spectacles. A distinguished gentleman of robust frame, thick and much pomaded black hair, caterpillar-fat eyebrows and an exquisitely groomed mustache, Mervin Pettyjohn managed the reception desk at the Arabella. Despite his occasional absent-mindedness, he ran the desk efficiently, and I didn't know what I would do without him.

He held up a finger to get my attention, but I couldn't let hotel business distract me at that moment.

"Can it wait?" I asked with some gravity, hoping he wasn't alerting me to some kind of new calamity.

He hesitated when my mother caught up with me. I didn't want to take the time for introductions. Quietly, he gave me a nod, and I headed for the stairs. Once we got to my rooms, I held the door open for her.

We entered to find Cordelia sitting at the desk, penning some correspondence.

"Mrs. Janes!" she said with nervous excitement, obviously as surprised as I with Mother's arrival. "You're . . . here."

Her eyes, showing her astonishment, darted in my direction and I responded with a brief upturn of my lips. Then she noticed the sling and her face clouded with concern. "Good heavens, Arabella! What's happened?"

"I had a little riding accident," I said dismissively. "I'm fine."

"Oh," she said, not sounding entirely convinced. She turned her attention once again to my mother. "Forgive my manners. How are you Mrs. Janes? Welcome." She gave my mother a quick hug.

"Hello, dear," she said to Cordelia. "Arabella and I were just about to settle in and have a visit."

Cordelia glanced over at me with a questioning look on her face. I knew if I asked her to stay to provide a buffer, she would, but I didn't feel it was necessary. I gave her a quick nod.

"Of course," she said. "My goodness, you two must want to catch up. I was just about to go to Archer's Dry Goods to purchase some more stationary. We are nearly out. Come, Bijou!" she said to my little dog, who jumped up from her bed under the window and ran to Cordelia.

When they left, I indicated with a tilt of my head that we sit on the loveseat under the bay window. I should have asked if she wanted any refreshment, but that could wait. She ceremoniously unfurled her shawl from her shoulders and held it in her hands. We sat down.

"Why didn't you tell me when you were coming? You've taken me quite off guard," I said flatly.

She shrugged a shoulder. "I wasn't sure myself. Our schedule is a little . . . erratic."

I studied her face. She was still beautiful, but her complexion was more wan than I recalled. Her Irish roots had bequeathed upon her a ruddy complexion, but there was no trace of it now. Her eyes carried a heaviness that aged her.

"A traveling theater troupe. I never would have thought," I continued. "How long have you been doing that?"

She looked down at her hands resting in her lap. "For a few years. Victor and Roger are old acquaintances of mine from London. They started the troupe there and then brought it to New York. They contacted me, and the rest is history. Seeing as you had no need for me at your theater, I jumped at the chance. And I wanted to travel." There was a tinge of sadness in her words, but I wasn't sure if it was genuine, or manufactured.

She continued. "Since I didn't have the means to start

something myself, I've had to partner with Roger Thompson. He's the financier and—"

"I've provided you with a rather generous allowance, at least until I had to come here. Have you spent all your savings?" I didn't intend to sound accusatory, but it came out that way.

Her eyes flared with indignation. "I am helping to support a good number of people, Arabella. There are eleven of us in the troupe, including four stage hands. You've never had to manage your finances. I did it for you for years, and then you married William who took over, and now you have that theater manager in New York. I don't expect you to know how costly it is to keep a business afloat."

I nearly choked on my anger at her words. I knew all too well, thanks to the stipulation in my late husband's will. I'd had to have Mr. Tisdale, my husband's estate lawyer, inform her of my new situation because her allowance had needed to be reduced.

"What exactly is it you think I'm doing here, Mother? Eating bonbons and drinking champagne all day long? I am running a business. I know the challenges, the hardships, the terror of it all going wrong."

She raised her chin. "It's probably the best thing William ever did for you."

I scoffed at her statement and shook my head. I didn't want to engage with this line of conversation. It was none of her business.

"What are you doing here, Mother? Why did you come? I don't have any money to spare at the moment. I'll resume your allowance once things are settled here and I'm back in New York."

She looked at me, aghast. "Is that what you think? That I've come here for money?"

"Well, you just happened to mention your lack of means.'"

"It's not why I'm here."

"Then what?!"

Her face softened. "I wanted to see you. It's been so long. I don't like our estrangement. When your father left, it was always just you and me——"

"Don't bring Daddy into this." I warned.

A glint of hardness pierced her gaze. "Have you heard from him?"

I swallowed down my disappointment. "No. But we aren't talking about him."

She bit her bottom lip, probably in an effort to restrain herself from disparaging my father—whom she loathed.

She cleared her throat. "I just thought that we could, you know, get reacquainted. I miss you, darling. I miss working with you——"

"You mean, you miss *working me*. Do you ride Celine as hard as you did me? Besides, when did she show up? How did you get involved in her career—sad as it is?"

I instantly regretted my words. Celine was talented, I knew that. She'd had some bad breaks when she was getting started, and then I'd heard through the theater grapevine she was involved with an older, married man, who ruined what was left of her fledgling career.

"I saw her perform in a theater on Staten Island. It was a shabby little place, but when I saw her name on the marquis, I was curious. She was always such a vibrant child. Not as talented as you, of course."

I gave her a dubious look at her attempt at flattery.

"Anyway, she was amazing on that stage. She had this

quality of . . . authenticity that she brought to the role. I was quite astonished at how she'd grown as an actress and—"

"So you thought you'd hitch your wagon." The words flew out of my mouth with an anger that surprised me.

My mother frowned. "That's not fair Arabella. You know I am good at managing talent, building a career, making a star. It's what I want to do with my life, and now that you won't have anything to do with me . . ."

My chest tightened with a strange anxiety, and suddenly I felt threatened. She was right. She excelled at star-making —and she had replaced me with someone who could easily eclipse me in the eyes of the world, and that didn't sit well with me. Especially as I was now out of the public eye, save for the articles written about me in the New York City Times. I had arranged with the editor, Mr. Theodore Rankin, to chronicle my life in the West—with notes supplied by Cordelia—to keep me, and my celebrity, relevant. But now, with the power of my mother behind Celine Dubois, I stood a chance of being edged out entirely.

My mother was also right about something else. I had shut her out of my life. Was she here to make me regret it?

Suddenly, she winced, as if in pain, and settled a shaking hand over her stomach.

"Mother? What's the matter?" I said, wary of her ways of manipulation.

She shook her head. "It is nothing. I believe I got hold of some spoiled food a few days ago. I'm getting better. She reached out and put her hand on mine, the trembling gone. "Please, darling. I've missed you. Can't we just enjoy some time together?"

I tried to quell the flutter in my stomach. I wasn't sure how I felt about the whole prospect.

"I'm sorry," she said with some finality at my silence.

"This was a bad idea—coming to see you. I'll tell the troupe we need to move on."

I took in a deep breath, reconciling with the turbulence of my emotions. Even though I was angry with her—for myriad reasons—she was my mother. It would be heartless to turn her away.

"It's all right. You can stay," I said reluctantly.

She raised her brows. "You're sure?"

I nodded. "We have room at the hotel if you and your troupe would like to stay here for a few days. The town has no theater, so you'll probably want to move on to Addison. It's a larger town, and I believe they have one there."

"I see." She pulled her hand away. "We'll pay for our rooms, of course."

"Yes. Of course." I gave her a tight smile. I wasn't ready to be that generous with her. And as there were several people in her troupe, I really couldn't afford to give away rooms other travelers might need. They would pay like anyone else.

Chapter Four

I kept to my office in the annex for the rest of the day, convincing myself that I was catching up on paperwork and the bills that seemed to double by the minute. In reality, it was difficult to do much one-handed, and my shoulder pained me a little, so I busied myself shuffling papers around. The bills that didn't need immediate attention, I placed in a drawer of the old rolltop desk.

The truth of the matter was, I wanted to avoid my mother. I knew Mr. Pettyjohn and Maggie would see to her, and the rest of her troupe's needs in getting settled into their rooms. Staring at the drawer where I'd placed the bills, I was lost in my ruminations about my mother and all the feelings she brought up in me.

After an hour of simply staring into space, I decided it was time to emerge from my hiding place.

I left the annex and made my way to the hotel. When I reached the lobby, I turned to the reception desk, where Mr. Pettyjohn was busy organizing some papers.

"Good evening," I said to him. Then I recalled he had

wanted to speak with me earlier. "Mr. Pettyjohn, I believe you wanted a word earlier?"

He looked up at me over the rims of his round spectacles, his dense caterpillar brows raised. "Good evening, madam." His mustache twitched as the corner of his mouth raised in what passed for a smile. "It was a trivial matter. I have resolved the issue."

"Oh. I see. I'm sorry I wasn't available. My mother and her . . . friends arrived earlier than I expected, quite taking me off guard. I do apologize. I hope you didn't have to scramble too desperately to assign them rooms. Is everyone settled?"

"We've got them taken care of, madam. I've put your mother in one of the third floor suites, and a Mr. Roger Thompson in the other—at her request."

Hmm. I wonder what that is all about?

"Mr. Shay and Miss Benavides, along with some of the crew, decided to stay in their caravans. Mr. Langston and Miss Dubois are on the second floor, madam."

"Thank you, Mr. Pettyjohn. Do you know where Cordelia is?"

"I believe she is in the saloon."

I considered going up to my rooms, but the slight rumbling in my stomach reminded me I hadn't eaten since breakfast. I'd better pop into the Bella for a quick bite. I gave Mr. Pettyjohn a nod of my head and then made my way toward the beveled glass door that led to the pub.

I entered to find it full to the brim with patrons, including my mother and her troupe of players. They had set two of the round tables together and were in deep discussion. To my surprise, Andrew Archer; a local artisan and craftsman and nephew to Mr. Archibald Archer, the founder and acting mayor of La Plata Springs, Sally Dean, ex-sporting girl now barmaid, and Cordelia were sitting with them.

Archibald Archer and Atticus Brooks, a former theater critic turned journalist—and my arch nemesis—sat at one of the booths in the back of the saloon; the one that was next to my favorite, which was always reserved for me. My heart sank. I would find no refuge here. I was about to turn and walk out when Cordelia rose and came over to me.

"Arabella, are you all right? I haven't seen you all afternoon," she said with some concern.

"I'm fine. Just a little rattled." My eyes trailed over to my mother, who had just loudly laughed at something someone said.

"I know this is difficult for you." She rested her hand on my arm. "But don't shrink into the background. Be the strong woman I know you to be."

Her words bolstered my resolve. I took in a deep breath, put on my best show smile, and went to the table.

"Arabella, do join us!" my mother said.

One of the men, the younger, golden-haired one, jumped up from his seat and dragged an empty chair from another table over and set it between him and my mother. He flashed me his charming smile, which was disarmingly boyish and bore a hint of impishness, and his yellow-green eyes sparkled the promise of mischief. I quickly surmised that this young man was potentially a handful.

Reluctantly, I sat in the chair he offered and let him help me scoot it in under the table. Cordelia reclaimed hers.

"We haven't formally met, Mrs. Pryce. I'm Edmund Farley." He sat down and offered his hand. His grip was strong yet gentle.

"How do you do?" I replied.

The salt and pepper haired man, who was the most

distinguished of the three men, addressed me. "Are you quite restored from your fall? I hope your arm isn't broken," he said with a tilt of his head toward my sling.

"No," I said. "Not broken. Just a sprain."

"Ah. That is good news. Forgive my manners. I'm Roger Thompson."

I nodded a greeting to him.

"And you know Celine—our ingenue."

"Yes."

"And this is Miss Gloria Standish. Celine's understudy." He nodded toward the middle-aged woman sitting opposite my mother. She darted a look at Mr. Thompson. An attractive woman, she had loosely swept up her auburn hair into a twist at the back of her head, leaving wavy tendrils to frame her face. Her expression was hard to read and bore a mix of contemplation and a guarded resilience. Her measured smile revealed the mark of radiance, should she let it bloom.

"We were just discussing their performance in La Plata Springs," Cordelia said with some enthusiasm.

"But we have no theater here." I said matter-of-factly, hoping to encourage them to move on—with my mother.

"Boss has an abandoned warehouse on the outside of town," Andrew piped in. "It's near the area where they've parked their caravans."

I knew the building. I had seen it on one of my rides with Clayton.

Victor Langston clapped his hand over Andrew's shoulder. "This good man said he might convince his uncle to let us fix it up and use it." He grinned. "I've written a fabulous play, if I say so myself, and the audiences we've encountered thus far have loved it. Our company's presence and performances would be a boon for your town, and I daresay for your hotel."

I glanced at Cordelia, who raised her brows at me. She obviously agreed it was a good idea. And Mr. Langston did have a point. More guests at the hotel would be beneficial. I certainly could use the money.

Mr. Thompson cut in. "Your mother tells me you have your own theater in New York. Quite a profitable enterprise, from what I understand. We'd love your expertise in making the warehouse a fine theater in which to perform our wonderful drama."

I looked over at Mr. Archer and Atticus Brooks, who were sharing a laugh about something. Their coziness put me on edge. I knew Mr. Archer would have dollar signs in his eyes at the prospect, and Mr. Brooks would also love to write about it, no doubt. As much as I missed theater life, I wasn't too keen on the idea because it meant more time with my mother.

"I really know nothing about building a theater," I said, hoping to discourage them. "Besides, I'm not sure I'll have time. The hotel keeps me very busy."

"Oh come, Bella," my mother said. "You would serve as an adviser of sorts. It won't require much time. We'll do all the work." She gave me her most manipulative smile, and a spike of anxiety stabbed me in the chest.

"She's right," Andrew said.

I gave a shrug of my shoulder, which must have signaled to him I had agreed, because suddenly he got up from the table and went to his uncle. I refrained from rolling my eyes.

In moments, both he and Atticus Brooks approached the table. Andrew made the introductions.

"Well," Mr. Archer said, puffing up his barrel chest. "It

seems I have been negligent in welcoming you all to the town. I'm Archibald Archer." His pale eyes settled on my mother. "Have we met before? You look familiar."

Noting his attentions, my mother smoothed the back of her hair and put on her most dazzling smile. "I don't believe so."

Mr. Brooks cleared his throat. "Millicent Janes's reputation precedes her. She was once an actress. Perhaps you'd seen one of her performances, long ago."

Mr. Archer nodded. "That must be it."

Mr. Brooks continued. "But then, she turned her talents to managing her daughter, Arabella Pryce."

"Ah yes. I see it. The resemblance." Mr. Archer's gaze darted between the two of us. "Now I know where your beauty comes from, Mrs. Pryce." He focused again on my mother and she practically purred at the praise.

He dragged his eyes away from her and ran his hand down his pointed gray beard. "I think your merry band of players performing in La Plata Springs is a grand idea." He turned to Andrew. "You are welcome to use the warehouse." Andrew beamed at his uncle.

Mr. Archer clapped his palms together. "Very well then. My nephew here says he will help you in any way he can, and I assure you, you will be in excellent hands."

"So, it's settled." Victor Langston stood up and shook Mr. Archer's hand.

"I'll take you to the warehouse, and we can see where we need to begin," Andrew said, his enthusiasm spilling over. This kind of thing perfectly suited his talents.

"Wonderful!" Mr. Langston said.

"And since Mrs. Pryce is versed in the running of a theater, I'm sure her insights will be quite valuable," Atticus Brooks gave me a forced smile, echoing my mother's sentiments which I found unnerving, knowing that they both had their own agendas. Hers, to get back into my good graces, and his to torment me with his knowledge of the falling out between my mother and me. Unfortunately, it had been quite public. I knew he was baiting me.

I shook my head. "I'm afraid I'm quite busy at the hotel. Especially with the potentiality of new guests arriving in town."

"But we need your input," Mr. Thompson said.

"Oh, please," Celine implored with her honeyed voice. "I've always been such an admirer of yours. I aspire to your success. I'd love to spend some time with you."

Feeling entirely put on the spot, I glared at Atticus Brooks, who was grinning like a fool. I then turned to Mr. Thompson with a demure smile.

"I'll see what I can do," was what came out of my mouth, but the sentiment brewing beneath was something quite different. Lord, help me.

Chapter Five

The next afternoon, Cordelia, Bijou and I summoned Mr. Ellis, the driver of the hotel's coach, to take us to the warehouse. According to Mr. Pettyjohn, the troupe had gone there after enjoying an early breakfast. They must have been eager to get the restoration started.

Despite my reservations about the entire enterprise, the warmth of the afternoon sun and the rocking of the coach lulled me into a relaxed state as I watched the peaceful scenery slip by. Suddenly, a wave of coolness washed over me. I turned my gaze from the window and nearly jumped out of my skin to see Percival seated next to Cordelia, directly across from me.

"Goodness, Percival. We've talked about you surprising me like that."

"Sorry, my dear," he said. He looked over at Cordelia. "Good afternoon." He greeted her.

"Hello, Percival."

"So, where are we going?" Percival asked.

Cordelia explained.

"Ah. That's exciting. You must be thrilled, Arabella. A theater, in our own La Plata Springs. Your very element!"

"Yes." I gave him a tight-lipped smile, still conflicted about the whole matter.

"You don't seem pleased," he said.

"I'm a little worried."

"Oh, about what?"

"About my mother's intentions for coming here with the troupe. I can't shake the feeling there's more to her intentions than simply wanting to rekindle our relationship. I do not trust her."

"I see. But, to have a theater here in town—you'll be able to be on the stage again."

I curled my lip. "It will hardly hold a candle to my theater in New York. Besides, I think it's a temporary arrangement. Just for the troupe's visit."

"Oh, I'd love to see you perform," he said with a devilish grin.

"Well, then you'll have to come to New York sometime." I glanced at Cordelia, who gave me a nod and a half-hearted upturning of her lips. She had grown to like La Plata Springs more than I could have ever imagined, and didn't enjoy talking about our eventually leaving it.

The coach came to a stop and jostled as Mr. Ellis jumped down from his perch. I raised an eyebrow at Percival, who, catching my meaning, popped out of sight. Although, I had a feeling he would not float his way back to the hotel.

"Here you go, ladies." Mr. Ellis opened the coach door for us. He was a bear of a man with a ruddy complexion and thick, sandy-blond hair that was graying at the temples. Likely seen as intimidating by others because of his size, I found him to be a bear of a different sort—a cuddly-type of bear.

Getting out of the coach, I noted the warehouse was certainly large enough to be a theater, and the brick exterior seemed in good shape, although simple in its design.

"Thank you, Mr. Ellis."

"Should I wait for you, ma'am?"

"No. You should get back to the hotel. In case any of the guests should need your services. Why don't you come back in an hour and a half or so?"

"Yes, ma'am."

Bijou leaped down from the coach and toddled off after new smells.

"Come, Bijou," I called after her.

We entered the single room warehouse to find the entire troupe there, my mother included. She and Victor Langston were in deep discussion, presumably over the script in her hand, which she kept pointing at emphatically.

Edmund Farley, Andrew, and Roger Thompson were standing on a raised wooden platform about four feet off the ground, which encompassed the entire back section of the building. Six or seven steps at one end provided access to it. Crates were lined up against the wall, both on top of it and beneath it.

Mr. Shay and another two men, whom I assumed were the stage hands my mother had mentioned, were in the process of removing the crates and taking them out the back door.

Over in another corner of the building, Celine Dubois, Miss Standish, and Miss Benavides were dragging empty burlap sacks into a pile near the front entrance. Bijou ran over to them, eager for some attention.

Two other men were also gathering debris and hauling it out a back door, under the direction of Andrew.

Percival reappeared directly over Celine and Gloria's heads and performed a little jig. Cordelia giggled, and I jabbed her in the arm with my elbow. I wasn't in the mood for his antics. The last thing I wanted was for my mother to find out I had been associating with ghosts again. Her warnings about anyone finding out about my secret and my imminent ruin loomed over me like a dark cloud.

"Mrs. Pryce!" Andrew called out, excitedly. He turned his body and spread his arms wide, demonstrating the length and width of the raised floor. "What do you think? Doesn't this platform make for a perfect stage?"

"It certainly does," I had to agree. No wonder this building immediately came to his mind when the troupe had presented their plans. The place could easily seat about fifty to perhaps one hundred audience members.

"It's filthy," Gloria Standish said, brushing dust from her hands. "It's going to take us a lifetime to clean this up and get it ready."

"I bet we could get some of the townspeople to help," Andrew said. "Especially if they knew we were preparing for a performance."

"Gloria, maybe you could head that up," the blond Adonis, Mr. Farley, suggested. His tone indicated that it was not a question. "Andrew here tells me there is a printing press in town. You could make flyers, pass them around. Ask for volunteers."

Miss Standish set her fists on her hips and glared at him. She then stormed from the warehouse and went outside.

"Not to worry," Andrew said, trying to diffuse the situation. "I can do it."

"Edmund!" Celine scolded.

"What?" the golden boy shrugged. "She's not the lead. You are."

"That will be determined," Victor Langston called out. His eyes traveled to the ingenue. "Celine has not been performing up to her usual standard lately."

The young woman's face fell, and her eyes clouded with emotion. She went over to a basket on the floor, picked it up, and then she, too, fled the scene.

"Now look at what you've done, Victor. You wrote the play for her!" my mother said in that tone that had so many times made me flinch. Andrew quietly slipped away and busied himself with the crates.

"Which you keep trying to change," Mr. Langston shot back at her.

She narrowed her eyes at him and slowly crossed her arms over her chest in that menacing way of hers, which signaled that their previous conversation was by no means over.

"I won't play opposite Gloria. We have no chemistry," Edmund stated emphatically.

"You will play opposite whomever I choose." Victor gave him a pointed look.

"You've been off your game as well," Roger Thompson said to Mr. Farley. "Perhaps if you spent less time gallivanting with whores and gamblers in every town we land, you wouldn't be teetering on the edge of being fired."

Mr. Farley laughed. "Fired! Oh, that is rich. This troupe would be nothing without me. It's me everyone comes to see. Me and Celine. Together. And she won't do this play without me."

"You seem very certain about that." Mr. Thompson gave him a dubious look.

Mr. Farley leaned forward, thrusting his arm out and pointing it toward the door. "Go ask her!"

Percival had moved to the edge of the platform near the steps and sat down. He quietly observed the situation with his thumb and forefinger resting on his chin.

"It seems we've come at a bad time," I said, growing more uncomfortable by the minute, not only because of Percival, but because of the icy tension among the players. I wished we could leave them to their devices, but Mr. Ellis had just taken the coach.

"All right, everyone," Mr. Langston said, holding out his arms in a placating manner. "Let's just take a break. Meet back here in fifteen minutes."

My mother strode directly over to me and Cordelia, a weary look on her face. "I'm sorry you had to see that. Things have been a little—well, fractious. We've been on the road for a couple of months."

I understood all too well that even when performing in one place, there could be strife among a theater company. So many creative minds in one space was a recipe for disagreement and dissention. Especially when it came to something everyone was equally passionate about.

"Why don't the three of us step outside, Mrs. Janes?" Cordelia suggested. "Perhaps you need some fresh air?"

My mother nodded. "I'm afraid I'll need more than that."

———

We stepped out into the sunshine and my mother marched directly toward a fallen down pine tree and sat down. She set what I assumed was the script on her lap and pressed her fingers against her temples, clearly upset. I didn't remember her ever showing duress. When she was upset or stressed, she usually hardened her veneer to such a degree her expression remained stoic.

Cordelia and I caught up to her. Suddenly realizing Bijou was not with us, I scanned the area. I was relieved to find her with Celine. The young woman was sitting on a patch of grass near the river, Bijou at her hip. I smiled, well aware of the comfort that little fluff ball could bring.

"Are you all right, Mrs. Janes?" Cordelia asked.

My mother lowered her hands from her face and put on a placid smile. "Yes. Just a bit of a headache. It will pass."

"You mentioned things have been fractious with the troupe," I said. "Perhaps you all need to take some time off? Are you sure you want to pursue this performance?" My question was part concern for her and the others, and part self-preservation.

"No. We don't need time off," she said. "Celine has a great deal of momentum right now, and I don't want to stop that. She deserves this chance."

"Would Celine really choose not to perform without Edmund Farley?" I asked, curious at the actor's emphatic statement.

My mother scoffed. "His arrogance is staggering, and his influence over her is maddening."

"His influence?"

She sighed. "They were in a relationship for a brief time. He's completely wrong for her, by the way. He is exceedingly demanding and domineering."

Hmm. The pot and the kettle came to mind.

I looked down at the papers on her lap. It was indeed a script, held together in the usual fashion with brass brads. There were several markings in her handwriting. In fact, they filled the page. I recalled that she and Mr. Langston had been discussing it with some fervor.

"But Miss Dubois and Mr. Farley are not in a relationship now?" Cordelia asked.

"No. She said he was stifling her, which he was."

"That must make for some awkwardness between them, traveling and performing together," I said.

My mother shot me a look. "They're professionals. And Edmund has a point—their chemistry is undeniable. It enhances her appeal."

And it's all about appearances, isn't it, Mother?

I wondered how Celine felt about all of this. Working with an ex-lover would only cause added stress.

"Millicent!" a voice boomed from the warehouse. It was Victor Langston. "A word?"

Mother's face took on its usual stoic veneer, but her eyes carried a look of impatience. "If you will excuse me," she said with measured politeness. "The king calls."

"The king? You don't care for him?" I found her edginess toward him interesting. She was usually so unflappable —almost to the point of seeming indifferent, a trait that made it easy for her to manipulate others.

"He's brilliant. But, some of this—" she held up the script "—isn't working for Celine. Victor says that she is 'off' but it's because he hasn't really captured the essence of the character in a way that relates to Celine's talents."

"And you have better ideas?" I nodded at the thing.

I shouldn't be so confrontational with her, but her presence brought up so many unresolved feelings. I was finding it hard to control myself.

She raised a brow in annoyance with me. "Yes, I do." She marched off toward Mr. Langston.

I sighed, admonishing myself for my impulsive tongue.

"Are you all right?" Cordelia ventured quietly.

"Yes. She just gets under my skin."

Edmund Farley emerged from the warehouse, catching my attention as he made his way over to Celine.

"You have some unresolved feelings regarding your mother," Cordelia said, pointing out the obvious. "Which is completely understandable, given how difficult she made things for you. But that was a long time ago. Think of all you've accomplished on your own. You're a different person now, a stronger person. Don't let the past control the present. Life is too short..."

I pulled my lips between my teeth. I knew she was right, but I was wrestling with my stubborn streak. I kept my eyes fixed on Edmund and Celine. She stood facing him, engaged in an animated discussion. He reached out to take hold of her arms, but she pulled away and turned her back on him. His gestures became more exaggerated, and his raised voice echoed in the air, but I couldn't hear what he said. Suddenly, Celine burst into tears, picked up her basket and, running away from him, headed in our direction.

Confused, Bijou looked from Celine to Edmund, as if deciding who needed comfort the most. She trailed after Celine.

"Oh no," I said. "I wonder what happened." I walked toward her and when we met, she shocked me by dropping the basket and flinging her arms around me. I gasped as a spike of pain stabbed my injured shoulder. I was never one to be so demonstrative, thus my surprise, but gritting my teeth against the pain, I hugged her back—the best I could —none the less.

"There, there," I murmured. "What is it, Celine?"

She pulled back from me and wiped her tears from her face. Her eyes went to my sling. "Oh dear! I'm so sorry,

Arabella. I don't know what came over me. Please forgive me."

"It's all right. There is nothing to forgive."

She shook her head, her anguish palpable. "I don't know if I can do this anymore. It's too much."

"What's too much?"

Cordelia had joined us. Bijou lay down on the ground between the three of us.

"Edmund and—" she looked away from me.

"And?"

She met my gaze again. "Millicent. I know she means well and only wants the best for me, but . . . "

"It doesn't feel that way?" I ventured, all too familiar with the phenomenon.

She gave a sheepish smile. "Yes. I'm exhausted."

"I understand." I smiled back, sympathizing with her plight.

She chuckled softly. "I'm sure you do."

"And Mr. Farley?"

She hardened her jaw. "He's just the same—but in a different way. He's constantly criticizing me. There is just no pleasing him."

"I understand you were in a relationship?"

She nodded. "We were, but Millicent . . . "

I raised my brows, urging her to continue.

"She told me to break it off with him. Said he wasn't right for me and that he would jeopardize my career. I didn't like to be told what to do, but she's right. He has a reputation for womanizing, gambling—many vices that—"

"Would tarnish your image," I finished for her.

"Yes. But, it's hard to turn off my feelings for him, even though he can sometimes be cruel. And he doesn't want to take no for an answer."

The basket fell over, and a white, leather-bound book fell out of it. Celine bent down and shoved the book back inside and then grasped the handles of the basket and straightened again.

Out of nowhere, the transparent figure of an older woman appeared behind Celine and placed a hand on her shoulder. Paralyzed by the apparition, I froze. The ghostly presence was small in stature, and wore a white, Grecian style garment. Her hair was partially pulled back with a wide band, leaving tendrils to hang loosely around her face. With a tilt of her head, she gave me a knowing smile, and a shudder ran through me. Celine seemed unaware of her presence. And then, as suddenly as she had appeared, she vanished.

I looked over at Cordelia, wondering if she, too, had seen the apparition, but her expression was only filled with sympathy for Celine. Had I imagined it?

Celine lowered her hands from her face and straightened her spine. "But," she said with a sniff. "The show must go on. I need to get back inside. We have a lot to do to get this warehouse ready."

"Yes," I agreed, still a little shaken. "We'll come with you."

When we walked back into the warehouse, the rest of the troupe had gathered near the platform. Things had seemed to calm down as the others were in quiet conversation. I noted that Gloria Standish stood a bit removed from the group, her arms crossed over her chest, and a sour look on her face. Her eyes were fixed on Mr. Farley. Celine joined them and went to stand next to my mother, who regarded her with a mixture of stern tenderness. The group seemed oblivious to our presence.

I looked at the pendant watch I wore on a gold chain

around my neck. The ninety minutes had flown. Mr. Ellis would be back at any moment.

Mr. Thompson pulled himself from the group and approached us.

"Well, Mrs. Pryce, I think this space will do quite nicely. We will need some lumber to erect a proscenium. We will also need some velvet fabric for the curtain, and other hardware supplies. Some additional man-power will be required as well, but from what I understand, that might be a bit of a challenge. Andrew informed us that many of the men here in town work in the mines."

At hearing his name, Andrew strode over to us. "Yes, they do, but I believe my uncle is keen to see this theater built, so he might be able to temporarily spare some of the miners. And, I'm sure Bob Parkhurst and perhaps Everett Emerson and Sam Crawford could help."

Seeing as the blacksmith, the Dry Goods store manager, and the Post Master all worked for Mr. Archer, I'm sure they would do whatever he required. Even if it meant taking some time away from their current jobs.

"It sounds like all is in hand, then," I said, realizing that there was no stopping this train. "What do you need of me today?"

"Nothing at the moment." Mr. Thompson placed his hands behind his back. "We just wanted you to see the space. As we get further along with the plans, I'd like your input."

"Of course," I said, feeling a little reluctant, but I supposed it wouldn't be difficult to offer my opinion when they were ready for it. "How long do you think it will take you to have it ready for a show?"

He rubbed his chin, contemplating the question for a

few seconds. "I'd say, depending on the man-power, two to three weeks?"

"So soon?" I said, thinking the time frame sounded optimistic.

"We've managed the same feat, with much less than a built-in infrastructure like this, in a month's time. I believe we can do it in less time than that."

"Well, you certainly would know better than I, Mr. Thompson," I conceded. "Now, if nothing else is required of me, I do have to get back to the hotel."

"Of course, of course," he said. "Thank you for coming out. We are very excited about bringing our show to your lovely town."

I nodded and smiled, and was about to respond that it really wasn't my town, when the apparition appeared once again. She was hovering over the dais, and her transparent gaze cut through me like a knife, producing in me an odd and inexplicable feeling of trepidation.

Who was she and what did she want?

Chapter Six

Mid-morning the following day, as I was gradually working through some correspondence in my suite, Percival's reflection appeared in the mirror above my desk.

While reflected in the mirror, he appeared as solid and tangible as any living man. It was only when he stepped away from the reflective surface that his form became transparent. Although I had grown accustomed to his ethereal visage, seeing him in the mirror always lent a more grounded, less otherworldly quality to his presence.

"Hello, my dear," he said, pulling his pipe from his pocket. With a flick of his fingers, the bowl of it glowed red and immediately the spicy fragrance of tobacco filled the room. "Why aren't you wearing your sling?"

"Good morning," I said. "It's too restrictive while I'm trying to organize these papers. I'll put it on later."

Seeing him now reminded me of the apparition I'd seen yesterday. "Percival, when we were out at the warehouse, did you see another ghost?"

He frowned, giving me a look of disapproval. "If you mean spiritual entity, yes, I did."

"I'm sorry. Spiritual entity."

Percival preferred referring to himself and his kind as spirits rather than ghosts. I didn't quite understand it, but on the other hand, I didn't like to be called madam. It wasn't entirely rational, I knew, but I didn't care for it all the same.

"Who is she?" I asked.

He shrugged. "I don't know." He stuck the stem of the pipe into his mouth, taking in the smoke. He then blew a series of rings into the air that wafted from the mirror and into the room.

"Did you speak with her?"

"No."

"Can you tell me anything about her?"

He cocked his head, thinking. "She seems to have attached herself to the young actress."

"Celine?"

"Yes."

"So, she's not connected to the warehouse?"

"No."

"Ah." It hadn't occurred to me that a ghost—spiritual entity—would attach themselves to a person, as the only encounters I had had with them were in specific places; Oliver Shrewsbury, my first encounter as a child, resided in a place in the woods where we used to play. Leticia Crookshank had been at my theater in New York since she'd passed on many years before my husband had purchased it for me. And Percival seemed to be attached to the hotel.

"Could she be Celine's relative? A parent, grandparent?"

"It's possible, but not necessarily the case."

Just then, Cordelia breezed into the room, Bijou on her heels. My pup scampered over, happy to see me. I picked her up and set her on my lap. After a few wet kisses, she curled up and rested there quietly.

"Hi Percival," Cordelia said. Her cheeks were rosy from the exertion of her walk.

He gave her a polite nod.

"You're not wearing your sling," she said to me with a look of disapproval on her face. With a sigh of acquiescence, I picked it up and secured it around my neck once again.

"Cordelia," I said. "Did you happen to see a spiritual entity yesterday while we were at the warehouse?"

Her brow pressed down over the bridge of her freckled nose. "No. Was there one?"

"Yes," Percival and I answered in unison.

Cordelia shook her head. "I had no idea."

"Interesting." I then asked Percival, "Why do you suppose she didn't see her?"

"Given your—" he spoke directly to Cordelia. "Highly pragmatic nature, the phenomenon would only present itself to you in an extreme situation—in your case, with a near-death experience. Others, like Arabella and even Constance Chatterley, have high sensitivity, and are much more susceptible to the anomaly, especially in times of duress. The only reason Cordelia continues to see me is that she and I have a bond because—"

"You saved my life." She smiled at him.

"Yes," he said quietly.

I watched as both of them shared a moment. Even though I had been alarmed at Cordelia knowing my secret at first, it had also come as a welcome relief. As if my best friend knowing somehow lifted the heavy burden of such a secret.

"Celine did not seem aware of her presence either," I said, turning back to the subject at hand. "From what I know of her, she is highly sensitive as well. Can you explain that, Percival?"

"It could be for that very reason. There are varying degrees of high sensitivity. Perhaps Celine's psyche borders on fragility. The spirit may know this and does not make herself visible to Celine for fear of damaging her mind."

"I see." I wondered if this was what had happened to my relative, who'd been committed to the insane asylum. Perhaps the ability to experience paranormal phenomenon had caused her insanity.

"What are you working on?" Cordelia asked me, breaking my train of thought. "Ideas for the theater?"

I shook my head. "No. Hotel business. I hope the troupe does not expect much more from me than my opinions regarding the theater. I'm quite overwhelmed as it is—"

"It will be fine, Arabella," she consoled. "Offload anything you need here at the hotel to me. This is a chance for you to reconsider your relationship with your mother. Reflect upon and address past grievances to potentially cultivate a healthier, more harmonious bond. You must take advantage of that."

I scoffed, perturbed at her suggestion. "Must I? Really Cordelia. You make it sound so simple, and it is anything but. The woman is impossible."

Although I had been on my own for quite some time, the fear of my mother's control and manipulation had never left me. I worried about getting caught up in the cycle that had kept me oppressed for much of my life.

"But you are not impossible," Cordelia said. "You don't

have to change her, only she can do that. Instead, you can strive to overcome your own negative sentiments toward your mother, for they serve only to harm you."

I shook my head, doubtful at the notion.

"If you ask me, I think turning this warehouse into a theater is an ambitious undertaking," Percival said, thankfully changing the subject. "Architecturally, I'm not sure how they will have things ready in a mere few weeks."

As a former architect, I'm sure Percival saw all manner of flaws in the old building. Based on the structure of the Arabella, it was obvious the man had been a perfectionist.

I shrugged. "They said they've done it before, and if they can enlist the help of the townspeople — "

There was a knock at the door. Cordelia answered, and the sheriff stepped into the room carrying a burlap sack. He swept his hat off his head and ran a hand through his thick sandy hair. His indigo eyes settled on me.

"Clayton." I rose from the chair. "What a surprise." An annoying flutter of butterflies traveled from my stomach to my chest. I did my best to ignore it.

"Arabella," he greeted me, and then nodded to Cordelia. Percival had made himself scarce. The sheriff's gaze settled on the sling encasing my arm. "How's the shoulder?"

"Feeling better," I said. "Thank you."

"Glad to hear it," he said. "I'm not here for a social visit. I'm afraid I have some bad news."

"Oh?"

"Edmund Farley has been shot."

Stunned by his declaration, both Cordelia and I gasped.

"Andrew found him at Archer's warehouse," he continued. "Apparently, he had gone there late last night, or sometime early this morning."

"So, he's dead?" Cordelia asked.

"I'm afraid so—and there's more." He pulled a rolled stack of papers from the inside pocket of his leather duster and handed it to me. It was the script I'd seen my mother holding. Her name was typewritten in the upper right-hand corner, and staining the left-hand corner, there was a smear of blood. "It was found next to the body."

I blinked up at him, not comprehending.

Clayton pulled another piece of paper from his pocket, its wrinkled appearance suggesting someone had previously crumpled it up. "He was holding this in his hand." He gave it to me and I read.

"Leave the company, or else." Dread oozed over me as I noted the curling loops of my mother's handwriting. Just to be sure, I compared it with the annotations on the script. The handwriting was the same.

Still mute, I gazed into Clayton's lovely eyes, which were filled with a mixture of compassion and concern.

"What does this mean?" I asked, knowing full well the answer. I just didn't want to speak it.

"I've taken your mother in."

"You've arrested her? She's in jail? But anyone could have put that script next to Mr. Farley."

He reached into the sack. "There's something more," he drew out a stunning Paisley shawl I immediately recognized. A vibrant mix of red, blue and green hues was incorporated into the elaborate teardrop and floral pattern. My mother was fond of wearing shawls. In fact, they had always been a part of her ensemble. This particular shawl had been handed down from my great-grandmother to my mother.

"We also found this at the scene. He pulled a revolver from the back of his pants pocket. "A Colt 1860 Army. It was lying a few feet from the body."

I scoffed, shaking my head in disbelief. "What are you implying? That my mother shot Mr. Farley? My mother would never own a gun." The words gun and my mother used in the same sentence seemed as paradoxical as anything I'd ever known before.

"You're sure about that? It's been some years since you've seen your mother. Am I right?"

"Well—yes—but . . . I can't believe she would do something like this. I mean, my mother is many things, and I'll admit, she can be a difficult person, but . . . to kill someone? It makes little sense. And why—if by some very unlikely chance that she did kill him—why would she leave the murder weapon there?"

"Perhaps she shot him in a fit of passion, and shocked at what she'd done, dropped the gun and fled the scene."

"Oh! This is beyond the pale!" I exclaimed. "You can't be serious!"

Cordelia came over to me and placed a gentle hand on my shoulder. "Arabella is right. Mrs. Janes wouldn't kill anyone."

I took in a deep breath, trying to steady myself. "There was a lot of tension within the group," I said, finally finding my footing again. "And much of it seemed to be caused by Mr. Farley. My mother wasn't the only person who had a grievance toward him. Are you going to question anyone else regarding his death?"

Clayton took in a deep breath and looked at me with a good deal of consideration, mulling over my statements.

"What if he killed himself?" I asked. "Have you considered that?"

He nodded. "I have. But the revolver was lying to the left of him. At the Bella, I saw him with Andrew. Farley was writing something down for him. He used his right hand. If he had shot himself, fell to the ground and dropped the gun, it would have landed on the right side of his body."

"That makes sense," Cordelia said.

"I'm going to have to search your mother's belongings. To see if there is any ammunition among her things."

I sighed. "Of course," I said resignedly. "But I'm certain you won't find any. Please look further than my mother into this matter. She didn't do it."

He exhaled loudly. "That's what I aim to find out, Arabella."

I rose from the chair and took hold of his hand, looking into those sea swept eyes. The room seemed to tilt as confusion swept over me, leaving my knees weak and trembling. My fingers tightened around his hand, seeking stability. "I understand you're just doing your job," I managed to say. "But I know my mother is innocent."

He reached out, his touch gentle as he traced a finger down my cheek. "We'll uncover the truth, Arabella," he assured me, his voice firm yet sympathetic. "But as things stand, the evidence isn't in her favor."

Chapter Seven

I accompanied Clayton to the jail that also served as his office. We walked in silence; he likely felt remorse for having incarcerated my mother, while I was engulfed in a whirlwind of confusion. My mother, accused of murder? The thought was staggering. Yet, she had a history of taking extreme measures to secure her clients' needs—a fact I knew all too well from personal experience.

As we entered, the sight of my mother perched on the sparse cot in the cell made my heart plummet, my body suddenly weak. The impact was unexpected, leaving me struggling to draw breath.

"Mrs. Pryce." Dirk Fleming, the sheriff's new deputy rushed over to me and took hold of my elbow, obviously sensing my duress. He was a strapping man in his late twenties with an eagerness in his dancing dark eyes and a head of thick ginger hair. He hadn't been in La Plata Springs long, but already he had many of the young ladies in town in a flutter.

"Would you like a chair?" he asked.

I shook my head. "No. Thank you, Deputy Fleming."

Still holding onto my elbow, he escorted me to my mother's cell. Clayton came up behind us holding the keys.

"I'll give you ten minutes," he said somberly. He opened the door for me and I went in. My mother rose from the cot and embraced me. Like an automaton, I stood stock still, my body stiff as a washboard. As I had not returned the gesture of affection, she reluctantly released me.

"Is there anything I can get for you, Mrs. Pryce?" Deputy Fleming asked, concern written in his face. He really was very sweet.

"I think she'll be fine for ten minutes," Clayton said, with an edge to his voice. He then looked at me. "We'll give you some privacy." He closed the cell door and he and Deputy Fleming stepped outside.

Now it was just my mother and me, standing face to face, yet I couldn't bring myself to meet her eyes. Her presence was as commanding as ever, and I felt the familiar wave of intimidation wash over me.

"I didn't do it, Arabella," she asserted, her voice hoarse and subdued.

I met her gaze, but found I couldn't speak.

"Someone is trying to implicate me for this," she continued. "You have to believe me."

I blinked at her, trying to find my voice. I cleared my throat.

"Do you own a gun, mother?"

She bit her lip, and her gaze shifted from mine. Her hesitation and the shift in her eyes were as telling as a confession.

"Mother! Why?"

Her eyes, settling on me again, flashed. "Because I am a woman, traveling from town to town. There are any numbers of dangers out there. Outlaws, marauding Indians, wild animals. I can't count on anyone else to protect me. Never have. You know that."

My jaw tightened at her insinuation that 'anyone' included my father, but I refrained from addressing it. Although I didn't like the implication of her possessing a firearm, her reasoning seemed plausible.

"But, what about the script, and the shawl found next to the body?"

"Someone obviously took them from my caravan."

"And, the note?"

She paused, biting her lower lip once again. "I wrote that, but it was weeks ago. Edmund was stifling Celine. I knew she would flourish without him. I was trying to scare him off."

"What else had you done to scare him off?"

"Nothing, I assure you! He knew the note was from me and confronted me about it. He declared he would never leave Celine, even if he could not have her romantically. He was utterly fixated on their collaboration. I presumed he had discarded the note. Someone else must have acquired it, along with the script and the shawl."

I let out a breath of exasperation. "Why would someone want to falsely accuse you of this, Mother?"

"Because of Celine."

"I don't follow."

She folded her hands at her waist and straightened her spine. "Gloria sees me as a threat because I push so hard for Celine's top billing. She also holds a grudge."

"For what?"

"I agreed to take her on as a client as well, but I've found that my efforts are much better placed with Celine.

The girl has more talent in her little finger than Gloria has or ever will have."

I scoffed. There it was. Her ruthlessness.

She placed her hand over her mouth and coughed. It was a thick, heavy cough that seemed to come from the pit of her lungs. Had she been ill of late?

I proceeded. "And the others?"

"Victor resents my closeness with Celine. He, like Edward, is possessive of her and wants her under his complete and utter control. He despised the closeness between Celine and Edward. I believe he, too, harbors affections for her, yet to both men, she would merely be another conquest in their string of women across the country. She deserves far better."

"And what of Mr. Thompson? Why would he want to implicate you for murder?"

She shook her head and let out a sigh. "Roger and I— well, we—"

I raised my eyebrows, encouraging her to continue.

"We have a past. I broke things off with him long ago, and I don't believe he's ever gotten over it. He could be punishing me."

I swallowed. I'd never considered that my mother would have had a romantic entanglement. She was so bitter about my father I assumed she had sworn off all men. She'd always said there had been no use for them, however it hadn't stopped her from throwing me in my late husband William's path. The match was advantageous to her because he had been extremely wealthy. Little did she imagine he and I were more aligned than she'd anticipated, and he helped me to escape from her clutches.

"What about Mr. Shay and Miss Benavides? Do they have something against you?"

She shook her head. "No. I don't believe so. They were grateful to get their roles in the play—Victor was uncertain about Helene, but I pushed for Dale, and as they are a married couple, they come as a package. And, she has quite risen to the occasion. It's challenging playing ensemble roles, but it can also give them more range in their abilities. They are both indebted to me."

"And what about the stage hands?" I asked.

She shook her head. "They have no reason to dislike me."

"Well then, that leaves Celine," I said. "Would she want to incriminate you?"

My mother darted a look at me. "Heavens no. She appreciates me. She would be lost without me."

By the look in her eye, it was clear she was upset that I was not lost without her anymore. It made me realize how far I had come on my own. Without Mother or William.

"You say some of the others harbor resentment toward you and might want to implicate you in Edmund's murder, but who would actually want to kill Edmund? It was clear some of you in the troupe had problems with him, but whose grievance was so strong they would want to end his life?"

"The man was a liability in every sense of the word. Talented yes, but volatile, moody, given to a number of vices, he—"

A fit of coughing overtook her, racking her body. She doubled over, clutching her chest.

"Mother? Oh, my goodness." I took hold of her arm and encouraged her to sit down on the cot. I sat next to her and waited until the siege had stopped. She took a moment to catch her breath. Her face had gone pale and glowed with a sheen of perspiration. I put my hand on her forehead. It was clammy and warm. "You're ill," I said.

She shook her head. "It's nothing. Just a chest cold."

It seemed a little worse than that to me. "Have you seen a doctor?"

"It's not necessary, I—"

Suddenly, she slumped against me, falling unconscious.

"Mother!" I gently shook her. She was unresponsive.

"Help!" I shouted. In seconds, Deputy Fleming came through the door.

"She's fainted," I said. "She's not well. We need Dr. Tate!"

The deputy swiftly unlocked the cell and in an instant, he had lifted my mother in his arms and was moving through the office door. I hurried after him, impressed by his strength. My mother was not a small woman. I glanced around for Clayton, but he was nowhere in sight.

Deputy Fleming hurried to the infirmary next door, with me close on his heels. Reaching the door first, I pushed it open for him. Inside, Dr. Tate was busily organizing medicine bottles on a shelf behind his reception desk.

At our swift and noisy entrance, he whirled around, confusion on his face.

"Deputy Fleming—Who—?" he inquired, peering at the two of them from beneath his spectacles.

"It's my mother," I said. "She was coughing and then lost consciousness. I believe she is suffering from a fever."

Dr. Tate motioned for the deputy to take her into his examining room. "Bring her back here."

Gently, Deputy Fleming laid her on the padded leather table. A smaller table beneath the curtain-adorned window held an array of supplies. Dr. Tate went to work while we stood by.

Deputy Fleming shot me a concerned look. "Let's wait outside. You look like you could use some air."

I nodded my agreement. He was not mistaken—I felt unsteady, my emotions a tangled mess.

Outside, we settled on the narrow bench on the front porch. The deputy kindly placed himself on the opposite side of my injured shoulder. The space was tight, barely accommodating us both, making our proximity unavoidable. I could feel the warmth of his arm and thigh pressing against mine, sending a subtle thrill through me.

"Are you all right?" he murmured, his voice low. As he leaned away slightly, resting his elbows on his knees to afford me a bit more space, his glance returned to me. His face, handsomely youthful and marked by sincerity, held my gaze a moment too long.

"I think so," I said. "My mother has always been such a strong woman. It's strange to see her vulnerable like that."

"I had a strong-willed mother, too," he said with a chuckle, the intensity of his expression softening. "A person did not want to get in that woman's way."

"She's gone?" I asked.

He looked down at his boots, now avoiding my gaze. "Yes. Last year."

"I'm sorry."

"Thank you. We weren't very close. She wasn't the warmest person. It was impossible to please her—but I know she loved me, in her way. And I loved her, too."

"Ah. Yes. Well, we have that in common, you and I," I said with a smile. He smiled back, his mahogany eyes twinkling.

The sound of someone clearing their voice startled me. I looked up to see Clayton standing there, hands on hips and a knee cocked. I wondered how long he'd been there.

"What's this all about? Why are you at the doc's?" he asked, his indigo eyes sweeping between the deputy and me.

Deputy Fleming straightened, his arm again pressing against mine. "Mrs. Pryce's mother fell ill. She's unconscious. The doctor is taking a look at her."

Clayton's gaze again bounced between the two of us, smashed together on the bench. "I see. All right, deputy. I'll take it from here. You go back to the office and finish that paperwork."

"Yes, sir," he said rising. He glanced at me again and gallantly tipped his hat. "I hope your mother will be all right."

"Thank you, Deputy Fleming," I returned, appreciative of his polite solicitude.

As he left with a respectful bob of his head, I faced Clayton's intense, granite-like scrutiny, suppressing a smile.

It seemed the good sheriff's concern was tinged with more than professional duty.

Chapter Eight

"Tell me exactly what happened," Clayton said, the sternness in his gaze melting away.

"My mother started coughing, and then she fainted. I couldn't rouse her, so the deputy helped me get her to Dr. Tate."

As if right on cue, Dr. Tate appeared at the door. "She's regained consciousness. She's resting."

"What's the matter with her?" I asked.

He took in a deep breath and then let it out slowly. "Her heartbeat is a little irregular, and her lungs, well, I'm afraid she's consumptive."

"Oh, no!" I raised my hand to my mouth. *Consumption. Tuberculosis. A death sentence.* The pulsating of my heartbeat rang in my ears. My mother could be dying.

"She's in the early stages. She said her doctor in New York suggested she come out West—to take in the mountain air."

So, that's why she's here. Still gaping at the doctor, my eyes brimmed with tears. I hadn't wanted my mother in my life for quite some time, yet the notion that she might be gone forever from this earth struck me with a blow for which I was wholly unprepared.

Obviously sensing my fear, the doctor gave me a sympathetic smile. "With proper rest, exercise, good nutrition and clean, dry air, there's no reason she should not enjoy many years to come. I've known people who have lived for a decade or more with the disease."

I remembered how she had clutched at her belly earlier. "Did she mention anything about pain in her stomach?"

He shook his head. "No. Nothing. What do you know about it?"

"Not much. I just thought it might be related to her illness."

"In my experience, stomach ailments are not directly related to TB."

"I see." I stood up and found that my legs were a little shaky. "May I see her?"

"Of course," he said.

I went through to the examining room. The doctor had propped her up on some pillows. Her usually robust complexion had paled, and her eyes carried a weakness I had never seen before.

"Arabella." She held out her hand.

Clasping it in mine, it was cold and damp to the touch. "Why didn't you tell me you were sick?" I asked.

She gave me a hesitant smile. "I didn't want to burden you. And I've hardly had the chance."

It was true. Our previous conversation had been quick and filled with tension. And then Edmund had been killed, and my mother arrested.

"How long have you known about the illness?" I asked.

She cleared her throat and then coughed. "For a couple

of months. We'd been touring the east coast, and I thought I'd caught a chest cold. It just kept getting worse, so, when we got back to New York, I went to my physician."

"And that's why you're here? To get better?"

She blinked at me. "That's why we came to the West, but we came to La Plata Springs so that I could see you. I've missed you and . . . " Her voice faltered.

"And?" I braced myself. I should have known there was a condition.

"There's something else I should tell you. It has to do with Edmund's murder and why I think someone is trying to make me look guilty."

She pulled a folded piece of paper from her pocket and handed it to me. I opened it up and read it.

"Millicent,
Your days of commanding the stage are numbered. The spotlight you so greedily bask in will soon turn dark. Remember, the final curtain call comes for everyone, and yours is overdue."

"Where did this come from?" I asked.

"I found it in one of my trunks when we first arrived in town. But it's not the first."

"Not the first? How many of these threatening letters have you received?"

"One other. It was when we were in Kansas, about two months ago. It said something to the effect of: In the theater, every act has its consequence, and then, 'The script of the past may yet have a twist. Tread the boards carefully.'"

"Do you think it was from Mr. Farley? In retaliation for your note?"

She shook her head. "No. The note I'd gotten in Kansas was before I'd written the note for Edmund."

I looked at the note she'd handed me. It had the same tone as the one she'd just described.

"I thought little of it at the time," she continued. "I thought it had come from someone who'd been to one of our performances. As you well know, fame can bring with it a degree of fanaticism."

I knew too well. I'd had more than one encounter with an obsessed follower who'd made me fearful for my safety. My mother has had a long history in theater, as an actress herself before I was born, and then as my manager from the time I was seven or eight. She, too, was fairly well known.

"The sheriff needs to know about this," I said.

A faint knocking sounded on the door and then Dr. Tate peered in, followed by Clayton. "I'm sorry to interrupt, but I wanted to check your pulse one more time," he said to my mother.

"Can I have a word, Clayton?" I tilted my head toward the door.

He nodded, and we went back into the reception area. Deputy Fleming had returned and was sitting in a chair reading the La Plata Herald. He set it back down on the table and rose to greet us.

"I finished the paperwork," he said to Clayton and then focused his attention on me. "Everything all right here?"

I gave a slight nod. "Her illness is more serious than I'd thought, but she's okay for the moment." I didn't feel like going into the particulars with him.

"That's good. I'm glad to hear it," he said with a smile.

"You had something to say?" Clayton asked me, his tone slightly impatient with the interruption.

"Yes. It's about Mr. Farley's murder. I think someone is trying to implicate my mother."

"What makes you say that?"

I handed him the note and gave him a moment to read it. He handed it to Deputy Fleming, who also read it.

"She said she'd received another, prior to this one," I said. "It sounds as if someone is trying to get rid of her."

Clayton sighed. "Maybe. But, these letters might have nothing to do with Farley's murder."

"But what if they do?" I asked.

"I'll have to look into it." He tucked the letter into his vest pocket. "After we search her caravan."

"About that," I said, and then hesitated. He looked at me with raised brows, waiting for me to finish. "She told me she does own a gun. It's for protection."

He blew out a breath. "I see. So, she lied to me, then."

I looked at him imploringly. "I am aware she presents a rather stern exterior, but I believe she is frightened. She recognizes she is in a predicament."

"We'll need to examine the gun to determine if the caliber matches the bullet that killed Mr. Farley," Deputy Fleming stated. "She could very well be innocent," he added to give me some hope.

"Obviously," Clayton said, his voice tinged with annoyance.

"What are you going to do with her?" I asked Clayton. "Are you taking her back to the jail? She's ill, she can't—"

He held up a hand to stop me. "I know. The doc said she's overworked and needs rest—and that means a comfortable place to stay. I'm going to let her go back to the hotel. But, she's still under investigation. We'll have to monitor her."

"She's not going to flee, if that's what you're thinking," I said, bothered he thought my mother a hardened criminal who would skip town if unsupervised.

"It's also for her safety, Arabella, if we are to give these threatening letters any credence."

"Oh," I said, contrite about my previous irritation. "Of course."

"I can keep an eye on her," Deputy Fleming chimed in.

Clayton shot him a look, perhaps a little perturbed at his suggestion.

The deputy continued, "I mean, I know you're occupied with investigating the murder and town business, Sheriff."

He didn't respond, so I pressed my case that she didn't need to be guarded against escape. "I can assure you, Clayton, my mother has no reason to leave. She didn't murder Edmund Farley."

He clicked his tongue. "I hope you're right."

"I am right." My voice had an edge to it that surprised me, but it was difficult to hear his doubts regarding my mother's integrity—although, I had doubted it in the past, and perhaps still did, but not insofar as murder. In truth, I wasn't sure how I felt about any of this at all.

Clayton raised a brow at my tone, but remained unmoved and said, "The truth will out, Arabella. It always does."

Doctor Tate lent his carriage to Deputy Fleming so he could escort my mother and me back to the hotel.

Upon our arrival, we found Cordelia at the reception desk, busy reviewing documents with Mr. Pettyjohn and Kitty. My mother, still frail from her episode, leaned heavily on Deputy Fleming's sturdy arm as we entered.

Once we got up to her suite, Deputy Fleming left us at the door.

"I'll be downstairs should you need anything, Mrs. Pryce."

I appreciated his attentiveness, and also that the sheriff didn't feel it necessary to post him outside my mother's door to keep her under lock and key, like he'd done with me on two separate occasions. While I had understood the reasons behind the enforcement, I hadn't liked it all the same.

Cordelia helped my mother to her bedroom, while I got the fire going in the parlor. Soon Kitty arrived, bringing us a pot of tea and an apple tart that Lottie, our cook, had made.

A statuesque woman, Kitty Carlisle's raven hair and keen, dark eyes, lent her a severe, schoolmarm-like appearance. Despite her stern exterior, she was kind-hearted and possessed a warmth that belied her austere facade. Kitty ran the bordello in the annex—something I was still getting accustomed to, and she also managed the Bella Saloon for me.

"How's your mother?" she asked with a lowered voice. "I hear she took a turn down at the jail."

I nodded. "She's consumptive. But Dr. Tate said if she gets the proper rest, her condition should improve with the mountain air."

She set her hands on her stout hips and, darting her gaze toward the bedroom whispered, "Do you think there is something to her being involved in that actor's murder?"

I could have taken offense at her bluntness, but this was simply her manner. And in truth, my mother's ambition and ruthlessness did create a shadow of doubt in my mind.

I sighed. "I don't think so—I certainly hope not."

"You have doubts?"

"My mother is . . . Well, let's just say she will stop at nothing to get what she wants. But I can't imagine she would be so determined to have her way as to actually kill someone."

"How are you holding up?" she asked.

"I'm a little numb," I admitted. "This is all a bit overwhelming."

She laid a comforting hand on my arm. "Well, you let me know if there is anything I can do. Even if you just need a friendly ear, you know where to find me."

"Thank you, Kitty."

She left the room, and instantly, the spicy smell of pipe tobacco filled the air. Percival appeared in the parlor mirror, holding his pipe to his mouth. He took a puff and then blew a smoke ring in the air.

"Sounds like your mother is in quite a fix, my dear."

I sighed. "Yes. I don't know what to make of it all."

The bedroom door opened, and Cordelia came out. "I assisted her into her dressing gown and settled her into bed. She fell asleep the minute her head hit the pillow." She quietly shut the door. "Hello, Percival."

"Cordelia." He nodded to her in greeting.

"I'm so glad the sheriff has allowed her to come back to the hotel," she said. "The woman is exhausted."

"From what I've gathered, he didn't really have enough solid evidence to hold her for long anyway," Percival said with a tinge of disdain.

"Well, in his defense, not only was my mother's script found at the scene, her shawl was found there as well," I said, trying to be logical and pragmatic about the situation. It was much easier than giving way to anxiety. "There could have been some kind of struggle, and in the process, the shawl fell off."

"But, Mr. Farley was shot. Have you ever known your mother to have possessed a gun?" Cordelia asked.

I told her what I told the sheriff.

"Oh, I see," she said, a look of surprise crossing her features.

My gaze slid over to Percival, who seemed to have wandered from the conversation. His head tilted the way it did when he was deep in thought.

"Percival?"

He held up a finger to silence me, as if he was listening to something. Cordelia and I shared a puzzled glance.

"I can feel her," he said.

"Who?"

"The spiritual entity we saw at the warehouse. The woman. Her presence is becoming stronger."

"What? Now? Is she here?" Cordelia asked.

"She's not in this room, but she is definitely in the hotel."

"What do you mean, stronger?" I asked.

He hesitated for a moment, continuing to listen. He then shook his head. "Well, it's gone again. When I saw her at the warehouse, her visage was faint, like a whisper, and I felt nothing. But, just then, I could definitely feel her. She is becoming bolder."

"You mentioned she might be connected to Celine Dubois," I said. "Celine has a room on the 2nd floor."

Percival moved to the window and looked outside. "Ah. That explains it."

Cordelia and I made our way over to his side. Down below, Celine was leaving the hotel with something tucked under her arm. She turned her head to look up the street and then down, as if worried someone might be watching her, or attempt to follow her. She then hurried along the boardwalk, heading north.

"I wonder where she is going?" Cordelia asked. "Is that a book she's carrying?"

"Could be a script," I said.

"It's a book," Percival said.

"Oh yes," I said. "Was it a white book?" I explained how I'd seen it fall from her basket at the warehouse.

"Yes." Percival stepped away from the window. "I saw her with it the other day at the caravan she shares with your mother. She was reading it and making notations."

"You were there, at the caravans?" I asked.

He shrugged. "I was curious. I followed her in."

"You went in the caravan?" I asked for clarification, a little irritated that he might have accidentally revealed himself to her, or worse yet, my mother.

"Was my mother there?" I asked, slightly horrified.

"No. The young woman was quite alone."

I let out a sigh of relief. If my mother ever found out I had been in communion with another ghost, I'd hear no end of grief, scolding, and warnings from her.

"She interests me," he continued. "She has an innocence about her I find quite attractive."

I sniffed. Yes, that was the allure of Celine Dubois. Sweet, innocent, utterly feminine—and talented. That spike of envy stabbed at my gut again. My appeal had been—well is—a bit more glamorous, sophisticated, less earthy. It was the image my mother had created for me and, over time, I had morphed into it. I wondered what lay beneath Celine's public persona?

"Well, do be careful, Percival. You must steer clear of my mother. Do you understand? It will not be good for me should she know of your presence or our relationship."

He frowned. "But what of the other spiritual entity? Are

you going to warn her away as well? You can't control these things, Arabella. What are you so frightened of?"

Clearly, he did not understand the dynamics between my mother and me. While she had not wanted my secret exposed for fear of it damaging my career, thus her power and income — she also, in the past, threatened that exposure to keep me under her thumb. It was paradoxical, I know, but sadly, it had been effective—for a long while. And now that I had, in essence, rejected her, I feared her retaliation. It was partly why I'd given her such a generous allowance once we'd gone our separate ways—and also because she was still my mother and I was making every attempt to be a decent human being.

"I never underestimate my mother's motives and the actions she will take due to them—and neither should you. If you care for me at all."

He considered me with those large, luminous eyes for a moment, and puffed on his pipe, creating a fragrant cloud around his head.

He lowered the pipe and bowed his head in deference. "Very well, my dear. I will be careful."

"Thank you, Percival."

A knock sounded on the parlor door. Percival popped out of sight and Cordelia went to open it.

"Hello, Clarence," she said.

"Hello, Miss Danson." The young bellman stepped inside and took his cap off his head and crushed it nervously between his hands. A gangly teenager, with freckled skin and a mop of sandy hair, Clarence was extremely efficient and took his job seriously. "Sorry to intrude, ma'am, but Miss Chatterley is here to see Mrs. Pryce."

"Oh," Cordelia turned to me. "I wonder what she wants?"

I sighed, knowing all too well. Constance Chatterley was a reporter, after all, and she'd undoubtedly heard of the murder and my mother's alleged part in it.

"Information," I told her. "Thank you, Clarence. I'll follow you downstairs."

Cordelia gave me a sympathetic smile. "I'll stay with your mother for a little while."

I thanked her and made my way out the door, preparing myself for the inevitable barrage of questions.

Chapter Nine

I descended the stairs to find Constance standing at the reception desk, making conversation with Mr. Pettyjohn. Or rather, she was doing all the talking, and he was listening with a patient but wilted look on his face. Once the woman got going, it could be difficult to get a word in edge wise.

"Good day, Constance."

Known for her flamboyant fashion, today she donned a vivid pink outfit with white highlights, reminiscent of a peppermint candy. Her oversized hat, extravagantly adorned with feathers and perched at a jaunty angle on her head, looked as if it might tumble off at any moment.

Her face brightened upon seeing me. "Arabella, dear!" she exclaimed. Then, almost instantly, her expression shifted to one of deep concern, her brows knitting together. "This must be so difficult for you."

Out of the corner of my eye, I caught Mr. Pettyjohn rolling his eyes before he feigned busyness with the organizing of papers.

"What can I do for you, Constance?" I asked.

"Well, I'm working on a story about the theater troupe —and your mother—and I had some questions."

I took in a deep breath, searching for calm. I let it out and gave her a well-practiced smile. "Let's go to my office, shall we?" I didn't want this interview to take place within earshot of others.

"Hello, Mrs. Pryce."

I turned to see Deputy Fleming standing behind me. He'd seemed to come out of nowhere.

"Hello Deputy," I said.

"Is everything all right, here?" He asked in a tone of concern, clearly taking his job of surveillance quite seriously.

"Yes, yes, of course," I said. "I just have some business with Miss Chatterley. We are going to my office."

"I won't keep you, then," he said with a dazzling smile. "How is your mother?"

"She's resting."

He nodded. "Good. I'll be right here in the lobby, should you need anything."

"Thank you," I said, suddenly feeling claustrophobic. Was his presence at the hotel really necessary?

I guided Constance along the lengthy corridor toward the hotel's annex while she prattled on, filling the air with mundane details about town business and local gossip.

Bright sunlight assailed us as we entered the exterior wing of the hotel, an area consisting of a grassy courtyard framed with several small houses where some miners and their families lived, and two larger, two-storied dwellings where Kitty and her "sporting girls" resided.

I didn't relish the idea of a bordello being run in my hotel, but Kitty's business had been operating in the annex many years prior to my arrival. When I had first arrived in

La Plata Springs to take possession of the grand Victorian lady, I had wanted to shut down the hen house immediately. I did not want the Arabella's reputation, or mine, endangered by association with a house of ill-repute, but now I found myself thinking of eviction less and less. I had grown terribly fond of Kitty and her girls, and the thought of throwing them out pained me. Besides, in six or seven months, I would put the hotel up for sale, and in time, the problem would no longer be mine.

Taking the ring of keys from my dress pocket, I fumbled with my free hand to open the door to my office, the first and smallest one-roomed domicile on the west end of the courtyard. The sling was becoming quite tiresome, and my shoulder was feeling better. Once in the office, I pulled it over my head, releasing my arm.

"Should you do that, dear?" Constance asked in a motherly tone—which I could not abide. Though she was likely ten years my senior, one mother was quite sufficient, thank you very much.

"It's feeling much better," I assured her with a placid smile.

The office was sparsely furnished with a desk and chair, a file cabinet, and two armchairs flanking the wood-burning stove. I motioned for Constance to take one armchair, and I took the other.

"Now," I said, smoothing my skirt. "How may I help you?"

"Well," she said with a Cheshire cat grin. "I've been doing some research on you, my dear."

"Me? Goodness whatever for?" This was not what I had expected.

"Well," she fluttered her eyelashes. "I started looking into Celine Dubois, of course, as she is here in our midst, which led me to your mother and her illustrious career, which inevitably led to you."

"Oh, I see," I said with some trepidation. Information in the hands of any reporter was ominous, but Constance Chatterley and her penchant for gossip made goose pimples rise on my skin.

"I knew you were quite famous, dear, but I did not know that it began when you were so young. A stage prodigy you were called."

"Yes. I did start very young."

"Such a pity about your father abandoning you. I imagine your parents' divorce caused quite the scandal."

I gave her a tight smile. "Not really. They split before I became famous."

"Yes, but surely, everyone knew the story. Your mother was quoted in several—"

My heart thudded in my chest, drowning out her voice. I did not want to discuss my painful childhood with her, or anyone. My mother, embittered by my father's betrayal, had used it to garner sympathy and admiration. The poor jilted wife, rising above rejection and poverty to create a star. The memory of her exploitation settled like a stone in my stomach. I needed to put a damper on this conversation.

"Constance, I thought you wanted to speak with me about the troupe. About Celine and my mother. I really am rather pressed for time, so . . . "

"Right," she said. "Your mother. I understand she has fallen ill?"

"I'm afraid she has. But with some rest, she should be better soon."

She clicked her tongue. "Shame about Mr. Farley. I'd heard your mother was the last to see him alive, and Sheriff Marshall has put her under house arrest?"

"Dr. Tate said she needs complete bedrest for the time being," I said in an attempt to deflect from the murder case.

"Good. That's splendid news," she said. "Anyway, in some of my research I stumbled upon a story that was quite interesting."

"Did you?" I said with some impatience.

"Yes. It claimed your mother contributed to a young actress's death. A Kathy Macarthur." She stared at me blankly.

My mouth dropped open. "What?! Where did that come from? It's preposterous."

"You know nothing about this?"

"I've never heard it before. Where did you get this information?" I asked again.

"It was a brief article, in some little-known theater publication—I forget the name—but I believe the year was 1863. It mentioned that the young actress's manager and your mother were each vying to secure a particular role for their performers—your mother's performer being you, of course—anyway, during this, the young actress became ill. So ill, in fact, that she could not work, and thus, you got the part. The girl later died from this illness. People said your mother somehow played a part in this tragedy."

"You mean poisoned her?" I said, appalled at the very idea. It was absolutely ludicrous. It reminded me of the type of vitriol that—

"Wait," I said. "You said 'some theater publication,' but you couldn't remember the name. I find that very unlike you, Constance. As a journalist, you pay attention to details. Where did you obtain this publication? Was it in your archive?"

She sheepishly lifted a shoulder. "Well, not exactly."

"Constance?"

She sighed. "All right, I got the information from—"

It suddenly seemed very clear to me now, and a sinking feeling hit my stomach.

"Let me guess," I said through gritted teeth. "You heard this from Atticus Brooks."

Pulling her lower lip between her teeth, she did not respond. It seemed that for once, the cat had the woman's tongue.

"Constance?" I pressed. "Did you hear this story of my mother's alleged part in that girl's death from Atticus Brooks?"

She blinked rapidly, and her mouth twitched at the corner. "I make it a policy to never reveal my sources—"

"Oh, please, Constance!" I couldn't contain my impatience any longer. "It is nothing more than a rumor."

"All right, all right," she said, holding her hands up in surrender. "I may have heard it from Mr. Brooks. He said he covered the story."

My jaw clenched, and I fought to keep from lashing out at her further. Could Mr. Brooks be attempting to sway opinion about my mother regarding the recent murder of Mr. Farley?

I put on a polite smile. "Constance, as a journalist, you know you can't believe everything you hear—or read. If there was no proof of my mother's culpability, then it's clear to me the story was a complete fabrication. Surely, if it was true, I would have heard of it."

She put a finger to her chin. "Yes, perhaps. But, like I said, he wrote it for a rather small publication."

"If he wrote it at all," I said, annoyed with this revelation of hers.

"Why do you say that? Are you implying he lied?" Concern flickered across her features.

Indeed, that was precisely my implication. The man harbored a rather tenuous relationship with honesty. He was, without question, a cheat. My husband had him expelled from his club after Mr. Brooks had been found cheating at cards there. Consequently, he embarked on a mission to tarnish my reputation. And, now apparently, my mother's.

I immediately regretted my accusation, knowing that Constance held the man in near reverence, and the last thing I needed was to be in another journalist's sights.

"I'm just saying I've heard of no such story. Was there anything else you wanted to ask me?" I asked, eager to change the subject.

She hesitated and fidgeted her hands in her lap. "Well, since I have you here, I was going to ask you—do you remember when I took a turn at the party for the Stewarts?"

My stomach clenched. She was referring to the night she'd caught a glimpse of Percival and collapsed.

"I do," I said with some caution. "You'd had too much to drink, and you stayed the night here."

"Right." Her fidgeting became more pronounced. "Well, I—"

I held my breath.

"Oh," she swatted the air with a wave of her hand. "Never mind. It's nothing."

I let out a sigh of relief. "Ah. Well, then, if there's nothing else, I really do need to get back to the hotel."

"Yes. Yes, of course," she said, rising from the chair. "I won't keep you."

The entire conversation had been unsettling. The ridiculous story provided by Atticus Brooks in which my mother had poisoned some young actress was beyond the pale. It was true I never knew of such a story, but I was at a disadvantage because I had been sheltered from such things in my youth. My mother wanted my sole focus on acting, singing and dancing, and it left little time for anything else. And that this information came from Mr. Brooks suggested to me he might have fabricated it.

As I bid farewell to Constance in the lobby, Celine Dubois descended the stairs, the white book and some papers tucked under her arm. Surely, this was the same book I'd seen her with before. It must be good reading.

"Good day, Celine," I greeted her.

"Hello, Arabella." She offered a weak and trembling smile. She seemed downcast, which was completely understandable given a fellow castmate had been murdered, and her manager accused of the crime.

"Is there anything I can do for you?"

She shook her head. "No. I am going to the warehouse. The others are there already. Victor is insistent we continue our renovation of the building. He wants the show to go on, as they say."

I pulled my chin back in surprise. "He wants to continue? But you've no leading man."

She let out a nervous laugh. "He offered the part to Mr. Shay, but he declined. Mr. Shay likes playing both of his roles. He thinks it will be better for his career. He is a lovely man, and a talented actor, but he's really not right for the part. So, Victor said he's going to hold auditions for the lead. If he can find a suitable replacement soon, they will have ample time to acquaint themselves with the role while we proceed with the preparations for the theater."

"I see." It all seemed rather callous, with Mr. Farley not

even cold in the ground, his murderer at large, and one of the principal owners of the company under house arrest.

Celine went on. "I've just been to see Millicent, to ask that she try to talk him out of it, but she is of the same mind. She says it's too important to the momentum of my career. We hope to perfect the show by the time we reach San Francisco. We are booked at the Theater Royale for the summer. And I believe she and Roger have plans to make it the troupe's permanent home."

"They do?" Why had my mother not mentioned this before? "How so?"

"Edmund told me he overheard them talking. Roger intends to buy the theater."

I blinked. This was news indeed.

"But everything is rather in disarray at the moment." She put her fingers to her temple and shook her head. "This is all quite upsetting." Attempting a feeble smile, the young woman seemed undone.

"Would you like to take some tea with me before you go? In my rooms? You look like you could use some refreshment."

She let go a sigh. "That would be lovely, Arabella."

I glanced over at Mr. Pettyjohn, who had been intently listening to us. "Would you like me to have Lottie prepare a tray, madam?" he asked.

"Thank you, Mr. Pettyjohn."

Soon we were up in my rooms sipping Earl Grey and nibbling slices of soft molasses gingerbread that Lottie had made that morning.

"So, how are things, really?" I asked her after setting my teacup down, quite satisfied with the mixture of bergamot and ginger on my tongue. "Working with my mother, that is?"

Startled, she stopped mid-chew and looked at me from beneath her long, sable lashes. It seemed I had caught her off-guard with such a direct question. Or perhaps she didn't know how to answer without somehow offending me.

"I'm sorry," I said. "I don't mean to pry."

She nodded and finished chewing. After taking a sip of tea to wash it down, she said, "That's all right, but I'm surprised you asked. Surely you know."

I shrugged. "I was just wondering if it was different—for you?"

"I know she was quite demanding of you," she said. "Everyone talked about it when we were growing up. I was always a little envious that your mother took such an interest in your career. I had little support at home. But, now, I have Millicent's support. It's difficult at times, but she only wants what's best for me and my future on the stage."

"Yes," I said, somewhat skeptically, and took a sip of my tea.

"I never knew she'd been an actress once," Celine went on. "I suppose that's what makes her such a superb manager. She knows what it's like. She never talks about it, though."

"No, she doesn't," I concurred. "How did you find out about it?"

"I—well," she hesitated. "I read about it somewhere. I was amazed to learn she'd once been in a play with Lily Beaumont."

I nearly choked on my tea. I'd never heard of this before. Lily Beaumont had been one of the stages' biggest stars. She also owned and managed her own theater. The woman was a legend. But her life had been cut short. She'd tragically died in her dressing room right before a performance.

"Ah. Yes." I tried to regain my composure. I was a little embarrassed. I had not known this about my mother.

"It was only a small part. Even so, Lily Beaumont!" Her eyes grew wide with amazement.

My mother shared little about her time as an actress. She had struggled for success and was never given a leading role during her brief career. I knew enough to know it was something she'd always been bitter about. I believe it's one reason she had pushed me so hard.

"Anyway, that doesn't matter," she went on. "To have been on stage with such an admirable actress must have been thrilling. When I found out about it, I brought it up in one of our rehearsals, but I wish I hadn't."

"Why is that?"

"Because when I did, Gloria sniggered. And then Edmund joined in. I think it hurt Millicent's feelings."

I recalled what my mother had said about Gloria resenting her for favoring Celine, and the contention between my mother and Mr. Farley. There certainly was bad blood between them.

"My mother and Gloria don't get on?" I knew the answer to the question, but I was curious to hear Celine's take on the matter.

She set her teacup down. "Gloria is a prickly one. She doesn't really get along with anyone."

I waited for her to elaborate, but she didn't, so I asked, "And, Mr. Farley? How was my mother's relationship with him?"

"He charmed her at first. In fact, she was actually quite taken with him. Edmund had that effect on people. Particularly women. He had a way of making you feel like you were the most important person in the room. He used to flirt with her, and she flirted back. It was all in good fun. But when Edmund and I became romantically involved, their relationship changed. They argued a lot."

I raised an eyebrow. It was evident that my mother disapproved of the influence Mr. Farley had over Celine. However, a darker thought began to form in my mind.

Could she have been jealous of his attentions toward Celine? So jealous, indeed, that she might have killed him in a fit of passionate rage?

Chapter Ten

A couple of hours later, after I had made my rounds in the hotel to see that all was running smoothly, I went to my mother's suite to check on her, my mind whirling anew with the story of my mother's rumored culpability in the death of the young actress, and the surprising revelations I'd learned from Celine.

I discovered her sitting in bed, script in hand, a pen poised, and a myriad of notes spread all around her. She wore a beautiful peacock themed dressing gown.

"Shouldn't you be resting?" I asked.

She didn't look at me, but scoffed. "I am resting."

"You're working." I adjusted the knot of the sling behind my neck. It really was becoming quite cumbersome, but I was doing my best to be a good patient.

"I'm fine," she snapped. "I can't bear to lie here idle. You know how I like to keep busy."

I sighed. "Yes. I do."

"As soon as that handsome sheriff discovers who killed Edmund, I shall be able to resume my work properly. There is so much to be done. At least I can work on the script and attend to my correspondence while I am confined here."

"Does your correspondence have anything to do with the Theater Royale in San Francisco?" I asked, my words more clipped than I intended

She finally raised her head, surprised at my knowledge of her plans. "As a matter of fact, yes."

"So, you mean to stay there? Permanently?"

She let out a small laugh. "Oh, darling. Nothing is permanent. You should know that. But we have a marvelous opportunity there I intend to pursue."

"Yes, of course," I said, trying to be agreeable. I wasn't sure why the notion bothered me. Was it because she seemed to have moved on with her life? No longer striving to get back into my good graces. Could it be that she didn't want me in her life any more than I wanted her in mine? I didn't like to admit it, but the idea pained me.

She gave me an apologetic look. "I was going to tell you, darling, but things have gone a bit sideways lately, as you know. How did you find out?"

"Celine told me."

"Of course. What was she doing? Was she here at the hotel?"

"She was on her way to the warehouse. She seemed a little discomposed. I asked her to join me for tea."

"No doubt upset about Edmund," she said with nonchalance.

I studied her as she perused her papers. If she'd once had feelings for Edmund Farley, I wondered at her indifference at his death. I recalled the note she'd left him, warning him away from the show. It was clear she wanted him away from Celine. Whether she was jealous of his ardent feelings for Celine, or protective of her budding star, I still couldn't fathom she would kill him. But, then again, she'd always been an enigma to me.

"Yes. I'm sure she is upset about his death," I agreed. "And, are you?"

She looked up at me again, disappointment flickering across her face. "How could you ask such a thing, Arabella? Of course, I'm upset about it. You act as if you don't know me at all."

Well, she was quite right about that.

I pressed on with my queries. "Celine also mentioned someone from your past. Lily Beaumont. I didn't realize you knew her."

She blinked at me and then got back to her notes. "Yes, I was in a play with her, in Chicago," she said, now again preoccupied with her work. "I was a great admirer of hers, and she was very kind to me."

"Why didn't you ever tell me about it?"

She shrugged. "It wasn't important. Just a moment in time. It was long ago." She scribbled something on the script. I suddenly had the feeling I was intruding, but I hadn't finished.

"I need to ask you about something else."

"What is it, dear?" she asked absently.

"I've just heard of a story written about you."

"Me? My goodness. Is it recent? It might be good for the show—"

"No. Not recent. And definitely not good for the show, if it is brought back to light."

I suddenly had her full attention. "What story?"

"That you were thought responsible for the death of a young stage actress. A girl who was up for the same part as me."

Her brows pressed down over her nose, and her mouth hardened. "Where did you hear about this story?"

"It was secondhand, but originated from something Atticus Brooks supposedly wrote long ago."

She rolled her eyes. "Ugh! Vile man. You can't believe anything that malcontent writes."

"But was there a story about this?"

"Yes," she said impatiently. "But the accusation was proven completely false. It was later determined the young woman died of some kind of bleeding in the brain. Of course, Brooks never followed up on the story with that bit of information."

I regarded her with a mixture of skepticism and concern. "But why would someone believe you'd do something like that?"

"Because of you, dear."

I sucked in a breath, shocked she would say such a thing. "Me?"

"You were the talk of the town—your brilliance, your beauty, your talent. You landed that part because you were simply better than the other actress, God rest her soul. There was no other reason. Yet, people blamed me. Had a man been managing your career, that absurd rumor would never have surfaced. But many found it unseemly for a woman to be working in that capacity. A woman with even the slightest bit of power is threatening to people. You know that, darling."

I did, in fact, as I had only recently been accused of murder myself. Still, people believed what they wanted to believe.

"Yes, but that story circulating here in La Plata Springs could be damaging to your reputation regarding Mr. Farley's murder," I said.

"Oh, don't look so worried, darling. I am innocent of this crime and that girl's death. The truth will come out."

I had to admire her belief in herself, and her faith that she'd come out of this unscathed. I, myself, wasn't so sure.

"But what about the threats you've been receiving?" I asked.

Her expression hardened. "I refuse to be cowed by them. I won't live in fear."

I blinked at her, amazed at her resoluteness. She bent her head and once again perused the script, silently dismissing me.

"Well, I can see you're busy," I said, still mystified by her lack of concern.

"I'm sorry, darling," she said without looking up. "I've got to finish this letter and then go over the scripts sent from the theater director in San Francisco."

Her confidence that a guilty verdict for murder or a severe illness would not deter her was either admirable or arrogant—I couldn't determine which. But one thing was true to form. Either way, my mother was tenacious and she would not go down without a fight.

I left the bedroom and went into the parlor. Something sticking out from under the door caught my eye. It was a large piece of thick paper, curled at the ends. How strange. It wasn't there when I came in.

I opened the door and picked it up. It was an old-fashioned show poster. At the top it read, Grand Theatrical Performance, and below that, the larger text read, *The Merry Wives of Windsor.* Beneath the title was the image of three women in elaborate 15th century dress.

Familiar with the Shakespearean play, I figured the three women were the characters Mistress Page, her daughter Anna Page, and Mistress Ford. Disturbingly, the image of

Anna was circled, and beneath it, the handwritten word "KILLER," and then under that "KILL HER."

My heart plummeted to the pit of my stomach at the violence in the words and I sucked in a breath to regain my equilibrium.

"Mother," I said, going back into the bedroom. She ignored me, still absorbed in her work. "Look at this," I handed it to her.

She studied it for a moment. The fortitude she'd earlier shown melted from her face. With enormous eyes, she raised her gaze to meet mine.

"What does this mean?" I asked.

She looked down at the poster again. "I haven't seen one of these for years."

"I found it under the door." I said. "What does this have to do with you?"

Holding the poster in her now trembling hands, she studied it carefully. "I was in this play. When I was first starting out on the stage. I played Anna."

She raised her gaze to mine again, and our eyes locked. There was no way she could slough this off. I gently took the poster back from her.

"Whomever sent you the previous threats is getting bolder. We have to take this much more seriously, Mother. Someone is out to do you harm."

Chapter Eleven

I left my mother amidst her papers, but now it seemed she wasn't as eager to return to her work. She lay back on the pillows and threw an arm over her face. Clearly, this most recent message upset her more than the previous ones, and I could definitely see why. It was more than just an idle threat. It was chillingly personal.

I rolled up the poster and headed down to the lobby. As I arrived at the second-floor landing, a woman's sharp, insistent voice startled me. The sound echoed from further down the hallway. I cautiously peered around the corner—no one in sight, yet the voice continued. Driven by curiosity, I crept along the hallway until I reached a room with its door slightly ajar, open by about six inches. The voice was emanating from inside.

A shiver snaked down my spine, and suddenly, Percival appeared in my path, making me jump.

"Percival!" I hissed.

"Sorry, dear. I'm so glad I found you. I have something to tell you."

"Can it wait?" I tilted my head towards the open door. Another voice joined the first—this one higher-pitched and gentler. I immediately recognized it as Celine's.

Percival was undeterred. "Well, it's actually about—"

"Shhh!" I hushed him and proceeded down the hallway. From the coolness wafting over my back, I knew he followed me.

I peered through the gap in the doorway. Celine and Gloria Standish stood facing each other, with the ghostly apparition I had seen before hovering nearby. I drew in a sharp breath.

"That's what I was trying to tell you," Percival whispered, his icy breath at the back of my neck. I shivered.

"—But she wouldn't do such a thing," Celine implored.

"Don't you remember when we were in Cincinnati?" Gloria said, her fists at her side, her body tense and rigid. "She threatened him. Said his days were numbered."

"She was angry with him. We've all been angry with him. He tests—tested—everyone's limits, especially yours! Does that mean you killed him?" Celine challenged.

"Oh, please! No, I did not, Celine. I don't have the stomach for it. But Millicent! Millicent would go to any length to get what she wants. Remember how she nearly tore down the director in New York for not giving you the lead? Or what about that actress she slandered in Virginia? The poor thing will probably never work again. She would do anything to protect you—to advance your career. Isn't that why you agreed to work with her?"

Celine went silent.

"And don't forget about her affair with Edmund, brief as it was. She was furious when he turned his attentions toward you."

My stomach folded in on itself. Celine had mentioned

there had been flirting between Edmund and my mother, but I assumed it had been harmless. But an affair?

"Oh my," Percival whispered behind me.

"She wasn't jealous," Celine shot back. "She was protecting me."

"Exactly!" Gloria flung her arms wide.

Celine didn't seem to have anything more to say about that. She bit a thumbnail and began pacing the room. The ghostly apparition's eyes followed her.

"I'm just saying, don't be blind to Millicent's ambitions, Celine. For you or for herself. Just keep that in mind when the sheriff questions you."

Gloria took her handbag from the desk, ready to depart. I hurried back to the stairway. The sound of a door closing followed by another opening and closing reached my ears. Gloria must have entered her own room.

I sighed, shaking my head. "I don't know what to make of what we've just heard."

"Your mother is definitely someone to be reckoned with," Percival said.

Instinctively, with a protective urge, I wanted to scold him for speaking about my mother in such a way, yet I couldn't deny the truth in his words. A wave of nausea swept over me, causing bile to rise in my throat.

"What is that?" Percival pointed to the rolled up poster in my hands. I unfurled it and showed it to him.

"God's teeth!" He exclaimed. "Who's the woman circled in ink?"

I raised my eyes to meet his, and he instantly got my meaning.

"Ah. I see. Your mother?"

"I have to go," I said.

"Are you all right, my dear?" He laid his hand on my shoulder, sending a wave of coolness into my arm.

I shook my head. "No, Percival. I'm not. I wish she and her troupe had never come."

I descended the stairs to the lobby. Mr. Pettyjohn stood behind the reception desk, pulling mail from a canvas bag designated for the hotel by the post office. Likely, Cordelia had retrieved it earlier. She too was at the desk, methodically sorting the mail into cubbies for the guests. Deputy Fleming, meanwhile, lounged in one of the lobby's round-backed, armless salon chairs, exuding a profound boredom. He had tipped the chair backward so that its front legs lifted off the floor while the back rested against the wall. Spotting me as I entered, he quickly righted the chair with a loud *thunk* and sprang to his feet.

"Mrs. Pryce," his face beamed. "Is everything all right? How is your mother?"

I shook my head, not wanting to go into detail, as I was still processing the conversation I'd heard between Celine and Miss Standish.

"I'm worried about her." I handed him the poster and explained the significance of the marred figure.

"When did she get this?" he asked.

"Just a few moments ago. I noticed it as I was leaving her rooms. It wasn't there when I first went in."

Cordelia came from around the desk to look at the poster. She gasped. "Oh, how awful! Who could have done this?"

I sighed. "I don't know. She has received some threatening notes over the past few months. Whoever it is, they are with her or following her. Certainly, someone familiar with her past," I said, my mouth going dry as I spoke.

"She said that people follow the troupe to see their performances," Cordelia added.

"Yes, but they haven't sent out an announcement about the play yet," I said.

She shrugged. "Still, someone could be following them."

"Right." She had a point. "Mr. Pettyjohn, have there been any new guests at the hotel since the troupe arrived?"

"The sheriff asked the same question," he said. "No. Not here."

"I see." That, of course, didn't mean that anyone who might have followed the troupe wouldn't have checked in at the General or any of the other, smaller, boarding houses in town.

"Deputy Fleming, have you seen anyone go up or down these stairs since you've been here?" I asked.

"No ma'am. Not a soul."

"It has been rather quiet," Mr. Pettyjohn added.

"Then it had to have been someone who is here." I mused. Gloria Standish immediately came to mind. Celine said Gloria was bitter about my mother's professional attentions toward her, and Gloria seemed to be convinced my mother was indeed the murderer of Edmund Farley.

"I need to see Sheriff Marshall. I'll be back soon," I said.

"Shall I accompany you?" Deputy Fleming offered eagerness in his eyes.

"Uh. No. I think you should stay here. To watch out for my mother."

"Oh, right. Of course," he said, his cheeks growing pink. "You can count on me."

"Thank you."

I glanced over at Cordelia, who was suppressing an amused smile—obviously the deputy's little crush was apparent to her as well. While it was indeed flattering, considering he was quite a few years my junior, I put it up to admiration of my fame—not of me personally. Sometimes people fell in love with their imagined idea of me—not necessarily my person. After all, how well did he, or any of my other fans, truly know me?

Upstairs in my rooms, after grabbing my hat and a light coat, I retrieved Bijou's leash from its peg by the parlor door and tried to clip it to her collar. Her excitement for our outing made it a challenge, as she jumped and wiggled so much that finding the little hook became a minor ordeal. Despite Cordelia having taken her out earlier that morning, Bijou acted as if she'd never been on a walk before. Her eagerness, however, lifted my spirits.

Out on the boardwalk lining the street, I was struck by the freshness of the spring air and the beauty of the mountains. It grieved me that my heart was so heavy during this usually buoyant time of year. I again lamented my mother's visit. Had she not come, none of this would have happened—but then again, if she really was intent on killing Edmund Farley, wouldn't she have done so anywhere? Why here? Unless it was in a fit of rage. And, I supposed, whomever was sending these threats to her would have continued no matter where the troupe landed. It had been going on for a while.

Although she hadn't brought herself to admit it outright, she had come here for my help. I could have refused, I suppose, but then, what kind of person would that have made me? Someone who was not true to myself, that's who.

I looked up from my musings to see Andrew striding toward me, a broad smile on his face.

"Hello, Mrs. Pryce," he said. "How are you today?"

I raised my brows at his joyfulness. "Getting by, Andrew. You look pleased."

"I've rounded up several volunteers to help transform the warehouse. It won't take much time at all now to make it a workable theater."

"I see." I was a little affronted at his cheerful mood, considering that one of the principal players in the troupe was dead. He must have read my disconcertedness.

"I know this is a difficult time for everyone. Especially you, as your mother . . . " He let the rest of the sentence drop, then continued in another vein. "But I'm excited for the town. We've needed something like this. A social outlet. Entertainment. The miners' lives are so dull. My uncle works them hard. And, if he wants to put La Plata Springs on the map as a vacation destination, we need some frivolity. Wouldn't you agree?"

"I suppose so, yes." His charm and enthusiasm were infectious, and I couldn't help feeling lighter in his presence.

"I know the timing isn't optimal, but I'm looking toward the future. And I hope we will see you perform one day."

Flattered by his words, I smiled, although, sadly, I couldn't really envision fulfilling his wish. I only had a little over half a year left here, and my time would be occupied with further renovating the hotel and preparing it for sale. And, once it was available for purchase, I would have to keep it maintained until the transaction was complete. I didn't see having any time for performing, although the thought of returning to the stage made my heart sing. Perhaps . . .

I shook the notion away. I would have plenty of time for the stage when I returned to New York and my theater. "Good for you, Andrew. Your concern for the people of La Plata Springs is admirable."

"I'm thinking of auditioning for Mr. Farley's part in the play. I know you are busy with so many other things at the moment, but I was wondering if you might give me some acting tips?"

I blinked at his request. How could I sum up all the years of learning, training, pulling out of myself some of the most intense emotions I never hoped to feel in real life? The blood, the sweat, the tears in simple "tips?" Rolling all of it into a few single pieces of advice was overwhelming.

"Well, Andrew, I-I—"

And then something Leticia Crookshank said popped into my mind and I recited it from memory. "Acting is all about walking in someone else's shoes. At its very essence, it is raw vulnerability. If you can be honest in that vulnerability, you transform a character from the page into a real-life, breathing, human being."

He stood looking at me with his mouth agape. "That's beautiful," he said.

I chuckled at his expression of awe. "I wish I could take credit for it, but it has served me well in my career. Now, if you will excuse me, I have some important business with the sheriff."

"Of course," he said. "I'm sorry to have detained you."

"It's quite all right, Andrew. Good luck."

Bijou tugged at the leash, and I yielded to her insistent urging that we continue walking. From afar, at the Sheriff's office, I saw Clayton exiting the building. He walked over to

Queenie, preparing to mount, but paused when he spotted me crossing the street toward him.

"Arabella? Is there a problem?"

"Yes," I said. Bijou pulled again at the leash and I let her go. She scampered over to Clayton and jumped up on his legs, eager for attention. He knelt down and tousled her ears. I held out the rolled up poster for him to take.

"My mother played that role years ago." I pointed to the encircled figure.

"I see," he said, leaving Bijou to her own devices.

"What do we do?" I couldn't hide the desperation in my voice.

A pained expression overcame his features, and his sea-blue gaze met mine. "I'm afraid that's not the worst of it."

"What? What do you mean?"

He pulled something from his vest pocket and handed it to me. It was a tintype photograph of a young woman partially in profile, her arms raised aloft, framing her face. Her hair, entwined with flowers and ribbons, cascaded down her back. It was a beautiful image, but made hauntingly terrifying as the eyes were etched out. My mouth went dry, and a trembling overtook my hands.

"Is this you?" he asked. "I couldn't be sure."

"Yes, that's me," I croaked. It was a publicity photograph taken of me while I'd been playing Shakespeare's Ophelia. I was seventeen.

"Where did you find this?" I asked.

"I found it on the ground, near the caravans. I had gone there to question some of the troupe. Mr. Shay and Miss Benavides opted not to stay at the hotel. They wanted to remain with the caravans and the crew."

"Have you questioned them about Mr. Farley's murder?"

He nodded. "I've done an initial round."

"And?"

"Mr. Shay and Miss Benavides claim they had been in the caravans all night. The stage hands say they were at Kitty's all night."

"Do you believe them?"

He shrugged. "The four stage hands all have alibis. I've spoken with Kitty's girls. Mr. Shay and Miss Benavides can only vouch for one another, so that might need more exploration."

I looked down at the photograph in my hands again, and my throat tightened.

He took it back from me and put it in his vest pocket again. He gently laid his hands on my shoulders and gazed deeper into my eyes. I was so transfixed by the intensity of his gaze, I barely noticed the twinge in my injured shoulder.

"I won't let anything happen to you," he said. "I promise I'll find out who is behind this."

The sheer determination in those captivating eyes, and the hardened set of his jaw, gave me a resoluteness I needed in that very moment. I swallowed down the fear that had balled up in my throat and raised my chin defiantly. I could not abide this kind of threat, nor the fear it produced. I would not cower from it. I would meet it head on and confront this menacing hatred.

"I know," I said with confidence. "And I'm going to help you."

Chapter Twelve

"It seems to me the threats to Mrs. Janes and Mrs. Pryce are related to the death of Mr. Farley," Deputy Fleming said.

We had convened in my mother's parlor with a select group assembled. Present were the deputy, Clayton, my mother, and myself. We also included Maggie, the hotel's head maid, Kitty, and Sally Dean. Their roles in the hotel kept them acutely aware of the guests' movements, habits, and personalities, providing them with valuable insights that could prove crucial.

Clayton nodded in agreement with the deputy's observation. "It's possible, but in what way? Mrs. Janes has been receiving the threats for some time. They might be taking advantage of his death for their own agenda."

"Which is?" Cordelia asked.

"To get rid of me," Millicent said. "One way or the other."

"But what about the photograph of Arabella?" Cordelia said. "Why would they threaten her?"

"I'm assuming it's to put more pressure on Mrs. Janes," the deputy added.

"There's no better way to get to a person than through their children," Kitty piped in.

Sally, seated next to me, took hold of my hand in a comforting gesture. I wasn't in need of any such sentimentality, preferring to deal with a crisis in a more pragmatic rather than emotional way, but I appreciated her kindness. Especially since, when I'd first arrived in town, Sally had been particularly bristly with me. She and the sheriff had shared some kind of relationship in the past—I never knew to what extent, but she'd clearly felt she had some kind of claim to him.

I never considered myself a threat, as I had no intentions of romance, (or so I kept telling myself) but she obviously had.

But that all ended when she and Mr. Emerson, the manager of Archer's Mercantile, started a romance. It was then she quit Kitty's employ as a 'lady of the night' and refocused her attentions on her other job of barmaid. She was glowing with happiness, and I was happy for her.

"You're right, Kitty," the sheriff said. "Which means Arabella could be in danger as well. We are going to have to pull together and see that neither one of them, or anyone else in town, comes to any harm."

"I did not kill Edmund Farley," my mother stated with her head held high, directing her words at Clayton. "But someone is trying to make it look like I did. I must have my name cleared. You must find out who the killer is."

The sheriff didn't respond to her demand, but simply regarded her with a blank expression on his face.

"You don't believe me?" She challenged.

"I believe in the truth, ma'am. And I aim to find it," he said.

Sally offered my mother an assuring smile. "You can count on the sheriff, Mrs. Janes. And, Arabella." She squeezed my hand. "She has brought several criminals to justice here in town. She and the sheriff work well together. She's a good detective."

My mother turned her gaze on me, and I nearly wilted at the disapproval in her eyes. "You're a detective now?"

"No," I blurted out, embarrassed by her demeaning tone. "I'm running the hotel. It just so happens that I—"

"Don't let her modesty fool you," Kitty said. "She is quite talented."

My mother cut a glance at her. "Yes. She's the most talented stage actress I have ever known. I'm just surprised to hear she's been directing her 'talents' elsewhere."

I knew she felt I had debased myself with police work. Appearance and status meant everything to her.

"I'm just trying to help," I said meekly, all the while seething inside. Not so much at my mother, but at myself for letting her make me feel so diminished.

"And she has been a great help," the sheriff said, coming to my rescue. "But I've been thinking about it. It might be best if you stood down on this one, Arabella."

The smug look on my mother's face made my blood boil. Even though I had shut her out of my life, stood on my own two feet, maintained an amazing and successful career as an actress, and had solved several crimes—all without her, she was still trying to dictate what I did with my life. I leveled a glare at her.

"I'd rather not," I said. "Someone is now threatening me, and I won't stand idly by and let them continue." I redirected my attention to Clayton. "It's important for me to do something about it."

He reached up and rubbed the back of his neck, and then ran his hand over his jaw, thinking. I knew he was concerned for my safety, but he also couldn't deny the fact that I'd been helpful. Especially when he was laid up with a bum leg last fall.

Deputy Fleming, who'd gone quiet, cleared his throat to get the sheriff's attention, and then said, "I think the more people we have on this case, the better, Sheriff. From where I'm sitting, Mrs. Pryce has made a valuable contribution with her investigative skills in the past. I'd be happy to team up with her. That way we can widen our net, so to speak. I assure you, I'll see that no harm comes to her."

Clayton raised his brows and scoffed, making it clear he didn't appreciate the deputy's offer. "Thank you, deputy, but I need you at the hotel, to keep an eye on—er, to watch over Mrs. Janes."

"But, sir," Deputy Fleming protested. "Don't you think you'll need more man power—and woman power—on the ground? Perhaps you could employ someone else to watch over Mrs. Janes. Maybe deputize one of the able-bodied men in this town."

"I could do it," Kitty said.

"No one messes with Kitty," Sally said with relish. "I've seen her take down a man inside of thirty seconds. She could definitely do the same with a woman if she had to."

Maggie raised her hand to speak, which wasn't necessary, but so like her. "My maids and I could report anything suspicious we see going on to Kitty. We also have access to everyone's rooms, so we could be on the lookout for some kind of evidence."

"And I can keep things running smoothly at the hotel," Cordelia added.

Clayton tugged at his bottom lip with his thumb and forefinger, pondering the proposal.

He cast a glance at me. "If I allow this, I'm afraid we may have to tell any incoming guests the hotel is full. We must ensure everyone's safety here."

I couldn't really afford to turn people away. I was having trouble making ends meet already. We were behind on some of our bills. Thanks to the kindness of many of the shopkeepers, our credit had been extended. It would only be a matter of time before Mr. Archer, who owned said businesses, would find out and run out of patience. But I understood Clayton's concerns. I nodded my agreement.

"Does that mean Mrs. Pryce can work with us?" the deputy said, his voice hopeful.

The sheriff let out a deep breath. "Yes."

I ventured a quick glance at my mother, whose frown declared her frank displeasure at what she surely deemed an act of rebellion on my part.

"Excellent." The deputy clapped his hands together.

Clayton gave him a withering look. "But she'll be working with me."

The following day, I had arisen early after a restless night. After dressing, I tiptoed through the bathing room and through Cordelia's room to go into the parlor.

I took up the shawl I had draped over one of the armchairs next to the fireplace and wrapped it around me. I wanted to build a fire to ward off the early spring chill in the room, but noted there were no logs in the bin. Disappointed, I comforted myself knowing that Maggie would soon arrive with wood in tow to build the fire for me.

I settled myself at my desk, where I busied myself with some of the mail Cordelia had placed in my letter box. As usual, there were a number of bills. One of them I looked at with particular dread.

"Oh dear," I said to Bijou, who had followed me out of the bedroom. She raised herself on her hind legs and placed her paws on the edge of my chair. I reached down and held her face in my hands. She looked up at me with loving, dark, button eyes.

"Oh, Bijou. If only you were a rich puppy dog and could take care of this for me."

She licked my hand and then gave me her canine grin, her tail wagging furiously. I gave her a quick pat on the head, and she then went over to her bed under the window and curled up for a nap.

The invoice was from Billings Building & Co. The construction company had placed a lien on the hotel for services rendered a couple of years ago. Mr. Bledsoe, the former manager, had been negligent in paying, and thus, the company held me hostage for an amount I could not readily pay in full at the moment. In fact, with the interest it had accrued, I would in all likelihood not be able to pay it off until my time in La Plata Springs was up and I could claim my full inheritance.

Unable to face it, I left it for Cordelia, who helped me manage the books. I tossed it to the side and went through a few more of the less auspicious correspondence.

A knock on the door signaled to me that my breakfast and tea had arrived. Lottie, our cook, greeted me with a smile.

"Your tea and scones, Mrs. Pryce." She was a tall woman, all arms and legs, and moved with an unusual, birdlike grace. She had a delicate, heart-shaped face framed by a thick halo of curls that stuck out from beneath her mobcap. The scent of lemon wafting from the scones and the woodsy fragrance of bergamot made my stomach rumble with anticipation.

Bijou jumped out of her bed and scampered over to Lottie, dancing on her hind legs.

"I've got your breakfast, too," she said, looking down at the little beggar. A small bowl of last night's beef stew had been placed next to the scones.

Maggie, who stood behind her, followed her into the parlor. After a quick greeting, she tended the fire until it was blazing. Once satisfied, she brushed the dust from her hands and smoothed down her pinafore.

"Ma'am, I think I saw something worrisome late last night before retiring for bed."

"Oh? What is it?"

"I saw Mr. Langston and Miss Dubois outside her room, and he—he accosted her."

"What?!" I said, alarmed.

"Well, he took hold of her arms and said something like, 'Come back to me. I can do more for you.'"

"What did she do?" Lottie asked, setting the tea tray down on the coffee table. Bijou danced impatiently for her stew.

"She pushed him away and told him to leave her alone. She went into her room, and I heard the door lock. He stood there for a moment and then went to his room."

"I see." My mother had said Mr. Langston had designs on Celine, but the words, as they came back to me, gave me pause. They indicated they had once been together in some

113

fashion or another. But, in the context of I can do more for you made me think perhaps their relationship had been more professional than personal—if he had been referring to my mother.

The more I learned about the dynamics of this troupe, the more convinced I became that the perpetrator or perpetrators of Edmund Farley's murder and the threats to my mother were from within the group—not from the outside. However, I couldn't be too sure.

"Anything else?" I asked the two women. They exchanged a knowing glance, but neither one of them spoke.

I blinked at them. "Well?"

Lottie bent down and picked up something tucked under the plate of scones. She handed it to me. It was Constance Chatterley's news publication, the La Plata Herald. The story, front and center, was titled: *The Magnificent Millicent Janes.* The air froze in my lungs when I read the byline: Atticus Brooks.

I quickly scanned the story. It highlighted my very public troubled history with my mother. It also mentioned that she'd sent me away for a time—alluding that something had been "wrong" with me.

It was true she'd sent me away. But how had Atticus Brooks found out about it?

After I had innocently notified my deceased playmate Oliver Shrewsbury's parents that I had seen and spoken with him in the woods, my life changed forever. The couple did not take the news well. In fact, they were furious. My mother sent me to a spiritualist to teach me how to shut down my ability to commune with the dead. The story didn't mention this, thank goodness, leading me to believe Mr. Brooks did not actually know the reasons I had been 'sent away,' even so, it rankled. This was deeply personal information, and it had been a difficult time for me.

"Are you all right, Mrs. Pryce?" Maggie inquired.

"Yes," I lied. In truth, I felt quite betrayed by Constance. Why had she allowed this? It was one thing to write about the troupe coming to town, and even about my mother, but why hadn't she edited out something that could be so potentially damaging to me?

"Nobody takes the paper seriously," Lottie said. "Everyone knows Constance likes to gossip. The paper is always filled with it."

I smiled at her attempt to make me feel better. I was relieved that neither one of them asked about what Mr. Brooks had been alluding to, although I wouldn't have expected it from them. They were both very discrete.

"It's all right, Lottie. This kind of thing comes with fame. It isn't pleasant, but I'm used to it."

I read on. The story detailed my long career and my mother's aggressive management of it. The way in which he wrote about her appeared to be an admirable report, but beneath the effusive words lay a condescending undertone, which Mr. Brooks had mastered. To my horror, he'd briefly mentioned the story about the young actress who had come to a premature demise. He alluded to hearsay that my mother had something to do with it, but also added that she had not been charged with any crime. He concluded with his assumption that the rumor had arisen from professional jealousy, thus not directly placing blame on my mother. This was only a way for him to deflect any accusation of slander on his part.

I closed my fist around the paper, crushing it into a crumpled heap before throwing it into the fire.

"Thank you for the tea and scones, Lottie. And thank

you for building the fire, Maggie," I said, politely dismissing them.

"Yes, ma'am," Maggie said. "Do you need anything else?"

"No, I don't think so," I said, trying to convince myself. "I'll be fine."

Chapter Thirteen

Shortly after Lottie and Maggie left, Cordelia came out of her bedroom, fully dressed and ready for the day.

"You're up," she said. "And you've been busy." She nodded at the tea and scones.

"Yes. There's plenty left for you," I said. "Drink the tea while it's hot. I'll take Bijou out to do her business." I took the leash from the hook by the front door. Immediately, Bijou got out of her bed and rushed over to me, dancing and yipping with joy. Still upset by the story I'd just read, I didn't mention it to Cordelia. I didn't want to give it lip-service.

"Do be careful, Arabella," she cautioned. "I'm concerned about the threats made against you."

"I will be," I assured her, attaching the leash to Bijou's collar.

Upon entering the lobby, Deputy Fleming, who was at the reception desk with Mr. Pettyjohn and Kitty, sipping a cup of coffee, immediately greeted me with enthusiasm. "Good morning, Mrs. Pryce."

"Hello, Deputy, Mr. Pettyjohn, Kitty."

Both Kitty and Mr. Pettyjohn nodded their hellos, their expressions wary.

"Is everything all right this morning?" I inquired.

Mr. Pettyjohn averted his gaze to the La Plata Herald spread out before him. Kitty offered a sympathetic look, which I found hard to bear.

"Oh, yes," I responded, forcing a casual smile. "Quite the interesting article, isn't it? By the way, is everything all right in the hotel?" I asked again, shifting the focus from the earlier topic.

"Nothing amiss, madam," Mr. Pettyjohn said, in his usually stately way. "It's been rather quiet."

"Very good," I said. "I'm taking Bijou for a walk. I'll be back shortly."

"I'd like to stretch my legs as well," the deputy said. "Mind if I join you?"

"Not at all, but—"

"I'll keep a lookout here." Kitty patted the pocket of her dress, and then discretely reached in and pulled out what looked like the handle of a pistol.

Mr. Pettyjohn rolled his eyes. "Lord, help us," he muttered. I stifled a smile. Kitty's stern presence and no-nonsense attitude reassured me.

Still stinging from the article, I had half a mind to march down to Constance's office and give her a piece of my mind, but I knew making a fuss would only make things worse. I had to find out who killed Mr. Farley, and who was behind the threats to my mother and myself. The sooner I did that, the faster my mother and this drama would leave us, and I could get back to a semblance of normalcy.

I made my way to the doors of the lobby. Deputy Fleming strode ahead to open them for me.

Out on the street, Deputy Fleming and I fell into step. Bijou pulled on the leash, excited to be outdoors.

"I didn't realize you'd started acting at such a young age," he said.

"Yes." I stiffened. I didn't want to talk about it.

"Your mother is quite the businesswoman."

"Not really." I gave him a terse smile. "But she's good at getting what she wants."

"I should think—"

"Deputy," I cut him off. "I really would rather not talk about my mother. Unless it pertains to the murder case or the threats."

"Oh, all right," he said, a bit surprised. I didn't mean to be rude, but I didn't want to discuss my past.

"Have you discussed with the sheriff what you will be covering on the case?" I asked, to soften any tension I may have created.

"Not really. He's redirected me. He wants me to help keep law and order in the town while you two investigate the case. Apparently yesterday, at Boss's Saloon at the General, there was a bit of a scrape up between some of the Tavani tribesmen and one of the ranchers who were playing cards there. Mr. Archer asked the Tavani to leave, and they didn't take kindly to it. Said the rancher was cheating, but Mr. Archer took his side. The sheriff thinks there might be some kind of retaliation. The Tavani aren't fond of Archer from what I understand."

"Yes. I've heard they're not pleased with his expanding of the town on land they feel belongs to them."

"That about sums it up," he said.

Suddenly, a man came rushing around the corner of the haberdashery, knocking into Bijou. She let out a yelp. It was Mr. Thompson.

"Dammit! Can't you keep that dog—" He looked up, and upon seeing that Bijou was attached to me, his eyes grew wide with mortification.

"My goodness. Dear Arabella. Please forgive me." He knelt down and gently took Bijou's face in his hands. "I'm sorry, little dog. Did I hurt you?"

The assault quickly forgotten, Bijou stood up on her hind legs and placed her front paws on his knee, panting happily with a grin on her face.

"She seems fine," I assured him. "But, are you? You seem a little shaken, Mr. Thompson."

He stood up and Bijou toddled off to a nearby bush to piddle.

Mr. Thompson adjusted the points of his waistcoat. "Oh, it's just that I was in a rush. I needed to run an errand before heading to the warehouse. Victor expects me at the meeting in twenty minutes, but I just wanted to grab a coffee at the Bella and then be on my way. I'll be late, but Victor can wait a little longer."

"I see. Is everything okay between you two?" I asked.

He sighed and shook his head slightly. "The man is reckless with money. Acts like it grows on trees and expects me to simply hand it over whenever he asks."

I was curious to delve deeper into the dynamics of the troupe, but I didn't want to hold him up.

"I think I'll join you for that quick cup of coffee," I suggested. "Would that be all right?"

A warm smile spread across his face. "That would be wonderful," he said. "As a matter of fact, I'd like to get your opinion on an idea I have."

"What about walking the dog?" Deputy Fleming interjected.

"Oh, yes. Would you mind?" I handed him the leash,

pointing to a nearby field. "Just keep her away from that area; I don't want her picking up fox tails."

The deputy looked at me, slightly taken aback by the sudden responsibility. I had put him in a tough spot to refuse, but I couldn't miss the chance to talk to Mr. Thompson alone.

I slipped my arm through Mr. Thompson's. "Shall we?"

We headed back to the hotel. I felt a twinge of guilt for my hasty exit from the Deputy and for burdening him with Bijou's necessary business. I resolved to make it up to him later.

Once seated in the Bella, me with a cup of Earl Grey, and Mr. Thompson with his dark, aromatic coffee, he pulled some papers from an interior breast pocket of his coat, and spread them on the table.

"I've been thinking about the seating in the house of the new theater. Please excuse my crude drawing, but what do you think of this arrangement? Do you believe it will provide a good view of the stage from every angle?"

I studied the sketch. "It might be problematic for viewers at the back," I said. "Perhaps you could design some raked seating to ensure that each row is elevated above the one in front of it. It would involve more work and expense, but it would be quite effective."

"Yes, yes indeed," he said with a slight frown. "It's a splendid idea, though. I'll have to discuss it with Victor— and your mother."

This was a perfect opportunity to steer the conversation toward the relationships among the troupe. Touching a hand to my mouth, I adopted a look of deep concern.

"Goodness, child. Are you all right?" Mr. Thompson leaned forward in his chair.

I lowered my hand and blinked my eyes rapidly, as if fending off tears. "I'm so worried about my mother."

"Of course you are," he said. "This is a terrible business about Edmund. And with your mother accused of the murder, I'm sure you are quite frightened."

"Yes. I can't believe she would do something like that, do you?"

He bit his lip, hesitating. "It was no secret she despised Edmund. They argued constantly."

"But do you really believe she would kill him?"

He shook his head. "I honestly don't know. Edmund had a knack for bringing out the best and the worst in people. He had a way of getting into the good graces of certain... influential people in our circle." His upper lip twitched in what felt like annoyance. "Especially the good graces of women. Bless his soul, he had such a talent for drawing attention—sometimes unwarranted, I might say. He seemed to have a particular charm for those already spoken for, if you take my meaning. Not that it's my place to judge the loyalties of others."

"No, of course," I said, bewildered at the rawness of his words—as if Edmund's finesse with women had somehow affected him personally. I found it curious, but continued with my line of inquiry regarding my mother.

"Mr. Thompson. I'm sure you know that my mother and I have been estranged."

"Yes. It is well known."

"And I realize she can be a difficult person."

He scoffed. "Quite."

"Did you know she is receiving threatening notes and messages?"

He blinked at the question and then raised his eyebrows. "Is she?"

"Yes," I said emphatically. "I believe someone is out to harm her, or make her look guilty. Or both. Someone wants to be rid of her."

A shadow of concern crossed his features. "What do these threatening messages say?"

After I told him what they said, he leaned back in his chair and ran a hand down his beard in contemplation. "Good gracious."

"Do you think there is anyone in the troupe who might want to target my mother?" I asked.

He clicked his tongue. "Well—I'll admit, we have our challenges with one another. We all have rather strong temperaments—with the exception of Celine. The girl seems quite fragile at times. But the rest of us do knock heads once in a while."

"Is there anyone in particular with whom my mother does not get along?"

He stroked his beard again. "She and Victor clash over the material. Always have. And she and Edmund—well . . . "

He hesitated, and his jaw flexed under his whiskers.

"What about her and Edmund?" I prompted. I detected a slight narrowing of his eyes.

"They also had creative differences, of course," he finally said. "Celine often crumples under the scrutiny your mother places on her. The poor girl really needs to learn to stand up for herself."

"What about Mr. Shay and Miss Benavides?" I asked.

"They are relatively new to our troupe, so they keep their thoughts to themselves, mostly. I don't think they would do anything that might jeopardize their jobs."

"And, Gloria?"

He scoffed with a snort. "The woman is unstable. She

seems to have a quarrel with everyone, especially your mother. Although, in fairness to her, Millicent does treat her with a measure of indifference, which is unkind, considering she agreed to manage the woman's career."

"Yes, I suppose so," I said. I then remembered my mother told me she and Mr. Thompson had once been romantically involved—something I was still trying to reconcile. She also mentioned that in the end, he had not taken her rejection of him well.

"And you, Mr. Thompson," I proceeded cautiously. "What exactly is your relationship with my mother?"

Surprise flitted across his face. "Me? Oh, well—we are business partners. It's the two of us who keep this traveling theater troupe afloat. Your mother provides a stabilizing influence. She also helps creatively. And I handle the money."

"Does she also have ownership of the business?" I asked.

"Yes. She, myself and Victor."

"I see. And that's all? I mean, with you and my mother. There is nothing—more?"

He chuckled. "I'm sorry. I don't get your meaning."

"What I mean is, has your relationship with my mother been anything but professional?"

Having just taken a sip of his coffee, he nearly choked on the directness of my question.

Setting his cup down, he cleared his throat. "Millicent and I, well, yes, we were sweethearts. But that was long ago. We met when we were young; we had gone to the same acting academy. But it didn't last. She met your father soon after." His face took on a wistful expression. "Then some years later, after he'd left, I thought we might have a chance again, but it wasn't to be."

"I see." I sipped my tea, studying his face. He seemed sad, lost in the memory. Suddenly, he snapped out of his musings. "Well, I really must be going. Victor doesn't like to be kept waiting."

I smiled at him. "Of course. Please don't let me detain you further."

He set some change on the table to pay for our beverages, and I opened my mouth to protest.

"I insist," he said with a smile.

I nodded my thanks and watched him walk away, my mind swirling with countless thoughts. Yet, one loomed larger than the rest. Could Mr. Thompson and Mr. Langston have plotted to remove my mother from their business arrangement? Was the plan to eliminate Mr. Farley, a known liability, and pin the murder on her? The friction between her and the director over the script and her management of Celine was clear. Moreover, if my mother's account of Mr. Thompson's bitter reaction to her rejection held any truth, could his lingering resentment have driven him to finally enact his revenge?

Chapter Fourteen

I finished my tea and passed through the saloon's rear door into the quiet lobby. The guests must still be tucked away in their rooms. At the reception desk, Mr. Pettyjohn and Clarence, the bellboy, were engaged in conversation. Clarence enthusiastically showed Mr. Pettyjohn an item he had just taken out of his pocket.

"The Tavani chief, Standing Bear, gave this to me." He pulled from his pocket something resembling a turquoise stone. "He said it would protect me, as I don't have parents anymore."

I was about to greet them but became distracted by my mother coming down the stairs, pulling on her gloves. Kitty was trailing behind her, an exasperated look on her face.

"Mother? What are you doing? You should be resting."

She avoided eye contact with me. "I have rested. I need to speak with Gloria."

Kitty reached the bottom of the stairs and pulled me aside. She said in a raspy whisper, "I'm sorry, Arabella. I tried to stop her, but the woman is as pig-headed as I am."

I turned to my mother. "Why do you need to speak with Gloria?"

She raised her chin defiantly. "It's a personal matter."

I remembered how Gloria had tried to convince Celine of my mother's guilt in Edmund's murder. Had Celine told my mother about it?

"You can't go alone," I said. "It isn't safe—and you are still under investigation."

"Your sheriff can arrest me then," she said. "I will not be held hostage by fear, Arabella. If I allow that, whomever is out to get me gets their way, and I'll be damned if I'm going to let that happen."

My sheriff? Not her, too. Percival was fond of referring to him as my personal possession as well.

"He's not my sheriff," I said with annoyance, "but if you won't be talked out of it, I'm going with you." Once she made up her mind, there was no changing it.

Just then, Clayton and Deputy Fleming came through the front entrance of the hotel. They strode toward us, looking every bit a dashing cavalry of two. Clayton was noticeably taller and broader, while the deputy possessed a lithe, athletic elegance. Their combined presence was enough to make any woman's heart flutter. Quickly, I refocused on the matter at hand.

"The sheriff will probably not let you go," I said to my mother.

"What's this?" Clayton said. "Good morning, Mrs. Janes. Arabella. Kitty."

We all nodded a greeting to the two men.

"My mother says she's going to go find Gloria," I said with a degree of irritation. "And I said I'd go with her."

"Ah. Well, I was going out to the warehouse myself. I can accompany you."

My mother gave me a smug raise of an eyebrow and then offered Clayton a coquettish smile. "That would be delightful."

I sensed Deputy Fleming's gaze and turned to meet his eyes. He greeted me with a radiant smile. "I'm getting a quick cup of coffee and some breakfast at the Bella. Would you like to join me?" he asked.

"Well—I—" I was about to tell him I'd just had my usual light fare when Clayton interrupted us.

"You don't have time for a social call, Deputy. You need to get over to the General, to see if there have been any guests coming or going, like we discussed."

The younger man's face flushed and his jaw tightened, but then he graciously acknowledged the Sheriff's reminder with a dip of his head. "Right. Well, then, I must be going." His gaze fell on mine again. "Another time."

Clayton released a faint snort of contempt as the deputy walked toward the Bella. He then turned to my mother. "There is something else I need to ask you, Mrs. Janes."

"Yes?" She blinked up at him innocently.

"We did not find the gun in your caravan."

"Oh?"

"Do you know where it is?"

A blank expression crossed her face. "No. I keep it in the drawer of my nightstand. It wasn't there?"

"We canvased the whole place. We found no trace of it. Not even any ammunition."

"See!" she said triumphantly. "Someone obviously took it. Someone who is trying to make me look guilty."

I met Clayton's gaze and didn't like the glint of dubiousness in his eyes. I knew what he was thinking. If my mother killed Edmund, she could have very well disposed of the gun, but he let the subject drop for the moment.

"Clarence," I said to the young bellhop, who was still enthusiastically recounting his story to Mr. Pettyjohn. "Please find Mr. Ellis and have him bring the coach around."

He snapped to attention. "Yes, ma'am."

"Thank you, darling," my mother addressed me in her most charming voice—obviously on show for the sheriff. "Let's get together later for lunch."

I gritted my teeth. The last thing I wanted was my mother alone with Clayton. Lord knows what she might say to him about me. I then said in my most charming voice. "Perhaps. But the sheriff and I are working together, right Clayton? I'm coming with you."

His sea-blue gaze swept from me, to my mother, and then back to me again. I smiled sweetly.

He held my gaze and then cleared his throat, clearly uncomfortable at the underlying tension in the room. I widened my eyes, awaiting his response, hoping he would back me up.

"Yes, that's right," he said, finally. "Arabella is coming with us."

When we entered the warehouse, I was astonished at how much work had been accomplished in such a short time. Alongside their small crew of four, I recognized several townspeople, both men and women, busily engaged in various tasks. Mr. Langston was directing some men as they erected the frame of the proscenium on the large dais. Three women were simultaneously working on a large piece of heavy fabric, obviously the curtain. The crates and burlap sacks and other various items that had once littered the place were gone. Another group of men were building walls on either side of the proscenium. I assumed it would be to allow for a backstage area. Not terribly deep, but certainly long. I must say, I was impressed.

Mr. Thompson, having arrived before us, sat at a small table with a ledger book and a stack of papers strewn across the surface. He watched the workers with a great deal of interest. I wondered if he was calculating in his head how much all of this would cost.

Andrew was standing in a corner of the warehouse with Celine, each with a script in their hands. When he saw we had arrived, he quickly came over. Celine followed him.

"Hello, Mrs. Pryce," he greeted me, his eyes wide with excitement. He nodded to the sheriff and my mother and then turned his attention back to me. "I have wonderful news. I got the part!"

"Oh. I see."

Mr. Langston suddenly appeared next to us. "The young man is a natural. And perfect for the part. Celine is thrilled, aren't you, dear?"

Celine bobbed her head but said nothing.

"That was quick work, Victor," my mother said, her eyes boring into him. "I thought we were going to see the auditions together. Did you even consider anyone else for the part?"

I flinched at her bluntness and slid my gaze over to Andrew, who seemed unaware that he'd received the brunt of her remark. I wished she would have a little more tact. Still, Andrew seemed unfazed.

"You were indisposed, Millicent," Mr. Langston said matter-of-factly. "You wanted the show to go on, so I was facilitating the issue of a leading man. I thought you would be pleased." His words were placating, but his expression was not. His eyes glittered with venom.

"Does he have any experience?" She asked between gritted teeth.

Andrew stepped in. "Well—not really, per se. I performed in a play or two when I was younger. At school."

My mother flicked her gaze over Andrew. "I'd like to hear you read with Celine. The chemistry has to be right."

Andrew looked over at Celine, perhaps for approval. She gave him a tightlipped smile.

"Sure," he said.

Victor clapped his hand on Andrew's shoulder. "If he pursues his talents, he will go far in the theater world. I can guarantee it."

I raised an eyebrow. Natural talent was one thing, but skill took years to hone. I couldn't help but think Victor might be doing this to irritate my mother. She was an equal partner in the troupe. I had to agree she needed to be consulted before making this kind of decision. But I really didn't want to get involved in this little tug of war.

"Very well, Andrew," my mother said, ignoring Mr. Langston. "I just need to speak with Gloria first about another matter." She scanned the warehouse. "Where is she?"

Celine darted a sour look at Mr. Langston and then pointed to the back door. "She stepped outside. She said she needed some air."

My mother headed for the door. I trailed after her, leaving the sheriff with the rest of the troupe.

Up ahead, Gloria sat poised on a boulder near the river's edge, her attention absorbed by the rushing waters. Bijou scampered ahead and when she reached her, placed her front paws on the boulder. Startled at first, the woman jumped, but then reached out and stroked Bijou's little head.

"I'm so sorry," I said. "She can be impulsive."

Gloria turned around, and when she saw my mother, she shot to her feet.

"Millicent. What are you doing here?" she asked.

"I have some good news for you," my mother said triumphantly. "I've heard from Harvey Milt, the director of the Blaine theater in San Francisco. He's offering you a part in A Doll's House."

A puzzled look clouded Gloria's features. "The Blaine theater, but I thought we were—"

"It's a wonderful opportunity," my mother insisted. "Harvey is brilliant. It would be good for your career."

Gloria pressed her lips into a thin line. "What role?"

"Anne Marie," my mother stated.

Gloria scoffed. "The nanny? She's ancient! And it's a minor role."

My mother shrugged. "It would show your range. I think we should take it."

"We?" Gloria's eyes grew wide. "But what about your golden child, Celine?" she said with sarcasm. "Are you leaving her to come with me to the Blaine?"

My mother's jaw tightened. "I can manage the both of you, like I've been doing. It's just that you will be at the Blaine, and Celine will be—"

"With the rest of the company at the Royal," she spat. "Why do I get the feeling you are trying to dispose of me?"

"Don't be silly," my mother remarked nonchalantly. "I thought you'd be pleased to have a supporting role again, to move on from understudy."

Miss Standish crossed her arms. "I know what you're

doing, and it won't work. Victor won't allow it. He'll want me to stay with the troupe."

"Victor and I are partners," my mother said. "He'll see that this will be good for you—"

"Don't!" Miss Standish held up a hand. "I can't listen to this." She left us striding toward the caravans.

My mother shook her head. "Foolish woman."

"Are you trying to get rid of her?" I asked, feeling sorry for the woman.

My mother took in a deep breath. "When she fills in for Celine, she pales in comparison. Celine's shoes are just too big to fill for an actress of Gloria's caliber. She plays the role flat, and . . . she doesn't have that youthful spark. I want to find another understudy and Gloria needs roles that are—"

"Older?" I said. "Don't you think that's rather harsh, mother? You certainly know what it's like—"

"It's best for the company," she cut me off, obviously not wanting to discuss the fact that the very same thing happened to her once—and actually caused her to quit acting. It was a play we were in together when I was just seven years old.

"You haven't changed," I said, disappointed she always put her agenda in front of anyone else's, regardless of the situation. "Come on, Bijou."

I left my mother and went after Gloria. I wished to see if she was all right, and then also to question her about Edmund's murder. I wasn't sure it was the right time for the latter, but the investigation was underway. The sooner we got to the bottom of the murder, the sooner the troupe could perform their play and be on their way, taking my mother with them.

I arrived at the cluster of caravans and attempted to

determine which one belonged to Gloria. I approached the nearest one and ascended the two steps at the entrance.

"Miss Standish?" I knocked and then pushed the door open. Leaning in, I scanned the interior. She wasn't there, and when my eyes caught sight of men's clothing draped over the bedpost, I instantly knew it was the wrong caravan.

I went to the one next door, which definitely had a more feminine air, with a few lovely hats, and a pair of lace gloves resting on a bureau. Miss Standish was not in this one either. I stepped inside and took a closer look. I recognized a coat of my mother's hanging in the partially empty wardrobe. This was the caravan she shared with Celine.

I entered the third caravan. Littered with more feminine furnishings, it told me I was on the right track, and the poster of Gloria tacked to the wall assured me I'd found the right one, but she was nowhere to be seen.

The caravan felt claustrophobic, with the bed set against the longer wall, making room for a large bookshelf at the narrow end, which was full to bursting. Miss Standish obviously could not be parted from her book collection. And, it was clear neatness was not one of her better qualities.

Upon closer inspection of the bookshelf, I observed that many of the books were Shakespearean plays and other classic novels. My gaze traveled to what appeared to be a worn, leather portfolio. It seemed very out of place among the books. I reached for it, and suddenly the air cooled and the familiar smell of spicy tobacco filled the caravan.

"Hello, my dear." Percival said. I turned to see him in the full-length mirror beside the wardrobe.

"What are you doing here?" I asked.

He shrugged. "It seems we are never alone anymore. Now that Cordelia and I are acquainted, we don't have to sneak around as much. I rather miss the adventure of it."

I gave him an impatient look. "Isn't that what you wanted?"

He puffed on his pipe and then blew a series of smoke rings into the air. "Yes. But only because I thought you and I could be together more."

I sighed. "Well, maybe we can—after we get this murder solved."

"I see. Have you made any progress?"

I shook my head. "Not really. Everyone seemed to have a motive for killing Edmund, including my mother. And, quite frankly, everyone also has a motive for pinning her with the murder. It's quite puzzling."

"Indeed. What are you looking for?" He tilted his head toward the portfolio in my hands.

"I was looking for Miss Standish."

He pointed to the portfolio. "What is that?"

"I was just about to find out. Could you ensure she isn't heading this way? I'd hate for her to find me snooping."

Percival emerged from the mirror, taking on his transparent form, and disappeared through the wall of the caravan. He then reappeared shortly thereafter.

"I did not see her," he said.

"Very well. Thank you." I opened the portfolio. There was a stack of papers inside, held together by brass brads. A script. I pulled it out.

"It's a play," I said. "Written by a Grant Colston IV. I've never heard of this playwright. It's entitled, *The Death of Ambition*."

Looking through the portfolio again, I realized there was something I'd missed. It was a one-page summary of the play.

Percival wafted over and stood behind me to read over

my shoulder. The coolness of his presence sent a shiver down my spine.

Together, we briefly scanned the summary. The play centered on Hans A. Lechim, an ambitious actor, playwright, and theater director with dreams of fame and fortune. He is enamored with a young actress, Dariann Roth, who reciprocates his feelings, though she is married to another man and remains out of his reach. Dariann is also under the control of a powerful impresario, Clint Neil James, who keeps a vigilant eye on the actress's life and career. Hans's life is turned upside down when his own career is destroyed by another actress Emily Boulant, one who exerts much power in the theater world—who, in revenge for not getting a desired role in one of his plays, blackmails him for fraud. Frustrated by her control over his life, Hans plans to destroy the disgruntled actress, who dies under mysterious circumstances. With Emily Boulant out of the way, Hans kills Dariann's husband, thinking they will now be together. But, he has underestimated her love for her husband, and she retaliates by reporting him to the police, leading to his capture and execution by hanging for his crimes.

"Egad," Percival said over my shoulder. "That's a rather dark story."

"Yes," I agreed. "This has all the makings of a fine tragedy."

I scanned the summary again. The details of the romances, rivalries and revenge were very familiar in the theater world—usually not with the added details of murder. But then again, a murder had been committed in my mother's theater troupe. I wondered, with a shudder, if Edmund's murder might have any parallels to this epic tragedy, and did Gloria have anything to do with it?

Chapter Fifteen

I carefully put the script and the summary back in the portfolio and then, just as I placed the portfolio in the bookshelf where I had found it, Gloria entered the caravan. She was startled to see me there, and I was equally startled that Percival had not popped out of sight as he usually did—at my request—when others interrupted us together. Perhaps Gloria had taken him by surprise as well.

"I beg your pardon!" she said. "What are you doing in here?"

"I—I—well, I was looking for you."

"What is that smell?" she asked, sniffing the air. "Have you been smoking in here?"

I darted a look at Percival, who quickly put his pipe back into the front pocket of his coat. He then sheepishly raised his shoulders in apology.

"Smoking?" I said in mock disbelief. "Absolutely not. I smell nothing."

She crossed her arms over her chest. "Anyway, what do you want?"

I could see she was still angry.

"I wanted to make sure you were all right. I know my mother can be a little——"

"A little?" she scoffed. "Your mother is never 'a little' of anything."

"You aren't happy with her management of your career, I take it," I said. "Have you considered seeking another manager?"

"Which would mean leaving the troupe for good?" she said. "No."

"Then, have you considered that you might benefit from having her manage your career at a distance? Perhaps working at this other theater is the freedom you need to flourish." I was speaking from experience. My mother's domineering nature was nothing if not stifling.

She shook her head. "I've been with this troupe, and Victor, longer than she has. She can't just come in with her little darling, and her big city ways and change everything. She and Edmund are two peas in a pod!"

"Edmund?" I said. "You mean *were* two peas in a pod."

She rolled her eyes and scoffed. "Very well. *Were*, then."

"Was Edmund trying to change things?" I asked.

She laughed. "Oh, yes. He was just as difficult as Millicent. I was initially in the lead role, and Celine was playing a minor one. But Edmund and Millicent insisted she have the lead. Victor, the poor man, is so smitten with the girl. He'd do anything to keep her happy, so Edmund and your mother got their way, leaving me with nothing. The understudy. It's insulting." Her jaw flexed and her lips flattened into a sneer.

I wondered if her displeasure with Mr. Farley had culminated in murder. And, if so, could she be plotting the same thing for my mother?

"Miss Standish, where were you the night of Mr. Farley's death?" I asked.

She flinched, taken aback at my question.

"I beg your pardon?" she asked, affronted.

"The night of Mr. Farley's murder, where were you?" I repeated.

She set her hands on her hips. "I was at our campsite, at the caravans. All night."

"You weren't at the Arabella?" I was a bit surprised at her claim, seeing as the troupe had paid for rooms there.

"No," she said, flatly. "I wanted my privacy. I opted to stay here at the caravans, with Helene, Dale, and the crew."

"I see."

"Now, if you don't mind?" She folded her arms.

"Of course," I said. "One more question."

She sighed impatiently. "What is it?"

"If things are so terrible for you here with the troupe, then why are you so determined to stay?" I asked. "Other than you were here before my mother."

She didn't answer right away, but then said quietly. "Victor needs me here. Besides, it's only a matter of time before . . . " Her voice trailed off.

"Before what?" I queried.

She huffed. "Never mind. Now, if you will, please leave?"

"Of course, I'm sorry to have intruded." I glanced at Percival and gave a quick tilt of my head, signaling that I wanted him to go, too. Getting my meaning, he popped out of sight.

I placed my hand gently on her arm. "If you should require anything of me, just let me know."

She shook off my hand and turned her face away from me. I wasn't sure why I had incurred such hostile behavior from her, but decided that her anger made her blind to anything else. Kindness included. I stepped outside the caravan and nearly ran through Percival, who was waiting for me at the bottom of the steps.

"Don't do that!" I whispered, exasperated at him.

"What do you think she meant by, 'it's only a matter of time?'" he asked, ignoring my admonishment. "Sounded very cryptic to me."

I looked around, hoping nobody would see me speaking to a person who wasn't there—like a madwoman. Luckily, everyone still seemed to be in the warehouse, Clayton included. Mr. Ellis must have retreated into the coach to take a snooze, as he often did while waiting for his passengers.

"I thought so as well," I concurred.

"And she also said that Victor 'needed' her. In what capacity, I wonder?" Percival placed his hands behind his back.

"Right. She also made it sound as if Edmund and my mother were scheming together to take control of the troupe."

"And now, he's dead," Percival said.

Movement at the warehouse caught my attention. Clayton had stepped outside.

"You'd better get going," I said to Percival.

He let go a weary sigh. "Banishing me to the hinterlands for your sheriff, are you?"

"Don't be so dramatic, Percival. And he's not my sheriff."

He glanced over at Clayton with a smirk on his face. "If you say so."

And then he was gone. I shook my head in annoyance. I wondered if he had been so petulant when he was alive.

Catching sight of me, Clayton raised his hand in greeting. As I walked toward him, he pointed to the fallen down tree, indicating we should meet there.

He arrived there first and leaned against the massive trunk, his legs casually crossed at the ankles. He took off his hat, and the sun glistened on his sandy brown head. My heart stuttered a moment—as it was want to do in his presence—and I did my best to ignore it.

"Where'd you go?" he asked.

"I went to look for Miss Standish, to see if she was all right. She was pretty upset with my mother."

"Did you find her?"

"I did. She is one angry woman."

"What did you find out?"

"Well, there was certainly no love lost between her and Mr. Farley, that's for sure. And you saw how she was with my mother."

"Yes," he said.

I told him about the script and what the story entailed. "Whomever this Grant Colston was, he surely understands the rivalries in theater life."

"I'm sorry to be so blunt, Arabella, but what does this have to do with Farley's murder, or the threats your mother is receiving?"

I shrugged. "I'm not sure." I couldn't articulate the niggling feeling that there was some significance in it.

"Well, we need concrete evidence. So far, all we have it what was left at the scene of the crime, and unfortunately, it points to your mother."

"Which means we need to find out who is threatening her. They might be the same person who is trying to make her look guilty of the murder."

His eyes squinted in the sunlight, and he put his hat

back on his head. "What do you know of this story in *The Herald* and *The Denver Times* about your mother's involvement in a young actress's death?"

I looked up at him, startled that he'd brought it up. *The Denver Times*? For heaven's sake! That means Atticus Brooks had sold the story outside of La Plata Springs. My heart plummeted to my stomach. Where else had it been printed? Clayton had made no mention of the part in the story of my "going away" which left me feeling both relieved and apprehensive at the same time. This could be disastrous—not only for my mother, but for me in association.

"You can't believe anything Atticus Brooks writes," I continued. "Especially when it comes to me and my mother. You remember I told you he had a personal vendetta against me for my husband getting him kicked out of his club for cheating at cards?"

"Yes. But if there is no truth in the story about your mother, that's slander. And in selling that story, he risks a lawsuit—and so do the newspaper companies who printed it. Do you think he would actually take that risk?"

I crossed my arms over my chest in frustration. "Don't underestimate him. He's very well connected. I'm sure he could find a loophole somewhere."

That he was in the inner circle of the Archer/Stuart family didn't help either. Archibald Archer's power was daunting, but it was nothing compared to that of his sister Bertha Stuart, whose reach was much wider.

"We just have to get to the truth of Mr. Farley's murder," I said.

Clayton plucked a long stem of wild grass from the ground and put the end in his mouth. His face bore a pensiveness that made him seem a million miles away.

"I took the opportunity to further question the members

of the troupe about their whereabouts on the night of his murder," he finally said.

"And?"

"Dale Shay mentioned he thought he saw someone leaving the warehouse at around 11:30 pm., which according to Doc Tate, was around the time of Farley's death, but he couldn't be sure."

"Could he identify who it was?" I asked, surprised at this. The warehouse was definitely in view of the caravan site, but it would have been dark.

Clayton shook his head. "No. He said it was too dark, and he couldn't be absolutely sure."

"So far, the only people with alibis are Mr. Shay and Miss Benavides, correct?" I asked.

"Yes," he concurred. "Victor Langston claimed to be in the Bella. He also made mention he couldn't have killed Farley because he is a pacifist—and has nothing to do with firearms. Said he didn't even know how to use one."

"Do you believe him?" I asked.

A shadow of doubt passed over his features. "I'm not sure. There's something about his character I find dubious. But Sally said she saw him that night at the Bella, but couldn't remember the time."

"Did anyone else see him there? What about Kitty?"

"She was attending to some business in the annex," he said, the stem of grass bouncing up and down with the movement of his lips. "I've got Deputy Fleming questioning others who were there that night, but so far, we've got nothing conclusive."

"Right," I said. My encounter with Gloria played in my mind. "What about Miss Standish?"

"She claims she was in her caravan, sleeping," he said.

"Miss Benavides said Miss Standish went to bed at around 10:00 p.m."

"She could have waited until they went to bed and then gone out again," I ventured.

"That's true," he agreed. "I guess we can't rule her out yet."

"All the same, this is feeling a little hopeless," I said, wishing I could account for my mother's whereabouts at the time of the murder that night.

Still chewing on the stem of grass, he gave me no words of comfort. I wanted to believe that my mother would never stoop to something so evil, but I knew if something, or someone, stood in the way of her ambitions, they would pay.

Clayton and I made our way back to the warehouse to find my mother. As we approached, the sound of shouting inside warned us that something was amiss. Clayton dashed toward the door, and I hurried after him as best I could, navigating the rough ground in my high-heeled shoes. Mr. Ellis stepped out of the coach and followed the sheriff inside.

When I finally burst through the door, I was alarmed to see that Gloria had my mother cornered and held something up to her face. Light glinting off the object gave me a sinking feeling in my stomach. It was a thin blade of some kind. Clayton, Mr. Ellis and the rest of the troupe surrounded them, their faces etched with fear. Clayton approached them, hands raised.

"Miss Standish, I know you are angry, but you don't

want to do that," he said, his voice stern but soothing at the same time.

"She's insane!" My mother spat. "Get her away from me!"

Gloria's face tensed, and she moved closer.

"I am so sick of your insults," Gloria said, her voice low and menacing. "Sick of your promises, your lies, your schemes, which are all so self-serving. You killed Edmund. I'm certain of it. He was standing between you and your precious Celine. And you are trying to ruin my career. You need to stop."

My mother's eyes flared. There was no trace of fear in her face, only defiance. "You are washed up, Gloria. Face it!"

Mr. Thompson stepped forward, his eyes blazing. "Millicent, bite your tongue. Victor and I have discussed it. Gloria isn't going anywhere."

My mother's face registered shock and surprise. "But—but we agreed this was best for the troupe." Her gaze bounced between Roger and Victor.

Clayton approached the two women. "Miss Standish, give me the knife. Violence will not solve anything."

"We can discuss this rationally," Mr. Langston added in an effort to help.

Still brandishing the knife, Gloria remained unmoved. "Only if she promises to leave the company," she said.

"Ha!" my mother laughed. "That will be the day."

Gloria's whole body tensed and she raised the blade high above her head, ready to strike when Clayton leapt forward, grabbed her raised fist and twisted her arm behind her. She yelped in pain and the blade clattered to the floor. He kicked the weapon toward me. With my heart pounding and my hands shaking, I quickly picked it up.

"Let go of me!" Gloria cried.

With his free hand, Clayton took the shackles from his belt and handed them to Mr. Ellis. "Open these please," he said.

Deftly, Mr. Ellis got them opened and assisted Clayton with securing them around Gloria's wrists, despite her attempts to free herself.

"All right," Clayton said. "Let's get back to town."

I went to my mother, who had semi-collapsed against the half-built proscenium. Her complexion was ashen, but rage still burned in her eyes. I took hold of her elbow. She clutched at me for support.

"Do you need to sit down?" I asked. Without waiting for her answer, Celine pulled over a chair. There were several of them, all miss-matched and grouped together on one side of the building. I guided her into the chair.

"The woman is mad!" my mother said once she got settled. Celine stood by quietly. A wave of coolness washed over me. I turned, expecting to see Percival, but it was the other ghost. The woman. She stood next to Celine, her hands primly folded at her waist. She must have been a delicate creature in life, but in her face, I saw resilience and strength. I glanced over at Celine, who seemed unaware of her presence. I wanted to speak with the apparition, but now certainly wasn't the time. I turned my attentions back to my mother.

"Would you like some water?" I asked. "Mr. Ellis usually carries a couple of canteens on the coach."

She shook her head. "I'm fine," she said stubbornly. Her shoulders were trembling, and I noticed several strands of her hair had become detached and rested on her collar. I wondered if Gloria had grabbed her by the back of her head, but her coif was still neatly arranged. Absently, I reached out and brushed the errant hairs away.

Mr. Ellis came back inside. "It's time to go," he said to me.

"What? All of us together in the coach?" I wasn't sure how wise it was to have my mother and Gloria in the same small space.

"Miss Standish is restrained. Clay's got her under control."

I heaved a sigh, wanting to protest, but decided to put my trust in Clayton instead.

Chapter Sixteen

We traveled back to the hotel in a wave of icy silence. I occasionally caught Clayton's glance, but we exchanged no words. There was really nothing to say at that moment, and we all wanted to get back to the hotel as quickly as possible.

When we finally arrived, Mr. Ellis helped me and my mother out of the coach.

"I'm taking Miss Standish to my office for a little chat," Clayton said to me. "I'll join you later."

I nodded and helped my mother into the lobby. Cordelia was passing through on her way to the Bella, but stopped short when she saw us.

"My goodness," she said, approaching us with concern. "Is everything all right?"

My mother's complexion was still wan, and she leaned heavily on me.

"Mother needs to go to her room," I said. "We've had a trying day."

"Is there anything I can do?" Cordelia asked.

I shook my head. "She just needs to rest."

My mother pulled away from me. "You needn't talk about me as if I'm not here!" she snapped. "And stop fussing. I'm perfectly fine."

Cordelia glanced at me with surprised confusion. I ignored my mother's outburst. "I'll take her upstairs."

"Mrs. Pryce!" a voice trilled behind us. "Mrs. Janes!"

I turned to see Constance Chatterley bustling towards us. As usual, her flamboyant and garish attire seemed to take on a life of its own, rendering her merely a passenger within its bold confines.

The dress she wore was more subdued in color than her usual palate, rendered in shades of gold and ivory, yet its design was strikingly unusual. It featured two diamond-shaped panels, one on the bodice and another on the skirt, each bordered with a deep gold silk trim. Rows of dangling green tassels reminiscent of miniature curtain swags adorned the panels. These tassels bobbed and swayed with her every movement, drawing attention to her already prominent bosom. The overall effect was dizzyingly dramatic.

"I'm so glad to have found you," she said, her face beaming with enthusiasm. "I'm working on a story about you and your troupe, Mrs. Janes and—"

"Not another salacious story," my mother said sharply. "I'm not sure my reputation can handle it."

Constance looked stricken. "Oh—well—"

"Atticus Brooks wrote the story, remember mother?" I said, fearing she would find yet another victim for her sharp tongue. I, myself, was none too pleased with Constance for printing the scandalous story, but adding fuel to the fire of my mother's anger would only make the situation worse.

She once again jerked out of my grasp. "Of course I

remember the penny-a-liner wrote it, but she printed the slanderous thing. I have half a mind to have my lawyer—"

"Oh, dear," Constance said with a waver in her voice. "It really wasn't wholly my decision—I—"

"Not your decision? Don't you own the paper?" I asked, a little confused at what she'd just said.

She bit her lip and diverted her gaze from mine and instead addressed my mother. "I am a journalist, Mrs. Janes," she said. "It is my job to see that the public is informed."

"Not a journalist worth your salt!" my mother bit back. "If you were, you would report the facts, not rumor and gossip." Her face paled even more, and a sheen of perspiration had broken out on her upper lip. I needed to get her to bed.

Constance shrank into the bulk of her stiff ensemble at my mother's ire. Although the delivery was harsh, I couldn't disagree with the sentiment, and it took some will-power not to join in on the tirade. However, Constance's wounded expression tugged at my conscience. The woman often got on my last nerve, and she should have never published Mr. Brooks's article, but the recent vulnerability she had shown in the presence of Percival made her a little more worthy of sympathy in my eyes.

"Mother, I really think you should go upstairs."

She fired a look at me. "Keep that woman away from me," she said. She pointed at Constance with a shaking finger. "And don't you dare go near Celine, do you hear me?"

Constance's face reddened with embarrassment, and her lower lip trembled with emotion. It was becoming increasingly evident to me that the woman was not a seasoned reporter, as I had suspected, and she lacked the necessary fortitude for the job. Either that, or she was on the verge of some sort of breakdown.

Cordelia, quietly observing the scene, quickly came to the rescue. "I'll accompany your mother upstairs, Arabella."

Fortunately, my mother did not protest. From the lines of weariness around her eyes and mouth, I could tell she was completely done in. She let Cordelia guide her up the stairs.

"Oh, my goodness," Constance said, looking affronted. "I—I didn't mean to cause such a commotion." She raised trembling fingers to her throat.

"Shall we go to the Bella, Constance? I could have Kitty bring us some tea."

Her face grew redder, and she scrunched up her eyes, clearly holding back a sob. She was more upset that I'd realized.

"Perhaps something stronger?" I asked, feeling that a stiff drink was definitely in order—for the both of us.

With our arms linked, I led her into the Bella. Once comfortably seated in my preferred booth at the back of the saloon, I signaled for Kitty to come over. The worry etched on Kitty's face deepened as she noticed Constance's nervous state.

"Is everything all right?" Kitty inquired, hands on hips.

"Apparently, I've ruined everything!" Constance erupted, her emotions finally breaking free.

"Could we have some wine, please?" I asked Kitty softly.

"Whisky," Constance interjected abruptly. "I need whisky!"

Kitty's chin retracted slightly in surprise, and she glanced at me with widened eyes. I nodded in confirmation. "Two glasses, please."

Constance retrieved a handkerchief from her purse and

dabbed at her eyes, then she blew her nose loudly. I gave her a moment to compose herself before speaking. "I'm sorry my mother upset you. She's not herself lately and—"

Constance interrupted with another honking blow of her nose and looked at me through saddened eyes. "I've never had the chance to work with a journalist of Mr. Brooks's caliber before. He's so distinguished, and so are your mother and Miss Dubois."

I managed a strained smile, mindful of the questionable reputation of Atticus Brooks. "Mr. Brooks is not quite so renowned, Constance," I remarked dryly. "And he's known to . . . well, let's just say he tends to exaggerate the truth. You must admit the article you published is slanderous. It was proven that the young actress's death was due to a brain hemorrhage, not because of any evil act committed by my mother."

At that moment, one of Kitty's servers arrived with two glasses of whisky and placed them before us. I nodded in appreciation, while Constance took a large gulp, wincing as the potent drink went down.

"Oh, my!" she exclaimed, choking, and then sniffed several times, steadying herself. "I'm sorry," she then said, looking contrite. "I—I didn't realize there was more to the story. I just assumed Mr. Brooks had all the facts."

That was your first mistake, I wanted to say, but instead took a sip of the whisky. Initially, the liquor burned, but soon mellowed on my tongue.

"Anyway," I continued, "the entire story, then and now, was based on hearsay. It shouldn't have been printed."

She shrugged. "Archibald thought it would bring attention to the town."

"Mr. Archer? So it was his idea to publish it?" I asked,

irritation creeping into my tone. "What possible benefit could that story bring to the town?"

"He says there's no such thing as adverse publicity. Your mother is well-known—as are you—and a little controversy goes a long way. Like the story about your Pryce Theater."

Startled, I wondered how my theater tied into this. "What story?"

She took another large mouthful of the whisky, her eyes widening in shock. It seemed she was seeking liquid courage.

"I have been meaning to ask you about this," she said, her voice hoarse from the stringent liquor. "I came across a small publication that mentioned your theater. It detailed a story about Leticia Crookshank, an actress who died on your stage."

"Yes," I replied cautiously, aware of where this conversation might lead. "That was before my time. Quite tragic, really. Her heart gave out on her, I believe."

"Yes, but what intrigued me was the mention of sightings."

"Sightings?" I feigned ignorance, though a knot of dread formed in my stomach.

"Of her departed spirit. On the stage, in the rafters," Constance pressed, leaning in closer.

I blinked, but willed the muscles of my face to remain placid.

"It seems they are everywhere you go," she continued, looking up at me with a questioning gaze.

"They?" I asked, again knowing full well what she'd said, but stalling in order to come up with a reasonable response.

"Ghosts," she said. "At your theater, and of course, the

ghost who supposedly lives here at the hotel. The architect Percival Blank. Tell me, are there others?"

"Oh, don't be silly. You don't believe in ghosts, do you, Constance?"

She leaned back, her expression contemplative and silent, which unnerved me, as she usually prattled on incessantly. Rallying my acting skills, I adopted a confident tone. "I assure you, any rumors of hauntings connected to me are mere coincidences."

Her silence lingered before she leaned forward again. "I also found another story about when you briefly left the stage when you were a young girl—right as your career was ascending."

She seemed to have recovered from her repentant feelings rather quickly. A tremor of apprehension rose in my throat. "Really?" My voice cracked slightly.

"Yes," she continued, her gaze piercing. "It mentioned your mother attending a social event for Dr. Edward Clapper, a child psychologist and a well-known spiritualist."

I quietly sucked in a breath. This was the man who'd taught me to manage my otherworldly abilities. I then took a rather large gulp of the whisky, seeking some liquid courage for myself, and instantly regretted it as my eyes suddenly felt like they were on fire.

I cleared my throat. "Yes? What of it?"

"I find it very interesting," she mused. "Is your mother a spiritualist?"

"No," I stated firmly, my patience wearing thin.

"Are you?" she pressed.

"No."

"The story suggested you three were quite close."

I bristled. "Constance, I think you're reading too much into things that aren't there. You know how stories get blown out of proportion. Like Mr. Brooks's story, for instance," I said, defensively trying to veer the conversation back to her lack of good journalistic judgement in printing the thing.

My mother had tried everything to get the story of our association with Dr. Clapper retracted. She feared if word got out about our association with a child psychologist, or spiritualist, my secret would be known and I would be labeled insane or a witch, and my career—and her principal source of income—would be ruined. Despite her efforts, which ultimately failed, she successfully turned public opinion against the writer. He never worked again.

"Well, yes, I know how some stories are sensational-ized," Constance agreed, obviously oblivious to my attempt to derail her. She eyed me dubiously. "It's a shame people might have gotten the wrong impression about—"

"What impression?" I challenged, my anxiety morphing to a slow burn of anger at this line of inquiry.

She blinked, taken by surprise at my quick response. "W-well," she stammered. "You know, about you and your mother and—"

"Tread carefully, Constance," I cautioned, feeling a little desperate at this point. "I had hoped we could be friends—but I find your digging through old gossip alarm-ing, if not intrusive. Let us not let such matters come between us."

"Oh, well, I just meant—" she tried again, but sensing she might continue with this line of inquiry, I cut her off.

"Besides," I said. "You don't want to get on my mother's bad side. As you witnessed, she can be testy—and tenacious. Those who have gotten in her way have deeply regretted it."

She visibly gulped, and I felt hopeful I'd gotten my message across. Indeed, my mother was not one to be trifled with, especially when her income or her reputation was threatened.

Because of the whisky and my warning, Constance left the Bella a good deal more sedate, yet her pensive look troubled me. I pondered whether she might have discussed her suspicions about my connection to the supernatural with Atticus Brooks. Perhaps he was spurring her on to delve deeper into this story? More likely, her curiosity had been piqued by her encounter with Percival. The coincidence of his being at the hotel, coupled with the rumored sightings of Leticia Crookshank at my theater, was too compelling for someone as drawn to scandal as she was.

And what of Mr. Archer? Was he aware of her theories? Brooks would relish the chance to see my downfall, and Archer had been openly covetous of the hotel. He might use this harmful information as leverage.

Despite my efforts, I couldn't rid myself of the nagging paranoia. I suspected Mr. Archer might be orchestrating the mishaps that had plagued the hotel since I assumed ownership, though I had no proof. The fact that he and Brooks were close—and that both seemed to have Constance under their influence—only intensified my unease.

The sheriff and I needed to make headway in this investigation and get to the truth of the matter, to put all of this speculation and innuendo about my mother—and me—to rest.

Even if she was guilty of murder.

Chapter Seventeen

The following morning, the sound of arguing voices from somewhere below roused me. A sharp knock on my bedroom door—the one leading to the hallway—banished any hope of returning to sleep.

I took the silk dressing gown hanging from the bedpost and wrapped it around myself. I went to the door to find Kitty standing there, dressed in her usual black attire, her complexion ashen and her dark eyes flashing with anxiety.

"We've got a bit of a situation," she said stiffly.

Instantly, my mother came to mind. My heart missed a beat, and my breath caught in my throat. "Kitty, what is it?"

"I think you need to come see."

My feet seemed to be stuck to the floor. What if my mother was hurt, or gravely ill—or dead? A sudden and terrifying hollowness overtook me. Even though I'd pushed her out of my life, I knew she was always somewhere out there, moving and shaking the world in her drive to succeed. What would it be like if that force ceased to exist?

"Arabella?" Kitty touched my sleeve, bringing me back to the present.

"Right," I said.

She led the way down the stairs to the third floor landing. Mr. Pettyjohn, in his robe, and Maggie, dressed for the day's work, stood with their backs to us, looking down at something. When they heard us coming, they parted to reveal the lifeless body of Gloria Standish.

"Oh, my stars!" I gasped. "What happened?"

"We don't know," Kitty said. "There's no blood anywhere. It's like she just dropped dead."

I knelt down to get a closer look at her. Her eyes were closed as if she was merely asleep, but the ghastly pale shade of her lips and face told me she was most likely dead.

"We need to go get the sheriff," I said.

"I've sent Clarence to fetch him," Mr. Pettyjohn assured me.

"Good."

"If you require nothing further of me, I'm going to get dressed," he said. "The guests will wake soon."

"Of course. Please go."

With a bob of his head, he made his way downstairs.

I looked over at Maggie, who was anxiously twisting her hands together. "You can tend to your duties as well," I said to her. "Are you quite all right?"

"Yes, ma'am," she nodded. She, too, left Kitty and me to stand guard over Gloria's body.

"What do you suppose she was doing up here?" Kitty asked.

"She was obviously coming up here to see Mr. Thompson, or my mother." I shook my head. "She must have come very early in the morning. I do my final rounds at 11:00 p.m. and Mr. Pettyjohn follows at midnight. Maggie starts her day at five o'clock in the morning, so she must have come up here between those hours. An odd time for a social call."

"She might have been on her way to see you," Kitty added. "She knew you were investigating Farley's death. Maybe she had important information?"

"Maybe." A horrible thought crossed my mind. "Or maybe it was something more sinister."

"You think she was delivering the threats to your mother?" she asked, getting my meaning.

I nodded. "She was furious with my mother. Perhaps she had come up here to make good on those threats."

"She has no weapon, from what I can see," Kitty said.

I knelt down and peered closer at the body, examining it for any clue. She was crumpled on her side with her right arm tucked under her torso. It was hard to tell if she had any kind of weapon in the concealed hand. Her face was made up, her lips, as usual, tinged with carmine.

"We'll know more soon," I said. "The sheriff will no doubt bring Dr. Tate with him."

As if on cue, the two of them strode up the stairs.

"You all right?" Clayton asked me. I was touched by his immediate concern for my well-being.

"Yes, I'm fine. But this is dreadful," I said, gesturing toward Gloria's prone body.

Doctor Tate nodded a greeting to me and Kitty. "Did you touch her or move her in any way?" he asked, his intelligent eyes meeting mine. He was an elderly man, his hair gray and his frame stooped and slender, yet his mind remained as sharp as an archer's arrow.

"No," I said.

He bent down and moved her head from side to side. He then gently pushed her shoulder over, turning her onto her back, revealing the arm below. There was no sign of a weapon. He lifted her skirt and, with a small knife, he cut open her stockings to reveal deep purple skin below.

"What do you know, Doc?" Clayton asked.

"Livor Mortis. The dark mottling of the skin in her lower extremities tells me she's been dead for two to four hours, but that's all I can say for now. I've got to get the body to the infirmary to properly examine it."

"What's all this noise?" Mr. Thompson had stepped into the hallway. Suddenly, he realized what was afoot. "Oh, dear god. Gloria."

Clayton gave him a few moments to take in the horrible scene, and then asked him, "Did you hear anything out here during the night?"

"No. I took a sleeping draught. Slept like a baby."

"I really must get the body to the infirmary," Doc Tate said. "I've got my carriage out in front of the hotel. Clayton, give me a hand, please?"

"Right," Clayton agreed. Together, they hoisted her body, the sheriff handling her upper half and the doctor managing the lower. They proceeded down the stairs. It was still quite early, so, with any luck, none of the guests would see them.

The last thing I needed was more scandal associated with the Arabella.

Chapter Eighteen

Two hours later, Clayton came back to the hotel. He and Deputy Fleming had assembled members of the troupe, along with some of my staff in my parlor. The space was tight and there weren't enough seats for everyone. Cordelia and I, along with Clayton and Deputy Fleming, opted to stand.

"Why are we here?" my mother asked. "I have much to do."

The sheriff cleared his throat. "It concerns a recent development. I wanted to gather you all to inform you of this development and also to ask some questions."

"Well, where is Celine, then?" my mother inquired, her voice weaker than usual. Her complexion had grown paler since the day before. Dark purple crescents had formed under her eyes, and her normally full cheeks appeared sunken. It didn't seem possible, but it looked as if she'd lost weight in the last few days.

"I went to her door," Deputy Fleming said. "She said she'd be right up."

"The girl loves her sleep," Victor Langston said. "God forbid we should have an early morning rehearsal!" he chuckled.

"We'll give her a few more minutes." Clayton rocked back and forth on the balls of his feet. "I'd like to wait until everyone is present."

"We have much to do, Sheriff," Mr. Langston said.

"It won't take long once Miss Dubois arrives."

We waited another ten minutes. Mr. Langston and Mr. Thompson got up and started pacing the room. My mother fidgeted with the green fan she'd been carrying; opening and closing it. Mr. Shay and Miss Benavides were having a whispered conversation. The group was growing restless.

"I'll go check in on her," I offered. Clayton gave me a nod, and I headed downstairs to the second floor.

I approached her door and knocked. "Celine?"

The door latch clicked open.

"Celine?" I peered inside. She was nowhere to be seen. However, the spectral figure was present. Perched on the desk, her translucent feet hovered above the floor. She was small in stature, almost childlike.

I stepped in and closed the door behind me. "Hello," I said. Not surprisingly, the temperature of the room was much cooler than the hallway.

The apparition said nothing, but looked down at a book resting on the top of the desk.

"I'm Arabella Pryce." I realized introducing myself was a little silly. She'd seen me before and must have known who I was.

It struck me as odd that she was here when Celine was not. Percival had said the spiritual entity was attached to the young woman.

"Do you know where Celine is?" I asked. "She is needed upstairs. Apparently, she was here a few minutes ago."

She didn't answer, but laid her hand on the book. It was the book Celine had been carrying around.

"Are you trying to tell me something about that?" I asked.

She nodded and then vanished. Suddenly, Percival appeared.

"I'm beginning to think she's avoiding me," he said.

"She does seem rather shy. I've not encountered very many spirits, just you, Leticia and Oliver, and you've all spoken to me. I wonder why she is so silent?"

He gave a shrug of his shoulder. "I'm a rather solitary spirit myself. I've never spoken to anyone but you—well, and Cordelia."

"But I would have thought she would speak with you."

He frowned. "Would she have in life? Perhaps not. We aren't so much different in death. We just don't have our earthly bodies anymore." He paused and tapped his finger on his lips, thinking. "Either that, or she may be transitioning into a different realm—existing in a liminal space that exists between the living world and the afterlife. But I can't say for certain."

"Well, it seems she was trying to tell me something about this." I approached the desk and looked down at the book. Bound in ivory leather with a gold embossed border gracing the top and sides, it was both beautiful and well-worn, clearly cherished by its original owner. It must have been quite expensive.

I picked it up and flipped through the pages. The entries were penned in an elegant hand, and there were lovely illustrations in watercolor; depictions of landscapes, colorful costumed figures, and theater stages. Some of it read like an instruction manual for acting. Many of the entries spoke of plays, and characters, and thoughts on how to best portray those characters. There were notations in the margins, written in brighter, fresher ink.

"It's a diary," I said.

Percival peered over my shoulder, causing a draft of cool air to skitter across the back of my neck.

"It seems Miss Dubois is quite the writer and artist."

"But, look," I said, pointing to the first page of the diary. "It's dated February 13, 1850. It couldn't be Celine's diary. That was the year I was born, and Celine is younger than I am. These notes in the margin might be hers, though."

I flipped through the pages again and landed on an entry toward the end of the diary. It stopped abruptly in the middle of the page. The remaining pages were blank. "The last page is dated November 1869—but there is no entry."

I turned back to the beginning and started reading.

"You mustn't hold out on me, my dear," Percival said. He had moved to the desk and perched where the lady ghost had been sitting. "What does it say?"

"This entry mentions a man named Michael Nash," I murmured, scanning the diary's aged pages. "He was mixed up in some shady dealings."

There was clear animosity penned here; the diarist bore no fondness for Nash. They claim he resented their clout in the theatrical circles and their mentorship of someone called Adrian N.

I turned back to the diary and flipped forward a couple of pages. An illustration captured my attention—it was of an intricately drawn theater stage, bordered by lush red curtains. Two figures, both women, stood prominently. My heart skipped a beat as I read the names beneath the sketch.

The name 'Adrian' was inscribed under the figure on the left, while 'Millicent' adorned the right.

"My goodness, you've gone quite sallow, my dear. What is the matter?"

I held the book out toward him and pointed at the figure on the right. "Could this be my mother?"

He studied the illustration. "Hmm. The face isn't drawn too clearly. Could be another Millicent. It's not that unusual of a name." He stated matter-of-factly.

"I suppose, but . . ."

It seemed too uncanny. I flipped through the pages again, then closed the book, looking again on the front cover and the back. "I wish I knew who this belonged to back then."

"Perhaps Miss Dubois knows."

"And the ghost—er," I looked up at him sheepishly, remembering he didn't like the word. "I mean spirit—she seemed to want me to look at it. She must be trying to tell me something. Percival, do you think you could get her to communicate with you?"

"I suppose I could try again. She may not be able to communicate with me. If she is able, she hasn't been too keen on the idea so far."

"Maybe you've offended her?" I queried.

He scoffed and looked at me as if I'd fallen from the moon. "I beg your pardon. How would I have offended her?"

I shrugged. "Maybe she doesn't like your smoking. Or maybe she doesn't like it that you play pranks on the guests. Have you lately?"

"What pranks, pray tell?"

"You know. Making noise in the attic. Moving things in their rooms."

"Oh, that." He wafted his transparent hand in the air. "That's only for the guests I don't like."

"Exactly!" I said. "Did you play one on Miss Dubois?"

"I like Miss Dubois. Very much indeed."

I gave him a sly smile. "Maybe a little too much?" I remembered his comment that she 'intrigued' him. "You haven't tried to appear to her, have you?"

He turned his gaze from mine.

"Percival?" I drew out slowly. "Have you been behaving yourself?"

He sighed. "She doesn't even seem to see the spirit who is following her around. Why would she see me?"

"I know you can be very determined to get your way."

"Well. Miss Dubois is entirely unaware of my presence, I assure you."

"If you say so," I said. "But that's the strange thing. Why would the spirit be here in the room if Celine was not, if she is attached to her?"

"Perhaps it's the book," he said.

"The diary? Do ghosts, I mean, spirits, attach themselves to objects?"

"They do indeed."

"How fascinating. I never would have thought." I turned the diary over in my hands again. "Well, I'd better get back to the sheriff and the others."

"Don't let me keep you," he said with a hint of displeasure. "You mustn't keep him waiting."

He'd made it no secret that he did not approve of my friendship with Sheriff Marshall. It was rather amusing that he should be jealous. In fact, it was a little flattering, but how could I promise myself to a ghost? Not that I wanted to promise myself romantically to anyone, but a ghost would definitely be the last on the list.

I went back upstairs, hoping that Celine had shown up, but to my dismay, she was not there.

"She wasn't in her room," I said, closing the door. Quietly, I slipped the diary onto my desk.

"I wonder where she could be?" My mother said, her concern evident. She winced, bending slightly at the waist as if her stomach pained her. I was about to ask her if she was all right, but she quickly regained her composure.

"She might be down by the river," Victor said. "I know she goes there when she is overwhelmed or anxious."

If that was the case, it occurred to me she might know something about Miss Standish's death. Perhaps a little too much. "Or she could have fled the scene," I murmured, thinking out loud.

"What did you say, Arabella?" My mother's voice broke my train of thought. The woman's keen hearing never failed her.

"Nothing," I assured her. I cast a glance at the sheriff. He nodded to Deputy Fleming, who took his silent cue and left the room, presumably to search for her. I was half tempted to go with him because I wanted to ask Celine about the diary. If he could find her. If he couldn't, her disappearance would definitely complicate things. Had she been responsible for Gloria's death? And why? With the support of Victor and my mother, her position in the troupe was solid. Gloria was no threat to her. But maybe there was another reason?

"Can we just get on with it, Sheriff?" Victor asked, not bothering to hide his impatience.

Clayton hesitated a moment, and then acquiesced.

"Gloria Standish was found dead this morning on the hotel's third-floor landing."

"Oh, good Lord," my mother exclaimed, fluttering the green fan rapidly in front of her face.

Miss Benavides released a sharp cry of distress, and Mr. Shay clasped her hand in support.

"Dreadful, absolutely dreadful," Mr. Thompson declared, sinking back into his chair.

"What happened?" Victor asked.

"We don't know," Clayton said. "The cause of death was not apparent at the scene. Doc Tate is examining the body as we speak."

"I don't understand." Mr. Shay put his arm across Miss Benavides's shoulders to console her. She was quietly sobbing into a handkerchief. "We saw her last night, and she seemed fine."

"Where did you see her?" Clayton asked.

Mr. Shay seemed startled by the question. His gaze flitted to Victor Langston and then quickly back to the sheriff. "It—it was at the caravans. She said she'd forgotten something she needed at the hotel."

Miss Benavides stiffened and shot a look at him. His knuckles whitened on her shoulder, and she glanced down at the handkerchief in her lap. I wondered at the odd exchange.

"What did she forget?" Clayton asked.

"She didn't say," Miss Benavides answered. "She was just in and out."

"Were you in your caravan?" He asked.

"No," Mr. Shay said. "We were outside, sitting by the fire."

"Was there anyone else at the caravans at that time?"

Clayton asked, directing his question to everyone in the room.

"I was in the Bella," Mr. Thompson said. "Having a drink with Mr. Brooks."

My stomach sank at the notion. Lord knows what they'd been discussing. Both had a past with me and my mother, and that past was filled with unpleasantries.

"What time did you return to your room?" the sheriff asked him.

"I think it was around eleven o'clock. I was exhausted."

"And you, Mr. Langston? Where were you last night?"

"In my room. Working on a new play."

"And you were there the entire night?"

"Yes, of course. I was deeply entrenched and had my dinner brought up."

"Did any of you notice anything odd about her behavior?" Clayton asked the group.

"She'd been very unhappy lately," Miss Benavides said. "Preoccupied and a little testy. She told me she felt unappreciated as an actress, and that she deserved the lead role in our current show—because she was more experienced than Celine." Her gaze flitted to Mr. Langston.

"I'm not the one who had a grievance with Gloria," he cast a withering glance at my mother.

"Just what are you implying?" my mother shot back at him.

"It was no secret you and Gloria were at odds because of Celine. In fact, weren't you trying to get rid of her? She was found on the third-floor landing. Right in front of your room."

"Come now, Victor," Mr. Thompson piped in. "I believe you, too, wanted her gone. I saw you arguing the night of Farley's murder. I wouldn't be surprised if you were in on

Millicent's little scheme to hand her over to another theater. You told me she was as good as washed up. Quite frankly, with the way you've been talking about her lately, I'm surprised you've kept her on this long."

"You were no better, Roger," my mother said. "You felt both Edmund and Gloria were liabilities. With Edmund's drinking and carousing, and Gloria's instability—"

"But there was evidence at the crime scene of Farley's murder that points to you," Victor said, glaring at her.

"There has been no proof of my guilt!" my mother said in a raised voice.

"All right, all right," Clayton said. "This isn't getting us anywhere."

"And where is Celine?" Roger Thompson said, staring daggers at my mother. "Don't you find it interesting that when the deputy told her we were all meeting up in Mrs. Pryce's suite, she's now nowhere to be found?"

"You're saying Celine killed Gloria?" My mother fired back.

"Gloria tormented the girl," Victor said. "Celine might have snapped."

"You are all assuming Miss Standish was murdered," Cordelia said. "The doctor has not yet confirmed her cause of death."

"Then why is the sheriff interrogating us?" Miss Benavides asked, her voice wavering with emotion.

"I am just trying to understand where all the members of the troupe were last night. I find it an odd coincidence that right on the heels of Farley's death, another member of your troupe has died."

Just as Mr. Langston was about to say something, Deputy Fleming entered the room. He went directly to Clayton and whispered something in his ear.

The sheriff then addressed the group. "That's all for now. You may go, but I'll need to speak with each one of you individually."

"But where's Celine?" my mother asked.

"She's safe," the deputy said. "I've taken her to the jail."

My mother inhaled sharply. "The jail? But why?"

"Do you think she's responsible for Gloria's death?" Mr. Thompson inquired.

The sheriff interjected, "Not necessarily. As Miss Danson pointed out, we haven't yet determined Miss Standish's cause of death."

"Speak plainly, man," Mr. Thompson said. "Does that mean you think she killed Edmund?"

"I've made no conclusions yet, Mr. Thompson," Clayton said. "I will be in touch with the rest of you soon."

"Is Celine all right?" my mother implored Deputy Fleming with a tone of worry in her voice that I'd never heard before. At least not regarding me.

"She's fine," the deputy assured her. "I'll help you to your room, Mrs. Janes."

"I don't need help," she snapped at him.

I cringed. Poor deputy Fleming was simply trying to do his job and be helpful.

"All the same, Mrs. Janes," the sheriff said, and gave the deputy a tilt of his head.

"You still think I had something to do with Edmund's death, don't you? That's why you have me under lock and key?"

"Nothing has changed, Mrs. Janes, except the fact that Miss Standish is now dead," Clayton said.

"Have you forgotten about the threats, mother?" I said,

growing weary of her caustic tone. "The sheriff is trying to protect you."

She glared at each and every member of the troupe in turn. "No, I haven't."

"Very well, then. Thank you, deputy," I said, hoping she would comply.

"Before you go," Clayton raised a hand, "I'll need Miss Standish's next of kin. If anyone has that information, I'd—"

"She didn't have anyone." Miss Benavides looked up at him with sad eyes. "She was all alone in this world. The troupe was her only family—and it pained her you were all so against her." Her gaze swept over the room. No one said anything further.

Indeed, it seemed as if Gloria Standish would not be mourned.

Chapter Nineteen

I showed the last of the group out of the parlor, their footsteps muffled by the thick, ornate rug that adorned the floor. The door clicked shut, leaving behind a silence that seemed to swell, filling the room. I turned to face Clayton and Cordelia, who'd remained behind.

"Did Deputy Fleming arrest Celine?" I asked.

He shook his head. "No."

"Where did he find her?" Cordelia asked.

"Down by the river, as Langston said."

"Well then, why did the deputy take her to the jail?"

He released a deep breath. "She said she didn't want to be with the troupe at the moment. She said she needed some space."

"Did she know anything about Miss Standish?" I asked him.

"Dirk told her about it and said we had some questions for her. She agreed to go to the jail so I could speak with her."

"I understand," I said, my mind suddenly snapping to

another matter. "There's something I need to show you." I walked over to the desk and retrieved the white leather-bound book.

"I've seen Celine with this. It's a diary with entries that date back to 1850. I can't say to whom it originally belonged, but I found something intriguing inside." I flipped through the yellowed pages until I reached the one with the illustration. The drawing of what I assumed was my mother, her name penned neatly beneath it. I held it out for him to see. Cordelia, standing next to him, craned her neck eagerly to catch a glimpse.

"Does this person look familiar?" I asked.

"Oh, my!" Cordelia gasped.

Clayton squinted his eyes to get a better look. "Your mother?"

"It appears so. Unless it's another Millicent, but the resemblance is remarkable."

"It is," he agreed with a nod of his head. "And there is no indication of to whom the diary belonged prior to Miss Dubois?"

"Not that I can tell, so far. But—and I'm not sure it has any bearing on the case—both the script and the diary have some parallels to what's been happening within the troupe —the murder of an actor, the threat of a strong and over-bearing woman—"

"The woman being?" he asked.

I shrugged. "My mother? And, the rivalries among the players are similar as well. I'd like to read this diary cover to cover, and further peruse the script."

"Well, it seems like a long shot, but it's not a bad idea. I'll speak with Miss Dubois about the diary. I'll get it back to you."

"All right. I'll go to the caravans to retrieve the script," I offered and turned to get my coat and hat. Clayton reached out and took hold of my elbow.

"I'd rather you not go alone. The threats to your mother were also indirect threats to you, remember?"

"I'll go with her," Cordelia offered.

"No offense, Miss Danson, but—"

"We'll bring Deputy Fleming," I said. "He won't mind."

Clayton let go a breath. "No, he wouldn't," he said with an undertone of annoyance. "But I think it would be better if Miss Danson and the deputy went out to the caravans. Besides, I'd like you to accompany me to speak with Miss Dubois. She might be more comfortable with you there."

I caught Cordelia's glance. She bit her lip, trying to suppress an amused smile.

"But they don't know where the script is," I stated, looking away from her. I did not want to indulge her in her teasing.

"Can't you tell Miss Danson where it is?" he asked.

She looked at me with raised eyebrows, the smile still playing on her lips.

"I suppose," I said.

"All right, then," he said with some satisfaction. "Miss Danson, please ask Deputy Fleming to escort you to the caravans."

Upon arriving at the jail, we found Celine sitting at Deputy Fleming's desk. Bijou, quick to spot her, scampered over and hoisted her front paws onto the chair, seeking affection. Celine leaned down and scooped her up. Bijou showered her with kisses on the chin. Yet despite the display of affection, Celine's expression remained somber and troubled.

"Hello, dear," I said.

She shook her head, her eyes filling with tears. "I can't believe she's gone."

I went to her and took her hand in mine. Bijou settled herself in her lap. "I'm so sorry."

She wiped away a stray tear. "I know she resented my relationship with your mother, but I never held it against her. I understood how painful it was for her."

"When you heard I wanted to speak with the troupe, why did you run away?" Clayton interjected, wanting to get on with the business at hand.

She sighed. "I didn't run away. I just needed a few moments. I've been feeling very overwhelmed. And when the deputy told me about Gloria, I wanted to speak with you privately, not in front of the others."

"Why?" he asked.

"Because—because I can't face Millicent."

"Why is that?" Clayton asked.

"Because, I'm afraid she—I saw her with the gun. The night Edmund died. I saw her take it out of the drawer of her nightstand and load it. I didn't really think anything of it because she put it back in the drawer. But then when Edmund was found dead—"

"Why didn't you tell me this before?" Clayton asked.

Her face twisted in anguish. "I—I don't know. I think I was in shock, and I was scared, but when I found out about Gloria—"

"You think my mother killed Gloria?" I asked, alarmed.

She bit her lip. "Gloria was blackmailing her."

I pulled my chin back in surprise. "What? Why?"

Gloria's gaze flitted between me and Clayton. "That's why she got her another part, at another company. To keep her quiet, and to get rid of her. Millicent thought Gloria would be happy about it—she's been so miserable with us—but she wasn't happy at all."

"What does my mother want kept secret?"

She hesitated a moment before saying. "A long time ago, in 1868, I think. Millicent had an affair. With a very prominent married man."

I blinked at her, struggling to grasp the significance of her words. 1868. My mother would have been thirty-seven then, and I, eighteen. It was difficult enough to fathom my mother having romantic entanglements, let alone with a married man. She, more than anyone, understood the havoc such an affair could wreak—having experienced firsthand the anguish of my father's infidelity.

"I see," I said at length.

"How did Gloria know about this?"

"I don't know," she shrugged.

"And how did you know about it?" Clayton asked.

She gestured with a tilt of her head towards the diary I still held in my hands. "That came from my room?" she asked.

"Yes." I answered. "Yes, when I went looking for you—I'm sorry for taking it, but I wanted to ask you about it."

"The story is in there," she said.

"Where did you get the diary?" I held it up. "I am assuming it isn't yours. It dates back to before your time."

"No, it isn't mine. I believe it originally belonged to the late actress Lily Beaumont. I was performing at the Youngstown Theater in Philadelphia, her home theater. I had the honor of being assigned her dressing room, which was a great privilege for me, as I've always admired Miss Beaumont, even though I was too young to have ever met her. One day, I discovered the diary hidden under the floorboards; one of them was loose and popped up when I stepped on it. When I went to fix it, I found the diary there. It's become quite a treasure to me, almost like a good luck charm," she said, smiling wistfully.

I understood the sentiment. I, too, had once cherished an object I considered a lucky talisman. It was a Forget-Me-Not ring given to me by my father before he left us for his Parisian benefactress. He said it would bring me great fortune, and for a while, it seemed to. But eventually, it became a crutch. I hoped Celine would not experience the same with the treasured diary.

"I've learned a lot about acting from Miss Beaumont's entries in the diary," she went on. "It's become a wonderful resource for me. And I feel like I've gotten to know her through its pages. It's like she's speaking directly to me."

Perhaps she was—in her silent way, I thought. The ghostly apparition Percival and I had seen had to be Miss Beaumont herself. I wanted to ask her if she could see the late actress's spirit, but didn't want to bring it up in front of Clayton.

"But then, how did you know Gloria was aware of the affair?" I asked instead.

"I overheard them arguing about it once. I'm not sure how Gloria discovered it, but, as you know, the theater world is quite close knit."

"Yes," I concurred.

She continued. "When Gloria was unhappy about the new role, your mother was beside herself. I assumed it was because she had this threat hanging over her head. And now Gloria is dead." Her voice caught in her throat.

Bijou, sleeping in Celine's lap, awakened from her little snooze and shifted to look up at Celine. She licked her chin.

Clayton had been listening intently, his arms crossed

over his chest. "We've heard from others that Miss Standish wasn't very kind to you. In fact, someone described her treatment of you as 'tormenting.' Is there any truth to that?"

Celine dropped her gaze to Bijou, who gazed back at her with adoration. "Yes. She was jealous. But only acted out towards me occasionally. Not all the time. Sometimes she was nice to me. I think she had very little control over her emotions. She was very troubled."

"So, you never felt the need to retaliate?" he asked.

She looked up at him. "No. When she was like that, I just tried to stay out of her way. I felt sorry for her."

"Other than Mrs. Janes, was there anyone in particular who was threatened by Miss Standish—that you know of?" he continued.

She bit her lip and looked away from him, refocusing again on Bijou. "No. Not that I know of."

Clayton and I shared a glance.

"Thank you," Miss Dubois," Clayton said. "This has been very helpful."

The idea that Gloria had been blackmailing my mother churned my stomach, suggesting she had an even greater motive to harm her. I could see that Clayton, too, was growing increasingly suspicious of my mother. And, reluctantly, I found myself harboring doubts as well. I remembered the article by Atticus Brooks in the La Plata Herald about the tragic young actress linked to my mother. Certainly, Clayton must have read it too.

What a tumultuous life Millicent Janes had led. And the situation with my father and her struggles with him was no less unfortunate. No wonder she was ill and exhausted.

Celine gently put Bijou down on the floor and stood up.

"Well, I suppose I must get back to the hotel." She held her hand out for the diary.

I gave her a gentle smile. "Would you mind if I held onto it?" I asked. I then remembered Percival say he'd seen her write in it. "Of course, if there is anything personal in it—"

A worried expression filled her eyes. "Well, there's nothing personal about me in it—but . . . "

"Yes?"

"There are some entries that include your mother, and well—it might not be information she wants people to know. That's why I've never told her about the diary."

"I see." *Curiouser and curiouser.* "I won't say anything to her," I assured her.

"And I'd really like to have it back," she added.

"Absolutely," I said. "Thank you for letting me borrow it."

She sighed. "I wonder if Victor will finally cancel the show?"

"I can't imagine he would continue," I said.

"You aren't to leave town, Miss Dubois," the sheriff said. "And neither is the troupe. Until we get this matter settled."

"Of course," she agreed. She took hold of my hand and pressed it between hers. "I'm so sorry," she said. "Millicent has done a lot for me. I hope I haven't gotten her into trouble—it's just that—"

I squeezed her fingers. "It's all right, Celine. We'll find the truth. I have every confidence my mother did not kill anyone." I gave her a sanguine smile.

If only I could feel so assured myself.

Chapter Twenty

Celine walked out of the jailhouse, leaving Clayton and me alone. He moved to his desk, took off his hat and sat down, his expression thoughtful. Bijou whined and jumped up against my skirts, wanting me to hold her. I complied, and she gratefully licked my cheek.

Clayton leaned forward at his desk, elbows resting on the surface. He brought his hands together, fingers interlaced, and rested his forehead against his thumbs.

"What are you thinking?" I asked quietly.

He lowered his hands and shook his head. "You don't want to know," he said, confirming my fears. The deck was becoming more and more stacked against my mother.

"I know it doesn't look good for my mother, but didn't you notice Celine's reaction when you asked her if anyone else might have reason to retaliate against Gloria?"

"I did. She didn't want to answer the question."

"Right," I said. "She's hiding something."

"Or protecting someone," he said. "But who?"

"Certainly not my mother." I added dryly.

"No," he agreed. "She might have been trying to throw us off, to steer us away from suspecting her."

I balked at his statement. "You don't think she did it, do you? I don't believe she could harm a fly. It has to be someone else."

From his sigh of resignation, it seemed he agreed.

"Dale Shay and Helena Benavides are new to the troupe," he said. "They wouldn't have any kind of past with Gloria, or, from what they've told me, with Farley," he said.

"Celine is fairly new, as well," I added.

He nodded. "The killer most likely has to be someone who's known Gloria for a while. How far back do the senior members of this troupe go?"

I shrugged. "I'm not sure, exactly. But, my mother knew Mr. Langston and Mr. Thompson in London, which was quite some time ago. Apparently, the two men started the troupe there and when they came to America, they reconnected with my mother. I can't be certain how long they've been together in this country—perhaps four or five years? William let my mother go as my manager about six years ago. We communicated little after that—other than the odd letters we exchanged now and then."

"So, Mr. Langston and Mr. Thompson started the troupe. How did they come to know your mother in London?" he inquired.

I shrugged. "Through the theater."

"Do you know the nature of the relationship between Mrs. Janes and the two men?"

I bit my lip, still uncomfortable with the idea of my mother in any sort of romantic relationship. "Apparently, she and Mr. Thompson had some kind of affair," I said. "It was short-lived, but my mother thinks he still carries a torch for her. Perhaps it's true, but it could also be her own vanity."

"And what about Langston?"

"I'm not sure how they met exactly."

"What do you surmise about their relationship?" he asked.

"From what I can tell, they appreciate each other's strengths—his creative mind, her nose for talent and business acumen, but like most powerful personalities, they sometimes clash."

The door opened, interrupting our conversation. It was Doctor Tate.

"Clayton, Mrs. Pryce," he swept his hat off of his head and held it between his hands.

"What's the news, Doc?" Clayton asked. "Do you know what killed Miss Standish?"

The doctor nodded. "Given the prior death among the troupe, I suspected she came to her demise by dubious means. I have tested the contents of Miss Standish's stomach, and I'm afraid the result has come up positive for poison. Arsenic."

"Oh no," I said. I had suspected as much, but hearing it confirmed was extremely unsettling. This was not good at all. "Are you certain, Dr. Tate?" I asked.

"Yes. There appeared to be no food substance in her stomach—she must have eaten well before her death—but the stomach lining contained a vibrant green hue."

"Green? What does that mean, Doc?" the sheriff asked.

"I believe she was poisoned with Scheel's Green, or Paris Green, dye—which is made of arsenic. It's used in a variety of things; draperies, articles of clothing, and it is occasionally used as food coloring. It's not used much anymore because of its toxic nature. Most often, the victim of such poisoning has been compromised over time, but in Miss Standish's case, I believe she ingested a single, lethal dose."

"But you said there was no food in the stomach contents," Clayton stated.

"I did. I imagine she ingested it through a drink. A cocktail perhaps. Mrs. Pryce, does the Bella serve Absinthe cocktails?"

"I—I don't know. You would have to ask Kitty."

I had heard of the drink. Right before I traveled to Colorado, at an afterparty following one of my performances, I met a young Irish playwright from London named Oscar Wilde. He had been in his cups with the drink —which he called 'The Green Fairy.' The effect upon him only added to his colorful personality and witty charm.

"But does Absinthe leave a green residue in the stomach?" Clayton asked.

"Not necessarily. But the color of the drink makes a great disguise for the dye."

"Indeed, it would," I said.

"Thank you, Doc." Clayton gave him a nod. "Is there anything else?"

"I noted something on the body of Mr. Farley, or rather, the absence of something on his body."

"Which is?"

"There was no gunpowder residue anywhere on his clothes or his person. There was, however, dirt in his hair and on the shoulder of his coat. There were even traces of some plant material; grass, leaves and the like."

"What does that mean?" I asked.

Clayton set his hands on his hips. "It means that Mr. Farley was not shot at close range, as the revolver found near his body would indicate."

"Yes," the doctor concurred. "In my estimation, he was shot from a distance, probably with a rifle, and then dragged into the warehouse."

"What kind of cartridge?" the sheriff asked.

".44-40."

Clayton nodded. "Right. Could be used with a rifle or a handgun."

"So, if he was shot with a rifle, that means that my mother probably did not kill Mr. Farley," I said with a great deal of relief. "And in her weakened condition, there is no way she could have dragged the body into the warehouse."

Clayton pressed his lips together, and a flicker of apprehension passed over his gaze. "If she knew how to use a handgun, using a rifle isn't that much of a stretch."

"You really think she did it," I said with an edge to my voice. It seemed he would not give my mother the benefit of the doubt.

"She has substantial motive for both murders, Arabella. More than anyone else. And with the items found near Farley's body, the script and the shawl, the evidence stacks against her as well."

"And the story about her past doesn't help matters," the doctor chimed in and Clayton dipped his head in agreement.

I inhaled sharply, taken aback that these two men, known for their practicality and reason, would give credence to a tale rooted in hearsay, especially one circulated by Atticus Brooks. Yet, deep down, I understood that my mother would go to any lengths to secure her future. Both Edmund and Gloria had posed threats to her well-being, and her ruthlessness was something I was aware of, though I found it hard to accept. I simply couldn't bring myself to believe it.

"But then, why was her revolver found near the body?" I asked. "Obviously, someone took it to make her look guilty. Celine said she saw Mother loading the gun. Perhaps Celine made that up, and she placed it by the body. She had motive to kill Edmund, he wouldn't leave her alone, and Gloria made her life miserable."

"We just need more solid evidence to rule out your mother," Clayton said.

I bit my lip, thinking. The diary and the script by Grant Colston that I'd found in Gloria's caravan and the parallels drawn between the story and Lily Beaumont's events of the past, echoed in my head. I wondered if one, or both, of those narratives held the key to solving this mystery.

"Mrs. Pryce," the doctor said, interrupting my thoughts. "How's the shoulder? I noticed you are no longer wearing the sling."

"It's a little tender, still, but it feels much better," I said, truthfully. "The sling was such an encumbrance."

He nodded. "I know it can be bothersome, but it seems to have done the trick. I'm glad you are feeling better."

"Thank you," I said, relieved he didn't feel it necessary for me to continue wearing it. He tipped his hat and left the office.

I turned to Clayton. "Cordelia and the deputy should be returning to the hotel soon, and I need to get back to check in on my mother," I said. In truth, I couldn't wait to dig into Grant Colston's script.

"I'll go with you," Clayton said. "It seems I am in search of green drinks."

Back at the hotel, just as we reached the last step onto the landing leading to my mother's rooms, the door flung open.

"There you are!" my mother exclaimed, her expression dark with anger. "It's happened again."

"What's happened?" I asked.

She held out another tintype photograph. It was a depiction of a woman I didn't readily recognize, but there was something familiar about her. It was in the eyes. Scantily clad, she lounged on a fainting couch, a smile playing on her lips. Written across her body was the word "fate."

"Where did you find it?" Clayton asked, taking it from her.

"On the dresser. It wasn't there before we went upstairs to Arabella's suite. I was looking for a hair comb and saw it."

"Who is the photograph of, mother? Do you know?"

She stabbed a finger at the woman. "That is Lily Beaumont."

Chapter Twenty-One

I took another closer look at the photograph of the woman my mother claimed was Lily Beaumont. The resemblance between her spectral appearance and the woman in the tintype was unmistakable.

"Fascinating," I murmured, still in awe of having encountered the ghost of such an iconic figure in American theater.

Clayton turned to me. "Is this the same Lily Beaumont of the—"

I gave him a sharp look. Celine had kept the diary from my mother for a reason. I didn't see the point in telling her about it now.

Thankfully, he registered understanding. "Uh—of the stage?" he finished.

Well recovered. "The very one," I said.

He took the photograph from my mother and studied it. "Did you know her personally, Mrs. Janes?"

"I worked with her once. She was a formidable presence in the theater world, one of those individuals who was adored or despised."

"Despised?" Clayton repeated with astonishment.

My mother fixed him with a piercing gaze. "She was a woman," she emphasized the word heavily. "The theater is dominated by men—a fact Arabella and I have worked tirelessly to change. It was even more restrictive for women in Lily's time. Directors and producers coveted her for her beauty and talent, yet they resented her too, especially as she amassed power."

"This woman is no longer with us?" he asked for clarification.

Well, I wouldn't say that, exactly, I thought. "She died mysteriously one night before a performance," I said. "I wonder if the word 'fate' here on her photograph pertains to that?"

"It's quite possible," Clayton said. "Did anyone else in the troupe know Lily Beaumont personally?"

"If they didn't know her, they knew of her," Mother said. "She was a legend."

I turned to Kitty. "Are you sure you did not see the photograph before the meeting?"

"Positive," she said. "In fact, I straightened the dresser for Mrs. Janes before we went upstairs."

"So, it was placed there while we were in my rooms?"

"Could be," Kitty said. "But, right after the meeting, we went to the Bella. I thought it would do Mrs. Janes good to have a bite to eat."

"And to take the air," my mother added with a hint of disdain, glaring at Clayton. "I've been cooped up in that room for far too long. But now I'm quite at my wits' end. I need to lie down."

"Do you need some help?" Kitty asked.

"I think I can manage to walk the three steps into my

rooms and get to the bed by myself," my mother said, her words dripping with sarcasm. "I'm not an invalid."

I rolled my eyes, and catching Kitty's gaze, I shook my head, offering her a silent apology. I didn't envy her role as my mother's caretaker. Kitty let out an amused chuckle as she watched my mother enter her rooms and slam the door shut.

"How long were you at the Bella after the meeting?" the sheriff asked her before I could verbally apologize for my mother's petulance.

She frowned, thinking. "I'd say twenty minutes. We had an enjoyable meal, but then Mrs. Janes felt faint, so I brought her back upstairs." Kitty remained unfazed by my mother's sharpness. "I had Sally bring a tray for some dessert and coffee. That's when I noticed the photograph."

"Interesting," I mused. "So, it was delivered after you left the room to come to the meeting, or after you went to the Bella."

"Could have been during the meeting," Clayton added. "And all were present except Miss Dubois. She was the only one in the troupe not accounted for before or during the meeting," Clayton said.

"Unless the person threatening her is someone who is not connected to the troupe," I added.

Clayton shook his head. "But you said the threats have been coming for some time—even before Mrs. Janes reached La Plata Springs. And, whomever this is has intimate knowledge of her life." He looked at me. "And possibly yours. I believe these threats are coming from within the troupe."

"Well, I guess that rules out Gloria, because the photograph was delivered after her death."

"Edmund, too." Clayton said. "We established that earlier."

"But are these threats connected to the murders?" Kitty asked.

"That is still unclear," Clayton said.

"What should we do next?" I asked.

He rubbed his chin thoughtfully, clearly pondering my question. "As much as I like to take action, I think we need to wait things out a little."

"What do you mean?" I asked.

"Whomever committed these crimes thinks they've gotten away with it. That will make them bolder."

"So, does this mean you believe my mother is innocent of the murders of Gloria and Edmund?"

He rubbed the back of his neck, suddenly looking very uncomfortable. "Not necessarily."

"What are you getting at?" Kitty asked.

His sapphire eyes met mine briefly before he averted his gaze. "I must entertain the possibility that she's using these threats as a diversion."

"Excuse me?" I interjected, anxious about his implication. "You don't mean . . ."

"That she's orchestrating them?" Kitty concluded.

"They have distracted attention from solving the murders," he said.

I raised my hands in protest. "Come now! You go too far, Clayton. The deviousness you are speaking of is even too evil for my mother. She would never—"

"You yourself questioned her reasons for coming to La Plata Springs. It's the ideal cover. She claims she's being threatened, convinces everyone she's a victim, and then eliminates anyone who poses a risk to her. Plus, she knows you would defend her, stand by her."

My mouth fell open in complete shock, a sharp pain piercing my chest so intensely it stole my breath. He was speaking about my mother. Yet, I couldn't completely dismiss his words. My mother had manipulated me before for her own benefit. But to commit murder?

I shook my head, raising my hands in protest. "I can't listen to this."

He reached for my hand, but I pulled it away. "Arabella, I'm sorry. But, we agreed to work on this together. We have to consider all the possibilities."

I crossed my arms tightly against my chest, my voice sharp with anger. "What do you propose we do?" I snapped.

"Like I said, we wait. Ease up on the vigilance with your mother. Let her move about. Interact with the others."

"But isn't that irresponsible? She could be in danger. And she's ill," I reminded him.

"We'll continue to watch her and investigate, but from a distance. If she is the killer, she'll want to cover her tracks. If she's not and someone is out to get her, they can't act if she's kept in a cocoon. We need to loosen the ropes."

I escorted the sheriff downstairs, still a little confounded about his plan and very disheartened that his opinion of my mother's guilt had not changed. In fact, he seemed more convinced than ever.

"Are you coming to the Bella with me?" he said. "Maybe we could have a drink and discuss the case further?"

"I don't think so," I said dismissively.

"All right," he drew out, sounding a little surprised. He must have sensed I was miffed. "Is something the matter?"

"No. I'm fine."

He gave me a wry smile. "You don't seem fine."

My unsettling feelings about his skepticism toward my mother's innocence had clearly shattered the facade of my composure. I narrowed my eyes at him. "It's very convenient for you, isn't it? Assuming my mother is guilty of murder would neatly wrap up your case."

"I am not assuming anything, Arabella. I'm following the evidence. And what do you mean, 'convenient'? What are you implying?" he countered with an edge to his voice.

"Well, it's obvious you don't like Deputy Fleming—even though you were desperate for another lawman in La Plata Springs."

He released a sardonic laugh. "What does that have to do with your mother or this investigation?"

I leaned in closer. "You want this case closed quickly so you can be rid of him."

He snorted. "If only things were that simple."

"So you admit it?" I said, my voice tinged with triumph. "Why don't you like him?"

"It's not about liking or disliking. He's simply not the right man for the job."

I folded my arms and gazed up at him with suspicion. "Really?" I challenged. "How so?"

I knew I was pushing him, but he hadn't outright denied my theory yet. His jaw tightened in obvious annoyance, and I knew I was playing with fire. In truth, he didn't need to justify his actions to me.

"He's a big city boy from Chicago, and very green behind the ears. He just finished police training and was sent to Denver to deal with drunks, gamblers, thieves, and prostitutes, not the hardened outlaws I've had to come up against."

"Oh, you mean like my mother?" I raised my eyebrows at him.

He frowned. "No, not like your mother. Like desperados, bandits, train robbers, marauding Indians. Fleming might handle a domestic case back in the city, but I doubt he can even ride a horse. Life here is worlds apart from the big city. Unfortunately, my hands are tied."

"Why is that?" I asked, curiosity piqued.

He sighed heavily. "Archer took him on as a favor to the police commissioner in Denver. Turns out, Fleming is the commissioner's nephew."

"Oh, I see," I replied, reminded once again that Mr. Archer was the puppet master behind the scenes in La Plata Springs.

"I didn't expect to have to train someone from the ground up," he continued with an air of resentment.

I understood his frustration, yet I found his judgment of the young man overly harsh. "He seems eager to learn. Perhaps you should give him a chance?"

"He's eager, all right," he replied, his tone dripping with sarcasm.

"What does that mean?"

"It means he's particularly keen on you," he explained.

I couldn't help but smile, though I tried to mask it. "And that surprises you? I assure you, Mr. Marshall, many men have been 'keen' on me."

"I don't doubt it," he conceded.

"But why does it matter to you?" I asked, flashing him my most disarming smile.

He furrowed his brow, clearly irritated. "It doesn't," he scoffed, but his tone suggested otherwise.

"Very well," I said, dropping the issue, yet the air

between us crackled with an unspoken tension. Clearly, I had struck a deeper chord than I intended.

Chapter Twenty-Two

After the sheriff departed, I retreated to my rooms, my mind preoccupied with Lily Beaumont's journal. Celine had mentioned an entry about my mother's affair, sparking my curiosity. Although I doubted its relevance to the recent murders, despite the threat of exposing my mother, I couldn't shake off my intrigue. The thought that my mother might have been involved with a man other than my father —even with his considerable failings—stung with a sense of betrayal.

I quickly stoked the fire and settled into one of the armchairs in front of it. Bijou left her bed and curled up at my feet. Notwithstanding the blaze of the fire, a familiar waft of cool air swept through the room.

"Hello, Percival," I said, and scooted my chair closer to the fire, disturbing Bijou. She padded her way over to her bed. When Percival didn't answer, I turned to find that the drop in temperature was not due to him, but from the presence of Lily Beaumont standing near the desk. Her elegant Grecian costume and the delicate wisps of hair framing her face danced as if caught in an unseen breeze.

"Oh, it's you," I said, unable to hide my bewilderment. Her gaze remained fixed on me, provoking an overwhelming sense of unease. I wished she would break the silence. As the room grew colder, the scent of pipe tobacco permeated the air. Much to my relief, Percival materialized in the chair beside me.

"Percival! I'm glad you are here. We have company," I said, gesturing toward the apparition of Lily Beaumont.

"So, I see," he responded, nodding to her in greeting. She remained motionless, her spectral face completely expressionless.

"Why doesn't she speak?" I whispered.

"I'm not entirely sure, but I think she exists in a different dimension of time and space than I do. I've attempted to communicate with her, but to no avail."

"What do you suppose she wants?"

He nodded toward the diary. "I think she wants you to read it."

I settled back into my chair, the fire finally making some headway in warming the room.

I skimmed the journal entries as I had briefly done before. Many pages were filled with acting techniques, apparently derived from seasoned masters of the craft. She detailed methods to express emotions authentically, avoiding melodrama or artificiality. Interspersed among these were more personal reflections. Miss Beaumont had engaged in romantic entanglements with several of her leading men. I must confess, some details in these entries were quite explicit, enough to make even me—a person seldom embarrassed—blush.

I felt Percival's transparent gaze boring through me.

"Everything all right?" he asked. "You look quite flushed, my dear."

I cleared my throat, feeling caught out. "Yes. Fine," I said and read on.

"These entries are cryptic," I said. "She doesn't name several of the people she writes about like she did in the earlier entries, but uses initials such as Mr. T., or Mr. J., or Miss S. Occasionally she uses initials for both first name and surname such as P.R., and the like."

He glanced over at Miss Beaumont. "Wise," he said, with a tilt of his head in her direction. "Probably in case someone got hold of the diary, which, in fact, someone did."

"Right," I concurred. "Some entries give her location, mostly London and New York, but some were written in Paris or Chicago."

"I'm sure she was sought after in many places if she was as renowned as you suggest." He blew a string of smoke rings into the air.

"She was. She was known the world over."

"Much like you?" he asked.

I smiled at him. "Yes. Like me."

I slowly flipped through the pages, pausing to appreciate the detailed illustrations of costumes, stage sets, and portraits. The portraits were predominantly men—likely her lovers? Among them, two profile views of a young man and woman facing one another caught my eye. The pair looked to be in their late teens or early twenties. Something about the jawline or the mouth of the man seemed eerily familiar. Sketched between the two profiles was a heart split in two. The young woman's profile bore no resemblance to Lily Beaumont. Her cheekbones were more pronounced, her nose pert and rounded, unlike Miss Beaumont's elongated, straight nose, and her chin featured a small indent suggestive of a dimple. Under the woman's portrait were the initials K. M. and under the man's Mr. L. As I turned the page, an entry from June 1872, London, grabbed my attention. Beside the text was another illustration of a woman. Underneath it, the initials "M.J." were neatly inscribed. I gasped in surprise.

"What is it?" Percival asked.

"Look." I showed him the page.

"Your mother?"

"Yes. The resemblance is uncanny."

The entry detailed that M.J. had been to visit. She and Miss Beaumont discussed a new play M.J. was interested in for her daughter. However, the part she wanted—Viola, the lead in *Twelfth Night*—had already been assigned to K.M.

I turned back to the page with the double portraits. Yes, the initials under the woman's portrait were K.M. It was the same woman. This had to be Kathy Macarther. Flipping forward again, I continued reading:

Upon learning that the role she desired for her daughter had been given to K.M., M.J. was greatly vexed. She asserted that when her daughter, A. auditioned, the director, H.T., had declared her perfect for the part. M.J. believed the matter settled. Therefore, upon hearing of K.M.'s casting, she stormed onto the stage during a rehearsal and threatened H.T. Frankly, I could hardly blame her. The gentleman is insufferably arrogant, although M.J. is no angel herself. She had been receiving favors from R.T., but she rejected him in favor of Mr. D. I suspect it's because Mr. D. is a wealthy man of significant influence. She has recently been entertaining visits and receiving gifts from Mr. D. which is playing with fire as he is a married man.

This must be the story Celine alluded to. She must have

worked out that M.J. was my mother, and A. was me. I read on:

M.J. declared she would ensure her daughter secured the role if it was the last thing she did. The next day, I heard that Mr. D. offered to finance the entire production. Suddenly, A. was cast as Viola. Shortly after, poor K.M. fell gravely ill and took to her bed. The following week, she was dead. Rumors of poison are rife, and everyone believes M.J. is responsible! Poor Mr. L. is quite distraught, as he had been recently courting the young woman. I'm afraid he's taken to drink to drown his sorrows.

Rapt, I turned the page.

I've just perused the Times. *There was an article regarding the demise of K.M., in which the author blatantly accuses M.J. of administering poison to the poor soul. I deem this writer's actions quite irresponsible, especially since the physician has withdrawn his initial assertion of poisoning. He now believes the young woman succumbed to cerebral hemorrhage. I am concerned about the reputation of that journalist . . .*

I leaned back, letting the diary rest in my lap. What a complex web of treachery this was. And to think, if M.J. and A. truly represent my mother and me, then I had been ensnared in the middle of this intricate tapestry of deceit and ambition without having any clue.

I certainly remembered playing the role of Viola, but I had been oblivious to any backstage drama. My mother had shielded me from the newspapers, fearing a negative review, although I later discovered that poor critiques of my performances were rare—until much later with Atticus Brooks.

This article, I assumed, was the one he had written defaming my mother. I shudder to think of how she may have reacted. And, then later, when Mr. Brooks had been expelled from William's club after the fated card game, he had even more incentive to take his frustrations out on me. If my mother had retaliated, then perhaps Mr. Brooks's crusade against me had been brewing earlier than I thought.

My mother had also kept me isolated from the other actors, worried about their potentially bad influence. In many ways, I was held captive for years. It puzzled me, though, how she kept her affair secret; she seemed to be with me all the time. Perhaps she slipped out while I slept, which was entirely plausible. If she was crafty enough to keep me in the dark back then, who's to say she wasn't still employing the same tactics now?

Chapter Twenty-Three

That afternoon, Bijou and I holed ourselves up in the annex office. I meticulously sorted through a stack of hotel bills while she snoozed at my feet.

Lost in the numbers, I jumped when a knock interrupted my focus. Bijou barked, and I quickly settled her.

"Come in?" I called out.

Mr. Pettyjohn peeked in through the barely opened door. "You have a visitor, Mrs. Pryce."

"A visitor? Who is it?" I asked, my tone edging on impatience. While I was hardly eager to wade through these bills with their looming payments, I was even less inclined to be interrupted. I needed to organize them and devise a plan to manage our finances.

"It's Boss Archer. He says it's important."

I sighed. "All right. Send him in."

I straightened the mess of bills into a neat stack and then slipped them into the desk drawer. No need for Mr. Archer to be reminded of the hotel's financial status. As the owner of the only bank in town, he knew too much already, and it made me uncomfortable.

As I slipped the last stragglers into the drawer, he entered the room with a gentle knock on the door.

"Mrs. Pryce," he said, flashing a broad smile. "Thank you for taking the time to see me. I realize how busy you must be with everything happening at the hotel."

I rose and gave him a tight smile. "It's no bother. How may I help you?"

His face took on a sympathetic grimness. "Well, my dear, it's actually I who have come to help you."

I blinked at him. "With what?"

With a tilt of his head, he gestured toward the chairs in front of the wood-burning stove. The fire was nearly gone, but the embers still emitted some warmth. "May we sit?"

"Of course," I said.

Once we settled ourselves in the chairs, he began. "I've become increasingly concerned about the hotel."

"I see. What exactly is it that troubles you?" I asked, although I had an idea what he was referring to. The dreaded finances.

"I guess I should say I'm concerned about its negative impact on the reputation of the town."

"Negative impact? I don't understand what you mean. The Arabella is the heart of the town. You know this."

He cleared his throat and looked at me from beneath furrowed brows. "That is exactly what concerns me. Her reputation is directly linked to the good standing of the town."

"Yes," I agreed, raising my chin. "Her reputation is sterling."

"Perhaps at one time, yes, it was. But, my dear, I'm afraid in recent months—with several murders within her walls and with the lien against her, not to mention rumors of terrifying ghostly phenomenon—"

"Terrifying?" I cut in.

He gave a nonchalant shrug. "There's been chatter among the townspeople—and even your guests—that the hotel is not just haunted, but cursed. Understandably, people associate the haunting with the many deaths that have transpired here."

The manner in which he spoke sent a chill through me, my heart plummeting to the pit of my stomach.

"She needs a new image," he pressed on.

Still shaken by his remarks about the Arabella's reputation, I managed a hoarse reply.

"Excuse me, did you just say cursed? You can't be serious. I've heard nothing about this."

He pressed his lips into a thin line, drawing a deep breath through his nose as if weighing his next words carefully. "There is also, well, I'm hesitant to mention it . . ."

"What is it? Please, continue," I urged, frustrated by his evasive manner.

He paused, letting his next words hang ominously in the air. "The unfortunate incidents at the hotel have escalated since your arrival—and now, with this situation concerning your mother . . ."

My chest tightened, and I clenched my fists, my ire quickly taking the place of my previous shock and dismay.

"So, you're saying it's my fault?" I drew out.

He didn't answer the question, but offered instead, "I can help with this matter."

I didn't like his ominous tone. The words would have been welcomed if I didn't suspect there was an underlying motive behind them.

"And how do you hope to help?" I asked.

"Like I said, the Arabella needs a new image."

I gazed at him, trying my best to suppress my anger, silently urging him to go on. He inhaled deeply once more before exhaling slowly.

"The only way to cleanse the tarnish is to start fresh."

"How?" I asked.

"She needs to be torn down and rebuilt."

I laughed, unable to hold in my emotions any longer. "Torn down? That's absurd." I paused before continuing. My heart ached at the idea. The hotel had meant so much to William, and it had been Percival's masterpiece. It would be an insult to their memories. "The Arabella is beautiful. An architectural wonder. You're suggesting that she be wiped from the earth?"

"The West is expanding," he continued determinedly. "And, as you're aware, my goal is to boost tourism here in La Plata Springs. We've already noticed a rise in visitor numbers recently. Plus, I have high hopes for the new theater Andrew is constructing—"

I raised a hand, cutting him off. "You mean the theater my mother's troupe is building with Andrew's help?" I reminded him.

"Yes, of course," he agreed with a condescending smile. "But, back to the hotel."

"It will not be torn down," I stated in no uncertain terms.

"Mrs. Pryce—Arabella—you are a marvelous talent, known nationwide; dare I say worldwide—"

"Worldwide," I said with emphasis. I sensed an unsettling undertone to his flattery and braced myself for the inevitable twist in his intentions.

"Your talent is being wasted on the hotel," he went on. "And any association with curses, murder and the occult could cause permanent damage to your public image. There has already been some bad press about your mother. I would hate for you to come under such negative scrutiny."

My shoulders stiffened at the subtle threat in his voice. He was no doubt alluding to his influence over his friend Atticus Brooks. Not that the smarmy theater critic needed any encouragement to show me in a bad light.

His words were like a dagger being driven into my heart. He'd cut to the core of my most dreaded fears; of being publicly disgraced and shamed, and of being deemed evil or insane. Both of which meant I was nothing, that I had no good or honest value in this world. It was like he saw right through me and it was terrifying.

He must have seen the blood drain from my face, because he reached out and took hold of my hand.

"My dear Arabella, use your fame, your brilliance, and your shining talent to do what you do best. I believe you can make this new theater a treasure. Not quite as grand as your theater in New York, I dare say, but with you at the helm, it will flourish."

I took in his words. He was flattering me for his own purposes, but the sentiment struck a pang of longing in my heart. The theater, either here, New York, or anywhere else, was where I truly belonged. I knew that with every fiber of my being.

"I will give you full control," he continued. "You can help make La Plata Springs a most desired destination. It would be very beneficial for the town, and for your own public image. We'll do this together."

His last words jolted me out of my yearning for the stage. *Do this together.*

I narrowed my eyes at him. "So, what you are saying is that I would work for you—running the theater?"

"Full control, my dear. Whatever you want to do. Spend as much money as you want. You'll have an extremely generous salary. I'm a wealthy man, Arabella. No expense spared."

I gritted my teeth at the insult. I knew his sister Bertha Stewart controlled the family fortune as the principal beneficiary of their late father's estate. Mr. Archer had made considerable money with the railroad and the mines, but he did not have authority over his entire fortune. And, once I had my inheritance, my wealth would be equal to his, perhaps superior. But I had to get it first. But the horrifying fact remained that even an enormous fortune could not repair a damaged reputation.

"And the hotel?" I asked.

He shrugged. "I'll buy it from you. As I have said before, I can give you a very attractive sum for it. You'll be rid of the scandal and I'll build a new hotel."

"So you will give me an 'attractive sum', as you say, for the hotel, and then destroy what you've just invested in? That doesn't sound like good business sense to me," I said.

His smile sent a shiver of unease down my spine. "I know it will pay off in the long run."

I regarded him thoughtfully, unable to dismiss his earlier warning that my public image might suffer irreparable harm. My heart pounded with fear at the thought. Yet selling now would mean losing out on my full inheritance. I found myself trapped between preserving my good name and securing my fortune—an excruciating dilemma.

Bijou emitted a low whine, and a sudden chill filled the room. I glanced up to see Percival sitting in the desk chair. He rested his elbows on the desktop and clasped his hands in front of his chin, interlacing his fingers. Our eyes met, and he slowly shook his head back and forth. My first instinct was to ignore him, to make him go away. I was afraid Mr. Archer might see him, giving him further ammunition for his quest of The Arabella's destruction, but then I realized Percival would not let this happen. He, of all souls, would not want the Arabella torn down, and he would not lead me astray. He knew what my reputation meant to me, and I knew he cared about me. I was also reminded that William had explicitly requested I not sell to Archibald Archer. Percival's unexpected presence gave me a measure of reassurance.

"I appreciate your offer, Mr. Archer," I said, mustering all the strength and courage I could, given the ominous threat hanging in the air. I sensed it would not be prudent to engage in direct confrontation here, but to deftly navigate these treacherous waters. "But, I cannot bear to see my late husband's work destroyed, and I owe it to him to ensure the Arabella's excellent reputation myself—for the time being."

His nostrils flared slightly and his jaw flexed. "I trust you know what you are doing, my dear."

"I do," I said with a smile I hoped conveyed confidence while my heart was in my throat. My head spinning with thoughts of impending doom, I glanced over at Percival, who gave me a nod of approval.

Mr. Archer stood up, clearing his throat. "Very well," he said stiffly. "Hopefully, you will not regret this decision."

I saw him to the door, my knees ready to buckle. He left, but his anger lingered in the room.

Raising my hands in the air, I turned to Percival. "Have I made a colossal mistake?"

"I don't believe so," he said, his voice soothing.

"But he has Atticus Brooks in his pocket. And Constance Chatterley. They could destroy me."

He shrugged. "But if you lose your inheritance, then

you lose the chance to better the world. You can use your gifts, and your money, to benefit many. Don't you think that's worthwhile?"

"Yes. Of course, but—"

"Good. So keep forging ahead. You have already benefitted this town with your ability to solve the unfortunate deaths that have befallen it—mine included. That has value, my dear Arabella. People recognize that."

"Yes, I suppose they do. But, if it gets out that I have psychic abilities?"

He shrugged. "Is that such a terrible thing? Hasn't it proven useful?"

"Well, yes, but I might be labeled a lunatic, or evil, like some of my relatives have been."

"I suppose you could. Anything is possible. Did you know these relatives?"

I shook my head. "No. They were quite before my time."

"Well, my dear, you know that spiritism is gaining popularity these days."

I recalled that several people in my social set in New York City had dabbled with seances and such, but I had steered clear, for obvious reasons. It was merely entertainment for them, while for me it had been a harbinger of something more threatening. My deep-seated fears of being discovered overruled any thoughts of joining in 'for fun.' My mother had seen to that.

"I think you are over worrying, Arabella. There are other distinguished people who have shared the belief in a gift such as yours: Charles Dickens, Mary Todd Lincoln, Mark Twain, and even Queen Victoria. No one has claimed they were engaging in witchcraft, or had lost their minds. Well, I take that back—people did question Mrs. Lincoln's mental health, but there were a number of reasons for that."

The tenseness in my shoulders relaxed slightly. He'd made a good point. I had heard the same thing about these people of influence, But I had been so consumed by my own fears, I couldn't perceive how others might view my abilities as advantageous. That fear had woven itself into the very fabric of who I was. So deeply embedded, I doubted whether I could ever be free from its hold.

Chapter Twenty-Four

Still preoccupied with my conversations with Mr. Archer and Percival, I made my way to the hotel kitchen. I needed some fortification in the way of some strong Earl Grey and one of Lottie's baked goods.

I walked in to see her hunched over a simmering pot, sniffing its contents before sampling a spoonful. Bijou padded her way toward her, letting out a chipper yip in greeting.

"That smells marvelous," I said.

Upon seeing me, Lottie quickly straightened and smoothed down her apron. "Good day, ma'am. I'm just making some mutton broth for your Mother. I'm sorry she's poorly."

"Thank you, Lottie. I'm sure she will be feeling better soon," I said, remembering Doctor Tate had said the clean air would improve her condition.

"Kitty said the poor woman hasn't been able to eat anything today, so I'm hoping this broth will do the trick."

"Really?" I said, alarmed at the news. I hadn't realized she'd gotten worse.

"Yes, ma'am. She hasn't been able to get out of bed today."

"I will go see her directly," I said. "Would you be a dear and have Clarence bring a pot of Earl Grey and a couple of your delicious scones upstairs to my rooms? When the soup is ready."

"Of course, ma'am. Shouldn't be too long."

I gave her a nod of thanks and made my way up the stairs to my mother's rooms. I found Kitty dozing in a chair next to my mother's bedside. Mother was asleep. Bijou went to the bed and set her front paws on the wooden frame to get a better look at its occupant.

I cleared my throat to get Kitty's attention. Her eyes fluttered open.

"She's worse?" I whispered.

Kitty straightened in the chair. "I'm afraid so."

"Have you called for Dr. Tate?"

"He's out in Masterson Grove, delivering a baby. I had Clarence leave a message for him at his office. Hopefully, he can come see her soon."

"Right," I agreed.

"Oh, I almost forgot to ask," Kitty said. "Have you seen your mother's fan? It seems to have gone missing. She has terrible hot spells. Is she going through the change?"

I shrugged. "I don't know. She's always run a little hot, but it does seem to have gotten worse with time."

"It's no picnic, I can attest to that. Starting the process myself." She shook her head in dismay.

Despite our loud whispering, Mother slept on, her breathing steady and rhythmic. Aside from the pallor of her countenance, she looked peaceful. I didn't want to disturb her.

"Please come for me when the doctor arrives?" I requested. Kitty gave me a nod of assurance.

"Let's go, Bijou." As we left the room, we ran into Cordelia, who was coming up the stairs.

"We've got the script," she said, holding out the portfolio.

"Wonderful." I took it from her. "Where is Deputy Fleming?"

"He's taking some refreshment in the Bella. Were you just in with your mother?"

"Yes. I'm afraid she's having rather a bad day, today. She feels quite ill."

Her brows furrowed in concern. "Oh dear, I'm sorry to hear that."

I nodded. "It's unsettling to see her in such a frail state. We've sent for the doctor."

"Good," she said. "Are you going up?" She lifted her chin toward our rooms.

"Yes. I want to dig into this script."

We went upstairs, Bijou taking the lead. She waited for us patiently at the door. Once inside, she scampered to her water dish and then went to the loveseat under the bay window. She hopped up onto it and settled in for a nap. Cordelia retired to her room, and I went to the desk, opened the portfolio and began to read.

Having skimmed the summary beforehand, I was briefly acquainted with the characters and plot. The narrative was exquisitely crafted, immersing me in the dramatic universe of Mantu's Theater. The protagonist, Hans A. Lechim, the director, emerged as a poignant figure whose tragic romance with Dariann Roth tugged at my heartstrings. His bitter relationship with her mentor, the notable actress Emily Boulant, intensified the story, casting a somber shadow over the narrative.

Emily Boulant, the chief antagonist, turns against Hans when he denies her a role in his masterpiece, citing her aging appearance. In retaliation, she accuses him of concocting a box office fraud scheme, stealing a hefty portion of the ticket sales with the manager, and promptly reports them to the authorities. Ensnared in this scandal, Hans's legal woes, combined with Miss Boulant's sway over Dariann and Mr. James's influence, drives the director to insanity and ultimately, a heinous murder.

The pages describing Miss Boulant's death scene were chaotic, with many lines heavily crossed out with ink. It appeared the writer had difficulty completing this part. Hans's method of murder remains undisclosed. The scene begins with Miss Boulant applying her makeup and powder before a performance. I couldn't read what came next, as many lines were scratched out. Then Miss Boulant collapses onto the floor, lifeless.

The scene ends with a Hans's soliloquy claiming he'd committed the perfect crime.

Confused by the demise of poor Miss Boulant, I stared at the passage, trying to make sense of it. Something about the doomed actress's name seemed familiar.

I paused at the spelling of her name: *E-M-I-L-Y B-O-U-L-A-N-T.* Where had I encountered this name before? Had this play crossed my path, perhaps at a theater where I had once performed?

A sudden chill swept through me. Bijou, still on the loveseat, let out a low growl and then barked. She occasionally did this when Percival appeared. He claimed she couldn't see him, but was sensitive to the changes in the environment, or my reaction to it. I looked up from the script, expecting to find him there, but was surprised to see Lily Beaumont seated on the corner of the desk to my left. Soon after, Percival showed up in the mirror above it.

"It seems you have a visitor," he said. With a flick of his fingers, he lit his pipe. The comforting smell of fruit, honey, and nuts filled the air. Cavendish. I knew it from my youth. One of the lead actors in a play I'd performed in loved the flavored tobacco.

"Yes," I said, still watching her. She regarded me with the same curiosity I felt towards her, but she remained silent. There was a tension in her shadowy countenance. Why had she appeared at this very moment?

"Has she spoken with you?" he asked.

"No. But, her timing is interesting. She also appeared when I was reading her diary." I held up the script. "Are you here because of this?" I asked her.

She nodded.

"What is she trying to tell me?" I wondered out loud. I set it down again and scanned the page. Her hand appeared in my periphery and then moved toward the document. She pointed to the name Emily Boulant. I blinked, trying to figure out the significance. I stared at the words so hard they blurred and danced on the page. And then, I noticed it. My eyes widened in astonishment.

"You found something?" Percival asked.

Too preoccupied to answer him, I grabbed a pen from its stand on the desk, dipped it in the inkpot and started writing out each letter of the name Boulant. Then the letters in the name Emily. I then reversed it to Emily Boulant, putting spaces between the letters. *E-M-I-L-Y*. I switched them around to *I-L-Y-M-E*. And then I sounded it out.

"Ilyme. Ily. Lily."

I gasped. "There it is."

"There what is?" Percival asked.

"It's an anagram. Emily Boulant is Lily Beaumont." I stared up at her ghostly visage. She merely blinked at me, but her transparent features had softened. I showed Percival my handiwork.

"Hah!" he let out a joyous chuckle. "So it is, my dear. Brilliant! But why would someone use an anagram for her name?"

I shrugged a shoulder. "They wanted her identity kept a secret?" I said. "But, why?"

She raised her hand, and with her finger, seemed to write something in the air. She then vanished and in her place, letters appeared in cloudy wisps, spelling out the name Hans Lechim.

"Hans Lechim," I said out loud. "Another character in the play. The director." I shook my head, trying to work it out. And then something dawned on me. All the strife in this story centered on a young, talented actress. Hans Lechim was in love with her, but she was under the control of her manager, and influenced by an aging actress, Emily Boulant.

"Hmm," I mused.

"What is it?" Percival set the stem of his pipe between his teeth and puffed on it.

"I can't tell if it's coincidental, but the relationship dynamics in this script mirror those within our traveling troupe. There's even a murder—the murder of an aging actress, Emily Boulant, or should I say, Lily Beaumont?"

"Are you saying there are parallels between the character Emily Boulant and Gloria Standish?" he asked, letting the pipe smoke linger in his mouth.

"Maybe," I said, my mind whirling with possibilities. "I think I need to speak with my mother about this."

"Why is that?"

"She worked with Lily. Perhaps she knew something about this script—or even the story behind it."

I went downstairs and, as I was about to knock on the door of my mother's suite, Victor Langston stepped out.

"Oh, hello Mr. Langston," I said, astonished to see him there.

He regarded me with his cool gray eyes and then smoothed the errant light streak in his long dark hair over his left ear. He was, as usual, dressed with an air of refinement and sophistication. He really did cut a dashing figure.

"Good day, Mrs. Pryce. I was just checking in on your mother. We had scheduled a meeting today at the warehouse—or I supposed I should say the new theater, but she didn't show. I did not know she was feeling so ill."

"Yes," I said. "I'd come to see her earlier, but she was sleeping."

"She is taking some soup right now," he explained. "Hopefully, it will restore her."

I looked at him skeptically, confused by this sudden concern. Recently he had chimed in on the accusation that she had killed Edmund Farley, and Gloria Standish.

"Yes, hopefully it will." I agreed. "I must admit, Mr. Langston, I'm surprised to see you here. I thought you believed my mother was guilty of the murders of your colleagues. I'd think you'd want nothing more to do with her."

A sheepish look passed over his features. "I'm afraid that was my grief speaking. I shouldn't have jumped to that conclusion so quickly. Millicent and I have had our trials, but we work well together. She is so very bright—and her insights are quite valuable to me. Although the evidence does point against her, I have every hope you and the sheriff will prove her innocent, my dear. I will let the results of your investigation, and the evidence, speak for themselves. It's not up to me to pass judgement."

"How gracious," I said, not sure I believed him. He and my mother not only 'had their trials,' their relationship had been quite volatile.

"Well, I won't detain you any longer," he said, offering a generous smile before descending the stairs. I lingered at the doorway, watching him go, his words still leaving me somewhat taken aback.

I walked into my mother's suite and proceeded to the bedroom. She was still in bed, but sat propped up, a tray resting on her lap. She wore an elegant Kashmir dressing gown patterned with peacocks. Gracefully, she spooned the soup Lottie had prepared into her mouth.

"I just saw Mr. Langston leaving," I said.

"Yes, he came to see me. He brought me this." She held up the folded fan, the edge of which, I noticed, matched the vibrant green and blues of her dressing gown. "I must have dropped it somewhere," she continued, shaking her head in dismay. "I've been so absent-minded lately. I thought I'd lost this, too," she said, pulling at the collar of her dressing gown. "The other day I was looking for it in my wardrobe of the caravan and couldn't find it. When I went back the next afternoon, it was there. I must have overlooked it."

"Well, it isn't surprising with everything that has been going on lately," I said. "Was that all Mr. Langston wanted? To bring you your fan?"

"No. He wanted to update me on the theater. Apparently, things are going well and they've made some notable progress. They've even found a way to create a raked seating arrangement, as you suggested. Nicely done, darling. We shall be able to perform on schedule."

"So, he intends to continue with the play?" I asked, surprised they intended to carry on despite the murders of now two of the troupe's thespians.

"Yes. It seems Archibald Archer has not only provided the use of his warehouse, but he has invested in our company."

A shiver of adrenaline spiked up my back and a sudden feeling of claustrophobia nearly took my breath away.

"Really?" I said, the sense of threat I felt at the notion draining the blood from my head. This would be catastrophic on so many levels. Archibald Archer sinking his claws of control into my mother's business? Was there nothing he didn't want to dominate?

"So, does that mean you are no longer going to San Francisco?" I asked, choking down my trepidation.

"No. We will come here in the off season. Mr. Archer thinks it will draw more visitors to La Plata Springs. Especially since you are here, my dear."

Suddenly, memories of my youth rushed back: the feeling of being a bird in a cage, put on display to be admired and expected to sing with perfect pitch. I would have to endure Archibald Archer, Atticus Brooks, and my mother crowding around me, suffocating me. I wanted to escape, to break free of the oppressive weight that threatened to snuff out my flame. I longed to return to New York, to my theater, and reclaim my freedom and my life; to flee this town, where the walls seemed to be closing in on me. But I was trapped—for several more months.

A familiar coolness settled over the right side of my body. I swiveled my head to see Percival standing next to me.

It's going to be all right. He didn't speak the words out loud, but I could hear him in my head. His smooth, buttery voice calmed the chaos in my mind, and the tension in my body released, allowing me to breathe again.

"What are you looking at?" my mother asked.

Startled, I caught her gaze. "Nothing," I blurted. The coolness ebbed from my shoulder. Percival had gone.

"You have that look in your eyes," she said, her eyes narrowing.

"What look?" I asked, feigning innocence. My anxiety had betrayed me.

"As if you're seeing something I can't," she said, her voice laced with accusation.

"Nonsense," I said, and silently chided myself. I must be more careful in the future. The last thing I needed was for her to suspect the reawakening of my abilities.

She lifted the fan and unfurled it. The handle was crafted to mimic a peacock's body, while the fan itself burst into the vibrant, colorful plumage of its tail. She then waved the fan gently across her face.

"That's lovely," I said, to divert the conversation.

She gave a half-smile. "Victor gave it to me, on opening night in Philadelphia."

"And did he also give you the matching dressing gown?" I pointed to it. I found it a little odd that he, as her business partner, would give her such an intimate and obviously expensive gift. Had they been lovers? If so, were they still?

"Yes," she said, not offering any other explanation.

"How generous," I said.

"He can be quite thoughtful. When he's not being difficult." She managed a weak smile.

I then remembered the other reason I'd come to see her.

"Mother, I wonder if you've ever heard of a play titled, *The Price of Ambition?*"

She stopped fanning herself and frowned. "No. Why?"

I shook my head. "Oh, it's nothing. Just a play I'd heard of, once." I didn't want to tell her I had it in my possession. "I recall it was a story about Lily Beaumont."

She set the fan down. "Really? You don't say."

"Yes. It's quite dark. A tragedy. Like Lily's life—and death."

My mother sighed. "Yes, poor woman. Although, she brought things on herself. She had a vicious streak. It was rumored she all but ruined Michael Nash's career—brilliant director, by the way."

"Michael Nash? I've never heard of him." I perched on the end of her bed.

"I knew him briefly," she continued. "He directed the play I was in with Lily Beaumont. He was taken with a young actress under Lily's tutelage, Adrian North. He and Lily fought bitterly over Miss North. Sadly, his career was cut short. He was Victor's uncle."

I blinked at her. Victor's uncle. This was intriguing indeed. It seemed the ghost of Lily Beaumont had many connections with our troupe—Celine through her journal, my mother, and now, Victor. Moreover, the script found in Gloria's possession bore striking similarities to our troupe's personal dynamics. Did Gloria have a connection to Lily Beaumont as well? It was regrettable I couldn't ask her. And I wished we could get Lily's ghost to share her side of the story. Maybe there was a way.

Meanwhile, I wanted to know more about Victor's uncle, Michael Nash.

Chapter Twenty-Five

Bijou and I left my mother's suite and went to my own to retrieve my hat, my gloves, and Bijou's leash. I had a mind to go pay Mr. Langston a visit and Bijou would love the outing. I finally managed to clip the leash onto her collar while she bounced around excitedly. I went down to the lobby where Mr. Pettyjohn was engaged in conversation with a young couple who were attempting to check in to the hotel. They had two little children with them, and a small dog.

My heart wilted as Mr. Pettyjohn explained there were no rooms available. The sheriff had not wanted to encourage any new guests during the investigation—for everyone's safety. Not only did I feel for the couple, but the hotel desperately needed the income. We simply had to get to the bottom of these murders, and fast.

Deputy Fleming was stationed near the foot of the stairs and upon noticing me, he sprang from his seat, quickly removed his hat, and greeted me with a radiant smile.

"Mrs. Pryce," he said, approaching swiftly. "You look lovely today."

I modestly dismissed the compliment, which he had already offered me earlier—twice, in fact.

Bijou tugged on the leash, excited to meet the other dog. They sniffed each other briefly before the other little dog retreated behind his mistress's skirts.

I introduced myself to the couple. "I apologize for the inconvenience," I said.

The woman thrust out her hand. "It's really you?" She was petite, with soft features and wide gray eyes, a pleasant-looking face. "You're Arabella Pryce?"

"Yes," I said with a gentle nod.

"We've seen you perform in New York. It's so thrilling to meet you," she said.

Standing only slightly taller than his wife, the man appeared fit and neat, with a clear-eyed gaze and distinguished cheekbones. He gave me a pleasant smile and said, "We are so pleased to find that the Arabella hotel lives up to its description in the papers."

My heart filled with joy at this welcomed news. Mr. Rankin's series of articles were having the exact desired effect I'd wanted.

"That's wonderful," I exclaimed. "Where are you from?"

"Ohio." The woman said. "When we read about you and your hotel, we just had to see it for ourselves."

"With your presence in town, it's no wonder you are full to capacity," the gentleman said. "But your reception clerk mentioned the General Hotel down the street. It will have to do."

It pained me to send business Mr. Archer's way, but there was nothing to be done.

"Again, I'm so sorry," I said.

"It's not all bad. We've met you," the woman beamed. "I'm still all a flutter. It was worth the trip."

The little boy, who I guessed was about six or seven, approached me. "I want to see a real Indian. And a lawman."

"Well, you're in luck," I said, tilting my head toward the deputy. "This is Deputy Fleming."

The boy's brows lowered, and his face took on a serious expression. "Have you fought the Indians?" he asked him.

Deputy Fleming grinned at me and then addressed the young man. "I'm pretty new in town. And, the Indians around here are pretty friendly. So, no."

The boy frowned with disappointment.

"It was a pleasure to meet you," I said, eager to get on with my errand. "Please step into the Bella for a meal. Our cook is the best in town," I boasted.

The boy and his sister shifted their focus to Bijou. Quickly forgetting the other dog's rejection, she basked in their attention. Although I could not accommodate them, it made me smile to think of their reasons for coming to the hotel. It was encouraging that word of its being 'cursed' had not become wide spread.

"Mr. Pettyjohn, please send for Mr. Ellis? I'd like to go to the new theater site."

"Certainly, madam. Mr. Johns has gone to the kitchens for a moment, but as soon as he returns, I will have him get Mr. Ellis."

"Thank you, Mr. Pettyjohn." Mr. Johns, our other bell-man, was a former miner who'd been unable to continue working in the mines. Mr. Pettyjohn had kindly offered him a position at the hotel, a gesture for which I was grateful.

"I'll wait outside," I said as I put on my gloves. Bijou

would need to piddle before the coach ride to the warehouse. It was now being referred to as 'the new theater' and I supposed I would have to get used to it, despite my trepidation at its existence.

"You're going alone?" Deputy Fleming asked with a measure of concern.

I shrugged. "Yes."

"I'm not sure that's wise, considering the threats you and your mother have been receiving. I'd like to accompany you."

I regarded him for a moment, the look of apprehension on his face quite endearing. I didn't really feel it necessary for him to come along, but I supposed it would be prudent to be careful.

"All right," I said.

Radiating with joy, he gestured I lead the way.

Together we strolled with Bijou around the corner to the grassy spot where she usually did her business. While waiting for her, I observed the main street bustling with townsfolk engaged in their daily errands. Down at the end of the street, near the sheriff's office, jail and Dr. Tate's infirmary, I noticed the sheriff, and the doctor engaged in conversation in front of the infirmary.

"Look." I pointed in their direction. "I wonder if they're discussing the case."

"Could be," Deputy Fleming agreed.

"Well, I'd like to find out." I hurriedly made my way over to them, the deputy close behind.

"Good day, gentlemen," I greeted them.

"Mrs. Pryce," Dr. Tate acknowledged me with a nod.

"Deputy," Clayton said. "Why aren't you at the hotel?"

The young man clasped his hands behind his back.

"Mrs. Pryce wanted to go to the new theater. I thought it wise to go with her. For her protection."

The sheriff's jaw clenched. I found it amusing that he seemed to find the deputy's lovesick behavior irritating. The young man was certainly harmless, yet it was entertaining to see Clayton slightly ruffled.

"Right," he said, somewhat dubiously, and then turned to me. "I was just coming to see you. We have some news about the case, concerning your mother."

I swallowed, hoping it wasn't bad news.

"As you know," Clayton began, "we've been trying to determine what firearm killed Edmund Farley."

"Yes," I said. "You claimed he was not shot at close range because of the lack of gunpowder residue on his clothing."

"But, the question remained, had he been shot with a rifle or your mother's Colt?"

"Go on," I encouraged.

"After taking another look at it, I spotted something I should have seen earlier. The firing pin is broken. It couldn't have been the murder weapon. Your mother claimed she'd never used it before, so it's possible she bought it in that condition."

"Oh!" I exclaimed with relief. "Then, for certain she couldn't have killed him."

"Right," he said.

The doctor intervened, "Furthermore, upon examining the body, the severe damage to his heart suggests that he was shot with a rifle, not a handgun."

"And why is that?" I asked.

"Because even with the same cartridge, a rifle is always going to have a higher velocity which would cause more internal damage."

"I see," I said, my heart lifting. I had struggled to accept the possibility of my mother committing murder, and I was overjoyed to discover that it wasn't true. "So we can rule her out?"

"For the shooting of Mr. Farley, at least," Clayton said.

"Right. Of course," I said, slightly disappointed. "Any more news about Gloria Standish and the poison?" I asked.

"Yes, actually." Clayton tilted his head toward Dr. Tate, passing him the torch again.

The doctor cleared his throat. "It appeared she died rather quickly, so I estimate the time of death at around midnight. I believe she drank the poison about an hour before that."

"Was it absinthe?" I asked.

"That's where it gets interesting," Clayton said. "It was not. The Bella has never served it or any other kind of green spirit, according to the barman and Kitty."

"How odd. But, she might have thought it was absinthe?"

"That is my guess," the doctor said. "However, the poison, Scheele's Green dye, is a much more vivid and vibrant shade of green. Either she had not had absinthe before, or she didn't seem to notice the difference in color."

"What if she intended to kill herself?" the deputy asked. "What if she shot Farley, had a guilty conscience about it, couldn't live with herself, so committed suicide?"

The sheriff shook his head in disagreement. "There is absolutely no evidence Miss Standish had experience with firearms—or could shoot someone with such accuracy at a distance."

"Besides," I said, "If she had been intent on killing herself, then why would she be wandering around the hotel in the middle of the night? She had opted to stay at the caravans."

"I think we can safely assume Miss Standish did not kill Farley. Same goes for Shay, Miss Benavides and your mother."

"So, that leaves Mr. Thompson and Mr. Langston," I said. "I was just about to pay Mr. Langston a visit at the new theater."

"Yes, and I am accompanying her," the deputy added.

Clayton's jaw tightened, and he hesitated before responding. "All right. I'll speak with Mr. Thompson, then."

The deputy grinned. "I suppose we should be off then. Are you ready, Mrs. Pryce?"

I glanced at Clayton who was glowering at the deputy. He caught my eye and then quickly straightened his face. I stifled a giggle as we left the office.

We arrived at the warehouse, to find Andrew busy directing several workers as they continued to build the necessary infrastructure of the theater. A group of them had already set up the proscenium arch and were currently hanging the red velvet curtain. The town dressmaker, Cynthia Mayes, was overseeing the task. Others were constructing the tiered floor. Constance Chatterley and—much to my dismay, Atticus Brooks—were there too, engaging Celine in conversation. From her overwhelmed expression it seemed they were bombarding her with questions.

"Ahh! Arabella," Constance said upon seeing us enter. "Isn't this exciting? It almost looks like a real theater, don't you think?"

"It is coming along nicely," I said stiffly, still a little annoyed with her.

"Miss Dubois was just sharing her inspiration with us— Miss Lily Beaumont," Mr. Brooks said, offering a prim smile. Trepidation gnawed at my stomach.

"I've always wanted to do a story about her," he continued. "Such a tragic figure. I understand your mother knew her? I'd love to speak with her about it."

I pondered whether Celine had revealed anything about my mother's affair—and the troubling suggestion that her lover had pressured the director to award me the coveted role of Viola over Kathy Macarther. Such information would only provide him more material to support his earlier claims that my mother killed Miss Macarther.

While my mother seemed to have been exonerated in Mr. Farley's death, the situation with Gloria's remained unresolved. I hadn't yet finished reading the diary and wondered if Celine might have learned of and disclosed any other details about my mother's past.

"My mother isn't feeling very well," I said to him. "I ask that you do not disturb her rest until she is better."

His mouth tightened, and he gave a reluctant nod of compliance. I hoped I could rely on his agreement.

"Miss Chatterley also reminded me of your connection with another tragic figure in the theatrical world," he went on. "Miss Leticia Crookshank? I had forgotten she met her demise on your stage. Silly of me to forget."

I glanced at Constance, who smiled and fluttered her eyelashes at Mr. Brooks. A shiver of icy fear shot through me. She was clearly infatuated with him, or perhaps just the prospect of collaborating with him. It seemed likely that she would disclose anything she uncovered while researching my theater, or my background.

"I suppose it's not worth remembering then, Mr. Brooks," I said trying to deflect. I did not want to further engage in this line of conversation. "If you will excuse me, the deputy and I are looking for Mr. Langston. Is he about?"

"Haven't seen him," Miss Chatterley said.

Andrew appeared at my elbow. "Hello, Mrs. Pryce." He greeted me with a wide smile. His sandy hair was mussed, and a sheen of perspiration showed on his forehead.

"Hello, Andrew. It looks like things are coming together well, here."

"Yes, ma'am, it is. We should be ready for a show in the next week. My uncle is eager to get the theater up and running. He and Mr. Langston have been burning the midnight oil getting the business side of things ready."

"I see." It appeared they were making these decisions without consulting my mother, which put me on the defensive for her. She had invested so much into the theater troupe. Was Victor Langston trying to edge her out of the business?

Andrew turned to Deputy Fleming. "Can I borrow you for a minute? We need an extra hand to stand up one of the walls for the dressing room."

"Happy to help," the deputy said.

Bijou jumped up onto my skirt and barked, telling me she needed to go outside. Seeing that Deputy Fleming might be awhile, I complied.

"Come on, girl."

Outside, we wandered over to the fallen down tree. I let go of the leash, allowing Bijou to wander. My gaze fell onto the caravans in the distance. I wondered if Victor was there, perhaps perfecting the script, or doing some paperwork.

"Let's go, Bijou." I took hold of her leash again.

Once at his caravan, I climbed the steps to his door and knocked.

"Mr. Langston?" I called out. I waited, but there was no response. As I turned to leave, I almost collided with—or more accurately, almost passed right through—Miss Beaumont, who had suddenly materialized. Her cold, wispy glow enveloped me. Bijou barked.

"Miss Beaumont," I said in surprise.

She pointed toward the door.

"He's not in," I said.

She thrust her bony transparent finger at the door again.

"You want me to go in?" I asked. She lowered her hand and nodded.

I turned the doorknob and stepped inside. From the coolness seeping into the back of my dress, I knew she had followed me in. Bijou jumped ahead and began a sniffing campaign.

At one end of the caravan, a raised bed sat atop a structure functioning as both a cabinet and bureau, with a curtain strung from the ceiling and drawn to one side. A long leather divan lined one wall, offering comfortable seating, while a bulky desk dominated the opposite wall. The desk, oversized for the space, featured drawers on each side and three smaller ones across the top. It was cluttered with papers, scripts, and books. Miss Beaumont glided over to it and perched herself on top of it.

"What do you want me to see?" I asked her. She didn't respond; she simply continued to stare at me.

Suddenly, the aroma of spicy tobacco filled the caravan. Percival had arrived. "Perhaps she wants you to go through the desk?"

"It seems so." I went to one of the drawers and pulled it

open. Inside were various writing supplies, ink bottles, and blotters.

I placed my hand on the pull of the next drawer, but it was stuck. I tugged, and it budged slightly—pulling harder, it finally opened. The drawer was empty except for a dark brown bottle with a cork, tucked away in the corner. I picked it up, noting its worn, faded, and partially torn label. Judging by its weight, it was about half full of liquid. I pulled out the cork and peered inside; it was too dark to see. Sniffing it, I detected no distinct odor. It seemed likely to be a large supply of ink, something any writer would certainly need. I went to another drawer and Miss Beaumont put out a hand to stop me.

"Not there?" I asked. She slowly shook her head. I looked over at Percival, confused. Suddenly, Bijou barked. I glanced down to see that she had gotten herself wedged behind the leather stool under the desk. No doubt the result of her quest for interesting smells.

"For goodness' sake." I pulled out the stool. She made her way out and smiled up at me. Unable to resist her adorableness, I ruffled her head. "You are a silly girl."

I was about to tuck the stool back under the desk when I noticed an envelope sticking out between the floor and the back of the desk. I reached in and pulled it out. The envelope was addressed to Mr. Victor Langston, and the seal had been broken.

"Must have fallen behind the desk," I mused.

"Arabella, look," Percival said. I glanced up to see Miss Beaumont emphatically gesturing toward the envelope. "I believe she wants you to open it," he said calmly.

I pulled the letter out and unfolded it. It was dated June, 1872.

"Dearest Victor,

I am so pleased to hear you are making progress with your play. Your uncle would be most proud of you, dear man. I am sorry to hear of his troubles. Miss Beaumont is indeed a force to be reckoned with. I do so admire her talent, but her ambition is like a greedy tyrant.

I am sorry to report I am still in hospital. I am growing weaker each day, and my head aches so, but I would not let it stop me from writing to you. I'm sorry it's taken me so long to respond.

Like your uncle, I, too, am afraid that I have come under the vengeance of blind ambition. The role of Viola has been taken from me and has been given to another, Miss Arabella Janes."

I gasped and looked up at Miss Beaumont. She slowly nodded her head. I dropped my gaze to the end of the letter. It was signed Kathy Macarther. The woman my mother had been accused of poisoning.

I went back to where I had left off.

"She is indeed a talented actress, but she and her mother seemed to have come out of nowhere. If I had not been ill, I'm sure Harold, our director, would not have even considered replacing me, but here I lie, in a hospital bed. Harold told me he'd wait for me to recover, but then suddenly changed his mind.

It is rumored that Mrs. Janes is involved with Mr. Dunham, a man with much power and influence who is also acquainted with Harold. In fact, Mr. Dunham has just offered to financially back the entire production. I suspect that Mrs. Janes has used her influence with Mr. Dunham to support Harold with some kind of bribery, to give her daughter the role. I am heart broken, Victor. Utterly heart broken. I await your return to give me strength. But for now, my headache gives me no peace. I must say goodbye. I look forward to your next letter. Forever yours, Kathy Macarther

I lowered the letter and looked up at Percival. "Victor was the Mr. L. in Lily Beaumont's diary. He and Kathy were sweethearts."

I tuned to the ghostly figure of Miss Beaumont who only offered a chilling, transparent gaze.

"Why did you want me to see this?" I asked, although I knew she would not respond.

"Maybe the letter has something to do with the murders," Percival said.

"Perhaps. Or at least, the threats to my mother. Could Victor Langston be out for revenge?" I opened another drawer. It was full of other various odds and ends. I then pulled open one of the smaller top drawers. Inside lay a single item. A large coin with a maroon, velvet ribbon attached. I reached in and lifted it out.

"Look at this," I said to Percival.

"It's a medal," he said.

I looked at it more closely. A large star dominated the design, the center of which was a lion's head inlaid with gold.

I flipped it over.

"Oh, my goodness," I said, glancing up at Percival. "It reads, 'For Bravery and Excellent Marksmanship, Victor Langston, 1862.'"

"Well, isn't that interesting?" Percival said. "He obviously fought in the Civil War."

"Yes. He'd earlier told the sheriff of his pacifist beliefs and had had nothing to do with guns."

Percival puffed on his pipe and then blew out a series of smoke rings. "It seems there is more to Victor Langston than meets the eye."

Chapter Twenty-Six

Still unable to locate Mr. Langston, the deputy and I went back to the hotel. When we entered the hotel lobby, I was surprised to see the sheriff standing at the reception desk.

"Clayton?" I said. "What's wrong?"

"I have some bad news," he said, a grave look on his face. "I'm afraid your mother has taken a turn for the worse. The doctor is with her now."

"What happened?" I asked, alarmed.

"I'm not sure. I had just finished with Mr. Thompson, and Kitty came downstairs saying your mother was complaining of extreme stomach pain. I went to fetch the doc, and by the time we arrived, she was unconscious."

I left both Clayton and the deputy and ran up the stairs, Bijou struggling to keep up with me. I burst into my mother's parlor to find Kitty pacing the floor, one hand on her hip, the other on her forehead.

"There you are. Thank goodness!" she said, striding toward me, her face etched with worry.

"Kitty, what's going on?"

"She said she wanted to sleep, so I came into the parlor to let her rest. Lottie had brought it upon herself to bring up some tea, and also to tell me there was a problem in the Bella between one of my girls and a customer, so I left to take care of it."

"You left Mother alone?"

"Only for a few minutes," she explained. "When I came back, she was in terrible pain."

I entered the bedroom where Bijou had hopped onto the bed and curled up at my mother's feet, trying to offer some comfort. Dr. Tate was listening to her heartbeat with his stethoscope.

"What's wrong with her, Dr. Tate?" I asked, still winded from dashing up the stairs. My mother's face had assumed a sickly chartreuse tint.

He looked at me sympathetically. "She's definitely worse, and she's having trouble breathing."

I went to the other side of the bed and sat down next to her. The vibrancy of the peacock dressing gown made her skin look even more bilious. She gripped the matching fan in her fist. I gently took her other hand. It felt cold and clammy. Bijou sidled up next to me. The tea tray, laden with a teapot and teacup and a plate of Lottie's delicious scones, had been placed on the nightstand. None of it had been touched.

"Mother, can you hear me?" I asked, hoping my voice would rouse her. A sickening feeling had taken over me. I had pushed her out of my life. Ignored most of her correspondence. Pretended she didn't exist. And now she was slipping away from me. Regret swelled in my chest, climbing up to my throat, and left me feeling choked.

She didn't respond.

I looked over at Dr. Tate. "Why is she worse? I thought

you said the mountain air would do her good—that her health would improve."

He shook his head. "I am as mystified as you, my dear. By all appearances, she was in the early stages of tuberculosis—I never would have dreamed she'd come this far along so quickly."

"What can we do for her?" I asked.

He shook his head. "Hope and pray, my dear. Hope and pray."

I could not imagine a world without my mother in it, bossing everyone around. How I regretted letting my bitterness push her away. But I supposed there was nothing to be done for it now except, as Dr. Tate said, hope and pray.

I shook my head, still unwilling to believe she was fading away. My mother was stronger than this. It made no sense to me. I pondered the threats she'd been receiving and how someone was attempting to cast her in a guilty light for the crimes. If there was one thing I could do for her, it would be to uncover who sought to tarnish her name and set the record straight. Should she depart from this world, the least I could do would be to prove her innocence. But it seemed I was running out of time.

When I left her room, Clayton was standing in the hallway, his back to me, looking out the window.

"You're still here," I said.

He turned around just as Bijou scampered toward him, rearing up on her hind legs for attention. He knelt down and scooped her up. She licked his chin and then, panting, looked up at him like he was the best thing she'd ever seen in her life.

"I wanted to make sure you were okay," he said quietly.

I gave him a brief smile, touched by his concern. "I think so. But I wish we'd made more progress in the case.

Did the deputy tell you about the medal we found in Victor Langston's caravan?"

"He did. We are still looking for him for further questioning. We'd heard from Betty Gilroy she saw Langston and Boss Archer headed out toward the mines. The two have become fast friends."

"Yes," I said with a sigh. "Apparently, Mr. Archer has invested in the theater troupe. He's become a partner."

The sheriff shook his head with a smirking grin. "Of course he has."

"What did you glean from Mr. Thompson?" I asked. "Anything conclusive?"

He shook his head. "Nothing. The guy seems clean as a whistle."

I sighed. "Well, will you let me know what you find out from Mr. Langston?"

"Sure," he said.

"Thanks for checking on me."

He gave me a nod, set Bijou down and descended the stairs. Bijou and I watched him go, both of us grateful for his friendship.

Back in my suite, I found Cordelia at the desk. Bijou went to her water bowl and then settled into her bed.

"Did you find Mr. Langston?" she asked.

"No, but the sheriff knows where he is. The deputy has gone to fetch him."

"Really? So, the sheriff wants to see him?"

I told her about the medal.

"Do you think it belongs to him? Perhaps it was a friend's, or a relative's."

"His name was engraved on it," I added somberly.

Cordelia regarded me with a sympathetic look on her

face. "Are you all right, Arabella? You sound rather defeated. It's not like you."

I then told her about my mother. "The doctor says there isn't much he can do for her."

"Oh, dear." Her expression was composed, but there was a fleeting sadness in her eyes.

"I don't want her to go," I said, unable to hide the waver in my voice.

Cordelia got up from the desk, came over to me and gave me a hug. "I know you don't. We mustn't give up hope."

"I know," I agreed. "I don't want her to go to her grave with a scandal on her head. I mustn't fail her."

She released her arms and gently took hold of my shoulders. "And, she won't. You will figure this out. *We* will figure this out."

I reached up and patted her hand, taking consolation in her confident assurance. I then went to the loveseat and picked up Lily Beaumont's diary. "After I found the medal in Mr. Langston's desk, I found something else."

I told her about the letter.

"My goodness. So, Victor and Kathy Macarther were acquainted?"

"More than acquainted. I believe they were sweethearts. The letter mentioned Lily Beaumont as well," I said, holding up the diary. "And my mother. I'm going to check if there's anything else in here that I've overlooked.

"Do you think the diary holds the answer?"

"I do. And the script we found. There are too many parallels between them and what's happening here. I just can't quite piece it together yet."

"It sounds like you could use some tea," she said with a smile. "I'll make us some. I'll be back in a moment."

I thanked her and then sat down with the diary and script. The diary gave insight into the fact that Victor Langston, Roger Thompson, and my mother all had connections with Lily Beaumont. Victor and my mother also had a connection to the young actress who had died, with my mother being accused of the crime. Which was similar to the situation now, with her being accused of both Edmund Farley's death, and Gloria's. Thank goodness she had been exonerated of Mr. Farley's death, but I still had work to do to find out who had poisoned Gloria.

The script, on the other hand, told a story. A story about an ambitious director whose career was shattered by Emily Boulant—a name that was coincidentally an anagram for Lily Beaumont—a woman of power who was not given her desired role in Lechim's play. Having eliminated one of his enemies, Lechim does away with his beloved Dariann's husband as well, thus—he thinks—solving all of his problems, but then Dariann turns against him.

I studied the unfinished scene where Emily Boulant dies at her dressing table before her performance. Lily Beaumont had also died in her dressing room, under mysterious circumstances, and the means of her death was never discovered. Perhaps that was why the very important detail of how Emily Boulant died had been left out. The writer, Grant Colston, was most likely trying to come up with the perfect method.

I then studied the scenes which highlighted Hans Lechim's romance with Dariann. It had been passionate, conducted in the shadows, with Dariann always conflicted about her feelings towards Hans and her husband, Phillip Richardson. Ultimately, she chooses her husband, whereby Lechim kills him by strangulation.

I set the script down and tapped my fingers on it.

Just then, Cordelia returned with the tea. "Here we are," she said, setting the tea tray down on the coffee table. I rose from the chair by the fireplace and went to the loveseat. I set the diary down on the coffee table, but held the script in my lap.

"Any insights?" she asked, pouring the both of us some tea. The familiar and comforting scent of Earl Grey filled the room.

"Not really," I said, sipping my tea and staring down at the script. The corners of its pages were now curled and worn from my constant leafing through it.

My gaze was again drawn to the name Emily Boulant. Boulant was indeed a strange surname—but it was an anagram for Lily Beaumont. If the writer wanted to maintain the name as an anagram, I'm sure there weren't many options in scrambling the letters.

"Lily is the key to all of this," I said.

"Indeed, she is," Percival's voice pervaded the room, but he had not yet appeared. Soon, the aroma of tobacco blended with the fragrance of Earl Grey tea as a chill permeated the room. He transformed beside me on the loveseat.

"Have you been able to get her to speak?" Cordelia asked him.

"No. As I mentioned before, I believe she is stuck either between the realms or within one."

"Is it because her murder was never solved?" she asked.

He shrugged. "Mine had remained unsolved for some time—that is until Arabella uncovered the truth—and I was not stuck. Although, I grew stronger afterwards—my options less limited."

"Meaning?" I asked.

"Meaning now, I no longer have to stay in the Ethereal Plane. I can move on to the Afterworld."

"So, does that mean you would leave us?" I asked, surprised at the feeling of loss that suddenly overwhelmed me.

"If I choose," he said. "But, for the time being, I choose not."

I smiled at him. "I'm glad of it."

"Tell us about these realms," Cordelia said. "Where do you think Lily is trapped?"

He clasped his hands behind his back, and his face took on a serious expression. "When we die, we must pass through four, sometimes five realms. The first, the Visible Realm is in the world of the living. A spirit in this realm often lingers around people, places or objects that are familiar to them."

"Like Lily?" Cordelia asked.

"Perhaps," Percival said. "The next is the Realm of Echoes. This is where the energy or essence of their past actions, emotions, and experiences are stored. In order to move on from this realm, a spirit must come to terms with all of those experiences, or they remain stuck. I believe Lily Beaumont is in this realm or caught between the two."

"That's fascinating," Cordelia said, her eyes wide with wonder.

Percival gave her a gentle nod of approval.

While I agreed his revelation was a matter of great interest, my mind strayed back to the script.

"In this story, it is never mentioned how Emily Boulant dies. However, since it alludes to murder, I would assume the means was poison. But there is no mention of her eating or drinking anything—so if it was poison, how was it done?"

"Let me see," Cordelia said. I pointed to the scene. "See here, she powders her face and neck and —"

I stopped short.

"Arabella, what is it?" Cordelia said.

"Powder. That's it!" I said. "What if the powder she used was poisoned? Or, her powder was laced with something, like strychnine?"

"Rat poison. Yes!" Cordelia said. "That is entirely possible."

"Is there anything about powder in Miss Beaumont's diary?" Percival asked.

"No." I shook my head. "But if that's what killed Miss Beaumont, how would she have known?"

"Well, there's another connection," Percival said. "Didn't Miss Standish succumb to arsenic?"

"Yes. But in the form of green dye," Cordelia said.

"So who is Grant Colston, and why did Gloria have this script?" I mused out loud.

"Perhaps she wrote it with a nom de plume?" Percival added.

I nodded. "She might have. Female playwrights are still not taken seriously. If she knew she was leaving the troupe, or, if she felt her acting days were done, she would have been worried about her prospects. She could have written this hoping to sell it—to secure her future."

"But why would someone want to kill her?" Cordelia asked.

"The better question is," I said, "If she took this story as inspiration—from the real-life event of Lily Beaumont's mysterious death, then perhaps she is exposing Miss Beaumont's killer."

"Which would be Hans Lechim," Cordelia added.

"And who is he?" My voice trailed off, and then

suddenly a though struck. "Whether coincidence or not, Emily Boulant is an anagram for Lily Beaumont. Perhaps Hans Lechim . . ."

I got up and went to the desk. Pulling out a piece of stationery from the paper tray, I picked up a pen and began writing the letters of his name. *H-A-N-S-L-E-C-H-I-M*. I studied my handiwork. But wasn't there something missing here? Oh, yes. The middle initial, A. I rewrote the letters *H-A-N-S-A-L-E-C-H-I-M*.

"What are you doing, dear?" Percival asked.

"Just a moment," I said.

C and H are often together, as are S and H, I thought. *C-H-A-L. No, S-H-A-L. No, again.*

I continued to work on the letters. Behind me I heard Percival chuckle at something Cordelia said. Although their talking made it difficult to concentrate, I was grateful the two got on so well.

Refocusing on my task, I then started from a different angle. *N-A-C-H*, then tried *N-A-S-H*. Nash!

"Oh, my goodness, I've figured it out," I said, turning around in the chair to face them.

"Really?" Cordelia asked.

"Yes. Hans A. Lechim is Michael Nash." I rose from the desk and showed them my work.

"And who is that, my dear?" Percival asked.

"Michael Nash is Victor Langston's uncle. An actor and director whose career was ruined by Lily Beaumont."

"Yes!" Cordelia's eyes went wide. "That's what your mother told you."

"Right, so is this script based on truth?" I mused.

"Either way, it's a very underhanded slander toward Mr. Langston's uncle," Percival said.

"Yes, but does Victor Langston even know about the

script? Miss Standish could have kept it a secret," Cordelia said. "She did have it tucked away in the portfolio in the bookshelf."

"I'd like to ask Mr. Langston about it," I said. "I wonder if the deputy has tracked him down yet? I'm going to the sheriff's office to find out. Besides, Clayton needs to know about this."

"Shall I go with you?" Cordelia asked.

I shook my head. "No. I'd rather you stay here with my mother. Kitty has been such a help in keeping watch over her, but I know she has other things to tend to. Perhaps you can spell her for a bit?"

"Certainly," Cordelia said. "I wanted to check in on Mrs. Janes myself anyway."

"Thank you, dear."

"Is there anything I can do?" Percival asked.

"See if you can locate Miss Beaumont and tell her of our discovery. If this story has unlocked the mystery of her death, perhaps it will have changed something for her, like it did for you when we discovered the truth behind your death."

"I will do my best," he said with a crisp salute.

I went to the hat stand at the doorway and took up my hat and coat. I then attached the leash to Bijou's collar. "Come on, little girl. Let's go see Mr. Marshall."

Chapter Twenty-Seven

Eager to depart, Bijou tugged on the leash, pulling me down the stairs. For such a tiny creature, she certainly possessed considerable strength in those short little legs.

When we reached the landing of the second floor, we turned the corner and nearly ran into the back of Mr. Thompson, who was going down to the first floor. Startled, he turned around to face me.

"Oh, my goodness, excuse me, Mr. Thompson!" I said. "We seem to keep running into you. Literally. I apologize."

"Ah, Mrs. Pryce. It is no matter. Your little dog seems to be on a mission," he said with a chuckle. Bijou looked up at him and smiled, her tail wagging furiously.

"Yes, she is excitable sometimes. I'm sorry to have startled you."

"It's no problem, I assure you. But where are you going in such a rush?"

"We were just — well, running an errand."

"I see. Don't let me keep you," he said, motioning for us to go down in front of him.

"Actually, Mr. Thompson, I was wondering if I could speak with you about something?" I was curious to find out if he'd known anything about the script.

He gave me a dubious look. "I'm afraid I am rather in a hurry. I was going to the Bella for some refreshment, and then I'm needed at the new theater."

"Oh, well, do you mind if I accompany you to the Bella?"

He beamed. "I'd love the company."

Once there, I led him to my favorite booth and waved Sally Dean over to us. With a pleasant smile, she obliged me. Today, she wore a simple dress of cotton muslin in a feminine floral print—I was still not used to her out of her scintillating barmaid costume. Since her engagement to Mr. Emerson, she had abandoned her previous role in Kitty's service to devote herself fully to her new position as Kitty's assistant manager at the Bella.

While we waited for her arrival, I spotted Atticus Brooks, Mr. Archer, and Constance Chatterley sitting at a table at the front of the saloon, by the window. Mr. Brooks was scribbling on his confounded pad of paper. What damnation was he conjuring up now?

Seeing them together, I gathered the deputy had indeed retrieved Mr. Langston from the mines—as he had been with Mr. Archer. If I kept this brief, I would hopefully catch Mr. Langston at the sheriff's office.

"Hello, Mrs. Pryce, Mr. Thompson. What can I do for you?" Sally asked, placing her delicate hands on her slim hips.

"Sally, Mr. Thompson needs to be on his way soon. Could you please see that his meal is brought to him quickly?"

"Certainly. What would you like, Mr. Thompson?"

He ordered the mutton stew and biscuits—a specialty of Lottie's, and a beer. I declined anything but a glass of water.

"Now, what is it you would like to speak with me about?" Mr. Thompson asked politely.

I pressed my lips together, not sure where to begin. "Were you acquainted with the actress Lily Beaumont?" I asked.

He blinked in surprise. "My goodness, but that's a name I haven't heard in an age. Yes, yes, I knew her. Briefly."

"I understand she was familiar with Mr. Langston and his uncle, the director, Michael Nash."

He frowned. "I do recall she had a very tenuous relationship with Nash. She was a formidable woman, and quite a talent. I auditioned for a play in St. Louis in which she had the starring role. It was a minor role, but I didn't care. The opportunity to work with such a talent would have been a great honor."

"Would have been?" I said.

"I didn't get the part."

"Oh my. I'm sorry."

He took in a breath and then released it, his face taking on a look of defeat. "Victor got it. In fact, Lily Beaumont had the play rewritten to give him a bigger role."

"Really? That's interesting, given her relationship with his uncle."

He looked at me conspiratorially from beneath his gray and sandy peppered eyebrows. "That was her modus operandi—divide and conquer. Victor was under her spell for a time, but when she started poking at Nash, he came to his senses. In fact, he grew to despise her."

"Did you ever get the chance to work with her again?" I asked.

One of the other barmaids appeared with Mr. Thompson's beer and silently set in on the table.

He nodded his thanks, took a substantial draught, and then answered my question. "No. I gave up acting shortly after that. I suffered a broken heart. Not entirely from not getting the part, but for another more personal reason."

"Oh, I see," I said. Was he referring to a broken heart over my mother?

His expression grew thoughtful, as if he was lost in a distant memory. Then, lifting his eyes to meet mine, he said, "The first love is never easy to get over, don't you agree?"

I stared at him blankly and found I couldn't answer the question. I'd never truly been in love. I had a great fondness for my husband and I missed him dearly, but he had never swept me away. It was a marriage of convenience.

"Yes," I said, indulging him. But I didn't want to delve any further into a discussion of romance. "Mr. Thompson, could you tell me a little more about—"

He raised a finger, silencing me. "You know, there's a certain kind of love that consumes you, where you become so intertwined with someone else's existence that thought of them with another, or living a life without you, it's . . . unbearable. It's like you're standing on the edge of a precipice, and the only thing that makes sense is pulling them back from anyone else's reach, even if it means standing there alone."

His gaze rested on mine, but it seemed he wasn't truly present; lost in his thoughts.

A chill ran through me. What a cryptic thing to say, "pulling them back from anyone else's reach." It had an air of resentment to it.

When I'd first met Mr. Thompson, I had considered him a jovial sort, but hearing this I could see the pain and suffering he had endured had left behind a wistful bitterness.

Finally, Sally Dean came back to our table with Mr. Thompson's stew.

"Here you are, sir," she said, setting it in front of him. It looked delicious and smelled even better. Had I not been in somewhat of a hurry, I would have ordered some myself.

"Would you like another beer?" she asked.

He looked at his half empty glass. "Sure, why not?"

She smiled and left the table.

During their exchange, I was still thinking about Mr. Thompson's puzzling allusion to his lost love, which could in all reality have been my mother. In fact, his odd sentiment had completely derailed me from my previous inquiry, which was leading toward Victor Langston and his uncle. Curious, I decided to follow his lead of his memories from the past, but from a different angle.

"Why don't you perform on stage anymore, Mr. Thompson? Do you miss acting?"

My question seemed to wake him from his reverie. He shook his head. "I was never graced with natural talent and suffusive charm like Edmund. It's fascinating, really, how fate seems to favor some more than others. That man walked into a room, and suddenly, the sun shone a bit brighter on him than the rest of us, casting long shadows behind those who stood too close. It was as if fortune's favor was his birthright. A gift, or so it seemed, yet not without its costs to those of us left in his wake."

I found it strange he'd brought Edmund into the conversation. I suddenly recalled what he had said about him before—that he had a way with women, hinting that the young actor didn't mind if they were involved with someone else. Was there a hint of envy? He had openly expressed that Edmund was a financial burden to the troupe, but was there also a personal grievance? I remembered Celine mentioning my mother's affair with Edmund. Could it be that Mr. Thompson harbored jealousy?

"It seems I've gone off on a tangent, my dear," he said with a smile. "I apologize. I believe you were asking me about Lily Beaumont and Michael Nash?"

"Yes, yes, I was."

"The story goes she ruined him. Claimed he was defrauding his theater company. Nasty business."

"Yes, and then she died shortly thereafter?" I added.

He nodded. "I believe you are correct."

"It's a fascinating story. It would make a good play—it has all the drama and intrigue for a great tragedy."

He chuckled. "Someone could make a mint with it! No one ever tires of hearing about Lily Beaumont. She'll always be a legend, seen as either beloved or notorious."

I was about to inquire further when two gentlemen, dressed in fine suits, walked into the front entrance of the saloon, causing a distraction. They seemed to look for someone, and then they spotted Mr. Archer, Mr. Brooks, and Constance Chatterley, who were sitting by the door, and began speaking with them. Mr. Brooks then pointed toward our table and the men strode over. Suddenly, inexplicably, a feeling of dread overtook me. From the stern expression on the men's faces, I had a feeling this would not be a welcomed visit.

The man who approached us first cut a commanding presence, appearing to be in his late forties. He removed his hat, revealing hair peppered with gray. His deep blue eyes, sharp and perceptive, seemed to miss nothing, suggesting a keenly shrewd nature.

"Mrs. Arabella Pryce?" His razors-edge gaze settled on me.

"Yes, that's me. How can I help you?"

Behind them, Atticus Brooks had turned in his seat to get a better view of the event and Constance was craning her neck to see around him. I was getting a sour feeling in my stomach.

"I am Edward Graham and this is Brent Wood."

His younger companion presented a more approachable demeanor with a slim build and an untamed mass of dark curls that defied conventional grooming. "Good day, ma'am," he said flatly.

"Mrs. Pryce," Mr. Graham began, "We are from Billings Building and Company, and we are here to collect on the lien against the hotel."

I blinked up at them, astonished at the request. My heart plummeted to my stomach and a wave of embarrassment coursed through me, inflaming my chest and face. I darted a glance at Mr. Thompson, who looked back at me with an expression of grave concern.

"Pardon?" I said, still in a state of shock.

"We have come to collect what you owe the company for construction supplies and services rendered," he said, a bit too loudly for my taste. Peering around him to see if anyone was within hearing, I noticed Atticus Brooks had taken from his pocket that offensive pad of paper and was furiously scribbling on it. Mr. Archer watched the spectacle with great interest. My mouth went dry. This was absolutely the last thing I needed at the moment.

Mr. Thompson came to my rescue. "I say, gentlemen, this is quite inappropriate to confront Mrs. Pryce in such a public place—her place of business. What's wrong with you, man?"

The younger man's cheek twitched, and he swallowed, obviously uncomfortable at Mr. Thompson's admonishment, but Mr. Graham seemed unfazed.

"You have one week to make the payment in full, or we will begin proceedings to take over the hotel." He put his hat back on his head, and then left us, his partner following him. I stared after them, unable to breathe.

I leaned forward, placing my elbows on the table and my face in my hands, trying to regain my composure. I was glued to the seat with mortification.

"My dear, what is this business?" Mr. Thompson asked.

I shook my head and lowered my hands. "I'm sorry you had to witness that, Mr. Thompson. "I'd rather not discuss it. If you will excuse me."

I got up from the booth and headed for the door that led to the lobby. In a flash, Constance met me there.

"Is it true, Arabella?" she said. "There is a lien against the hotel? What will you do?"

I could not tell if she was sympathetic or angling for a story.

"This is just terrible," she prattled on. "You've done such a fine job with it since you've arrived. Why, with all the improvements you are making and everything? Surely, with all your money, you can quickly pay off this lien. Did you not know of its existence? Did this happen on your watch, or previously under Mr. Bledsoe's—oh my goodness, but this is quite disturbing. By all appearances, it seems things at the hotel have been running better than ever, despite, of course, the rumors of it being cursed and haunted and such —but I just can't imagine—"

"Constance!" I exclaimed, more sharply than I meant to, but I couldn't let her continue, especially not with talk of curses and ghostly hauntings. I was already gasping for breath and didn't need her troubling statements to drown me further.

She blinked at me in surprise. "Yes, dear?"

"I can't speak about this right now, if you will—"

"Have you ever thought of having an exorcism performed?" she asked. "You know, to get rid of the spirits wandering about. I've heard that Father Green from Addison was quite successful in performing one over at—"

"An exorcism. I beg your pardon?" I said, offended at her insinuation that there was some kind of evil afoot in the hotel. Percival could be cantankerous and mischievous, but never evil.

"Well, yes," she said with a shrug of her shoulders. "Considering your recent troubles with your mother being accused of murder, and now your financial problems, I know you must be out of your head with worry, poor dear. The last thing you need is a ghost wandering around, and further word getting out about it. No one will want to stay at the Arabella, and it would be such a shame—she is such a beautiful—"

"Constance," I repeated, this time with more gravitas. It seemed it was time for a frank discussion with her about the matter of spiritual phenomenon, but I needed time to script what I would say, and I had more pressing difficulties to deal with at the moment. "I will speak with you later about these matters. In fact, if you will keep quiet about them, I will give you an exclusive story." I neglected to say about what, but I figured it would be enough to entice her penchant for gossip into silence for the moment. I only wished I had as much insight into Atticus Brooks's Achilles heel.

I made my way quickly to the hallway door across the lobby that led to the annex. I needed a moment of privacy to collect myself.

Once alone in the hallway, I leaned against the wall, closed my eyes, and tried to steady my shaking limbs. It felt as though the world was collapsing around me. How had things come to this? For the thousandth time, I wondered why William had done this to me.

Bijou barked, startling me. A coolness permeated my cheek, and I opened my eyes to see Percival standing before me, his transparent hand cupping my chin and a look of tenderness in his eyes. I wished I could reach out, put my arms around him, and rest my head on his chest.

"Did you see that?" I asked.

"Yes." He released my chin and placed his hands behind his back.

I shook my head. "I do not know if I can continue this, Percival. It is too difficult. I believe I must cut my losses and return to New York. I can earn enough to live comfortably if I resume performing. Indeed, that is likely what I shall have to do, as I cannot meet the stipulations of William's demands in his will."

"Oh, come now, Arabella. You have more resilience than you realize. I've never known you to give up so easily."

I shot him a look. "There is nothing easy about this."

"I'm sure a solution will present itself, my dear."

"Will it?" I laughed. "And how do you know this? Do your powers extend to fortune telling?" I asked, my words dripping with sarcasm.

He merely smiled. "Have faith, my dear."

"Well, I'm sorry, my friend, but faith won't fix this mess. And those busy-bodies, Atticus Brooks and Constance Chatterley, will make it worse. It seems the complications of my life are their favorite subject."

He lowered his chin, gazing steadily at me with those

luminous dark eyes. "You let me take care of Miss Chatterley."

I drew in an anxious breath. "Do nothing rash, Percival. Constance may be exceedingly vexing, but I do not wish her to be harmed or threatened in any way. She has been quite fragile since she caught a glimpse of you during the holidays."

He raised a hand. "Don't worry. Trust me, Arabella. Please." His eyes implored mine with a sincerity that melted the tension around my shoulders. I often wondered how he could provoke such visceral sensations in me.

"Carry on with your investigation," he instructed. "We'll deal with the matters of the hotel later."

"But—" I wanted to protest.

"Go on," he pressed.

I took in a breath and smoothed down the front of my skirt, feeling more steady. "All right," I said.

Sensing we were about to leave, Bijou, who had settled herself on the floor at my feet, stood up, her tail wagging. I bent down and picked her up, longing for the comfort of her warmth, and set out for the sheriff's office.

Chapter Twenty-Eight

Outside the sheriff's office and jail, Queenie, Clayton's beloved mare, was in her usual spot, dozing at the hitching rail. I greeted her with a scratch at her withers and she replied with a low knicker.

I walked into the office just as Mr. Langston was about to leave. He gave me a tight smile, and I noticed a stiffness around his eyes.

"Mrs. Pryce," he said, nodding slightly before brushing past me.

"Hello, Mr. Langston, I was wondering if I could—"

Before I finished, he shook his head and walked away.

"Goodness," I said to Clayton, who was still sitting at his desk. "He's unhappy about something."

He gripped a pen and drummed it against the notepad before him. "It didn't please him to discover someone had rifled through his caravan," he said, fixing me with a meaningful gaze. "I wish you had consulted me before acting. He's grown quite close to Archer, and that complicates matters for me."

"Did you tell him it was me who'd gone through his belongings?" I asked, hoping he'd used discretion.

"Of course not. I didn't tell him anything, which he also wasn't happy about. You need to be careful, Arabella."

"But, I was investigating, and in doing so, I caught Mr. Langston in a lie—a lie that could have a direct impact on the case."

"You did. However, you legally have no authority to do that."

"But Deputy Fleming was with me," I argued, sitting down at the chair on the other side of his desk.

"He shouldn't have let you go into the caravan," he said. "He should have searched it himself. If it gets back to Archer that you went into Langston's caravan uninvited, he'll hold me responsible."

I bit my lip. "Oh dear. I do apologize." The last thing I wanted was to get the sheriff in trouble.

"And why are you alone?" he asked, his tone mildly admonishing. "I thought we agreed you needed to be with someone at all times because of the threats to you and your mother."

My back went up at his statement. We had agreed, but I didn't need to be coddled like a child. "Come now, Clayton. I doubt I would come to harm in the street in broad daylight."

"You can't be too careful, Arabella," he warned.

"All right, all right. I'll be more careful," I agreed. "So, what did you find out about Mr. Langston's medal for marksmanship? What did he say about it?"

He shrugged. "He was definitely surprised at being called out in a lie. He apologized and didn't deny he was an expert marksman, or used to be. He claimed he hasn't touched a firearm since the war. He abhors them."

"I see. So, that's it?"

He rested his elbows on the desk and laced his fingers together. "I have no evidence that he shot Farley—unless we find a rifle in his possession and the ammunition matches, which we haven't so far."

I sighed. "We just don't seem to make any headway. And my mother is gravely ill. If she goes to prison, she won't get the care she needs."

He shook his head, a look of helplessness in his eyes. "I'm sorry, Arabella."

I held up the script. "I'm not sure it's significant, but there is more to this story than I'd initially thought." I tossed it onto the desk in front of him. "It's about Michael Nash and his professional and personal downfall at the hands of Lily Beaumont."

"That's the woman who wrote the diary," he said, swiping it off the desk.

"Yes," I confirmed.

He rifled through the pages, then gave me a blank look. "And this matters because?"

"Lily Beaumont had a terrible feud with Michael Nash and she ruined his career. But what's interesting is I've found out from my mother that Michael Nash is Victor Langston's uncle—I believe the story in this script is based in reality."

He went through the pages again. "I see no mention of this Michael Nash or Lily Beaumont."

"That's where it gets more interesting. Look here." I pointed to the name Emily Boulant. Then I reached across the desk, took the discarded pen, wrote the name on a piece of paper. Then I wrote the name Lily Beaumont below it and drew lines between the corresponding letters.

"It's an anagram," I said. "And Hans A. Lechim is an anagram for Michael Nash."

He studied my handiwork. "Okay. Again, what does this have to do with the case?"

I rested my arm on the desk. "I'm not exactly sure, but I'm guessing Gloria Standish might have written this under a pen name—Grant Colston. If the story is true, or even partially true—then she is revealing Lily Beaumont's killer —Michael Nash. And, if Mr. Langston knew about the script—"

"You're saying he had motive to kill Miss Standish? To protect his uncle?"

I clapped my hands together. "Yes!"

"But, if Langston did kill her, don't you think he would have tried to dispose of the script?" he asked.

"I suppose you're right, but if he didn't know about it, then perhaps Gloria was using the information to blackmail him? She wanted power within the troupe."

"I'll admit this information is intriguing Arabella, and it is something to go on, but we'd need more to prove anything definitive."

"I had a feeling you'd say that. Another thing: I think we should also look more closely at Mr. Thompson," I added. "I've just had a strange conversation with him. It seems he had somewhat darker feelings towards Mr. Farley than we first considered."

Clayton leaned back in his chair and folded his arms across his middle. "Well, he said he'd felt Farley was a financial liability for the troupe. Is that what you mean?"

I shook my head. "No, it's more than that. It felt like there was a deep resentment. When I asked him why he stopped acting, he instantly mentioned Mr. Farley, describing him as a golden boy who always got everything —and everyone—he desired. And, you might not know this, but Mr. Thompson once had deep feelings for my mother. He was quite in love with her, in fact. She chose my father over him, and later, she had a relationship with Mr. Farley."

Clayton listened intently and then spoke up. "All right, that might be further motive to get Farley out of the picture. I'll give you that, but we'll need some kind of physical evidence—for both murders—before I can act on anything."

"We have to keep looking," I said.

He took in a deep breath and let it out slowly. "I'll follow up with Thompson," he said. "To be honest, up to this point I hadn't seriously considered him as a suspect, but perhaps I was remiss."

"What would you like for me to do?" I asked.

"You've done enough, Arabella. Stick close to your mother. It sounds as if she might need you. I'll walk you back to the hotel."

"But—" I protested.

He fixed me with a warning glare. "It's not up for discussion. I'm escorting you to the hotel."

I rolled my jaw in annoyance that he felt I needed a bodyguard, but I knew I'd get nowhere arguing with him. We'd been down this road before.

"Very well," I said, sighing with resignation. "Come on, Bijou."

Clayton put on his hat and took his gun belt from the back of the chair, and after securing it around his waist, gestured for us to lead the way outside. We had just begun our walk to the hotel when a tow-headed, wide-eyed young boy came running toward us from down the street.

"Sheriff, you've gotta come quick!" he shouted.

"Matty? What's the matter?" Clayton said.

"There's a fight down at Ma's boarding house, and a man's got her held hostage. You gotta come, Sheriff!"

Clayton squeezed my elbow. "It looks like I've got to handle this," he said. "Promise me you'll go straight to the hotel?"

"Yes, I promise. Go!" I said with a wave of my arm, concerned about the boy's mother.

He grasped Matty by the shoulder. "We'll take Queenie. Come on."

They went to the horse and Clayton set the boy up on the saddle and then climbed on behind him. They took off like a shot, galloping down the road. Bijou barked at the commotion.

"It's all right, girl," I said soothingly. "Let's do as we're told and get back to the hotel."

We set off, my mind swirling with thoughts of how to uncover the evidence needed to solve these murders. Bijou trotted along joyfully in front of me, eagerly pulling on the leash. The sun shone brightly above, and I looked up to see billowing white clouds floating over the southern mountains. As we approached the hotel, I began to cross the street diagonally when suddenly the sound of thundering hoofbeats echoed from behind.

"Look out!" someone shouted.

I turned to see an enormous horse pulling a carriage heading straight toward me. The driver had his hat pulled down low over his head and the collar of his duster pulled up around his face.

Quickly, I bent to pick up Bijou when someone collided with me, knocking me aside. Bijou yelped as we both tumbled to the ground. Despite landing on the opposite side, my injured shoulder cried out in pain. When I opened my eyes, I was astonished to see the stocky frame of Everett Emerson, the dry goods store manager and Sally Dean's sweetheart, lying next to me.

"Mrs. Pryce, are you all right?" he asked.

"My shoulder," I said, wincing.

With a powerful hand, he helped me to my feet. Bijou, who had come through the ordeal unscathed, whined, sensing my discomfort.

"Let's go see Doc Tate," he said. Although he was a bear of a man with a growling voice and a frequently frowning face, there was a sweet nature hidden beneath his gruff exterior. Sally was gradually coaxing that gentleness to the surface.

I shook my head. "No, no, really. I'm fine. Thank you for pushing me out of the way. What happened exactly?"

"That crazy driver was heading right toward you. I couldn't tell if he'd lost control of the horse or if it was intentional."

I gripped my shoulder. "Did you see who it was?"

"I didn't. His face was all covered up. Are you sure you don't want to go see the doc?"

"I'm sure, Mr. Emerson. I'll be fine. It's already feeling better," I lied. I didn't want word of this to get back to Clayton. He needed no more reason to worry about my safety.

"Well, then, let me walk you back to the hotel," he said.

"It's unnecessary, really. The hotel is just right there," I pointed to it. "I'll be okay. I promise."

His eyes carried the worry of doubt, but I knew he wouldn't push. "All right, then, Mrs. Pryce. You let me know if there is anything I can do for you."

"Thank you, Mr. Emerson. I will."

He bent down, picked up Bijou's leash and handed it to me. She raised herself on her hind legs and set them on his shins, showing her gratitude. Tousling her head, he then bade us farewell.

"My goodness, Bijou, that was frightening. Let's get back to the hotel."

We crossed the street and made our way back. When we passed by the alleyway between the haberdashery and the laundry, I spotted the carriage that nearly ran me over down by the river. The driver got down from the carriage and started walking in the opposite direction. With the bulk of the coat and his hat pressed down low on his head, it was impossible to make out his build or features.

"Come on, girl. Let's see if we can get a closer look."

We went through the alleyway, and when we neared the end of it, I slowed. The man looked back toward town and I shrunk behind the corner of the laundry building. When he was a suitable distance away, I stepped out of the alley.

Common sense dictated that I go find Clayton and tell him what had just happened. But if I did that, the man who tried to run me down would surely get away. Unless I could identify him, I wouldn't be safe. Neither would my mother if I couldn't protect her. If this was the person sending her threats or setting her up for the murders, this might be my only chance to put the whole matter to rest. If only I could get a peek at his face.

I had to follow him.

"Let's go, girl," I whispered to Bijou, who was busy nosing around in some weeds. I picked up a brisk pace to ensure he wouldn't disappear from view.

We walked downriver to the south. My heart pounded as I realized we were headed toward the caravans and the new theater. After another quarter mile or so, he veered away from the river, away from the caravans, and headed toward a heavily wooded area. Bijou and I followed, but had to fall back as my footsteps caused the snapping of branches on the ground, threatening to give us away. The man went over a small rise and when we finally reached it, a shack came into view below. Had he gone inside? I hovered behind a large pine tree, watching.

"You had quite a close call in town." A familiar voice echoed behind me. I turned to see Percival.

"Yes, I did," I said.

"Why would someone want to run you down?" he asked.

"My guess is that either someone is making good on their threat to my mother, or I may be getting closer to finding our murderer than we thought."

"Or both," he added.

"Right," I had to concur. "I think he went into that shack. Percival, can you go check and see?"

"At your service, my dear."

He wafted toward the structure and then hovered above it, ready to slip down the narrow chimney when, suddenly, the man reemerged. I quickly picked up Bijou and sucked myself back behind the tree. Bijou licked my chin, thinking she was in for a cuddle.

"Good girl," I whispered, hoping she wouldn't make any noise. The man shoved something into one of the large pockets of his duster and headed back in the direction we came. I skirted around the tree as he passed by, holding my breath. After several seconds, I peered around the tree trunk, but he had vanished. I glanced over at the shack again. Percival left his perch on the roof and drifted over to me.

"Shall I go after him?" He asked.

"I'm curious about that shack," I said. "I'd rather you stay with me, to stand watch in case he comes back."

Bijou and I entered the small cabin, and she immediately began her sniffing patrol. The only furnishings in the place were a wooden rocking chair, covered in cobwebs, and a table with two chairs beneath a window at the back. All four pieces of furniture, along with the floor, were blanketed in a thick layer of dust.

"This place looks like it was abandoned years ago," I said out loud to myself.

Percival wafted into the room and settled himself on the fireplace hearth. He took out his pipe and brought the bowl to a crimson glow with the snap of his fingers.

"I thought you were standing guard for me," I said, a little annoyed at his lackadaisical manner.

"I will sense his presence if he nears. Don't worry, my dear. I am on alert."

The familiar, spicy fragrance of his tobacco filled the air and gave me a measure of comfort. Trusting in his extrasensory abilities, the tension in my shoulders eased.

"This cabin was probably built by one of the early miners," he added.

Through the grimy window, the afternoon sun illuminated several dark bottles, all of them the same shape, sitting on the table. As I drew nearer, I noticed these bottles were free from the dust that coated everything else. Several dark, wet stains had left marks on the dusty surface of the table.

"Look at these," I said, lifting one of the bottles. I shook it back and forth. It felt like it was partially filled with some kind of liquid. I uncorked the bottle and took a sniff. A faint, sharp smell escaped, but I couldn't pinpoint exactly what it was. I placed the bottle back down.

"What is that on your face?" Percival rose from the hearth and came so close I felt as if I'd been plunged into cold water. "There is something under your nose."

I touched the space between my lip and nose with my finger, then pulled it away to see a green smear on my fingertip. I drew in a sharp breath.

"What in the world . . . " I breathed out, and then it struck me. Scheel's Green dye. Arsenic. Quickly, I pulled a handkerchief out of my pocket and wiped off the offending liquid. Thankfully, I had only come into contact with a small amount.

"This is the poison that was used to kill Gloria," I said.

"Of course," Percival agreed, his luminescent eyes wide with wonder. "You've found it, my dear!"

"This is the evidence we've been looking for," I said, and then a cold realization hit me. In the script I discovered in Gloria's caravan, it was clear that Hans Lechim had poisoned Emily Boulant by tampering with her face powder. "And now I understand why my mother is ill."

"You do? How?" he asked.

"The peacock fan my mother has constantly in her possession, and the fine Kashmir dressing gown with the peacock design she wears every evening. It has this same green hue. My mother's fan went missing the other day, but then was returned to her—by Mr. Langston. She also said she wasn't able to find her dressing gown in her wardrobe, but the next day, it reappeared. And her condition has suddenly gotten worse. What if he was regularly using the dye on both items?"

Percival tamped out the ash from his pipe. "So, you're

saying that he regularly took the items from her possession, soaked them in the dye, and then returned them?"

"It's possible, isn't it?" I asked.

"I suppose so," he said, placing his pipe back in the breast pocket of his smoking jacket. "How very diabolical."

"Yes, it is," I agreed, re-corking the bottle. "Percival, we have to get back to town. And fast."

Chapter Twenty-Nine

Back at the hotel, Bijou and I hurried through the lobby together.

"Mr. Pettyjohn," I called out. He was sorting the guests' mail into the cubbies behind the reception desk. "Could you please ask Clarence to fetch Dr. Tate and have him come to my mother's room immediately?"

His spectacles had slid down his nose, and he blinked at me over the top of them.

"Quickly, Mr. Pettyjohn!"

"Yes, madam." He rang the bell on the desk and I quickly climbed the stairs.

Bijou, mistaking our rush for a game, sprinted ahead of me. Once we reached the third-floor landing, I hurried to my mother's door and burst into the parlor. Kitty, who was engrossed in the newspaper, looked up in astonishment.

"Arabella? What's the matter?"

"Come help me," I said. I didn't want to take the time to explain at the moment. I entered the bedroom to find my mother dozing. Her face was an ashen shade of white and her breathing, shallow.

"Mother. Mother, wake up!" I set the bottle on the nightstand and then pulled the covers off of her. She was wrapped tightly in the dressing gown, and she held the fan with clenched fingers. I took it from her and threw it across the room.

"Arabella, what are you doing?" Kitty asked with alarm.

"Help me get her out of this dressing gown," I said, untying it.

She looked at me as if I'd fallen from the moon. "But, why?"

"I'll explain in a minute. Please help me."

My mother's eyes flitted open and shut. "Arabella?" she muttered groggily.

"Hello, Mother." I tugged at the sleeves. "We need to get you out of this dressing gown. Do you think you can sit up?"

Her eyes glazed over with confusion. I gave Kitty a quick glance, and she sprang into action, helping my mother to raise herself up. We managed to remove her dressing gown, straighten her nightgown, and gently lay her back down. She appeared lethargic and weak, attempting to speak, but only mumbled.

"Arabella?" Cordelia had stepped into the room. "Is there a problem? What's going on? I was just coming back to check on Mrs. Janes."

"Yes, there is a problem," I said. "I think my mother—"

"Mrs. Pryce?" A male voice echoed from behind us. I turned to see Dr. Tate standing in the doorway.

"Doctor. Thank you for coming so quickly."

"I was just leaving the General when Clarence found me. Is everything all right?" He immediately went to my mother, who now seemed completely spent by the ordeal of undressing her. He took hold of her wrist and pulling his pocket watch out of his waistcoat, took a reading of her pulse.

I shook my head. "I don't think so, doctor."

He released her wrist and put his watch back into its place. "I would agree. Her pulse is weaker than before."

"I think I know why," I said. I showed him the bottle. "I found this, and several others like it, in a shack in the woods." I then explained my theory of how the poison had been administered.

"Oh, how awful," Cordelia exclaimed. "It's like the script's story about Emily Boulant's death."

"Right," I said.

Dr. Tate reached for my mother's hand again and examined her fingernails. "Interesting," he mused. "Do you see these white lines?"

I looked closer. On each nail, a white line ran parallel to the cuticle and the top of the nail, just below the center. "Yes. What of it?"

"They are called Mees lines, or leukonychia striata. They indicate some kind of internal ailment, such as kidney failure or heart problems—which are not consistent with her symptoms." He paused and then raised his gaze to meet mine. "Or they could suggest arsenic poisoning."

"Well, I never!" Kitty exclaimed.

The doctor gently pried open one of mother's eyelids. "Ah. I hadn't noticed this before," he said. "The whites of her eyes have taken on a slightly greenish hue, another indicator of poisoning by Scheel's Green dye. The recent change in the color of her eyes indicates that she's been exposed to the metal for quite some time. It's been a slow process."

The doctor rubbed his chin thoughtfully. "I'll need to examine the bottle's contents, and the garment and the fan, to be certain."

"Yes," I agreed, looking over at my mother. "Is there anything you can do to help her, now that we may have found what's making her sick?"

"Give her plenty of fluids," he instructed. "It will help to flush out any toxins. If the tests come back positive for arsenic contamination, then you will have to dispose of anything green in her possession—just to be safe."

Kitty let out a low whistle. "If someone was using the dye on her clothing, they would have to get it away from her. That would require some stealth."

"Yes," the doctor confirmed. "Given that the troupe travels together, everyone is in close proximity to each other's caravans and belongings. It would be relatively easy to sneak into her caravan, remove items one by one, and then replace them."

"But since they are in such proximity, I would think it would be more difficult. They are always together," Cordelia said.

Suddenly, I had a sinking feeling in my stomach. "Unless it was someone who lived in the caravan with her," I said.

"You mean Miss Dubois?" Cordelia said.

"Yes," I replied, feeling uneasy. The thought of Celine being involved was disturbing; she had always been so kind-hearted, and such actions would be completely out of char-acter for her. However, considering the immense pressure she had been under recently, I wondered if perhaps she had acted out to secure her freedom.

"She'd said she'd been feeling hemmed in and

oppressed by Victor Langston and my mother. She'd also felt stifled by Edmund Farley."

"You think she shot Edmund Farley?" she asked. "But the sheriff said the body had been dragged into the warehouse. She's no bigger than a mite. She wouldn't have the strength."

"That's true," I acknowledged. "The person who tried to run me down in the street, whom I followed into the woods, was not petite and clearly had the build of a man."

"Maybe she was an accomplice to the murders?" Cordelia said.

The same dreadful idea struck me. Could she have enticed Edmund Farley to his death with the promise of a romantic encounter? Did she position him within the killer's reach? And afterwards, did she assist him in hauling the body back to the warehouse?

"But had she done so of her own volition, or was she somehow forced under some kind of duress?" I said. Then I told them about the medal I'd found in a drawer in Victor Langston's desk. "It seems I need to speak with Celine again," I said. "But first, I need to tell the sheriff about what I found in the woods."

"How did you find the green dye?" Cordelia asked. "What prompted you to go into the woods?" Cordelia asked.

Reluctantly, I explained what had happened.

"Someone in a carriage tried to run you down!" Cordelia exclaimed, alarmed, as we hurried down the street. We were moving so swiftly that Bijou struggled to keep up.

"Yes," I said, absently reaching across my body to touch my injured shoulder.

"And you followed him into the woods?" She said incredulously.

"I needed to see who it was," I explained. "Unfortunately, his face was concealed."

"Arabella, that was extremely dangerous. You could have been killed. I can't believe you went out into the woods alone."

"Percival was with me."

She reached out and pulled me to a stop. "Percival? What if you had gotten into a physical confrontation? He's no help in a situation like that! Arabella, that was reckless. What were you thinking?"

I faced her head on. "I wasn't thinking, Cordelia. I was taking action. My dear, sometimes we need to take action to get to the truth—and I found something vital to the murder cases. Well, at least to Gloria's murder, and the reason my mother is so ill. I think it was a risk worth taking."

She sighed and let go of my arm. "Perhaps. But, really, you must be more careful."

The ache in my injured shoulder echoed her sentiment.

When we neared the sheriff's office, I spotted Clayton standing on the front porch. He was leaning against the column flanking the front steps, taking in the happenings on the street. From his expression, I could see he was deep in thought.

Bijou wriggled free from Cordelia's grasp on the leash and darted over to him, then began bouncing up and down on her hind legs, eagerly dancing for some attention.

Like most people, he could not resist her charm and bent down to ruffle her little head.

"Hello, girl," he said, his pensive expression vanishing.

He then straightened and tipped his hat to us. "Arabella, Miss Danson."

"Clayton, I need to tell you about something I found. I believe I know why my mother is so ill, and I think it has bearing on Gloria's murder and possibly Mr. Farley's as well."

"Let's hear it," he said, crossing his arms over his broad chest.

"I believe I've found the substance that was used to poison Gloria. The doctor is testing it right now."

"The green dye?" he asked.

"Yes. I also believe it was repeatedly used to dye some of my mother's clothing—and her fan. As we know, constant exposure to even small levels of arsenic over time can cause illness, and even death. The doctor is doing some tests on the items to find out for sure."

A wave of skepticism washed over his face. "And how did you find this dye?"

Knowing he would react even stronger than Cordelia had at my answer, I pulled my upper lip between my teeth, pondering how to phrase my response to minimize the perceived danger—and the fact that I had been alone. I certainly couldn't let on that Percival had been there with me.

I must have hesitated too long because Cordelia blurted out, "Someone tried to run her over in a coach, and she followed them into the woods."

His eyes darkened with concern. "What!? My god, Arabella. Are you all right? When did this happen?"

"Shortly after that young boy came to retrieve you—"

"Dammit!" he said. "I never should have left you alone."

I raised a placating hand. "I'm fine—Mr. Emerson pushed me out of the way."

Then that sea swept blue gaze of his darkened even more, like thunderclouds over the ocean. "And then you followed this person who tried to kill you? Alone?"

I gulped at the fierce expression on his face.

"Miss Danson," he said, still keeping those steely eyes fixed on me. "Would you give us a moment?"

A tense silence filled the air. I knew her loyalty to me would override any request anyone made of me, so I looked over at her and nodded. "It's okay, Cordelia."

"Very well," she finally said. "I'll take Bijou for a walk."

The sheriff motioned for me to go into his office. Once we were behind the closed door, he stepped closer to me until I had no choice but to look up into his angry face.

"Before you say anything," I said, "I realize that what I did was probably not such a good idea, and I shouldn't have gone alone, but—"

"It was extremely foolish, Arabella. You need to use caution. We've talked about this—time and time again. If you are going to be this imprudent—"

I flinched at his tone, which sounded like that of a scolding father. "I'm a grown woman, Clayton. I make my own decisions—foolish or not. And I think I've made that clear, 'time and time again.' I also think I've clarified that I am determined to get to the truth, and have been successful in several instances." The intensity of his gaze made me want to wilt, but I refused to look away.

"You have put your life in danger in several instances, too," he said. "And if something happens to you, it's on my head! You don't understand the position you are putting me in, Arabella."

I blinked at him, confused and a little annoyed at his

statement. Hands on hips, I straightened my spine. "Oh. I didn't realize this was about you. I'm trying to be helpful. Didn't we agree we would work on this together?"

Finally, he looked away, shaking his head. "I shouldn't have left you alone."

I knew he felt responsible for my actions, and that wasn't entirely fair. I relaxed my stance and hesitated a moment before saying softly, "I had to find out who it was. You must admit, you would have done the same thing."

He turned to face me again, his eyes flashing. "Yes, I would have. But it's my job to take those risks! Not yours. It was irresponsible."

I shook my head, baffled by his mixed signals. Was he feeling guilty? Concerned for me? Angry? Or perhaps it was a combination of all three.

"Well—you weren't there. And it seems you don't want my help after all." I turned and headed for the door and suddenly he reached out and took hold of my elbow. He pulled me in close and wrapped his arms around me. I looked up into those searching blue eyes and suddenly felt like I couldn't breathe. My heartbeat echoed in my ears, drowning out everything except his captivating eyes. And then his lips were on mine.

The door to the office opened, and we quickly broke apart to find Deputy Fleming gaping at us, a look of utter confusion on his face.

"Oh—uh—I-I'm sorry, I didn't realize—" he stammered.

My heart still in my throat, I absently smoothed my hair, the sudden awkwardness of the situation making me want to flee.

The sheriff, equally surprised, cleared his throat. "What have you got, Deputy?" he asked.

"I—I just ran into Doc Tate," he stammered, his dark eyes darting back and forth between us, clearly still baffled by what he'd witnessed. "He said to tell you he's confirmed the items he took from Mrs. Janes had large traces of the same green dye that poisoned Miss Standish."

"I knew it!" I said.

Clayton looked at me with skepticism.

"That's what I was trying to tell you!" I exclaimed.

Setting his hands on his hips, Deputy Fleming scoffed. "So, that's what you were doing just now?"

Oh dear, but this was uncomfortable.

Ignoring the heat in my face, I resumed my explanation. "When I followed that man who tried to run me down—"

The deputy stepped forward, his face now stricken with worry. "Run you down? When did this happen?"

Clayton shot him a glance. "I'll explain later."

"Anyway," I continued. "I followed him and he went to—"

"You followed him?" The deputy asked, as equally incredulously as Cordelia and the sheriff. "You were alone?"

"Yes—but—"

"My god, are you all right?" He reached out and took my hand in his. I glanced at Clayton, who rolled his eyes.

"Yes. Yes, I'm fine." I said patiently, pulling it gently away. I was touched by the young man's concern, but it was making the strange situation between the sheriff and me a bit more problematic. I found myself caught up in feelings I wasn't prepared to deal with at the moment, so I pushed them aside and pressed on.

"The man didn't see me following him. He went deep into the woods until he came to an old shack. He went inside for a few minutes and then came out, putting something in his coat pocket. After he left, I went in and found the supply of dye. There were three or four bottles of it. I brought one back to show to you and Dr. Tate."

The two men stood silently, finally taking in what I had to say.

Clayton spoke first. "We have to find out who this man is. You are obviously a threat to him, which means you are in even more danger than we first suspected. And, if he has any idea that you were following him—"

Before the sheriff could finish his terrifying thought, I interjected. "I'm almost certain it's Victor Langston."

I intentionally left out my earlier suspicion that Celine was his accomplice. I wanted to give her the benefit of the doubt, and to find out for myself first.

"What makes you think Victor Langston is the killer?" the deputy asked.

"It's the script I found in Gloria's caravan. The main character, Hans Lechim—whom I believe is Michael Nash, Victor's uncle, kills Emily Boulant—or Lily Beaumont, a woman who stood in his way, by lacing her face powder with some kind of poison, probably arsenic. I believe Mr. Langston is reenacting history."

"But why would he want to kill your mother?" Clayton asked.

"Because he holds her responsible for the death of Kathy Macarther."

"You mean the young actress from Brooks's story?"

"Yes. When I was eighteen, I had the opportunity to work under an extremely influential director for a coveted role. The role was promised to Kathy Macarther, but she fell ill. According to the letters I found in Langston's desk—"

"Wait." Clayton held up his hand. "You found letters? Why didn't you say so?"

I shrugged, shaking my head. "I had every intention to, but when the deputy and I returned from the caravans with news of the medal, you were waiting at the hotel to tell me my mother had taken a turn for the worst. I suppose I forgot to mention it. Besides, I didn't know if they had any true bearing on the murders. Now, I think they do."

He let out a sigh of frustration. "Go on," he said.

"The letters were from Kathy Macarther. She and Victor were sweethearts."

"So, because you got the role, Langston thinks—" Clayton started.

"I think he believed the rumors circulating at the time that my mother poisoned Kathy Macarther. He's slowly been enacting his revenge."

He rubbed the stubble on his chin. "And using her influence and money along the way," he added.

"Right!" I raised my hands in agreement. "And he either knew about the script that would expose his uncle for the murder of Lily Beaumont, or Miss Standish was using the information to blackmail him, which is why he killed her. He also lied about his ability with firearms—why do that unless he killed Edmund Farley? I'm telling you, Victor Langston is our man!"

Chapter Thirty

Clayton and Deputy Fleming stood silently, each one of them considering my theory of Victor Langston's guilt in the murder of Gloria Standish.

"You make an excellent case, Arabella," Deputy Fleming finally said. Surprised he'd addressed me in the familiar, both Clayton and I regarded him with raised brows.

He cleared his throat. "I mean, Mrs. Pryce."

"He's right," Clayton said, breaking the tension. "But we need to hear from Doc before we make any arrest. We need to be certain that the substance in the bottle you found is indeed arsenic dye. Let's go next door and see what he's got."

We located the doctor in a small room at the back of his infirmary, which he referred to as his chemical laboratory. He sat at a table cluttered with various-sized bottles, several mortars and pestles, and a large metal scale. Shelves filled with even more bottles stretched up to the ceiling behind him.

"Doc," the sheriff greeted him. "Do you have a result for us?"

He lowered his chin to look at us from above his round spectacles. "The contents of the bottle are indeed Scheel's Green dye—or a close copy, as the stuff isn't sold much anymore. In my estimation, someone used cobalt and zinc oxide to produce the green effect, and then added arsenic powder to the mix."

"So that was used on my mother's fan and the dressing gown?" I asked for clarification.

He nodded. "Yes. I've found arsenic in both items."

I turned to the sheriff. "When I went to visit my mother the other day, Victor Langston had just come from her room. She said he'd brought her fan with him—she thought she'd misplaced it. She also mentioned misplacing the dressing gown at an earlier time."

"So that was making Mrs. Janes sick?" Clayton asked.

The doctor nodded. "Partially—it was severely worsening her tuberculosis. Without a doubt, it would have led to her premature death."

"All right, then," Clayton said. "We've got enough to arrest him for the death of Gloria Standish, and the attempt on Mrs. Janes's life."

"I imagine he was the one sending the threats," I added.

"What about the murder of Farley?" the deputy asked.

Clayton pressed his lip together and scratched his head. "It would be helpful if we could find the rifle and his connection to it."

"But we've established motive," I said. "His professional, and perhaps personal, preoccupation with Miss Dubois—Maggie said she witnessed him accost her, begging her to 'come back to him.' And my mother says Mr. Langston is quite possessive of Celine, and was jealous of her relationship with Mr. Farley."

"We've discovered the means as well—his obvious skill with firearms," Deputy Fleming added.

"And we know he had opportunity, given his proximity to all the troupe members. He had plenty of chances to kill Mr. Farley." I finished.

Clayton gave a nod of his head. "It's enough to proceed. Let's go get him, Deputy Fleming. You check the hotel, and I'll head out to the new theater and the caravans."

"Yes, sir." The deputy tipped his hat to the sheriff in agreement and then turned to me with a brilliant smile. "Excellent detective work, Mrs. Pryce. You really are a marvel."

The sheriff cleared his throat. "At your leisure, deputy," he said with a hint of sarcasm.

"Yes, sir," he said, and with another smile in my direction, he left the doctor's office. Clayton and I followed him out.

"Well, it appears you have succeeded once more, Arabella." Clayton said as he pulled his hat down lower onto his forehead. His jaw was tight, and he avoided my gaze.

"Does that bother you?" I asked with some curiosity.

He gave me a sideways glance. "It bothers me you put yourself at risk."

I recalled his recent, but brief, kiss, which made his feelings for me quite clear. Yet, it seemed he had retreated from those feelings, just as I had. Jarred by the memory, I found I couldn't speak at the moment. We silently watched the deputy walk toward the hotel.

"You ought to temper your impatience with him, Clayton," I said finally, avoiding the subject.

"Oh, yeah?" he said. "Why is that?"

I shrugged. "You must admit, it's been good for you to have the extra help."

He shook his head. "The kid's too green. I need someone with more experience."

"Seems to me it's a great opportunity for you to mentor him. I've done that myself in my profession. It will pay off, I assure you."

He sighed. "Maybe. Well, I'd best get out to the theater."

"Yes," I said. "Good luck."

Without another word, he stepped off the porch and made his way toward the hitching rail in front of his office, where Queenie dozed in the sun.

I should have been more satisfied with the fact that I'd once again solved a murder—two, in fact—and I had hopefully prevented the premature demise of my mother. This should have given me a great deal of relief, but the whole thing left me feeling hollow. The possibility that Celine had helped facilitate the poisoning of my mother still hung in the air. Had Victor perhaps coerced her?

I knew Clayton would be furious with me for withholding my suspicions from him, but I wasn't absolutely certain, and I didn't want to cast any guilt upon Celine if she was innocent. I felt a tug of protectiveness over the girl —as we had shared the full force of my mother's domineering ways.

Looking up at me, Bijou let out a little whine.

"I know, girl," I said to her. "I have an odd feeling we're not completely done with this case."

A dense coolness at my feet roused me from sleep. I opened my eyes to discover the room cloaked in darkness, yet suffused with a chilling, icy light. As my eyes adjusted, I saw Percival and Lily Beaumont seated at the foot of my bed. Bijou also woke up and barked.

"Shh, girl, you'll wake Cordelia," I said. She settled in next to me and emitted a low growl at our guests.

I reached for my watch necklace lying on the bedside table and squinted to see the time. From what I could make out, it was four o'clock a.m.

"It's rather early, Percival," was all I could say—my tongue still thick with sleep.

"Miss Beaumont came to me and it seemed rather urgent," he said.

I glanced over at her. Her posture erect, she sat tall and proud, the wisps of her flyaway hair gently moving in an undetectable breeze.

"What is it?" I asked.

She pointed to my nightstand, and I realized she was pointing to the diary. I had left it there some days ago.

"The diary? What about it?"

She, as usual, didn't answer, but continued to point at the thing.

"She obviously wants you to read it," Percival said, as if I was daft.

"But, I have read it," I said. My gaze slid over to her. Her face remained placid, stoic.

"All right," I sighed as I sat up in bed. I opened the nightstand drawer and rummaged for the matches. Once I found them, I struck one and lit the oil lamp that was on the nightstand.

"What does she want me to read?" I asked, of no one in particular.

"I'd say start from the beginning," Percival said.

I shot him a sardonic glance, then opened the book. The initial entries described her journey to England for a new role at the Theatre Royal on Drury Lane in London, where she first encountered my mother. I skimmed through several entries, finding nothing noteworthy until I stumbled upon a mention of an R.T.V. According to the entry, Miss Beaumont considered this man eager and hard-working, yet lacking in talent.

Subsequent entries discussed Michael Nash and Lily's tumultuous relationship with him, and his unrequited feelings for Adrian North. As I had observed before, the dates then leaped forward to 1863, when I appeared in her journal. She wrote about accusations against M.J.; my mother, for making K.M.; Kathy Macarther, ill to secure the coveted role of Viola for A.; me. An R.T. was mentioned, along with V.L., whom I suspected was Victor Langston. By this time, Mr. R.T. had abandoned acting and attended one of Miss Beaumont's performances, appearing to be a very wealthy man. Could this have been Roger Thompson? Was he also R.T.V?

"I've read all of this before," I said to her.

Her eyes flared, and she stabbed her icy finger at the diary. Lowering my eyes to the page, I read more carefully and noticed a description I hadn't noticed before, or that I had skimmed over. She had detailed R.T.'s appearance.

Although his complexion was quite paler than I recalled, and always fleshy around the middle, he had slimmed down an alarming degree. Despite his altered appearance, his eyes gleamed with the satisfaction of success, as did his ensemble. He wore a finely tailored dark suit with a crisp white shirt and a silk ascot tie. The most eye-catching feature of his attire was a richly embroidered waistcoat with shades of green, signifying a new sense of style. He carried a silver pocket watch, which he continually pulled from his waistcoat, as if to draw one's attention to it. The chain was thick and prominently displayed across his waist-coat, showing his new financial status.

I am afraid, however, that this peacock's display of wealth and success was lost upon M.J., as she had eyes only for Mr. D.

The description matched Roger Thompson precisely.

Clearly, this was the point where M.J., my mother, was involved with her wealthy lover, Mr. Dunham, who possessed not only money but also influence over the director who ultimately awarded me the part. I read on until the diary ended, but found nothing remarkable. I looked up at the two ghostly figures at the end of the bed.

"I don't understand," I said, and then Miss Beaumont vanished.

I pushed out a breath. "Why did she leave?"

Percival shrugged a shoulder. "She's an enigma, that one."

"Have you gotten anything out of her?" I asked him.

"Not a word."

"She wants me to know something, but what? And why?"

Percival tapped his finger against his chin. "When did the troupe, as we know it, come together?"

My mother said they've been together for several years. Mr. Langston and Mr. Thompson were old friends, and we know they both knew my mother. She said they started the troupe in London and then brought it to New York. They became reacquainted with my mother, and the rest is history. Why?"

"I'm trying to determine what Miss Beaumont is attempting to tell us, just like you."

"Well, if you find out, please find me as soon as possible," I said with a yawn.

After dressing and enjoying some tea and scones with Cordelia, I paid my mother a visit. She was sitting up in bed, which was an improvement, yet her skin remained pallid, and her eyes reflected the lingering weakness in her body.

"Good morning, darling," she said, her eyes misting over. Her expression carried an unusual softness, and there was an ethereal quality to her demeanor that I found disconcerting.

"What is it, mother? Are you all right? Do you need the doctor?"

She shook her head and held her hands out to me. "Come sit," she said.

I obeyed and perched on the side of the bed next to her.

"You saved my life," she whispered.

I chuckled softly. "Oh, well, yes, I suppose I did."

She reached up to caress my cheek—something I don't recall her doing since I was a small child—when I had fallen and scraped my knee. It sent a shiver down my back.

"You still love me," she said.

My breath hitched in my throat, rendering me speechless. All I had wanted was to do the right thing, to solve the problem and ensure justice was served. Or so I believed. But at that moment, I realized that, yes, I truly did still love my mother—even after everything she had done to make me feel exploited, insignificant, and valued only for what I could achieve on stage and in life.

Choked up, I still couldn't respond.

"You're a good girl, Arabella. You always have been—deep down. I'm glad you've found yourself again."

I blinked at her, further stunned. *Found myself again.* Was this what William had been hoping for when he'd sent me out here to the mountains of Colorado? To find myself again?

She closed her eyes for a few seconds. I could see she was still tired and weak from the poison that had been coursing through her body for weeks, maybe months.

After she opened them again, she said, "I know I've always been rather tough on you, dear. And I fear it was because I could never be what you became—I simply didn't have that innate talent. Yes, I was a competent actress—but not like you. I could never touch people's hearts and make them feel the way you do. And then, when your father left, somehow I blamed you."

I flinched. "So, you think it was my fault father left?" Angry at her insinuation, I had finally found my words.

She squeezed my hand. "At one time, yes, but it was a very short time. You reminded me of all the things he had wanted me to be—but I just wasn't that person. When he left, my heart shattered. I was overwhelmed with sorrow, despair—and fury."

It was the fury I remembered. But I suppose I never considered it came from a place of pain and sorrow. I didn't respond, but let her continue.

"It hurts to realize that I turned away from true happiness with someone who accepted me unconditionally, loving me for who I was, flaws and all."

"Do you mean—?"

She let out a small chuckle. "Roger, of course. Through my illness, and now in my recovery, I've thought about him often. Yes, I've worked side by side with him for several years, but now . . . Now I see that I've been a fool. A stupid fool!"

Shocked and surprised at this declaration, I swallowed

hard. From what I had observed, she seldom gave him much attention, interacting with him only for the troupe's benefit. Her focus had always seemed squarely on Celine and her future.

"I didn't realize that you still cared for him . . . In that way."

She smiled and lay her head back on the pillow. "I think I kept it deep inside. I couldn't afford to get involved, well, seriously involved with anyone. When you were younger, it was all about survival, and ensuring that you had an amazing future. I suppose I forgot about that part of myself. The part that needed to love and be loved—truly loved—by a man. And then Celine came along, and well . . . " She closed her eyes again.

Couldn't afford to get involved with anyone. Her words rang in my head. How many times had I said that to myself since I'd arrived in La Plata Springs? Only every time Clayton Marshall looked at me with those fathomless sea-blue eyes or flashed that knee-melting smile that caressed his strong jawline.

Never in a thousand years would I have admitted I was anything like my mother, but hearing this . . .

"It's not too late," I said.

She opened her eyes. "What?"

"It's not too late. You're here, Roger is here. You work together. Tell him how you feel. Tell him you were wrong to have turned him away."

"Oh, well—" she weakly batted my suggestion away with a wave of her hand.

"I'm in earnest, mother. It's not too late."

Her piercing gray eyes studied me thoughtfully for a moment. She let go of my hand and laced her fingers together at her waist.

"Perhaps you're right," she said as a slow smile spread across her face. "Maybe I should talk to him. I mean, really talk to him—not about business, not about the future of the troupe. But talk to him about us."

"I don't know what you are waiting for," I said. "Would you like me to tell him to come visit you?"

She pressed her fist to her mouth with apprehension, but then she nodded.

"Yes. Yes, please go get Roger and bring him to me."

Chapter Thirty-One

Despite the nagging suspicion that Celine had assisted Mr. Langston in poisoning my mother, a renewed sense of optimism washed over me as I exited my mother's suite. I felt hopeful that my fraught relationship with her was gradually becoming more tolerable. If I could aid in healing her heart, perhaps she would no longer feel compelled to exert such stringent control over everything and everyone around her.

I only wished I could be more optimistic about other matters in my life, like the lien on the hotel. The uncertainty of how I would come up with the funds to pay it off was overwhelming, and I found myself teetering on the verge of hysteria whenever I thought about it. Unfortunately, I would have to most likely send a wire to Mr. Tisdale explaining the urgency of the situation, and given the stipulation in the will and the fact that I had not served my full year yet, I feared for my future—and that of the Arabella's. I vowed to do so as soon as I finished my errand.

Eager to retrieve Mr. Thompson for my mother, I knocked on his suite door, but there was no answer. I went downstairs to continue my search. After inquiring with Mr. Pettyjohn regarding his whereabouts, he informed me he was nowhere in the hotel. Naturally, I assumed he was probably at the new theater. I hoped Celine would be there as well, as I wanted a quiet word with her.

After arranging for Mr. Ellis and the hotel's coach, Bijou and I set off for the new theater. Upon arrival, I instructed Mr. Ellis to wait as I searched for Mr. Thompson. He assisted me in alighting from the coach, then contentedly settled inside for a brief nap. Meanwhile, Bijou darted ahead, eagerly sniffing the ground, savoring the intriguing scents nature offered.

Several men were hanging a sign over the entrance of the theater. It read "Aurora Mystique." I marveled at the irony of the name. The word 'aurora' denoted a new beginning. Unfortunately, the beginnings of this theater had been more akin to a finale, with two of the troupe's players dead, and one a murderer.

However, as much as it made me nervous, Mr. Archer's involvement promised to introduce something fresh to the troupe, and the town, perhaps signaling a new start, a rejuvenating beginning. I did my best to view it in a more positive light. If the hotel was taken from me and I had to sing for my supper once again, perhaps a job managing the theater might be beneficial. However, the idea of working under someone else's control again, namely Mr. Archer, or my mother, seemed daunting. The oppressive weight of overwhelm threatened my resolve, so I put the notion out of my mind for the time being.

Bijou and I entered the theater to find both Mr.

Thompson and Celine sitting at a small table, their heads bent in conversation. More of the townsfolk were busy putting the final touches on the stage, curtains, and lights. Two men were busy hammering together various stage props; tables, chairs, bookshelves and the like, making quite the din of noise. The raked floor had been completed, and the result was quite satisfactory.

The newly constructed stage was a sight to behold. A majestic proscenium arch crowned the performance area and commanded attention. Beneath it, the freshly re-floored oak platform served as a perfect setting for the dramas to unfold. Lush red velvet curtains framed the space, adding a touch of elegance and drama. Remarkably, this transformation had materialized in just three weeks—a testament to resilience despite the recent turmoil within the troupe. The theater had indeed surpassed all expectations, emerging as a beacon of artistic promise, and I wondered what it would be like to perform there.

Bijou ran up to Celine and rested her paws on the edge of her chair, warmly greeting her.

"Well, hello, you." Celine pulled Bijou up onto her lap. The little hound thanked her with several wet kisses on her chin.

"Mrs. Pryce, what brings you here?" Mr. Thompson asked.

"I was looking for you two."

"Ah," he said. "We were just discussing Victor's arrest. The sheriff and the deputy left here with him in handcuffs just moments ago."

"Yes," I said with some sympathy. This must have been a shock to them both. "I'm sorry you had to witness his arrest."

"We didn't," Celine said. "We were with Dale and Helene at their caravan, discussing the play. Andrew told us about it."

"Sad as it is, I must say, I'm not surprised to learn of his crimes," Mr. Thompson said with a doleful look on his face.

"Really? Why do you say that?" I asked, curious why he had said nothing to this effect before.

He glanced at Celine. "Farley's murder had to do with Celine, of course. Victor is completely infatuated with her. He couldn't stand the idea of Celine and Edmund getting back together."

I turned to her, surprised at this declaration. "So, you reconciled?"

"Not officially. Edmund asked me to marry him. I was considering it and told him I wanted some time to think. We agreed to keep it a secret, but Edmund said something to Victor and—"

"He obviously didn't take it well." Mr. Thompson finished for her. "I believe he was also terribly jealous of your mother's relationship with Celine. They argued about her constantly. He wanted to possess her completely, the dear girl." He reached over and patted Celine's hand. "But now, you won't have to worry about that anymore."

She offered him a grateful smile.

"And your mother will be safe, as well, thanks to you," he said with a satisfied smile.

"Yes," I agreed. I was eager to tell him about my mother's change of heart regarding her feelings for him, but there was still more I wanted to know about why he'd not been surprised about Vincent's guilt in the crimes.

"But, what about Gloria?" I asked.

Celine took the baton. "Well, initially, I brushed it off, but I overheard her telling him, 'I know what you've done.' I thought she was referring to the role Millicent and Vincent arranged for her at the Blaine Theater. They presented it as an opportunity for her to revive her career, but it was actually a ploy to oust her from the troupe. But now, I realize she must've been referring to Edmund's death. Someone was spotted leaving the theater that night, wasn't there? She must have known it was Victor."

"Agreed," Mr. Thompson said. "Because then, out of the blue, Victor and Millicent were in violent disagreement about letting her go. Victor said he'd changed his mind and wanted to keep her on."

"So, you think Gloria blackmailed Mr. Langston to keep her position in the troupe?"

"Yes," Mr. Thompson said. "I had agreed with Millicent and Victor that she needed to leave the company. Gloria created conflict and tension within the group."

"Mr. Thompson!" A worker shouted, standing beside the item he and two others had been diligently hammering away at. "Could we speak with you about something? We need you to come see this."

He gave me an apologetic smile. "Ah. Yes, if you will excuse me. I'll be right back."

He got up from the table, leaving Celine and I alone for a few minutes.

"So, you two are going to continue with the company?" I asked. "Even with Victor now gone?"

She nodded. "Yes, we are. And with Millicent, of course. I am so glad she is going to be all right. One of the workers overheard the list of charges against Victor; the murders of Edmund and Gloria, and the attempted murder of Millicent by poison. Just like Gloria. I can't believe it."

This was a perfect segue into questioning her about the fan and the dressing gown. "Well, it was a little different in that Gloria was given a large dose of poison all at once, and my mother was being poisoned more slowly—for weeks, even months. Her clothing was tampered with."

She shook her head. "It's just so awful."

"Yes," I agreed. "But I am trying to figure out how it could have happened. I mean, I suppose Victor could have gotten into the caravan the two of you share."

"Well, yes. Living as closely as we do—"

"Or perhaps he had help?" I ventured.

She blinked at me. "What do you mean?"

As the sheriff had mentioned before at another time, I wasn't all that good at subtlety, especially if I was after information—and I had to admit I was struggling to find some subtlety at the moment. So, I decided to just come out with it.

"Since you and my mother share the caravan—"

Her eyes grew wide and then filled with tears. "You mean, you think that I—"

"You admitted you were feeling hemmed in by her," I said.

"Well, yes! But that didn't mean I wanted her to die! And why would I help Victor? He caused most of my suffering, not Millicent. Yes, she can be domineering, but I owe that woman everything."

"Everything?"

"Yes. What she didn't tell you—what she said she would keep till the grave—was the real circumstances she found me in."

Confused, I opened my mouth to speak, but she continued.

"I was in a terrible way—a terrible way. She didn't find

me in the theater, she found me outside the theater—surviving on the streets, ensnared by opium's cruel grip. She recognized me from our childhood days, and out of kindness, she took me in and nursed me back to health. She stood by me as I fought to rid myself of the addiction." Her eyes burned with a fierce intensity. "So, as I've mentioned, my debt to her is profound. I would never dream of causing her harm."

Humbled by her words, I didn't know what to say.

"I'm sorry, Celine," I offered. "I had no idea. Of course you wouldn't hurt her—I shouldn't have assumed."

Tearing up again, she gave me a brief nod. "Excuse me," she said. Gently placing Bijou on the floor, she then got up and left the building. I felt awful for what had just transpired and was kicking myself for it when Mr. Thompson appeared at the table again.

"I apologize for leaving in the middle of our conversation," he said. "I think we've got the problem solved. Where did Celine go?" he asked.

The hammering suddenly intensified, and I pressed my finger to my ear. "I'm afraid I've upset her," I said, loudly over the noise.

"She's been rather emotional lately. Understandably so," he shouted back.

I nodded. "Could I speak with you about something?" I asked, eager to change the subject and to escape my feelings of remorse for having caused Celine's distress.

He cupped his ear with his hand. "Let's find a quieter place."

Glad to escape the din, I nodded and Bijou and I followed him outside.

"Ah, that's better," he said with a laugh. "I was just

about to fix myself some tea in my caravan. Would you like to join me?"

A cup of tea was just what I needed after my horrendous faux pas.

"That sounds marvelous," I said.

"Excellent. Do you like Earl Grey?" he asked.

I smiled. "Almost more than anything."

Chapter Thirty-Two

I stopped by the coach to tell Mr. Ellis I would be detained longer, but found him fast asleep on one of the coach seats.

"Well, I suppose there's no need to ask for your indulgence," I said to his sleeping form. He didn't stir, but emitted a loud snore.

I rejoined Mr. Thompson, and we walked to his caravan. The interior décor of it presented a stark contrast to that of Victor Langston's caravan. Whereas Mr. Langston's space overflowed with ornate decorations, Mr. Thompson's was more simplified, completely free of clutter, and meticulously tidy.

He retrieved a lantern-sized, single-burner cast-iron gas stove from the shelf that lined the wall. The stove, quaint and equipped with a handle for easy portability, was a charming artifact. Next, he took down a teakettle, and then gestured toward a striking blue and white ceramic water pitcher resting on the table. "Would you hand that to me, please?"

I obliged. Filled to the brim, its weight was considerable.

"I always keep some water on hand," he said with a chuckle. "I can't be without my tea."

"I know what you mean," I said. "Have you tried Mrs. Gilroy's Dandelion tea?"

He shook his head. "Only Earl Grey for me."

I smiled, pleased we had something in common in our love of good English tea. He took a tea tin down from the highest shelf and poured the ground leaves into a tea strainer and then set the tin back up on the shelf.

After completing his preparations, he placed the pitcher back on the table. Soon the water was rumbling in the kettle, and shortly thereafter, we each had a cup of the soothing brew in hand. He gestured for me to take a seat. Meanwhile, Bijou had positioned herself at the open door-way, resting her head on her paws, gazing out into the natural surroundings—likely in anticipation of spotting a squirrel.

"Now, what is it you wanted to talk with me about?" Giving me a wide grin, he held the teacup under his nose and then sipped gingerly, as the tea was piping hot.

I wasn't sure where to begin. "It's—well, it's about my mother and—"

"How is Millicent faring?" He asked flatly.

"Well, it was a close call, but thankfully I think we got the poisoned articles away from her in time. I hate to think of what would have happened had I not found the Scheel's Green dye."

"So, you're the one who discovered it?" he asked, showing a hint of interest. "You really are quite the detective, aren't you?"

I shrugged. "Someone was framing my mother for murder—and threatening her life at the same time. I had to do something."

I wanted to steer the conversation back to the topic of my mother and him, but struggled to find a smooth transition.

"I see," he said. "So you surmised Victor was guilty of all the crimes, just by finding the green dye?"

"Well, yes—and then there was the script as well."

"The script?"

"I came across a script in Gloria's caravan. It narrated a tale involving the actress Lily Beaumont, Victor's uncle, Michael Nash, and their intense rivalry that ended with her death. The story bore striking similarities to current events within your troupe. But it was the suggestion of how he killed Lily Beaumont that got me thinking. The story alludes to the possibility that Michael Nash tampered with something Miss Beaumont used every day—her stage powder. It inspired in me a chilling thought—that my mother might be suffering from poisoning through her clothing. It's quite a sinister notion. Anyway, what I wanted to talk to you about is—"

"So, the script was in Gloria's caravan, you say?" he asked. He then took another sip of his tea and then lowered the teacup, waiting for my answer.

"Yes—well, it was tucked away in a portfolio in her bookshelf. I stumbled across it quite accidentally. I think she was also using this script to blackmail Mr. Langston."

"Fascinating," he mused. "Who wrote the script? Anyone I might know?"

I shrugged. "It was written by someone named Grant Colston. But I think Miss Standish wrote it, using a pseudonym."

"I see. And how did she know that Michael Nash poisoned Lily Beaumont?"

"Well, that I don't know, exactly. But Gloria had worked

with both of them, as had you and my mother. Somehow, she must have either found out that it was true and used it in the story, or she just fictionalized it. Either way, it would be quite damaging to Michael Nash's reputation."

"And why was she blackmailing Victor?"

"Well, to keep her position in the troupe, I suspect. Or perhaps to secure a leading role. You mentioned Victor had a rather sudden change of heart about Gloria."

He leaned back in the chair. "Yes, I suppose so."

I wanted to get back to my reason for being here. "So, Mr. Thompson, the reason I've come is—"

"And, what about Edmund Farley?" He persisted. "What evidence convinced you it was Victor who shot him?"

Even though I had my own agenda, I supposed I should indulge him with my findings, since he was so interested.

"In his examination of Mr. Farley's body, Dr. Tate discerned he had been shot at long range with expert precision, likely with a rifle, as there was no gunpowder residue on Mr. Farley's clothing. The real tip-off was that I found a Civil War medal in Mr. Langston's possession—a medal for marksmanship. He had previously claimed to have nothing to do with guns. Unfortunately, we never found the rifle, but the evidence for Miss Standish's death was substantial enough for the sheriff to arrest and charge him with murder."

Mr. Thompson tapped his fingertips on the table, hanging onto my every word. "Yes, I suppose so," he said. "And tell me again about finding this dye?"

Suddenly, Bijou jumped to her feet and started barking.

"Bijou!" I said. "Hush, girl."

She stood completely still, staring at something in the distance.

"She's probably seen a rodent," I said to him. "Sorry for the interruption. You were saying?"

"How did you find the shack?" he asked.

"Well, I was in town, just leaving the sheriff's office, when a man driving a carriage nearly ran me over. Fortunately, I escaped with only a jolt to my already injured shoulder. But then, I trailed him to—"

I stopped, a sudden realization causing my breath to catch in my throat. How had he known about the shack? I hadn't mentioned where I discovered the dye. And he couldn't have heard it from the deputy or the sheriff; he and Celine weren't present when Mr. Langston was arrested, and surely the deputy would not have gone into the details. Tongue-tied with this new realization, I simply stared at him.

"You were saying?" he prompted.

"Yes," was all I could manage. He looked into my half-empty cup.

"Would you like more tea?"

"Um—" my mind was racing with the new realization that he might have been the man who'd run me down. I could have been completely wrong about Mr. Langston. I needed more information, to be sure.

"Yes, that would be nice, thank you."

He took my cup, got up from the table and went to the shelf, taking down the tea tin again. "Go on, dear. You were telling me about finding the shack."

I finished my story as he prepared more tea. He returned to the table, and as he passed me my teacup, I glimpsed something on his shirt sleeve that sent a shiver down my spine. There, against the crisp white fabric, was a smattering of tiny green stains.

Chapter Thirty-Three

"Your bravery is quite remarkable," Mr. Thompson remarked. "Venturing deep into the woods after that man, and with no form of protection."

My tongue was glued to the roof of my mouth and my heart beat such a staccato I thought I might faint. I couldn't tear my eyes away from the stains on his sleeve.

He must have seen my gaze because he abruptly tugged his coat sleeve down to cover the incriminating evidence. Our eyes met, and in that instant a silent acknowledgment passed between us—he knew I was aware of his secret.

"I'm not sure if it was brave, or foolish," I managed to say. Bijou's bark rang out again, this time with more urgency. Was she reacting to my fear, or had she sensed something else?

"Oh, goodness!" I looked at the small, jeweled watch pendant I wore on a chain around my neck. "I hadn't realized it was so late. I—I really should get back to the hotel."

His eyes still locked on mine, he said, "But you haven't

finished your tea. And you haven't told me what you wanted to speak with me about."

"Oh, you know, it's really not that important." I stood up, and he rose as well, his stature suddenly looming much larger than before. He moved away from the table, positioning himself between Bijou and me, effectively obstructing the doorway. I realized that if I panicked, all would be lost. If I could keep him talking, I might figure out a means of escape.

"I think it must have been important," he said, moving closer to me. "Or why would you have come all this way to see me?"

I swallowed down my fear and summoned the most stern expression I could muster. My gaze traveled down to the cuff of his sleeve again. There was currently no way out of this, so I decided my best option was to keep the conversation going. Hopefully, Mr. Ellis would soon wake and come looking for me.

"Why, Mr. Thompson?" I said through gritted teeth. "Why did you kill Gloria Standish? Why were you slowly killing my mother?"

"Kill your mother? I love your mother," he said, his voice low and menacing.

"I know," I said. "And she—" There was no point in telling him about my mother's feelings now. Once she learned he had tried to kill her, those feelings would quickly die. If I didn't die first.

"So, if you love her, then why try to kill her?"

His lips pressed together, forming a hard, thin line. He slowly raised his chin. "She would never be mine. She made that quite clear. I thought we had a chance before Farley. It was ridiculous! A woman her age with a rake like that."

"But their relationship didn't last," I reminded him. "He took up with Celine."

"He sullied that girl," he spat.

He obviously didn't know about Celine's sordid past, I thought.

"The girl has become like a daughter to me," he continued. "And Millicent continued to make a fool of herself, pining over that ratbag. I wanted to save her from herself."

"So, you admit it. You've been slowly killing my mother."

He let go a breath and inched closer. The walls of the caravan seemed to collapse in on me. I was trapped, like a helpless animal in a cage.

"It's what I said. I was saving her from herself," he said steadily.

"And it was you who were sending her the threatening notes, the poster, the photographs. Not Victor Langston. What did you hope to achieve?"

"She was afraid—it brought her closer to me. She never told me why she was afraid. But I knew she took comfort thinking I would protect her. She needed me—she just didn't want me. She wanted that . . . boy." His expression darkened.

"So, you shot Mr. Farley." I stated, refusing to be deterred by his intimidating bulk. I bit my lip to distract myself from my fear.

"He deserved it. I wanted him gone, but Langston and your mother were so enamored—and so were Helene and Dale, not to mention sweet Celine. It was like he cast a spell over everyone. He was draining money from the troupe with his philandering and gambling ways. He had to go."

"But Miss Standish didn't care for him. Just like you," I said.

He shook his head. "No, she didn't. Gloria was the only one, other than me, who could see right through him."

"But then why kill her?"

He gritted his teeth, as if the notion pained him. "She . . . knew things."

My eyes scanned the caravan for something I might use to either defend myself or to incapacitate him so I could escape. My gaze landed on a letter opener on the side table, next to an envelope with his name written across it. *Roger Thompson V.* Roger Thompson the fifth. *R.T.V.*

"What things?" I asked.

"Things from my past. And, more recently." To my utter surprise, his face crumpled with emotion and his eyes welled with tears. He had all but confessed to poisoning my mother and murdering Mr. Farley, the latter appearing to be his most recent offense. Miss Standish must have been aware of one or both incidents. But what exactly was this 'thing' from his past he mentioned?

"Miss Standish knew you killed Mr. Farley. Did she help you move the body?"

His expression shifted from anger to what seemed to be sorrow or perhaps distress. "She must have seen me dragging his body to the warehouse. She came to me, threatening to go to the sheriff with the information. She also mentioned something I'd done years ago. Something I thought no one knew about. It shocked me."

"Which was?"

A sob escaped him, and he pressed his thumb and forefinger to the bridge of his nose, closing his eyes tightly. "Something I deeply regretted," he said.

When he opened his eyes, his expression swiftly changed back to anger. His hand slammed down on the table, making me jump.

The muscles of his jaw twitched. "Something I did in vain!"

Frightened by his outburst, Bijou barked. I hushed her again, afraid he would turn on her.

"So, you killed Miss Standish because of something from the past that could have caused you trouble?" I asked, encouraging him to go on.

His posture suddenly wilting, he gazed at me with a look of helplessness in his eyes. "She said if I promised to fight to keep her on with the troupe, and secure the best roles for her, she'd keep my secrets. She knows I have some influence over Victor—the man can't hang onto a dime to save his life —he needed me to keep the troupe afloat, so I told her I would do it."

"But something changed your mind?"

"No. I couldn't live with that hanging over my head. I fully intended to kill her. I just needed some time." He shook his head. "That poor girl."

I blinked in confusion. Miss Standish was certainly no girl.

"Gloria?" I asked.

He sighed, the tears resurfacing. "No. Kathy Macarther. I only did it for you. Or rather, for Millicent. She wanted you to have that part so badly. And, it was a good thing you got it, don't you think? It launched your career. So, you see, my intentions were not all bad."

The blood drained from my head, and feeling woozy, I raised my elbow onto the table and rested my forehead between my thumb and fingers.

"You poisoned Kathy Macarther," I whispered, still not looking at him.

"Yes," he said, his voice shifting in tone once more, now edged with bitterness. "It gave you your start, and your mother a much needed income, but where did it leave me? Nowhere. I thought it would bring us closer, but—"

I snapped my head up. "My mother knew what you'd done?"

He shook his head, and anger flitted across his features once again. "No. I was going to tell her, but she wouldn't speak to me. She said we were through and she wanted nothing to do with me anymore."

"And later? Why didn't you tell her what you'd done for her later?" I asked, trying to keep him going until I could figure out a way to get past him to safety. Where was Mr. Ellis? I thought, impatiently.

He shrugged. "Suddenly it didn't matter. I was rich. You see, I came from a very wealthy family—but my father disowned me when I told him I wanted to be an actor. My mother, dear soul, always believed in me. Once my father died, she reinstated my inheritance. So you see, I finally had something to offer Millicent. I was still in England—as was everyone else who eventually made up the troupe. She must have heard about my reinstatement in my family and wrote to me. She said she knew about Victor's and my new venture, and that she had discovered Celine Dubois, and would I help her to launch the girl's career. So, I agreed. I notified Victor and Gloria and we sailed for New York. By that time, she had already hired Edmund, so there wasn't much I could do about that—at first."

"And how did Miss Standish know what you did to Kathy Macarther?"

"At that time, she was an errand girl for Lily Beaumont. I say, errand girl, but what I mean is spy."

I blinked in surprise at this revelation. She was never mentioned in the diary.

He went on. "Gloria claimed that Lily Beaumont

suspected I had killed young Kathy. She had no proof. Even so, it posed a threat. And after Gloria found out about Edmund . . . "

"You couldn't let her live to tell either tale."

He sighed. "I had no choice."

"So, you claim to have loved my mother, yet you let everyone think she had something to do with Kathy Macarther's death?" I shook my head in disgust.

He shrugged. "I'd done so much for her. And yet, she carried on with that plutocrat, Dunham."

Mr. D. The wealthy man who had financially backed the director.

"And, then, once you got to New York, you realized she was having an affair with Edmund Farley," I said.

His face pinched with anger. "Yes. I knew I had to do something."

"By using Scheel's Green dye on the fan and the dressing gown." I added through clenched teeth, unable to mask my repulsion.

"Bravo, my dear. You are correct," he gave me a satisfied nod, any hint of his previous remorsefulness gone. "I don't know why I'm telling you all this," he said with a laugh. "I suppose it's because it feels good to unburden myself. And I know it will go no further because you will never leave this caravan alive."

His words tore through me like a knife. I was trapped here, between him and the open doorway. My gaze fell to Bijou, who was silently staring up at us.

"But Mr. Ellis will come looking for me," I said, clinging to the desperate hope that he would awaken at any moment and would notice my absence. "You won't get away with this."

Mr. Thompson laughed and then turned to a tall

cabinet beside the door. He opened it and withdrew a rifle. "Not if he meets a bullet from this first."

He aimed it at me. "Now, sit down and drink your tea."

I slowly sat down again and watched while he pulled open a drawer and took from it a small bottle. He uncorked it with one hand and then poured the putrid green liquid into my teacup.

"Better drink it while it's hot," he said. "There's nothing worse than cold, Earl Grey."

Suddenly, Bijou started barking again and leapt from the caravan, chasing after something. Mr. Thompson reached over and pulled the door shut.

"I hope I won't have to force you to drink it," he said with a sinister smile. "I'd hate to ruin your dress."

I needed more time. I would have to distract him with my reason for coming to see him in the first place.

"I'll tell you why I really wanted to see you," I said, trying to keep my voice steady. "It's about my mother."

A flicker of interest sparked in his eyes. "Go on. But make it quick."

"I came to tell you that my mother wanted to speak with you. You see, this recent brush with death has made her realize she was wrong to have rejected you. She knows, now, that she could have found true happiness with you. She is filled with regret."

He snorted, leveling the rifle at me again. "You expect me to believe that?" His gaze travelled to my teacup. "Drink up."

Outside, Bijou continued barking. Whatever she'd been chasing must have gone into a hole, or climbed up a tree. I hoped the noise would wake Mr. Ellis.

"She said she'd been a fool," I added.

"Well, she's got that right, my dear. I would have done

anything for her. But it was too late. She needed to be saved."

"Yes, you've made that clear," I said. "You'd do anything for her. Even kill her."

His eyes flared with indignation. A sudden loud knocking on the door made us both flinch.

"Mr. Thompson!" It was Mr. Ellis. My heart leapt with joy. "You in there? I'm looking for Mrs. Pryce!"

"She's not here!" Mr. Thompson yelled back. "Said she wanted to walk back to town."

I pressed my lips together, overcome with relief at Mr. Thompson's mistake. Everyone knew Bijou would never leave me for any length of time. In fact, she'd probably led Mr. Ellis to the caravan.

The knocking grew more persistent. "Mr. Thompson!"

He rose swiftly and spun around, leveling his rifle at the door, poised to fire. In a desperate move, I grabbed the water pitcher and crashed it over his head. Porcelain shards and water scattered in all directions, soaking us both. He wheeled around to aim the gun at me once more, but suddenly, his eyes rolled back and he collapsed to the floor.

Chapter Thirty-Four

FIVE DAYS LATER

"Brava! Brava!" The audience roared.

Gazing out at the townspeople of La Plata Springs from the stage, I took Celine and Andrew by the hands and we bowed together. Soon after, Dale Shay and Helene Benavides stepped forward to join us, and together, we all clasped hands and bowed as one. Moments later, the three of them stepped back, leaving me alone on stage, and the crowd erupted in cheers once more.

Victor Langston emerged from the wings, bearing an enormous bouquet of roses. He joined me center stage, soaking in the applause. With a dramatic flourish, he bowed and then presented the bouquet to me.

"Thank you," I said when he rose.

"Oh, they aren't from me," he said with a smile, then gestured to the audience to encourage further applause. After a moment, he guided me and the others off the stage.

"Well, my dear, you've still got it," he remarked once we

were behind the curtain. My mother approached, her steps tentative with the aid of a cane the doctor had provided. Though still frail, her health was gradually improving, and for that, I was immensely thankful.

"You were marvelous, Arabella." She planted a kiss on my cheek. "Astounding, as always."

I laughed, the thrill of the performance still coursing through me. "It felt good to be on stage again. I've missed it so much." I turned to Mr. Langston and added, "Thank you for including me."

He nodded in response. "It just didn't feel right to go on with the play I had written for Edmund and Celine—with him, God rest his soul, now performing in the theater of the heavens. I wrote this play years ago, and you were the perfect fit for the lead role."

I blushed at the compliment, still surprised that he had offered me the role, especially after I had suspected him of being responsible for the deaths of Edmund and Gloria.

"It was such a thrill to work with you," Celine said, appearing behind me. She wrapped her arms around my waist and gave me a gentle squeeze. "I'm off to get changed now. Meet you at the Bella?" she asked.

"Yes, I'll head over as soon as I change too," I replied.

Glancing over at Andrew, I noticed he was reveling in the praise from several townsfolk who had ventured backstage to commend him. He had performed exceptionally well in his debut, and it was clear he had thoroughly caught the acting bug. This performance would surely not be his last.

He caught my eye, and I offered him a nod of approval. In response, his face lit up with a beaming smile.

Cordelia, with Bijou in her arms, squeezed her way through the crowd to get to us. "That was brilliant!" she said, her eyes wide with enthusiasm. "Everyone just loved it. You were all amazing up there."

Bijou barked in agreement.

Suddenly, my mother faltered, and I reached out to grab her by the elbow. "Mother, are you all right?"

She gave me a faint smile. "Yes. I suppose it's all the excitement."

I looked at Cordelia apologetically. "Would you mind taking her back to the hotel? She should rest."

"Of course," she said. She set Bijou down and took hold of my mother's other elbow.

"I'm fine!" my mother barked. "I don't need to rest."

"But you do, Mrs. Janes." Dr. Tate came around the corner.

My mother rolled her eyes. "All right. I'll go back to the hotel and rest for thirty minutes, but then I would like to attend the party at the Bella!"

I raised an eyebrow at the doctor, and he reached out to give me an assuring pat on the arm, letting me know he approved. He and Cordelia escorted her out.

Dale Shay and Helene Benavides also departed to change out of their costumes, and left for their caravan, leaving me and Victor alone.

"Well, my dear," he said, taking both of my hands in his. "Archibald tells me he's approached you about taking charge of this theater. I think you should consider it. He and your mother and I could sure use your talents, on stage and off. What do you think? You certainly shine in these environs."

Anxiety flared in my chest as I realized I might have no choice. I had sent a wire to Mr. Tisdale about the urgent lien situation with Billings Building and Company. He was attempting to secure a loan from a New York bank, but I hadn't heard back yet. If successful, I would be further detained in La Plata Springs, and I wasn't entirely sure how I felt about that. But, at least I wouldn't lose the hotel.

"I'm surprised by your eagerness to engage my services, Mr. Langston. I falsely accused you of two murders."

He shook his head. "You were only following your instincts—and some evidence. Having read the play you found in Gloria's caravan, I could see why you might think I was reenacting the past."

"I quickly realized that Emily Boulant and Hans Lechim were anagrams for Lily Beaumont and your uncle, Michael Nash, and now I realize that Dariann Roth was an anagram for Adrian North, his love, but I didn't connect that Grant Colston IV was an anagram for Victor Langston. The Roman numeral IV misled me, until I remembered the envelope on Mr. Thompson's desk addressed to Roger Thompson the fifth, using the Roman numeral V."

He stroked the stubble on his chin. "It was Roger's name—specifically that he was the fifth—that inspired the anagram for my name. I thought it was quite clever," he said, laughing.

"It was," I laughed with him, and then took on a more serious tone. "I have to ask you, Mr. Langston, did your uncle really poison Lily Beaumont?"

He shook his head. "No. My uncle was a gentle soul. May he rest in peace. He was quite tortured in his love for Adrian North, though, and might have done almost anything to have her, but never murder. I just thought having Hans Lechim put the arsenic in Emily Boulant's face powder would make for the perfect crime."

"So, do you know how Miss Beaumont actually died?" I asked.

He shook his head. "No one knows for sure. It was

rumored she suffered from asthma, but she was a very private woman and if she had the condition, she'd never admitted it. But, my uncle always thought that's what killed her—that she had an attack before a performance, but it was just speculation on his part. I suppose we will never know."

"I suppose not," I agreed. "But why did Gloria have your script?"

He sighed. "I asked her to look it over and give her opinion. She said she liked it but had some ideas on how to make it better. I encouraged her to play around with it. She might have been losing her spark as an actress, but she was a brilliant writer."

"So, did you really want to be rid of her? I mean, insofar as having her leave the troupe?"

He clicked his tongue. "Sometimes, a director must do what's best for the company. Gloria was not contributing positively to the troupe—and we weren't supporting her effectively, either. We all concurred that it had been a mistake to bring her on. But now, I understand why Roger suddenly insisted on keeping her."

"Yes," I said, "and he convinced me it was you who'd changed your mind." Guilt washed over me for my blatantly incorrect assumptions. "Again, I truly am sorry."

I didn't deserve his forgiveness, and he was showing himself to be incredibly gracious. However, one thing was still bothering me.

"Mr. Langston," I said, proceeding with caution. "It's none of my business, but your relationship, or should I say —your feelings—for Celine, are they . . . " I was struggling to find the right word. I didn't want the girl to fall prey to a man with less than honorable intentions.

"Respectable?" he finished for me with a frown.

I gave him an apologetic smile. "Yes. Respectable."

"Highly, my dear. I'll admit, she is beguiling, but my interest in her is purely professional. I can be a tad obsessive about the actors I work with—it's something that has always plagued me, and has always caused problems for me. I'm endeavoring to remedy that. Your mother will keep me on task in that regard, I assure you!"

"Of course," I said. "I didn't mean to pry—and again, I'm sorry for accusing you of—I just . . ."

He gently wrapped his hand around my elbow. "Let's not think of it again, my dear. Let bygones be bygones."

Moved by his kindness, a lump had formed in my throat, rendering me speechless.

"Now!" he said, with a spark in his eyes. "It seems we have a party to attend! You must get out of this costume and into a party frock, my dear. I'll see you at the Bella!" He gave me a kiss on the cheek and then made his way through the crowd toward Andrew—his new leading man.

Still holding the fragrant bouquet, I pressed my face into the roses, basking in their comforting scent. Something sharp hit my nose. It was a card buried deep within the cluster. I pulled it out and laughed when I read the inscription:

Congratulations on a masterful performance! Queenie.

Back at the Bella, Cordelia and I, along with my mother, Celine, Clayton and Deputy Fleming, all sat in my favorite booth at the back of the room. Clayton and the deputy had pulled up additional chairs for themselves, so we would all have ample room. Bijou had found a comfortable resting place on Deputy Fleming's lap.

The place was full to bursting with townsfolk and the troupe, several of whom stood next to Matt De Vries, the new musician Mr. Greer, the barkeep, had hired. He energetically played cowboy songs and gospel tunes on the piano, which was positioned on a raised dais along the south wall. Kitty, Sally, and the rest of Kitty's girls buzzed around, busily ensuring everyone had plenty of food and boiled peanuts. I pictured Lottie in the kitchen, a whirlwind of activity, as she prepared heartier fare for the crowd.

At his favorite table by the window, Archibald Archer presided over a group of people proudly boasting of Andrew's acting achievements. Andrew sat beside him, basking in the attention. Atticus Brooks was there too, of course, busily jotting down notes in his notebook. Constance Chatterley was also present, seated on the other side of Andrew, her face aglow with excitement as a crowd assembled around them to offer congratulations.

Deputy Fleming loudly cleared his throat and raised his glass of beer. "I'd like to make a toast to the most beautiful woman in the place, a first rate-detective, and a most talented actress, Mrs. Arabella Pryce!"

"Here, here!" said Celine, who was the next to raise her glass, followed by Cordelia and my mother. I glanced at Clayton, who shook his head at the deputy's exuberance, but then caught my eye and gave me a wink. He then raised his glass, and we all clinked them together in a toast.

"Now, it's my turn to raise a glass to Miss Celine Dubois, who has an incredibly bright future in the world of theater, and who will undoubtedly give me a run for my money!" I said jubilantly.

She blushed and glanced at my mother, who took her hand and gave it a reassuring squeeze. Celine had confided that she and my mother had reached a new understanding, granting her more freedom and a greater voice in choosing her roles.

Celine also shared that Mr. Langston, fearing he might lose her to another troupe, had also agreed to offer her more independence. I hoped he would keep his more amorous feelings for her in check—for her sake.

I couldn't help feeling envious of the young woman's newfound assertiveness, and regretted that I had never truly advocated for my own desires in my relationship with my mother. I supposed our situations had been quite different; my mother had been doing all she could to ensure our survival after my father left us. My previous resentment was slowly dissipating, though I knew I still had some distance to go.

The piano player launched into "Buffalo Girls," prompting Kitty and Sally to dash up to the dais and join in, singing boisterously to the crowd's delight.

As I watched them, my attention shifted to the saloon's front doors as two gentlemen entered. They were the same pair from Billings Building and Company. My cheerful mood instantly waned. Mr. Archer, Atticus Brooks, and Constance Chatterley also noticed their arrival and watched with keen interest as they made their way to the back of the room, heading toward my booth.

"Good evening, Mrs. Pryce," Mr. Graham said, tipping his hat. The sheriff and the deputy turned around in their seats, and then Clayton stood up.

"Gentlemen, can I help you?" he asked.

"We're here to see Mrs. Pryce," replied Mr. Wood, the younger of the two. "We are representatives from Billings Building and Company."

"What is your business with Mrs. Pryce?" Clayton inquired, his tone laced with defensiveness.

To my utter chagrin, I spotted Mr. Archer and Atticus Brooks approaching the booth. Constance tagged along behind them, her eyes wide with curiosity. The champagne in my stomach suddenly soured.

"It regards the lien placed on the hotel," Mr. Graham explained.

Once again called out in public, my embarrassment swiftly shifted to anger. I fixed the older gentleman with a glare, the intensity of which I typically reserved for my performances on stage.

I defiantly raised my chin and addressed them. "If you will excuse me, gentlemen. I hardly think this is the time or the place for—"

"We've come to tell you the debt has been paid in full, ma'am." Mr. Wood said. Shocked, I simply stared at him.

"We thought you'd like to hear the good news as soon as possible," he added with a grin.

Suddenly, a wave of relief washed over me. "Oh, then you received the funds from my bank in New York," I exclaimed.

"No, ma'am. Anonymous donor," Mr. Graham said.

I looked over at Cordelia, who raised her shoulders in confusion.

"What?" I said. "I—I mean—when?"

"Just this afternoon, ma'am. We were processing the paperwork, but just wanted you to know you are free and clear of the debt," Mr. Graham said.

"But—" I still couldn't work out what had just transpired.

"Paid off?" Mr. Archer interjected. "By whom? There's been no sizable withdrawal from my bank."

His sudden involvement in the conversation took me by surprise and I was about to say so when I noticed my mother, her head bowed, and her eyes fixed on the table. Initially, I worried she might be unwell again, but then a different, nearly as daunting, thought occurred to me.

"Mother?" I asked cautiously, suddenly all those feelings of entrapment resurfacing.

She raised her eyes to meet mine and gazed at me steadfastly. "You've always given me such a generous allowance. I've put some of the money by, just as a safety net. Just in case it was ever needed."

My indignation flared. "But, how did you know—?"

"I'm afraid I might have let something slip," Kitty said as she approached the table. "I knew about it from before. When Mr. Bledsoe was the hotel's manager. I got worried when these two men came in a week ago, and I said something to Sally when she brought Mrs. Janes some soup. I thought she was asleep, but she wasn't and asked me about it."

Feeling a sudden, urgent need to escape, I struggled to rise as I was wedged between the booth and Cordelia. The thought of being indebted to my mother again was unbearable. I had sworn with every fiber of my being never to return to that state. William had liberated me from the confines of her control, and I was determined never to go back.

I needed to get some fresh air. "Please let me out, Cordelia," I said flatly.

"Arabella," my mother pleaded.

"Cordelia?" I repeated.

With a sympathetic and helpless look on her face, she scooted out of the booth. "I'll come with you," she said.

"I need to be alone," I stated. Once I had managed to stand, I turned to Kitty, looking hard into her apologetic, ebony eyes.

"You had no right," I told her.

"I'm sorry—I just thought—"

Bijou hopped off Deputy Fleming's lap and, sensing my distress, scrambled over to me and whined for me to pick her up. Teetering on the edge of screaming, crying, or exploding, I brushed past her and the others and stormed through the door to the lobby. Hoisting my skirts, I dashed upstairs as fast as I could, taking the steps two at a time until I reached the fourth floor, both breathless and seething with fury.

Chapter Thirty-Five

The thud of her paws on the stairs caused me to whirl around. Bijou had scurried up after me. I scooped her up and pressed my face into the back of her neck.

I reached into my pocket for my keyring, unlocked the door, and stepped inside to find Percival and Lily Beaumont's spectral forms seated on the loveseat. A fire crackled warmly in the fireplace. Swirls of smoke surrounded Percival, pipe in hand, while Lily sat with her feet tucked beneath her, engrossed in a translucent book. They resembled a contented couple spending a cozy evening together.

"What is this?" I asked curtly, wanting to be alone and having no patience for this domestic scene.

"Hello, darling," Percival said. "You all right?"

"No, I am not all right!" I snapped.

Lily Beaumont lowered her book and looked at me with concern.

"It's my mother!" I said. "She's doing it again."

"Doing what?" Percival asked.

"Trying to take control of my life." I set my hands on

my hips and began pacing the room. "I won't let it happen," I declared. "I'll find a way to pay her back. I will not be beholden to her for even a week, much less seven months."

"Slow down, Arabella," Percival said. "Tell us what's happened."

I stopped my pacing and then sat down, perched on the edge of the chair next to the love seat. I explained what I'd just learned.

Percival blew a series of smoke rings into the air. "And you think your mother did that to control you?"

"Yes!" I said, perhaps a bit too emphatically.

"Millicent always was manipulative," Lily Beaumont said. "Even as a young woman. Had Roger Thompson running in circles."

Shocked that she'd finally spoken, my mouth dropped open. "But—you—" I started, but couldn't seem to finish.

"Yes, I've found my voice. Thanks to Percival." She smiled at him.

I pulled my chin back in surprise. "Percival? What did he do?"

"He facilitated a meeting," she said. "I couldn't quite figure out how to do it—how to enter the next realm, but he showed me the way."

"A meeting? What kind of meeting?" I said, astonished, if not quite impressed. I met his gaze. "Care to elaborate?"

Percival smiled, quite pleased with himself. "I explained to you I believed Lily was trapped between realms, or within the Realm of Echoes—"

"Which is where I was," Lily interjected. "In the Realm of Echoes."

"And in order for her to move on, she had to come to terms with her past," Percival continued.

"I was stuck in that diary," she cut in again. "My past was literally haunting me, and I couldn't find my way to the next realm until I could make amends with Michael Nash. He had moved on, but Percival called him back to the Echoes so we could hash things out. I could then join both of them in the Ethereal Plane. Now, I am free."

My gaze bounced back and forth between the two of them, who looked smug in their explanation as if it was the simplest thing in the world to understand. I sat there for some time, contemplating this otherworldly philosophy. Finally, I was about to pose another question when a sudden shriek distracted me.

Constance Chatterley stood in my parlor, staring into the mirror, her face pale as alabaster. I then realized I had left the door open. She glanced toward the loveseat, but Percival and Lily had disappeared. Turning back to the mirror, she found their reflections had vanished as well.

"Oh, my stars!" She said, her voice tremulous. "But— who?" She reached out into the air as if searching for something to steady herself.

Afraid she might collapse, I jumped up and grasped her arm, ready to support her in case her knees gave way. "Constance, come sit down."

This was the moment I had feared ever since she first glimpsed Percival at the Bella a few months ago. I had persuaded her it was all in her imagination, but that explanation was no longer viable.

"D-did I j-just see—?" she stammered, her voice climbing an octave.

"Sit down, Constance," I led her to the chair and then knelt down next to her. "Tell me what you saw." I said, trying to still the sickening swirl of butterflies in my stomach.

"There was a man. And—and a woman," she pointed to the loveseat, "Sitting right there. I saw them in the mirror, but now . . . "

"Are you sure?" I asked meekly. How was I going to get out of this?

She looked me directly in the eye, and her expression took on a frightening certainty. "I would bet my life on it. It was him. It was Percival Blank, and a woman. An older woman. Didn't you see them?"

I blinked at her, not sure what to say. Every fiber of my being told me to lie, to tell her that no, she must be daft; there was no such thing as ghosts, but I found I couldn't do it.

"I believe you did see someone," I said, finding a calm I didn't know I possessed.

She shook her head and then rested her forehead in her hand. "It's happened again. I think I must be going mad."

I took hold of her free hand and held it between my own. "You aren't going mad, Constance. I promise."

Her frightened gaze met mine. "You don't think I'm going crazy, do you?"

"No," I said.

"But then, how do you explain what I saw?"

I took in a breath, steadying myself. "You see, Constance, some people have special abilities, certain . . . sensitivities. It isn't well understood, and because of that, people who have these abilities are often misjudged. They are called insane—sometimes accused of witchery."

"Oh, dear!" she raised her fingers to her mouth, her eyes wide with alarm.

"Don't worry, Constance. Your secret is safe with me," I assured her.

She then squinted at me. "But how do you know this?"

I pulled my lips between my teeth, not quite ready to divulge the entire truth, but I wouldn't lie to her. "I have relatives who have those sensitivities."

"Really?" she squeaked.

"Yes. On my mother's side. We don't speak of it."

Her eyes took on a knowing look. "Right. Right. Best not speak of it," she said in a breathy voice. "Then, I suppose I should scrap my story of the ghost in your theater, and the ghosts here—Mr. Blank and—"

I blinked at her, unwilling to help finish her thought.

"No," she went on, shaking her head. "I wouldn't want to betray a family's confidence."

"No," I agreed. "And, thank you, Constance."

She tried to offer a smile. "And you will tell no one that I possess these . . . abilities?" she asked for reassurance.

I patted her hand. "I promise."

Her sigh of relief echoed mine, and her mouse-like eyes gazed at me appreciatively. "It will be our secret," she said, squeezing my hand.

"Our secret," I repeated, and then rose to standing. "Are you all right now?" I asked. "Is there anything I can get for you?"

"No, no," she shook her head and stood up. "I'm quite restored. I think I'll rejoin the party. Are you coming?"

I smiled at her. "I'll be down soon. I just want to freshen up," I said.

But in truth, I had to prepare myself to face the music downstairs. And my mother.

After seeing Constance out, I returned to the chair and

positioned it in front of the fireplace. Sitting down, I gazed into the flames, gathering my thoughts.

"Crisis averted," Percival said, leaning against the fireplace mantle.

I sighed, still trying to figure out how I could go downstairs and face everyone after storming out. "I suppose."

"It's just as well." He took his pipe out of his front pocket. "I don't want my name bandied about. I'm quite enjoying my anonymity."

I looked up at him. "Where's Miss Beaumont?"

"She had an engagement. With Michael Nash. Tea, I think."

I let out a snort. "Really?"

He nodded with a wry smile on his face. "Seems they've become friends in death. Everything is different once you pass on."

"I suppose so," I mused, then lowered my gaze back to the fire. A log, burnt down to its core, collapsed onto the hot coals beneath it. I let out a deep sigh, envying the absence of emotional turmoil in the existence of a spiritual being like Percival.

"You know, I think you are looking at this thing with your mother the wrong way," he said.

I gazed up at him. "Really? How so?" I asked, not agreeing with him in the least. I knew exactly what my mother was up to.

"You've supported your mother since you were a child, haven't you?"

I gritted my teeth. "Yes. I have. In grand style, I might add." I flicked my gaze back to the fire.

"And, this money that she's saved—it came from you, didn't it?"

I glanced over at him again. "Well, yes. I don't believe the troupe has earned much yet. They're still too new."

He held his pipe in one hand and raised the other to his face, turning his palm up and curling his fingers to inspect his nails. "Perhaps you could look at it as a repayment on a loan. A rather small payment on a rather large loan, that is."

I stared at him, trying to take in what he'd just said. "A loan?"

He shrugged. "For the span of your life in the theater. It's a large loan."

"Yes—Yes, I suppose it is."

"And you wouldn't expect her to pay it back entirely, would you?" he said, and then blew a large smoke ring into the air.

"Of course not. The sum would be enormous."

"Then you are still ahead, my dear. You are still in control—of your finances, and your mother's. You are not beholden to her. In fact, it is quite the other way around, and has been all along."

I blinked at him and then laughed. "You're right, Percival. You are absolutely right! I could kiss you!"

His face suddenly bore a very sad expression, and he gazed at me with those dark, luminous eyes. "As pleasant as that sounds, my dear, I'm afraid it's not possible, more's the pity."

"Oh, Percival, what would I do without you?" I extended my hand towards him, and as his fingers brushed mine, my pulse seemed to slow, as though the blood in my veins was being constricted to nothingness. Suddenly immobilized, I found myself unable to think.

Instinctively, I jerked my hand away and drew in a sharp breath. Life surged back through my body.

"See what I mean?" he said, his voice tinged with melancholy.

Dazed, I nodded. I had experienced this sensation before when, frustrated with him, I tried to walk through him. It was clear the distinct realms we each inhabited were fundamentally incompatible.

"But we will always be friends, won't we?" I asked, my heart breaking to see the look on his face.

He smiled and said, "As long as you will have me."

———

I made my way slowly down the stairs, reflecting on how valuable my friendship with Percival had become to me. He was my better half in so many ways. He need never worry about our friendship; I intended for it to last forever until I could join him in whichever realm he'd find himself.

When I entered the Bella, it was as if I'd never left, thank goodness. I went over to my booth, where my mother, Celine, Cordelia, Clayton, and Deputy Fleming still sat. It was clear they had enjoyed another round of drinks, and the table was littered with plates holding remnants of their meal.

"You're back," Cordelia said, patting the seat next to her.

"Yes," I slid in beside her. "I apologize for my abrupt departure. I'm afraid I behaved badly."

"It's been an emotional time," Celine added, as if that would explain away my tantrum—which it didn't.

"I didn't mean to step on your toes," my mother said. "It's just that you've been so generous with me—even when we weren't speaking. I wanted to help, in my small way."

I smiled at her. "I understand that now, Mother. I just

needed to think about it for a moment. I appreciate it. You will get it all back, I promise."

She shook her head. "I won't hear of it."

"But I need you to know that I run my own affairs now, Mother."

"Yes, my dear. I'm quite proud of you."

She'd never said that to me before. I blinked back tears that threatened to surface. Seeing my emotion, she turned to Celine. "I'm quite tired, dear girl. Please escort me to my suite?"

"Of course," she said with a bright smile. "I'm worn out myself. I think I'll turn in as well."

"I suppose I'd better feed Miss Bijou," Cordelia offered. "Is she up in our rooms?"

I nodded. "I left her asleep in her bed."

We said our goodnights, and I was left with Clayton and Deputy Fleming.

"Well, Mrs. Pryce," Deputy Fleming said. "Like I said before, it was a pleasure to see you perform tonight. You did not disappoint!"

"You are too kind, deputy," I said. "It was a terrific play. Mr. Langston is very talented."

"Oh, and the part where you gave that soliloquy? Magical, I tell you. Simply magical!" He beamed.

"Goodness—you quite flatter me," I demurred.

Clayton tapped his fingers on the table. "Have you had anything to eat, Arabella?" He said in an even tone.

"What? Oh—no, I guess I haven't. But, I'm not really—"

"Dirk, be a good lad and see about getting a plate of food brought to Mrs. Pryce, would you?"

Deputy Fleming hesitated at the request, but Clayton gave him a raised eyebrow.

"Oh, yeah, sure," he finally agreed. "Be right back."

He got up and left the table.

"Clay, you really didn't have to—"

Before I knew it, he seized my hand, pulled me up from the booth, and rushed me out the door into the lobby. We quickly moved down a short hallway to the right, through the south door, and into the cool night air. It all happened so quickly that I barely had time to catch my breath. He spun me around to face him.

"Clayton, what are you doing?" I asked, puzzled by his sudden urgency. He looked at me impatiently with those steely blue eyes. "I've been wanting to talk to you all night, but you've been surrounded."

"Oh," I said, laughing. "Well, you've got me now."

He laughed too. "The lengths I have to go to."

"What is it you wanted to talk to me about?" I asked.

He shrugged. "Nothing in particular. I just wanted to be alone with you."

A thrill went through me, and I smiled. "Thank you for the flowers—or rather, I guess I should thank Queenie for the flowers."

"Yeah. I thought that was pretty funny," he said, giving me that knee-melting grin of his.

"But what about Deputy Fleming, and the food?"

He shook his head. "He'll be fine. That kid needs to simmer down. He drives me to distraction."

"Oh, come now," I said. "Don't be so hard on him. You know he greatly admires you."

Clayton scoffed. "Not as much as he greatly admires you."

"Well," I said with a chuckle, "you might be right there."

"Modesty becomes you," he teased, and I gave him a playful tap on the shoulder.

"But, the overeager, love struck Deputy Fleming has one thing right," he said more seriously, setting his hand on the wall behind me, closing me in.

"And what is that?" I asked, my mouth suddenly going dry at his closeness.

He stepped closer to me still and looked deep into my eyes, his ocean blue gaze making my breath catch in my throat. "You are the most beautiful woman in the place. The town. The world."

My face flushed and a wave of heat coursed through me, threatening to make me crumple right then and there. "My goodness," I managed to choke out softly. "The entire world?"

"The entire universe," he said, and then he kissed me.

Closing my eyes, stars burst before me like fireworks at a carnival, blinding me with their brilliance, lighting the darkness, and sweeping me away to galaxies previously unknown.

Next in The Pryce of Murder Series

vinci-books.com/pryceofpride

A legacy at stake. A secret worth killing for.

1886, Colorado—As Arabella Pryce prepares to leave her family's
historic hotel, a controversial festival unearths deadly secrets. With
a ghostly ally and a town on edge, she must unravel a mystery
before history is rewritten in blood.

Turn the page for a free preview…

The Pryce of Pride: Chapter One

I stood on the front steps of the Arabella Hotel, taking in the view of the town's main street. La Plata Springs was alive with activity as the Cultural and Historic Festival had begun early that morning. Banners fluttered in the breeze and the street buzzed with a happy cacophony of voices and the clip-clop of horses' hooves as they pulled carriages and wagons carrying supplies and visitors from nearby settlements.

Down in the open field by the river, a group of children, both Tavani and Caucasian, engaged in foot races and a game of Tava-Ha, which consisted of passing around a ball fashioned of stuffed buckskin with broomsticks or long tree branches.

The festival was a time where the diverse cultures of the area came together to celebrate their mutual respect for one another. It was the brainchild of Eleanor Reynolds, a passionate local historian, who had worked tirelessly to bring the event to life. This year, it promised to be more spectacular than ever thanks to the collaboration with

Archibald Archer, the town's founder and acting mayor, and a businessman named Theodore Chase, who was from the neighboring town of Addison. Both men sought to boost tourism and economic growth in the area.

To the south, a large platform was being erected in front of the General, the rival hotel to the Arabella, whose grand reopening conveniently coincided with the festival. Archibald Archer, who owned the hotel, had convinced Miss Reynolds to plan the event at the time of his grand reopening for optimal exposure.

I smiled at the power play. Mr. Archer had made no secret that he wanted to possess all the businesses in the growing community, and owned about ninety percent of them. The jewel in his crown would be the Arabella, built by my late husband and the architect—my supernatural friend—Percival Blank. I had inherited the hotel at my husband's death, and had been directed by a stipulation in his will to run the hotel for one full year in order to gain my full inheritance, which was vast, to say the least. The other request by my husband was to never sell the hotel to Archibald Archer.

One full year. When I received the news of my assignment, I thought I'd never survive it. I had become accustomed to my lavish lifestyle in New York, my renowned theater, and the craft of acting upon the stage which afforded me more than just money. It had been my entire reason for living. To leave it was unimaginable, but leave it I did. Temporarily. And my year-long venture was nearly at an end. I could scarcely believe it. The time had flown.

However, because of the expense of sundry problems with the hotel, my stay had been extended and I would remain here another six months, which now seemed a mere blink of an eye. Having finally felt settled in the little community, the thought of leaving produced feelings in me that were hard to reconcile. I had grown fond of the town and the people who resided in it.

"My goodness, but this is quite impressive," a male voice echoed next to me. I turned to see Percival Blank standing to my left in his transparent, ethereal form. He ran a hand through his thick wavy hair, drawing attention to the hint of gray at his temples. His dark, luminous eyes regarded me with their moody, Byronic charm. Although not among the living, he was a permanent resident of his beloved creation, the Arabella, and he'd become my first friend in La Plata Springs. Clasping his hands behind his back, he rocked back and forth on the balls of his feet, surveying the scene before us. As usual, his pipe was clenched firmly between his teeth, and fragrant wisps of spicy tobacco encircled his head.

"Indeed, it is," I agreed.

He craned his neck to see past me down the street to the south. "It looks like Archibald plans to mesmerize the festival goers with a dazzling speech for the reopening of his flop-house."

I let out a snort. "Come now, Percival," I chided. "He's completely renovated the General. It's much more than just a flop-house now. It's a grand hotel."

Percival scoffed. "Grand, my foot. It will never measure up to the Arabella. I see he is determined at his attempts to steal her shine, since you've refused to allow him to get his grubby hands on her."

I shrugged. "He's making efforts to grow the town, Percival. The mines have attracted a good deal of men whom he's made rich because of those mines, and now he wants to put La Plata Springs on the map with tourism as well. You can't fault him for his ambition. He's a man who makes things happen—although, I will grant you that some-times his methods can be questionable."

A distinguished man, who looked to be in his early forties, and a lovely woman approached the entrance to the hotel. Percival popped out of sight. The man had a schol-arly appearance with short, neatly combed dark hair that was shot through with the occasional strand of gray. His well-fitted suit with bow tie gave him a formal and some-what pretentious look. His expression was serious and bore a confidence that seemed almost unshakable, radiating a self-assurance that commanded respect.

The woman appeared to be slightly younger than the man. Her auburn hair, the front of which was styled in loose curls framing her intelligent and determined face, shone brilliantly in the sun. Her chocolate brown dress, intricately embroidered in tan, sported lace details and a high neckline, which complemented her coloring and her kind, but slightly strained, demeanor. She wore a beautiful silver brooch at her neck. It depicted a majestic bird in mid-flight surrounded by delicate foliage.

"Excuse me, please," the woman said. "Is this the Arabella Hotel?"

"Why, yes, it is. I'm the owner, Arabella Pryce."

The woman blinked, as if confused. "Arabella Pryce … You mean THE Arabella Pryce? The actress?"

Pleased at her recognition of my name, I gave her a broad smile. "Yes, guilty as charged."

"My goodness." She laid her hand on her chest. "I've read about your travels to the West and your hotel, but I did not know you'd actually be here. I assumed you'd be in New York, or traveling somewhere abroad." She looked over at the man. "Isn't this amazing?"

The man gave her a polite—but not exactly sincere—

smile, and then he turned his attention to me. "Forgive my wife's exuberance. She has quite forgotten her manners. I'm Warren Baxter, and this is my wife, Bernice."

The woman pressed her lips together in irritation at being chastised by her husband. "Yes, please forgive me."

"It is quite alright," I said to her, wishing to deflect from the awkwardness of the situation. She nodded graciously.

"Mr. Baxter, you are the honored guest of the festival, I understand. I'm looking forward to hearing you speak this evening."

"Thank you. Yes, Archibald Archer reached out to me some weeks ago regarding the festival. He has a great appreciation for my work in native art, artifacts, and antiquities in both South and North America. Recently, I am dedicated to studying the culture of the Tavani. I was happy to comply."

"How lovely. I assume you will stay at the General?"

"Yes," his wife said. "I had hoped to stay here at the Arabella, of course—I've been so curious about your hotel —but since the invitation came from Mr. Archer … "

"Naturally," I said. "I completely understand. I hear the renovations he's made to the General are quite impressive." As I said the words, a niggle of worry edged its way into my bones. Even though the lien against the Arabella had been recently paid, I still had a lot of financial catching up to do to bring the hotel back to its former glory. It seemed with every step forward I took, I had to take two steps back. I needed to keep the hotel full to occupancy. We were nearly at eighty-five percent now, but I wanted it to be at one hundred percent. Hopefully, visitors for the festival would continue to trickle in.

From behind me, the door to the hotel opened and

Bijou, my little Havanese dog, came scampering over to me. She raised herself up, pawing at my skirts.

"There you are, Arabella," Cordelia, my assistant, companion and best friend, joined me. Her strawberry blond hair was slightly mussed. From this, I knew she'd been reading, or working on my correspondence, as she often had her hands in her hair while concentrating. "Bijou was searching for you."

Chuckling at my pup's smiling face, I picked her up. "Here I am, sweetheart." She happily settled in my arms.

"Cordelia?" Mrs. Baxter stepped forward, looking at her intently. "Cordelia Danson?"

Cordelia's hazel eyes appraised the woman and then grew wide with surprised recognition. "Bernice Madison!"

"Oh, my goodness! I can't believe it," the woman said. "And—it's Baxter now."

Cordelia's gaze bounced back and forth between Mrs. Baxter and her husband. "Yes, yes, of course," she said, apologetically. She clasped her hands together at her waist, and I noted her knuckles instantly paled. Despite her obviously forced smile, her upper lip twitched at the corner.

"You know each other?" The revelation caught me off guard.

"Cordelia and I, we—well, we went to finishing school together in Massachusetts, didn't we, dear?" Mrs. Baxter said.

"Finishing school?" I fixed my gaze on Cordelia, struggling to mask my shock. From what I knew of her background, which I had obviously assumed incorrectly, finishing school was something her family could scarcely afford.

Cordelia's face blanched, causing the light scatter of

freckles across her nose and cheekbones to stand out more vividly.

"Yes," her voice cracked. "Well, I suppose congratulations are in order?" She asked, neatly skirting the subject.

"It's been twelve years," Mrs. Baxter said, looking over at her husband.

He gave Cordelia a brief upturn of his lips and then cleared his throat. "Miss Danson. We had no idea you would be here in La Plata Springs."

"I—I work for Arabella—er, Mrs. Pryce. I've worked for her for ten years." She briefly glanced at me, but would not look me straight in the eye. I gathered this was because she had somehow neglected to mention she knew the famous artifacts historian and his wife, but for what reason? It had me more than curious, and I hate to admit, a little hurt. We'd known he'd be coming to town for a few weeks.

What in the devil's name was she hiding?

The Pryce of Pride: Chapter Two

After we said our goodbyes to the couple, Cordelia pivoted sharply and strode back into the hotel, leaving Bijou and me staring after her in complete bewilderment. Without hesitation, I hurried after her through the doors.

"Cordelia?" I called after her. She was rapidly approaching the stairs to go back up to our rooms. Either she didn't hear me, or she was ignoring me. Either way, her behavior was odd. This was not like her at all.

I passed by the reception desk where Mr. Pettyjohn, the clerk, was assisting a couple who were checking in to the hotel. Much to my delight, several others were waiting in line to do the same. The festival, so far, promised to be very beneficial for the hotel, and I hoped we would be at full capacity soon.

As I was about to climb the stairs to go after Cordelia, Sheriff Clayton Marshall and Deputy Dirk Fleming emerged from the Bella with another couple and came into the lobby. My heart lurched at seeing the sheriff—which was completely annoying and unsettling. My feelings for the man often had me confused, and I did not have time for such distractions. I had not seen him for a few weeks, as he had rather abruptly left town—a few days after we had shared a lovely kiss—and his sudden presence sent my emotions reeling. That he had gone away without mentioning it to me was a little inconsiderate. Not that I expected anything from him. The kiss was probably the result of exuberance at our success in solving a recent murder, nothing more. Yet, to my dismay, it felt like something more. I pushed the feeling firmly aside.

Calling upon my acting skill, I put on a pleasant, casual smile and approached the foursome.

"Clayton, Deputy Fleming, how good to see you!" I set Bijou down and she happily raised herself on her hind legs, dancing for the sheriff's attention. He bent down to pet her, and she immediately dropped to the ground and rolled over, exposing her belly. He gave her a few scratches and then rose again.

"Hello, Mrs. Pryce," the young deputy said, his expressive dark gaze meeting mine with a mixture of warmth and boyish charm. A faint blush tinged his cheeks. Tall, broad-shouldered, and with a shock of red hair, Dirk Fleming was a new arrival in town, and I'm afraid he'd become quite smitten with me. He was a darling young man, and while I appreciated his effusive personality and rugged good looks, I did not feel quite the same ardor for him.

"Arabella." Clayton greeted me flatly with a nod. His handsome, weathered face, which featured deep-set, piercing blue eyes, a neatly trimmed mustache and a hint of stubble on his square jaw, was void of a smile. I found it curious, and mildly disconcerting, that he'd addressed me in such an ambivalent manner, quite opposite from the eager deputy.

The gentleman with him, clearly from the local Tavani tribe, looked to be in his late sixties or early seventies. His noble countenance was lined with age and wisdom. Long gray hair swept away from his face and fell loosely over his shoulders. He wore a striped, cotton collared shirt, and a fringed buckskin vest. The woman, much younger—I guessed to be in her late twenties—was strikingly beautiful, with wide expressive eyes, high cheekbones, and glossy dark locks that fell to her waist. Her light tan buckskin dress was fashioned with a frontispiece of elegantly woven beadwork and small shells. Her beaded dangled earrings flashed with color, and a beautiful, almost iridescent deep blue and turquoise feather was threaded into her hair.

"This is Michael Two Trees," Clayton nodded toward the gentleman. "He's an elder and historian of the Tavani tribe, dedicated to educating others about the traditions and history of the native culture here."

"Ah, yes," I said. "You're here for the festival. Welcome."

His warm, kindly eyes settled on me, and he gave me a nod of silent greeting.

Clayton held his hand out toward the woman. "And this is Sarah Redhawk. She's an artist and activist and is passionate about land issues and cultural preservation. She's also on the festival's planning committee." He tilted his head toward me. "This is Arabella Pryce. She owns the hotel."

"It's a pleasure to meet you," Miss Redhawk said. "We are just about to check in to your fine hotel."

"Oh." My brows lifted. "You aren't staying at the General?"

Miss Redhawk and Mr. Two Trees shared a glance.

"No," she said, flatly.

"Ah. Well, we have a few rooms left. I'm sure the General is quite filled up."

Her lips twitched with an attempt at a smile. "I have no idea, but we'd rather be here."

An awkward silence fell among us. I suppose I was waiting for some kind of explanation. Mr. Archer had offered his rooms at a generous discount for the grand opening, probably to entice prospective guests. I had just assumed that anyone involved in the planning committee would stay there.

"I see." I blurted it out, eager to break the silence. "You are most welcome. Please let me know if there is anything I can do to make your stay more pleasant."

"Thank you, gracious lady." The corners of Michael Two Trees' eyes crinkled with gratitude.

The young woman gently took him by the elbow and led him to the back of the line at the reception desk.

"It looks like the festival is off to a good start," Deputy Fleming said. "Are you interested in native historic art and artifacts, Mrs. Pryce? I understand there are some very interesting lectures on the schedule. Will you be attending Mr. Baxter's this evening?"

"I am."

"His theories are quite controversial," he continued. "I'm sure his talk will garner some lively discussion."

"You're familiar with his work?"

"Yes. I dabble in cultural history myself." He straightened his spine and proudly puffed out his chest.

Clayton, not willing to engage in our shared interest, cleared his throat and pulled a watch from his vest pocket. "Deputy, I believe you're on patrol now."

Deputy Fleming's smile faded, replaced with a look of determined seriousness. "Right. Yes, sir." Placing his hat on his head, his fingers lightly touched the brim. "I hope to see you at the lecture, Mrs. Pryce."

"I'll be there," I assured him. His smile returned, and he strode away.

Clayton and I were again left in an uncomfortable and uncustomary silence between us.

"It's nice to see you, Sheriff," I said finally, still confused at his cool demeanor and rather bland introduction of me. Were we not friends? Perhaps more than friends? "You've been away."

He nodded, quietly appraising me with those dazzling blue eyes. "I had some business in Colorado Springs."

"Oh. Law business?" I felt somewhat like I was pulling teeth to get him to talk to me, which was strange. Our conversations in the past had usually come so easily.

He shook his head. "No. Personal."

"Ah. Well. I hope it was a successful trip."

Another awkward silence sucked the air from the room.

"I should get on," he said.

"Yes," I agreed. "Me too. There's a lot going on at the hotel."

He placed his hat back on his head, gave me a polite nod, and walked away. I watched him go with a knot in my belly. Had I done or said something to offend him? Had he regretted the kiss? Did he somehow feel an obligation to me he couldn't abide?

I shook my head, not wanting to face any of these possibilities. After all, what did it matter? I would sell the hotel and leave in six months' time. Leave all of this behind me. Leave him.

I couldn't let these silly emotions derail me from my

purpose, which was to get the hotel back on its feet, serve my allotted time here, and get back to my theater in New York. After all, that is where I belonged.

The Pryce of Pride: Chapter Three

After we said our goodbyes to the couple, Cordelia pivoted sharply and strode back into the hotel, leaving Bijou and me staring after her in complete bewilderment. Without hesitation, I hurried after her through the doors.

"Cordelia?" I called after her. She was rapidly approaching the stairs to go back up to our rooms. Either she didn't hear me, or she was ignoring me. Either way, her behavior was odd. This was not like her at all.

I passed by the reception desk where Mr. Pettyjohn, the clerk, was assisting a couple who were checking in to the hotel. Much to my delight, several others were waiting in line to do the same. The festival, so far, promised to be very beneficial for the hotel, and I hoped we would be at full capacity soon.

As I was about to climb the stairs to go after Cordelia, Sheriff Clayton Marshall and Deputy Dirk Fleming emerged from the Bella with another couple and came into the lobby. My heart lurched at seeing the sheriff—which was completely annoying and unsettling. My feelings for the man often had me confused, and I did not have time for such distractions. I had not seen him for a few weeks, as he had rather abruptly left town—a few days after we had shared a lovely kiss—and his sudden presence sent my emotions reeling. That he had gone away without mentioning it to me was a little inconsiderate. Not that I expected anything from him. The kiss was probably the result of exuberance at our success in solving a recent murder, nothing more. Yet, to my dismay, it felt like something more. I pushed the feeling firmly aside.

Calling upon my acting skill, I put on a pleasant, casual smile and approached the foursome.

"Clayton, Deputy Fleming, how good to see you!" I set Bijou down and she happily raised herself on her hind legs, dancing for the sheriff's attention. He bent down to pet her, and she immediately dropped to the ground and rolled over, exposing her belly. He gave her a few scratches and then rose again.

"Hello, Mrs. Pryce," the young deputy said, his expressive dark gaze meeting mine with a mixture of warmth and boyish charm. A faint blush tinged his cheeks. Tall, broad-shouldered, and with a shock of red hair, Dirk Fleming was a new arrival in town, and I'm afraid he'd become quite smitten with me. He was a darling young man, and while I appreciated his effusive personality and rugged good looks, I did not feel quite the same ardor for him.

"Arabella." Clayton greeted me flatly with a nod. His handsome, weathered face, which featured deep-set, piercing blue eyes, a neatly trimmed mustache and a hint of stubble on his square jaw, was void of a smile. I found it curious, and mildly disconcerting, that he'd addressed me in such an ambivalent manner, quite opposite from the eager deputy.

The gentleman with him, clearly from the local Tavani tribe, looked to be in his late sixties or early seventies. His noble countenance was lined with age and wisdom. Long gray hair swept away from his face and fell loosely over his shoulders. He wore a striped, cotton collared shirt, and a fringed buckskin vest. The woman, much younger—I guessed to be in her late twenties—was strikingly beautiful, with wide expressive eyes, high cheekbones, and glossy dark locks that fell to her waist. Her light tan buckskin dress was fashioned with a frontispiece of elegantly woven beadwork and small shells. Her beaded dangled earrings flashed with color, and a beautiful, almost iridescent deep blue and turquoise feather was threaded into her hair.

"This is Michael Two Trees," Clayton nodded toward the gentleman. "He's an elder and historian of the Tavani tribe, dedicated to educating others about the traditions and history of the native culture here."

"Ah, yes," I said. "You're here for the festival. Welcome."

His warm, kindly eyes settled on me, and he gave me a nod of silent greeting.

Clayton held his hand out toward the woman. "And this is Sarah Redhawk. She's an artist and activist and is passionate about land issues and cultural preservation. She's also on the festival's planning committee." He tilted his head toward me. "This is Arabella Pryce. She owns the hotel."

"It's a pleasure to meet you," Miss Redhawk said. "We are just about to check in to your fine hotel."

"Oh." My brows lifted. "You aren't staying at the General?"

Miss Redhawk and Mr. Two Trees shared a glance.

"No," she said, flatly.

"Ah. Well, we have a few rooms left. I'm sure the General is quite filled up."

Her lips twitched with an attempt at a smile. "I have no idea, but we'd rather be here."

An awkward silence fell among us. I suppose I was waiting for some kind of explanation. Mr. Archer had offered his rooms at a generous discount for the grand opening, probably to entice prospective guests. I had just assumed that anyone involved in the planning committee would stay there.

"I see." I blurted it out, eager to break the silence. "You are most welcome. Please let me know if there is anything I can do to make your stay more pleasant."

"Thank you, gracious lady." The corners of Michael Two Trees' eyes crinkled with gratitude.

The young woman gently took him by the elbow and led him to the back of the line at the reception desk.

"It looks like the festival is off to a good start," Deputy Fleming said. "Are you interested in native historic art and artifacts, Mrs. Pryce? I understand there are some very interesting lectures on the schedule. Will you be attending Mr. Baxter's this evening?"

"I am."

"His theories are quite controversial," he continued. "I'm sure his talk will garner some lively discussion."

"You're familiar with his work?"

"Yes. I dabble in cultural history myself." He straightened his spine and proudly puffed out his chest.

Clayton, not willing to engage in our shared interest, cleared his throat and pulled a watch from his vest pocket. "Deputy, I believe you're on patrol now."

Deputy Fleming's smile faded, replaced with a look of determined seriousness. "Right. Yes, sir." Placing his hat on his head, his fingers lightly touched the brim. "I hope to see you at the lecture, Mrs. Pryce."

"I'll be there," I assured him. His smile returned, and he strode away.

Clayton and I were again left in an uncomfortable and uncustomary silence between us.

"It's nice to see you, Sheriff," I said finally, still confused at his cool demeanor and rather bland introduction of me. Were we not friends? Perhaps more than friends? "You've been away."

He nodded, quietly appraising me with those dazzling blue eyes. "I had some business in Colorado Springs."

"Oh. Law business?" I felt somewhat like I was pulling teeth to get him to talk to me, which was strange. Our conversations in the past had usually come so easily.

He shook his head. "No. Personal."

"Ah. Well. I hope it was a successful trip."

Another awkward silence sucked the air from the room.

"I should get on," he said.

"Yes," I agreed. "Me too. There's a lot going on at the hotel."

He placed his hat back on his head, gave me a polite nod, and walked away. I watched him go with a knot in my belly. Had I done or said something to offend him? Had he regretted the kiss? Did he somehow feel an obligation to me he couldn't abide?

I shook my head, not wanting to face any of these possibilities. After all, what did it matter? I would sell the hotel and leave in six months' time. Leave all of this behind me. Leave him.

I couldn't let these silly emotions derail me from my

purpose, which was to get the hotel back on its feet, serve my allotted time here, and get back to my theater in New York. After all, that is where I belonged.

Grab your copy...
vinci-books.com/pryceofpride